WHAT KIND

of PARADISE

WHAT KIND

of PARADISE

A Novel

JANELLE BROWN

Random House
New York

Random House
An imprint and division of Penguin Random House LLC
1745 Broadway, New York, NY 10019
randomhousebooks.com
penguinrandomhouse.com

LIBRARY OF CONGRESS CATALOGING-IN-PUBLICATION DATA
Names: Brown, Janelle, author.
Title: What kind of paradise: a novel / by Janelle Brown.
Description: First edition. | New York, NY: Random House, 2025.
Identifiers: LCCN 2025000692 (print) | LCCN 2025000693 (ebook) |
ISBN 9780593449783 (hardcover) | ISBN 9780593449790 (ebook)
Subjects: LCGFT: Thrillers (Fiction) | Novels. | Psychological fiction.
Classification: LCC PS3602.R698 W53 2025 (print) | LCC PS3602.
R698 (ebook) | DDC 813/.6—dc23/eng/20250108
LC record available at https://lccn.loc.gov/2025000692
LC ebook record available at https://lccn.loc.gov/20250006930

Printed in the United States of America on acid-free paper

1 2 3 4 5 6 7 8 9

First Edition

BOOK TEAM: Production editor: Kelly Chian •
Managing editor: Rebecca Berlant • Production manager: Sandra Sjursen
• Copy editor: Kathy Lord • Proofreaders: Deborah Bader,
Annette Szlachta-McGinn, Frieda Duggan, Megha Jain

The authorized representative in the EU for product safety and
compliance is Penguin Random House Ireland, Morrison Chambers,
32 Nassau Street, Dublin D02 YH68, Ireland.
https://eu-contact.penguin.ie

To the Tiredlings and Salonistas
who changed the trajectory of my life

He who fights with monsters might take care lest he thereby become a monster. And if you gaze for long into an abyss, the abyss also gazes into you.

—FRIEDRICH NIETZSCHE

The cost of a thing is the amount of what I will call life which is required to be exchanged for it, immediately or in the long run.

—HENRY DAVID THOREAU

WHAT KIND

of PARADISE

Prologue

THE KNOCK I'D been waiting for finally happened early on a normal Monday morning, not long after my daughter left for school. It came almost as a relief. There she was, the stranger at the door who I'd been afraid of for so long: a woman maybe fifteen years younger than me, a rumpled linen blazer that advertised seriousness of intent, ergonomic sneakers tapping nervously at the planks of my porch, black hair yanked into a crooked ponytail.

How many strange knocks at the door had I heard over the previous decades? Each one accompanied by a corresponding knock in my chest, a surge of my pulse: *I've been found.* I didn't get many solicitors out where we lived, in the winding woodlands of Marin, but people sometimes made their way to me anyway. Neighbor kids selling raffle tickets, a particularly persistent Environment California fundraiser, real estate agents wondering if I was willing to list my covetable acreage. I ignored the strangers, answered the door when it was children, hid in the back when it was a man.

So why did I answer this particular knock? Why did I drift toward the entry, the cereal spoon from my breakfast still in my hand, impulsively compelled to open the door?

Probably I had felt the global temperature shift, despite my attempts to disregard it. Once you're aware of something's existence, you can't will it back into oblivion, no matter how hard you try. Or maybe some long-buried voice from deep inside me had sent up a smoke signal: *It's time.*

Gus was barking like a maniac, claws scrabbling at the door. I grabbed his collar as I twisted the doorknob and peered at the woman standing there, her laptop bag heavy across her thigh.

"Hi, I'm Yasmin Amadi. *San Francisco Chronicle?*" She had an eager squeak in her voice, her breath came fast even as she tried to keep her face calm. She stuck her hand out, a business card in her palm.

I stared down at it, at the fingernails chewed to the quick and the string bracelet on her wrist. I gripped Gus's collar tighter, forcing him to sit. "Sorry, but what's this about?"

"Is this you?" She held out a piece of paper with a sketch of me that I'd hoped I'd never see again. Her eyes scrutinized my face, and I could sense her measuring me up against my teenage self: noting the gray now threading the blond, the wrinkles that split my forehead like a cracked windshield, my nearsighted squint from too many hours staring at close objects. I could tell that she was looking for something in particular, could see the question mark in her eyes as she failed to find it. A renegade air, maybe. A criminal mien. But all she could see was a faded middle-aged lady with paint in her hair. It was possible she was questioning herself.

I could have answered no. Could have hidden behind the new name I'd given myself, the carefully constructed smoke screens I'd thrown up years before. Names are easy to slip on and off, like an ill-fitting suit. I've gone through so many. Personal identity, however— that's a whole different story. Identity is far harder to change.

I closed my eyes. Behind my lids I saw the same familiar ghosts flicker past, my life's movie on perpetual rerun. Blood spatters across a shiny red dress. The cold heft of a gun in my palm. A tower of flames, bright against the night sky.

"How did you find me?" I asked. Gus panted obediently at my feet, drool dripping on my bare toes.

To her credit, she didn't grin in victory. Instead, she bit her lip apologetically, clearly aware of just how much effort I had put into *not* being found. "A lot of research. It took a few months to connect the dots, piece together clues. And the internet was very helpful, of course."

"Of course," I repeated. Because the internet was how it had all begun. It had undone me, made me whole again, and then undone me once more. My savior, my nemesis, the harbinger of doom for us all.

"Considering everything that's happening, I thought maybe you'd want to talk to the press?"

"Everything that's happening?"

Her eyes opened wide, a little patronizing. "Oh. Maybe you aren't aware that your father has been in the news lately—maybe you don't have a television?" I wondered if she was thinking that after so many years of trying to escape my father's legacy, I had somehow ended up rebuilding his Arcadia.

"I'm aware," I interrupted her. I pointed the cereal spoon over my shoulder, to clarify. She glanced past me for the first time, noting the interior of our little cedar-lined house: the paintings that hung on every wall, little clay figures teetering on ledges, the novels flung open on the couch. Signs of a teenager, scattered shoes and clothes, abandoned breakfast plates. But also: a desk with a full computer setup and a television that was currently on mute.

"In that case, maybe you'd like to set the record straight," she persisted. "You haven't ever told your full story, not since it all went down."

"Thanks, but when it's time for me to tell my story, I'll do it myself. Please leave."

I released Gus's collar and he leapt happily at Yasmin, clambering up her thighs. She backed away, wiping off the drool on her slacks, then turned and walked to her car. I felt a little bad—she seemed nice enough. Smart and persistent, which would probably take her far. But I also knew that she was facing a futile task: How could an hourlong conversation with a reporter possibly capture the complexity of the story I had to tell? After all, the dichotomies of my childhood were a subject that even *I* struggled to wrap my head around: All these years later, I still wasn't sure I fully understood what had happened.

But as I turned back from the door, I found myself thinking of my daughter. She was almost the age that I had been when everything began; and her gaze was starting to settle on the territories beyond her familiar borders. I knew that for her sake—if not my own—it might finally be time for me to try.

Part One

JANE

1.

THE FIRST THING that you have to understand is that my father was my entire world. It had been that way since I was four and my mother died, leaving us alone together. Not alone in the typical bereaved-family sense, but truly *alone,* as in, just us two living out in the wilderness together. As a child, I had no understanding that our lives were not normal—it was simply the way things were. Our cabin, our forest, our woodstove surrounded by our towering piles of books and newspapers, and our potatoes that we dug out of our vegetable garden and roasted in the coals. My father, his long brown hair shot with gray, the side of his hand permanently smudged with ink, his worn-soft shirts with holes right where the fabric rubbed against his belt. His hugs, which smelled of smoke and the mint sprigs that he chewed.

There were so many things that were said about my father later, so many portraits that weren't at all accurate; but one thing that everyone felt the need to acknowledge was that he was very intelligent. A mind as sharp and bright and piercing as a nail. Think, *Mensa-level genius.*

Growing up, I sometimes thought I could hear his mind fizzing and popping, dendrites of connection whirring in his brain, an electric buzz coming off him that was almost audible in its intensity. I felt slow around him: a dim bulb compared to his incandescent filaments. I read the books he put before me, tried to formulate arguments that would impress him; and even though he would nod and smile as I stumbled my way through Nietzsche or Goethe or Baudrillard, I always feared that I was letting him down.

He never let me forget that he was an extraordinary man, either.

"They didn't know what to do with me at Harvard. Got three degrees in four years—engineering and mathematics and philosophy—and I wanted to get one more in history, but it was money I didn't have." "I quit a high-profile job after I exposed the underlying flaw in their thinking and they didn't want to listen." "I could have gotten sixteen patents for inventions, but I walked away from all of them because I didn't want to deal with the government bureaucracy of it all."

The subtext, of course, was that there were so many things he could have done, but he chose *me* over all of them. He chose *me*, and preserving my future, over his own blinding success. He'd given all that up to move us to the woods, so he could raise me in an Edenic paradise. That was how much he loved me.

How could I not trust that?

So yes, I grew up fully aware that my father was a brilliant man whose expertise I should never ever ever question.

Did I believe that he was a *good* man? That's another question entirely.

HE WASN'T *WITHOUT* goodness. When I think of him now—that is, when I try to remember the father I revered, not the man from the news—I often find myself reaching back to a March day when I was fourteen. My father shook me awake at dawn and told me that we were out of food and the snowstorms had made the roads impassable, so we were going to go hunt a deer. It wasn't hunting season, but that didn't bother my father a bit. He wasn't about to let the government tell him how to conduct his business on his land; and though the forest wasn't *technically* our land (our property was a small patch of woods-adjacent scrubland), my father certainly knew it better than anyone else.

And so off we went at dawn, my father's loaded rifle tossed over his shoulder, both of us bundled up in old Army Navy parkas. Snow started falling as we trudged through the drifts. I remember trying to fit my feet into my father's footsteps as we walked single file through the trees; and the effort it took me to fit my short girl's stride into his long man's one. Our breath formed clouds in the air, froze ice crystals into my scarf. I could see my father's head turning right and left, looking for signs. I kept following his gaze into the depths of the trees, and saw nothing.

And then he stopped so fast that I almost bumped into him. He pointed one finger up at the sky, signaling me to pay attention, and then he slowly lifted the Remington and fitted it to his shoulder. There in the path, less than twenty feet in front of us, was a magnificent buck, with at least twelve points on his rack. The deer wasn't a young one; but he wasn't old yet, either. His flank was crossed with violent-looking scars; his haunches quivered with muscle; the fur under his muzzle was matted with icicles. He looked like a creature that had just survived an epic quest from a Jules Verne story.

He stared at us. We stared at him. No one moved.

I braced myself, waiting for the rifle shot. But it didn't come. Instead, my father slowly let the rifle slip in his hands until it was pointed at the ground. And then I heard an unexpected sound: the soft huff of my father's tears.

My father never cried.

"Go on," he said to the deer; and his voice in the silent forest was shockingly loud. "Better you than us."

"*Dad!*" I objected in a whisper, already anticipating a familiar knot of hunger. My father hunted only once or twice a year, and only on these late-winter days when our food stores were empty and the roads were still unplowed. Without venison, I knew that all we would have to eat was oatmeal mush and canned beans and the last of the frozen potatoes in our storage shed.

My father ignored me. So did the buck. They stared at each other, and something seemed to pass between them, two battle-scarred veterans of life. The needles of the pine trees, swaying in the wind, seemed to be whispering secret messages to them both. Time slowed and stopped, as if the falling snow had frozen them both into statues. Half hidden behind my father, I was part of the moment and yet I knew I wasn't a part of it at all.

And then within a single breath the buck leapt away into the brush and was gone.

My father turned to me, his face glistening with frozen tears. "Every living thing on this planet, including human beings, are products of nature, squirrel," he said. "Humans may *believe* that we are in charge, but we shouldn't be, because we can't be trusted with that power. We need to acknowledge the things that are still wild, the things that have survived *us*. We need to remember that this"—he gestured at the trees around us, the falling snow, the vanished deer— "is what we are supposed to be part of. Instead, we've manufactured these precarious societies, ruining the earth with our so-called technological advances. Our guns and our biological weapons, television sets and computers. Making ourselves obsolete in the process, even." He wiped away the last of the tears. "Left alone, nature takes care of itself. But all we humans do is destroy. That's where this all goes eventually, you see? Apocalypse. So there was no way I was going to kill that deer. Not today."

My father had hunted deer before. I failed to understand why this day, this *particular* deer had affected him so profoundly; but my father's impulses were an enigma I often failed to understand. "Come on, Dad. It's just one deer, not the end of the world," I complained. "And I'm *hungry*."

"You're not listening, Jane," he said sharply.

My greatest fear was disappointing my father. So I looked, really *looked*, at the trail that the deer had left in the snow, and at the trees holding us close; and I felt my eyes welling up with tears, too—at the beauty of it all, how much would be lost if we destroyed it. And I believed him, even when my stomach twisted itself into a tiny little walnut of hunger later that day. I believed him, even as we ate oatmeal at every meal for the next week, until the plows finally came through and the roads were passable again. Nor did I stop to consider the hypocrisy when my father went into his office after dinner and turned on his TV, tuned it to the news, and began to write. Because in my heart I understood that my father was always right, and my complaints *were* a sign of my privileged position within a flawed modern society. That if we killed one deer, we might as well kill them all; and then where would we be? Once we lost our respect for nature, the world was on its way to an end.

My father, I told myself, was a pure man, a bona fide modern Thoreau who could see things in a way I never would.

Three years later, when I published his manifesto, I would recognize many of the same ideas that he shared with me that day—the same kernel of truth, but spun out until it was a thick, impenetrable web, encompassing all human existence. And even though the madness inside him had grown evident by then—evident to anyone who had a TV or a newspaper subscription or an internet connection—I could also still remember that moment in the forest and see the truth in it. The moment where he made me understand why he wept for a deer. And I was able to love him for that, despite everything he'd done to me.

2

On the day that everything began to change, I woke up to the sound of cursing men. Someone was pounding on the door of our cabin, the side of their fist a dull thud against the rough-hewn planks. I sat up with a jolt, already anticipating my father's command, ready to run.

Instead, from the kitchen, on the other side of my bedroom door, I could hear my father whistling as he cooked up bacon for breakfast. He'd burned it again; I could smell it from there. My father never quite understood when to turn off the heat.

The pounding stopped. There was one more massive bang it sounded like a steel-tipped boot against the door—and then a voice yelled hoarsely, "Asshole, we know it was you." This was followed by the sound of footsteps squelching through the mud in the driveway; more murmured conversation; a truck starting, wheels spinning against gravel.

The calendar on the wall across from me read November 12, 1996. I was seventeen years old.

Happy birthday to me, I thought. *I'm almost an adult now.*

It was an abstract idea for me, being an *adult,* probably because I had never particularly felt like a child in the first place. My father had always taken pride in treating me like an equal: giving me the same responsibilities, the same reading material, the same daily and weekly chores that he would do. As if we were partners, not father and child. The only things he didn't let me do were drive his truck alone or fire his gun without him by my side. Things that might, you know, precipitate my untimely demise or get me arrested. Otherwise, everything that he did, I did, too: cooking, cleaning, chopping firewood, proofreading his essays, debating the tenets of post-Kantian philosophy.

Growing up, I was aware that in other homes, kids were treated like delicate creatures, pampered and taken on beach vacations, and showered with toys and clothes that mostly ended up in the landfill. They read books with dragons and princesses on the covers rather than books authored by dead Russian thinkers. There was no point in longing for this, though; the few times I'd asked my father for something frivolous, like a dress or a doll, he'd gotten an expression on his face like I had just asked him to arm-wrestle with a ferret. And even if he later showed up with a gift vaguely along the lines of what I'd requested—a pink T-shirt with sequins on the front, picked up at the thrift store in Livingston, or a moldering stuffy shaped like a turtle—it wasn't ever *quite* right, and so eventually I'd learned not to ask. It was easier just to want the things that he wanted, too, because then I might actually get them.

Because it was my birthday I gave myself the luxury of an extra five minutes in bed, and then made my way to the kitchen.

The kitchen was warm and hazy with smoke from the bacon. My father, standing at the sink, was staring out at the muddy lane, looking inordinately pleased with himself. He turned to see me standing in the doorway.

"Happy birthday, squirrel." My father pointed at the table, where he'd placed a small rectangular gift wrapped in newspaper and yarn next to my plate. The table was set with pancakes and hot coffee and the carbonized nubs of bacon. Three out-of-date newspapers—today it was *The Wall Street Journal, The New York Times,* and *USA Today*—sat in a stack, part of my daily political science lesson.

I slid into my chair, ignoring the gift. I figured that it was going to be something intrinsically practical and utilitarian—a new pair of gloves, or a utility knife, or maybe a German-English dictionary so I could translate Heidegger myself. I poured maple syrup over my pancakes and took a big, sugary bite. "What was that?"

He pasted a studied blankness across his face. "What do you mean?"

"At the door, Dad. The men pounding at the door. Not the feds, I take it?"

"Ah," he said. He scratched his beard. "No. Hmmm. I think they were just the men who were working on the power lines up the road."

All week long, bulldozers had been busy clear-cutting a path through the forest, just a mile away from our cabin. You could hear the buzz saws from our property, a brutal cacophony that echoed off the hills. Some new variety of power lines was going in, something to do with the explosion in dial-up internet, and the gash in the forest stretched as far as you could see in either direction. Dad and I had walked up a few days earlier to assess the damage, watched the bright yellow machinery swarming through the cut. Felled pines lay scattered on the ground like beached whales, waiting to be dragged off and transformed into paper napkins and salad bowls and two-by-fours.

"This is what happens when people get addicted to technology, their television sets and computer monitors. They lose all perspective of what's important," my father muttered.

"*Every creature is better alive than dead, men and moose and pine trees, and he who understands it aright will rather preserve its life than destroy it*," I said.

My father smiled and inclined his chin in approval, which sent warmth all the way down to my toes in their thrice-darned socks. And then he shook his head. "Frankly, I'd have to disagree with Thoreau about that. Not all men are better alive than dead, considering."

A bulldozer drove past, and the man behind the wheel smiled and waved at us, believing us curious gawkers. In response, my father raised two fists to the sky and unfolded his middle fingers. The driver dropped the smile and flipped him the bird right back.

"So why didn't you open the door?" I asked now, even though I already suspected I knew the answer. There was, I had already noted, a suspicious silence coming from the cut today, even though it was already 8:00 A.M., well past the time when the machinery usually started up.

"Didn't think there was much that needed to be said to them, did I?"

"Dad. Did you do something?"

"What *something* might you mean?" He was trying not to smirk, and failing. "Like, say, sabotaging their equipment by putting sugar in the gas tanks? I suppose someone might have done that. I heard the interlopers rumbling about *something* along those lines as they tracked their mud on our porch and splintered our door with their boots. But is there evidence that it was me who did such a *something*? Absolutely not. No evidence at all." He picked up a black strip of bacon and crunched it, then winked.

The wink delighted me; there was nothing I wanted more than to be his confidante and keeper of secrets. "Way to show them, Dad," I said.

I sat and grabbed the closest paper—a two-weeks-out-of-date *New York Times*—and pulled out the Arts section, where there was a review of a film adaptation of *Romeo and Juliet* that I knew I would never get to see. When I looked up, my father was watching me read with an opaque expression on his face. "That's the garbage section. Read the National Report first. And aren't you going to open your present?"

Preparing myself for disappointment, I picked up his gift. I untied the knot and tore off the paper, revealing a box of colored pastels. Not at all what I had expected. It stunned me silent. My old set of drawing pencils were cheap Crayola crayons, worn to stubs; these were fancy, professional-like. Who knew where he'd even gotten them, or how he'd afforded them, or why he'd felt compelled to buy me such a frivolous gift.

"I didn't get the right kind?" he asked, breaking the silence. When I looked at him, I was surprised by the naked neediness in his face. He didn't usually seem this concerned about whether I liked something.

I lined the pastels up neatly against the edge of the table. "No. They're perfect. I'm just surprised."

"I thought you deserved something nice. You're getting so . . ." He didn't finish this sentence, and I was left wondering how it was going to end. Instead, he stood behind my chair and put his hands on my shoulders. He squeezed them, gripping me so hard that it felt like he was trying to pin me in place forever. Then he let me go, but not before I received his silent message, the one that he'd never been very good at articulating out loud. *I love you. This is for you. We are a team.*

AFTER BREAKFAST I took a blanket out to the ancient recliner on our porch—leaking stuffing, water-stained, the shape of our rears permanently dented in its fabric—and sat there, testing out my new pastels. The air smelled like woodsmoke and damp pine needles, rich and organic. The meadow below our cabin was frosted with dew; I could see the silvery tracks of the deer that had passed by before dawn.

Thanks to my vantage point, I had a perfect view of the wolf as he emerged from the tree line to lope through the clearing toward a thicket just beyond the meadow. He had been living in a den somewhere near our property since the previous spring; a lone silver-haired wolf, stiff with age and a little bedraggled. My father thought he'd been expelled from his pack by a younger alpha male; but the old wolf was stubborn and refused to die. Too slow to hunt deer, he'd instead been dining on the rabbits in our meadow or seeing what he could pick off from the farms beyond the woods. I'd wanted to name him— *Samson*, I was thinking—but my father said that would be infantilizing to a wild animal who was indifferent to human existence, and probably not long for this world anyway. So I kept the name I'd picked to myself.

I sketched Samson's matted fur, the lean muscles in his flanks; tore it up, tried again. My father emerged from the cabin with a cup of coffee in his hand. He handed it to me and we shared it in silence as the sun lifted above the trees and lit up the dew like a million tiny prisms. You'd think I'd have been used to the view after living my whole life in that cabin, but it never got old. It's a cliché, I know, but every damn day felt new.

I studied my father as he gazed out over his domain. He had a face that looked like it belonged on Mount Rushmore, all angles and crevasses. His eyes, as bright and black as a raven's, were set deep in his face; and his nose had a prominent bump on it from when he'd broken it in a childhood bike accident. His skin was tanned and leathery, with deep lines from all the time he spent squinting in the sun. He trimmed his beard only a few times a year—he couldn't be bothered to think about it until it started to catch in the buttons of his shirt, and then he'd hack it all off and start from scratch. He might have been handsome had he been interested in taking care of himself, but that was something only lesser men cared about.

I never drew him, because I knew I couldn't do him justice.

"So what do you want to do today?" he asked. "Walk out to Coyote Rock to check on our dam? Get the pickles going? Tackle the Spanish Civil War?"

It was a Tuesday, so technically a school day. But my father had let go of those kinds of formalities long ago. Officially, I was a home-schooled high school junior. Unofficially, I had been haphazardly taught some subjects (science, languages) and given college-level instruction in others (philosophy, mathematics, history) and missed others altogether (health and music). Every year he dutifully sent in the form testifying that I was being properly educated and received, in exchange, a packet of instructional materials that we used to start the fire in the woodstove. My father wasn't big on being told what to do with his own kid. That's why he'd moved us to a cabin in the woods in the most libertarian state in the nation when I was just four years old.

"What if we drive into Bozeman?" I asked. "We could go to the bookstore."

My father's face twitched. He did not particularly like going into Bozeman, where you could eat sushi that had been flown in from the coasts or buy lamps made from deer antlers or drink at a bar that had an entire wall of TV screens broadcasting different sports games. The place gave him hives. But Bozeman did have a great bookstore, whose manager saved him all the old newspapers; and several useful thrift stores; and the best farm supply store in a hundred miles. And so he toughed it out every few weeks and drove us in.

When I mentioned the bookstore, he glanced over his shoulder to regard the stack of zines that was sitting just inside the door, just as I knew he would. We'd been tripping over them every time we came in and out of the cabin: *Libertaire, issue 8,* twenty-four pages of essays and think pieces penned entirely by Saul Williams, most with titles like "The New Technological World Order" and "Power to the SHEEPLE" and "Dismantling the Autocratic Financial System." The stack by the door held exactly one hundred copies of *Libertaire,* printed out at the Kinko's in Bozeman and cut and stapled together by one Jane Williams, Saul's trusty copy editor and production assistant and occasional typist. Not that I was listed on the masthead.

"Sure," my father said, brightening. "I've been meaning to drop off the new issue."

3

I'M TRYING TO reconstruct all this for you with some purity of memory, but the truth is that I'm never going to be able to rid myself entirely of hindsight. What I see now, from the perspective of these decades later, versus what I felt and saw and experienced in the moment, are two distinct things entirely. My father was a brilliant philosopher king, the benevolent ruler of our tranquil domain; or he was a tyrant, a maniac, and a menace. My life was bucolic and happy; or it was bizarre and lonely.

Which is true? Is it possible it could be both? The more I seek clarity, the more entangled and confused my recollections become.

So let's start by focusing on facts.

Home for us was a seven-hundred-square-foot cabin in the middle of a patch of wild fields and shrubs, surrounded by national forest land, over an hour away from the nearest town. We were the longtime tenants of a man in Livingston who had used the cabin for hunting before he accidentally shot his own foot off. Our closest neighbor was a fifteen-minute drive up a rutted dirt road: a grizzled old carpenter named Shirley, who was as solitary and unsociable as Saul. The two of them drank beer together sometimes and discussed the merits of tax avoidance. That was the extent of my father's social life.

My own social life was even more pathetic. There weren't exactly a lot of teenagers living in the woods around us.

Behind the cabin was a modest vegetable garden and a henhouse, though our chickens kept dying from mange and foxes and general lackadaisical care on my part. Near the edge of the woods there was a garden shed with a solar array on the roof, which my father had built himself some years back and which provided power for us. Farther down the hill was a small pond, diverted from a stream in the woods, with a washing machine he'd jury-rigged out of a plastic bucket, a car battery, and some plungers. Beyond the pond spread a dense blanket of pine, covering the hills for hundreds of miles in every direction.

Once upon a time, you could walk for days through those woods and never come across a sign of civilization, just the occasional hunting cabin; but in recent years kids from the towns had started coming out with their ATVs and motorbikes and crashing their way through the forest. This made my father furious, of course. He'd threatened to put out beds of nails on the paths, or maybe string some wire between the trees, until I pointed out that if he did that and someone died, he would be held liable for murder. When I said that, he hesitated, a distant expression passing over his face; and for a horrible moment I'd wondered if that wasn't such an unappealing prospect to him after all.

Our cabin had four rooms: two tiny bedrooms; a great room with a woodstove, a tidy kitchen, and a leather couch that had been weeping foam for most of my existence; plus my father's study, which was the only room with a lock on the door. The study was where my father spent much of his days, writing on his dyspeptic Smith Corona, or reading, or tinkering with things that he called his "inventions." I wasn't allowed inside this room, though I had my ways.

When we'd first moved to the cabin, back when I was small, there had been no functional bathroom at all, just an outhouse. I could still conjure up the horror of that: the cold, dark maw below me, the spiders overhead, my terror that I might slip into the stinking hole and vanish. My father had finally built a bathroom after I'd cried too many times; he had paid for the septic tank and installed a toilet and clawfoot bathtub, a fact that he still lorded over me whenever I suggested improvements to our living situation.

"Pampered princess demanded a porcelain toilet, and I gave it to her, and that was my first mistake. I've been paying for it ever since. What's next, heated floors and crystal chandeliers?"

"A toaster is not a crystal chandelier, Dad."

"I don't see why you can't make toast under the broiler, the intelligent way. Toast is just heat plus bread. Why do we need a whole extra appliance, with only one function, that will inevitably end up in the landfill someday?"

I'd sighed and given up. I always did. It was impossible to win an argument against my father, though he liked me to try anyway. The man needed a worthy adversary, and I worried that it was never going to be me.

WE DID HAVE a telephone: an old black Bakelite beast, with a cracked rotary dial. My father had installed this in case of emergency, but he mostly used it to call the office of *The Bozeman Daily Chronicle* and suggest editorials about criminalizing ATVs or leaf blowers. I used this phone, now, to call my friend Heidi and let her know that I would be coming by the bookstore. Then I dressed quickly into my cleanest clothes, pulled my hair into braids and assessed myself in the mirror. There wasn't much else to be done.

The previous year, on a trip into town, I'd stolen a lipstick from a Walgreens—slipped it into my pocket while my dad was buying toilet paper—and tucked it at the back of my sock drawer once we got home. The next day, when my father was out in the shed, I hid in the bathroom and smeared it across my lips. The girl that stared back at me in the mirror looked foreign, clownish—the color was a garish, unflattering fuchsia—but I was fascinated by her anyway. As if I had just gotten a glimpse of a Jane from an alternate universe, one where there were school dances and double dates and afternoon matinees. Maybe even a girl who had a mother who taught her how to apply mascara and took her shopping and brushed her hair for her.

I wanted that so badly that it hurt to let myself think it.

"When you're an adult," the other Jane in the mirror said slowly, "you can go anywhere you want. You can leave here. You don't have to stay."

I gripped the edge of the sink, dizzy at the very thought, but then I could hear my father's boots on the porch, his voice calling my name—"Jane? Squirrel? Where are you? Come give me a hand."

I grabbed a tissue and swiped frantically at the lipstick, praying that my father wouldn't notice that the cheap tint had stained the cracks in my chapped lips. I shoved the lipstick deep in the back of my sock drawer and didn't look for it again for months.

When I did, I discovered that it had disappeared entirely.

4.

W E'D BEEN HAVING intermittent rainstorms for weeks; the meadows were vast seas of sludgy mud and there were already patches of ice in the shadowy recesses under the trees. The sky was the color of a damp stone. November was the saddest month, in my opinion, even though it was my birthday month. Or maybe *because* it was my birthday month, and birthdays always felt so anticlimactic. November was also the month that my mother died, my father had told me once. Which made it unbearably sad, even though I had no memory at all of her death.

My father drove the truck. He always did, despite the fact that I was a perfectly capable driver. Ever since my legs grew long enough to reach the pedals—at age twelve—my father would regularly stick me behind the wheel of his rusting Chevy pickup and have me drive up and down the dusty dirt roads that surrounded our property. *Just so you're prepared for when the worst-case scenario happens,* he'd say. Believing, it seemed, that it was an inevitability that it *would* happen. He never elucidated the precise scenario that he had in mind—clearly, one in which my father himself was incapacitated—so I filled in the gap with my own imagination. A forest fire sweeping in, me fleeing before a wall of flame. A hunting accident; me behind the wheel racing my father to the hospital, blood puddling up in the passenger foot well. And of course, government agents in black vests, surrounding our house, my father in handcuffs while I fled in the truck.

The feds were the shadowy threat that loomed over us at all times. My father wasn't particularly clear with me about who the "feds" were, exactly—the FBI, for sure, but other times this seemed to also include the state police, U.S. marshals, the ATF, and pretty much anyone who worked as a government authority of any sort. Nor had my father ever given me a clear answer to the question of why we were so concerned about them, just that the government was always looking for a reason to target the good guys. As in, "We represent a threat to the feds, we're smarter than them, and so it's just a matter of time before they come after us." This was supposed to be a sufficient explanation for why we'd lived out there in the woods for thirteen years, as far from the authorities as humanly possible; and it was also why I would never submit to a driver's test administered by some limp-mustached DMV stoolie.

Only on our property, far from the arbitrary rules of government and authority, did my father ever seem truly comfortable.

A few miles down the road, we passed the worksite, where the inoperable bulldozers sat idle inside the cut. The slash in the forest was quiet.

"Score one for the good guy," my father said, and we smiled at each other. The old Chevy truck rattled down the dirt road, rutted from the rain, the pines thick on either side. After twenty minutes, the track spat us out on a paved highway, with the beginning signs of civilization—a few houses, a small market, a shack selling smoked jerky.

We stopped at the intersection there, where a grille of mailboxes signaled the existence of the homes hidden in the woods beyond. It was a surprising number. Ours was a rusty steel oblong that locked with a deadbolt, as if there might be communication of true value stashed inside and an abundance of mail thieves nearby.

My father idled the truck and handed me a stack of letters. "Pop these in the box, will you?"

I glanced at the addresses on the envelopes as I shoved them in the mailbox. *New York Times Op Ed. Harper's—Editor in Chief. The Washington Post Submissions. Reason. National Review.* The usual suspects.

Our box was empty except for a dead spider. I blew the spider away and left the stack of envelopes for the mailman.

"Nothing in there?" my father asked when I got back in the passenger seat.

I shook my head. "I don't get it. I thought that last essay you sent in was really brilliant."

"It's because they're morons." He spun the steering wheel hard, throwing us back on the road so quickly that I nearly fell off my seat. I ignored his darkening mood, because my own was lifting with every mile closer to town.

Bozeman was still a modest college town back then, not at all the overpriced yuppie destination it was doomed to become. Main Street was a stretch of brick-faced buildings, many of which dated back a hundred years or more—a hotel, a theater, a hardware store, your standard small-town staples. Even then, though, there were already a few upscale boutiques and restaurants catering to the college students and ski bunnies who were building themselves mansions out at Big Sky.

We parked on the street outside the Country Bookshelf. My father pulled the paper sack of *Libertaire* from the bed of the truck, and together we went inside.

Heidi was waiting for me. Before I even made it through the door she threw her arms around me in a straitjacket embrace. "Happy birthday, Janey-Jane," she squealed in my ear, her breath smelling like strawberry candy. "You're so old!"

I was unpracticed when it came to hugs from people who were not my father. Each one I received—and I could count them on one hand—had come burdened by a minefield of unanswerable questions. How long were you supposed to hug someone back? What did you do with your hands, squeeze or pat or just let them lie there limply on the other person's back? Was it weird if you took a big sniff of the person you were hugging, to see what they smelled like? What about if your boobs got mashed against the other person's chest? If the other person let go first, did it mean they liked you less?

I went with the pat-and-release-first method. "Practically dead. Better prepare the coffin."

"God, you're so *mordant*. What are you doing to celebrate?"

"Visiting my favorite bookstore?" I looked around the shop. It was a pleasantly cluttered two-story space, open at the center, the shelves bristling with handwritten recommendations. You could buy a calendar, or a coloring book, or a fishing guide; there was a children's section with beanbags, and a long wall of magazines. At the far end of the room was a modest wooden shelf, jammed with self-published zines. They were hand-stapled and time-faded and curling at the edges, decorated with hand-drawn graphics, priced at a buck or two apiece. Somewhere on that shelf sat copies of *Libertaire, issue 7.*

Lina had emerged from the stockroom, drawn out by Heidi's squeals. She had a blue apron tied over her jeans and T-shirt, frizzy curls anchored on the top of her head with a Bic pen. "Well, if isn't the birthday girl," she said.

"Hi there, Lina."

"Call her Mrs. Murphy," my father muttered under his breath. "Be respectful."

Lina tucked her hands in the pockets of her apron and smiled at me. She was a round woman, who walked belly-first as though her soft paunch was a source of great pride. "Oh, no need to be so formal. Not that I don't appreciate it—good manners are hard to come by these days. But Lina is fine, Jane."

"Thank you, Lina," I said.

The four of us stood there awkwardly. Lina smiled brightly at my father, as if he were just an average customer and not a curmudgeonly recluse who lived in the woods. "You know, I was thinking of you two the other day. My cousin converted the barn on his property into a sweet little guesthouse, and he's looking for tenants. I thought, maybe this would be the year you two would want to move a little closer to town." I couldn't see my father standing behind me, but I could glean his reaction to this from the way Lina widened her eyes and held up a finger to slow his objections. "Wait, now, listen—you could try it just for the winter. I know how hard it is out there, once you get snowed in. Don't tell me it's not. And, Jane, you could enroll in a few classes at Gallatin High. Or even, Montana State, they have some extension courses for advanced learners like yourself. Now, Saul"—the finger was waggling in alarming circles—"I'm not saying that you're not giving Jane an excellent education at home. But this might be a nice change of pace. And Jane would get to meet some more local kids."

I knew there wasn't a chance in hell my father was going to take her up on this. The waggling finger wasn't helping matters. "Local kids? You're talking about the thugs that I see wandering around this town, plugged into their Walkmans, their jeans hanging down below their underwear? Tattoos and pierced noses and the intellect of a flea? What business would Jane want with them?"

"Oh, now, I wouldn't call them thugs. There are some very nice girls at the high school—"

"Who will fill Jane's head with frivolous nonsense. No thank you."

I could see Lina's expression deflating in the way that people's expressions sometimes did when my dad started to really get going. "No, you're right, we certainly wouldn't want *that*," she said. It was painful to watch other people try to argue with my father; didn't they know they'd never win? "Anyway, it was just a thought! Heidi's considering giving the high school a shot this spring. She'd love to have a friend with her." She put out a hand and caressed Heidi's cheek, lifting a stray hair with one finger and tucking it behind Heidi's ear. Heidi swatted Lina's hand away, but she smiled at her mother as she did it.

The intimacy between the two of them made something ache inside me. I had a vague memory of my own mother's hands in my hair, combing it into braids; but it was possible that was just cribbed from a scene I'd read in *Little Women*, Marmee fussing over Jo's locks. Whenever I was around Heidi and Lina, I couldn't help wondering what it must feel like to have a mother like Lina. Did Heidi's mom teach her what to do when she got her first period? Or did she just leave her a box of sanitary pads next to a dog-eared copy of *The "What's Happening to My Body?" Book for Girls*, like my father had?

I couldn't help wondering who I would be, with a mother of my own. How much easier my life might have been.

"We're just fine where we are," my father said. "We don't need any *thoughts*."

"I'm sure you don't," Lina chirped. "Now, Saul, how do you feel about letting the girls go get some coffee by themselves? It's a little early in the day for cake, but they have cinnamon rolls down at the diner that will do if they want a sugar fix. Besides, I have some business matters I need to discuss with you."

My father looked at me. I stared back at him, trying not to beg. I could see him making calculations in his head. Then he shrugged. "It's a free country, or so they like to say, though God knows most of its citizens are eager to throw away that freedom and hand it straight over to . . ."

I tugged Heidi toward the street, tuning him out. "I'll be back in an hour, Dad," I called and let the door slam shut behind me before he had a chance to respond.

5

Heidi clung to my arm as we walked the three blocks to the diner. This was as much about practicality as it was affection: She walked with a limp, the result of an old car accident that had left her bedridden with a fractured spine for much of her adolescence. They said she'd never walk again, but she refused to accept that diagnosis and eventually proved them wrong. Her pugnaciousness was one of the things I loved about her.

Our friendship was a much happier accident. Two years earlier, on one of our stops at the Country Bookshelf, the middle-aged woman at the counter had held up the copy of *On the Origin of Species* that my father was purchasing, her eyes running from the book cover to me and back again.

"Your daughter is homeschooled," she observed.

My father looked like he might snatch the book right back out of her hand. "Who told you that?"

"Well, it's Wednesday morning and your daughter isn't in school, and I suspect this reading material isn't intended for you." When he didn't disagree, she turned to me. "How old are you, sweetheart?"

"Fifteen," I answered.

She lit up. "Well, that's just perfect. I have someone you should meet." She turned and shouted toward the back of the store, "Heidi, can you come out here a second?"

A small round girl appeared in the door of the stockroom and walked toward us. She was redheaded and fair, but her face was so thick with freckles that it looked like she had a tan. She wore lavender head-to-toe, from her fuzzy angora sweater down to her striped knee-high socks. Even with the cane in her hand, she moved quickly, with a funny lopsided waddle that reminded me of a drunk penguin.

"My daughter, Heidi," announced the woman—this was Lina, the store manager, I was to learn. "She's been doing school at home, too, ever since the accident. We're always looking for other homeschooled girls to connect with."

Heidi's eyes met mine. I was acutely aware of my own pastel-free outfit, pieced together from trips to thrift stores and the Army Navy. Flannel shirt, cargo pants, boots with lug soles, everything selected for practicality rather than fashion. But this girl didn't stare or curl up her nose, the way the kids I passed on the Bozeman streets sometimes did. She just grinned, with teeth as crooked as her spine, and stuck out her free hand.

"Pleasedtameetcha," she said.

IF MY FATHER wasn't thrilled about my one-and-only friend, in all her conspicuous-consumptive glory, he was also wise enough not to discourage it. He knew, I think, that I had grown aware of the existence of other kids in the world, and my own isolation from them. Maybe he had calculated that keeping me secluded was more likely to fuel any burgeoning teenage discontent than a solitary friend would. It's possible he also reasoned that he shouldn't upset Lina, who managed one of the handful of bookstores in Montana that allowed him to stick *Libertaire* on its racks, and who also gave him all the out-of-date newspapers and magazines for free.

Friendship was a logistical challenge. I'd never been allowed to go to Heidi's house, and she certainly wasn't invited to mine. Distance and lack of transportation made it difficult to see each other, but at least there was the telephone. I'd tell her stories about life in the woods, about the raccoons that mated under our porch, and the geothermal cooling system my father was trying to build; she'd tell me about what was happening in town, the people she saw on the streets, and the plots of the Meg Ryan movies she'd watched. She complained about her mom, always hovering and anxious; and I think she expected me to do the same about my father, but I didn't exactly know how. What other reference points did I have to compare him to, anyway? I had never met any other dads. I didn't know what was normal.

Looking back, I have to wonder what Heidi found compelling about me. It wasn't my worldliness—I had the social-emotional intelligence of a toad, even if I could quote Baudelaire and knew how to kill a chicken—and it certainly wasn't that I was a fun gossip. Maybe she was taking pity on me, in my isolation; or maybe she didn't have any other options for friends, either. Possibly she just found me interesting, like a novelty act in a vaudeville show. Even in Montana, a state full of iconoclasts, you didn't meet a lot of kids who had been raised almost completely off the grid.

Whatever the reason for Heidi's enthusiasm, I certainly wasn't about to question it.

THE WESTERN CAFÉ was exactly what its name suggests, an old-school diner whose knotty-pine walls were hung with taxidermic turkeys and vintage rifles and handy illustrated diagrams of fishing lures. We sat at the counter and sipped black coffee that tasted like old pencils. The café was populated entirely by good old boys at that hour, butt cracks visible on every stool; but for a teenager who had spent most of her life in the same patch of woods, sitting there with an actual friend felt like the height of adult sophistication.

I picked at my cinnamon roll, slick with icing. "Is it true, that you're going to enroll in school?"

"Thinking about it," she said. "I'm sick of spending my days studying in the stockroom of the Country Bookshelf. God, I don't think I've spoken to a boy in, like, a year?" She looked at me, expecting me to be horrified by this revelation, though of course I'd never spoken to a boy in, like, *ever*? "Maybe you could move to town by yourself, even if your dad doesn't want to. We have an extra bedroom."

"My father is never going to let that happen, Heidi."

She took a big bite of her roll, sugar icing frosting her lips. "Yeah, I guess not. He was in a real downer mood today, wasn't he?"

"That's just his personality."

"Don't you get tired of it?"

I shrugged. "He knows what he believes. There's nothing wrong with that."

"My mom, she's always trying so hard to be upbeat and optimistic, I think she believes that a positive attitude is somehow going to erase all the bullshit from my accident. But gosh, it's not like you can smile away pain." When I looked at her with unease, she laughed. "Oh, don't worry. I've got opioids for *that*. Anyway"—she pulled a small box out of her pocket and handed it to me—"here. For your birthday."

Her gift was wrapped in butterfly paper and tied with a shiny gold ribbon, prettier than anything I owned. I stared at it so long that she finally elbowed me in the ribs. "You're supposed to *open* it, idiot."

I picked at the tape with a ragged fingernail, sliding the paper off carefully so that it wouldn't tear, thinking that I might fold it and save it. Inside was a white cardboard box, and inside that, a small silver chain with a dolphin pendant. A tiny blue jewel winked from its solitary eye.

"It made me think of you," she said.

I had no clue why the pendant made her think of me—I didn't own a piece of jewelry, nor did I care much about dolphins—and yet I was in danger of crying into my coffee. "This is the nicest gift I've ever been given."

"Don't be too impressed, that's not a sapphire and I'm pretty sure it's just plated. Don't wear it in a swimming pool or you'll end up with a green neck."

"That's not going to be a problem," I said. "As I've never actually been in a swimming pool and I don't see that changing anytime."

I lifted my braids so that she could fasten the chain around my neck. She sat back to assess it, then adjusted the pendant until it was centered on my sweatshirt. "I'm going to make my mom take me to the zoo when we go to Chicago. They have a dolphin exhibit there. Apparently, you can even feed them fish by hand, doesn't that seem wild?"

It did, but I was distracted by the other part of her story. "You're going to Chicago?"

"We're visiting colleges over Thanksgiving break. I'm looking at Loyola. It's not my top choice, though. I want to go live somewhere *warm* for a while. Like Miami. Or Texas. But my mom went to Loyola so I might be able to get a legacy scholarship."

I took a swallow of tepid coffee, feeling it sour in my stomach. "But that's so far away. You don't want to go to Montana State?"

"God, I think I'd die. Do *you* want to stay in Bozeman for college?" She hesitated, suddenly realizing: "Wait, you are going to apply to college, aren't you?"

I shrugged. I'd mentioned college to my father a few months earlier, and the conversation had ended just about the way that I expected. "I went to Harvard, the best college in America," he'd said. "I ended up completely in debt to some financial institution and what did I get for it? Nothing. College is a scam. You're not paying for an education. You're paying for a piece of paper that's supposed to quantify your value to society, an utterly arbitrary and meaningless valuation." He'd tapped on the pile of books I was studying. "This is what counts. I'm teaching you everything they taught me. Just as good as a Harvard education, but free, and no one judging you."

"College is a scam," I told Heidi. "You pay a fortune for the right to get drunk at frat parties and learn how to play bongos. Besides, we don't have the money for it, even if I did want to go."

"So you're going to, what? Just stay in the cabin with your dad forever, even after you finish high school?" She looked horrified.

"Not forever," I said, as if I'd put endless hours of thought into it. But honestly, I was still fuzzy on the alternatives that might be available to me without a driver's license or a monetizable skill set or a credentialed education. Would it be so bad, really, to stay in our cabin forever? My father certainly seemed to have no intention of us ever leaving. *You don't understand, this is the best place to be. I picked it special for you. The world is ugly and cruel, you are safe here with me.* He'd said this before, more times than I could count. And how could I argue with that? It was true that nothing bad had ever happened to me there, in our cabin. The horrors of the world at large—the wars and conflicts, the modern frivolities that rot your brain and make you soft, the mass murderers and government agents and people who would want to hurt you—existed only beyond the borders of our property, not within.

We hadn't always been so cloistered. When I was much younger, my father used to take me on day trips to strange towns, some of them quite a drive away. We'd eat ice cream cones and wander around the town's main street, looking in the shop windows but rarely going in. My memories of these trips were vague, but they came underlined by a tinge of anxiety: of waiting in a cold car while my father ran his adult errands, his palpable state of agitation at being out in the world, the sugar on my tongue soured by a sense of guilt. Maybe that's why my father eventually called a stop to them.

We'd stayed in our cabin ever since. And I always told myself that this was fine with me.

And yet. More and more lately I'd found myself fantasizing about getting behind the wheel of my father's truck and just *driving*. Across the Montana state line. Maybe even all the way to one of the coasts. To get a glimpse of the ocean; or a big city; or anything, really, besides the same patch of land that I'd been looking at for my entire childhood.

Heidi was staring at me. She leaned in so close that I could see the flakes of mascara in her lashes. "Please don't do this to yourself, Jane. Don't act like you don't care."

"I'm happy; it's fine," I told Heidi, a little too assertively.

"Remember, you'll be eighteen in a year, and then you'll be a legal adult," she continued. "He can't keep you prisoner after that."

"I'm not a *prisoner*," I retorted, defensive. Still, Heidi's words stuck to me, like a burr in fur: *Was* I? In thirteen years, I'd never left the property without my father. I barely left the property at all. That was an awful lot like prison, if you looked at it that way. I shook my head, trying to dispel the notion, and slammed back the last of my coffee.

"Want refills?" A waitress was standing over us, brandishing an ancient carafe.

I silently pushed my cup forward, just as the front door of the café opened with a bang. My father stood in the doorway, his arms wrapped around the paper sack—still stuffed with copies of *Libertaire,* I noticed with a twinge of concern. His eyes scanned the room, looking for me, but skidded across me as if I were a stranger of no interest. And then they sprang back, with a look of shock, and I realized that he hadn't recognized me.

He smiled at me, but his smile was like a coiled spring, tight and ominous. "You ready?"

I wasn't, but the expression on his face suggested that I didn't have a choice. I stood and fished in my pocket, wondering if a dollar might have magically materialized there.

"Don't worry," Heidi said, her hand grabbing mine. "I got this."

"Call me when you get back from Chicago?"

"Of course," she said. "We'll do something when I get back. Maybe we can go to the movies. I want to go see *Romeo and Juliet.*" She smiled encouragingly.

"We'll do that, for sure," I lied.

6.

My father was silent for most of the ride home. The day had turned dark, heavy cumulus clouds that threatened more rain collecting overhead. The heater on the old truck spat tepid air at us, losing a futile battle with the drafts from the floorboards. I turned on the radio and spun the dial until it tuned in to a classical station that I knew my father wouldn't object to. Mahler's fifth symphony was playing, and I closed my eyes and tried to let it lull me to sleep, but I could feel the electricity coming off my father, static that filled the cab. My own mood was equally sour, my birthday spoiled by Heidi's unwelcome prodding.

We were almost back to the cabin when he hit the steering wheel with his fist, jolting me alert. "She said they were phasing out the zine rack," he said, his eyes fixed on the road before us. "*Zine.* I hate that word. Equating *Libertaire* with the rest of the crap on that rack, comic strips and music reviews. They didn't sell a single copy of the last issue, can you believe that? Not a one! And someone had jammed a piece of *gum* between the pages of one copy and placed it right back on the rack."

"Which essay? Maybe it was the reader's commentary on your argument. A material metaphor about the stickiness of the subject."

He threw me a look. "She gave the copies all back to me and declined to take the new issue. They're clearing out the rack to make room for a new technology section. Apparently the *internet*"—he spat this word out, as if it were poison—"is more interesting to them than political philosophy and intellectual debate."

"Ugh. The internet," I said knowingly, although I still had only the vaguest understanding of what that was, mostly based on the snide articles that I came across in *The Wall Street Journal*. ("About 15 Million People Troll the Internet, a Study Finds." Or "Wall Street Whiz Finds Niche Selling Books on the Internet." And so on.)

"*So long as the machine process continues to hold its dominant place as a disciplinary factor in modern culture, so long must the spiritual and intellectual life of this cultural era maintain the character which the machine process gives it,*" my father said darkly. "Thorstein Veblen. He saw all this coming. The replacement of psychological health with inhuman computer logic. Our ruin is impending, unless we do something drastic."

We were passing the cut in the forest again, and when I turned to look at the sabotaged bulldozers I saw that two men in orange vests had the side of one of them open, working at the engine. I battled a queasy sensation as I realized that the workers would be back at it tomorrow, or the next day, and the new power lines would go in whether we liked it or not.

"Inevitability is the most important foe to fight," my father liked to say. But as we drove past the waiting coils of cable, I couldn't stop myself from wondering if that battle was ever winnable. Instead, the image of my father sneaking down in the dark to put sugar in the gas tanks was dredging up a different and wholly unwelcome word: *futility*. And then I felt guilty for having let the word into my mind at all.

Because of course my father was right, he *had* to be. I'd read all the books he gave me—Marx and Mao, Rousseau and Paine—and so I understood the teleological basis of his world philosophy. The world was going downhill, industry and technology were making men rich and lazy and self-destructive; and only radical, revolutionary leaders like my father would divert us from disaster. Sabotaging those bulldozers was just a skirmish, I reassured myself; we could still win the war.

Looking back now, can I blame myself for believing this? After all, I was a very good student, and I'd only ever had one teacher.

WE WERE ALMOST to the cabin when he slammed on the brakes. I jerked forward, almost hitting the dashboard with my forehead. A shape was lying just ahead, blocking the road to the house. It was an animal carcass, its fur so matted with blood and mud that it took me a long minute to realize it was the grizzled old wolf that hunted in the meadow. *Samson.* Three hunchbacked vultures were already circling nearby, eager to get first crack at their lunch.

My father got out of the car and went to stand over the body of the dead wolf. I watched as he prodded at the carcass with the toe of his boot. Then he grabbed it by one of its paws and dragged it through the mud to the edge of the road, heaving it toward the bushes. The vultures, undaunted, pressed in closer. He picked up a rock and threw it at them, then turned and climbed back into the truck.

He sat, staring through the windshield for a long time, before starting the truck again.

"How did he die?" I asked.

"Someone shot him."

I wondered who had done this. Could it have been the workmen in the cut, getting revenge for their ruined bulldozers? But how would they even know that this was *our* wolf? More likely it was a nearby farmer, protecting his livestock, and the wolf had slunk back to our property to die. That kind of thing happened all the time in Montana, especially to an old wolf that didn't have a pack to hunt with anymore. I knew I wasn't supposed to feel attached, any more than I felt attached to the chickens whose necks I so casually wrung for our dinners. But the idea of the old wolf being eviscerated by vultures left me feeling oddly bereft.

When we got home, my father went straight to his study and closed the door, locking it behind him. After a few minutes, I heard the television go on. I picked up an empty canning jar and pressed it to the door to listen. Through the wood I could hear a news anchor commenting on the elections that had just taken place the previous week. (The results— *yet more fools in charge*—had sent my father out to the woodpile with his axe, stormy-eyed and silent.) Louder than the television, though, came the syncopated rattle of my father's Smith Corona. I could hear his fingers striking the keys as if he were trying to punish them.

7

I woke up at some nameless hour of the night, roughly shaken into consciousness by a hand on my shoulder. Blinded by the dark, at first I wasn't sure if I'd crossed back over the threshold into reality or if this was just part of my dream. But then I registered my father's presence leaning over me, felt the heat of his nighttime breath against my cheek.

"It's time," he whispered in my ear. "They came for us."

I bolted upright, instantly wide-awake. "The feds? Is this because of what you did to the bulldozers?"

My father held a finger to my lips, silencing me. He was already moving toward the door, his stocking feet silent against the wooden floorboards. I slid out of bed and followed him.

We slept in our clothes for just this reason. *The day may come when we will need to flee without warning.* I had permanent rough patches on my belly where the buttons and zippers of my jeans rubbed my tender skin all night long.

There was almost no moon and our curtains were drawn for privacy, so I couldn't see what was happening outside our cabin. I couldn't hear footsteps on the porch, so the feds had to be farther down the lane or hidden in the tree line with their guns trained on our door. I wondered how my father had known that the feds were on their way: if he'd been up late, listening to the sounds of the night, or if he'd somehow been tipped off.

I grabbed my go bag from the hook where it hung outside my bedroom door; and then the rifle that hung on the wall beside that. These were my jobs. My father was already working at his, pushing aside the table in the living room, flipping back the threadbare rug to reveal the trapdoor beneath it.

I handed him the rifle and he moved aside so that I could climb in first.

The air in our secret tunnel was cold and smelled so strongly of earth that it made my nose sting. I got to the bottom of the ladder and crouched there, waiting as my father climbed down beside me and then pulled the trapdoor shut above us. He'd rigged up a clever little pulley to flip the rug back into place. Once it was closed, the tunnel was a black pit of darkness, devoid of light so completely that I couldn't see my hand in front of my face.

"Dad? Is this really it? Or is it just a drill?"

"It's real," he said tersely.

I fumbled in the pocket of my backpack, trying to locate the Zippo that was stashed there, my shaking fingers doing an inventory of the bag's familiar contents: Flint. Box of bullets. Extra batteries. Altoids tin with two hundred dollars in cash stashed inside. Pocketknife.

My father's flashlight clicked on next to me, just as I grasped the smooth metal of the Zippo. I recoiled from the sudden wash of light and flung out my hand to reveal the lighter in my palm.

"You want me to do it?" I whispered.

My father shook his head. "You go ahead. I'll set it and catch up with you." He pointed the flashlight down the tunnel. "Run."

Relieved, I turned and ran.

Not that running was really possible, of course. The tunnel was only four feet high and three feet wide, braced with two-by-fours, and only a hundred yards long, the distance to our shed. My father had spent more than two years digging it out with a pickaxe and explosives that he designed himself, starting not long after my thirteenth birthday and ending after I'd turned fifteen. My task had been to shuttle the dirt to the far edges of our property, using a rusty old wheelbarrow that rubbed my palms raw. The blisters had eventually popped and bled before turning into permanent calluses that I liked to rub with my thumb when I was reading.

I squatted and waddled as fast as I could toward the darkness that lay beyond my father's flashlight beam. The first time I'd been down here I'd been terrified of seeing spiders or rats or sightless moles; but the truth was that nothing lived down in this gravelike dark. Behind me, I could hear the pop and sizzle of my father's matches. I braced myself for the flare of light that would come when the ignition pile lit; I wondered how long it would take for the cabin to go up in flames. What if my father hadn't calculated it properly? What if the flames shot down the tunnel instead of exploding up through the vents that he'd designed? What if he set *us* on fire by mistake?

By the time I made it to the door beneath our garden shed, my father had almost caught up with me.

"Faster."

I was sweating through my T-shirt. Even through the dust in my nose I could smell the sharp tang of panic as I pushed against the door, trying to get the leverage to fling it open. It seemed to be stuck. I waited for my father to reach across and help me but he just crouched behind me, his arms braced against the dirt walls of the tunnel, waiting. The explosion kept not coming. Maybe it wouldn't come. Maybe we were seconds away from dying. Maybe the feds were already sitting on the other side of the trapdoor, guns pointed at us.

The trapdoor wouldn't budge.

Finally, I heaved my shoulder into it, jamming it so hard that I thought my collarbone had surely snapped. The door dislodged itself from the frame, and I managed to push it open and climb out into the cool silence of the garden shed.

My breath came shallow and fast. I retrieved tennis shoes from my go bag and pulled them on, tying the laces with fingers that remained stubbornly disobedient. My father materialized from the tunnel and slammed the door shut behind him. He went to peer through the dusty window of the shed back toward the cabin.

"Can you see anything?" I whispered. "Is it on fire?"

The shed had two doors: one in front that faced the cabin and a second that opened directly into the forest, shielded from view. Out the back door, then, and into the woods: There was a path there, just steps from the shed, that led for a mile through the trees. Eventually it would take us to an old logging road, rarely used, where my father sometimes hid his truck.

"OK," he said. "Let's go."

I opened the back door of the shed and began to run.

Shrubs whipped at my calves. My feet fumbled over rocks and roots. Tree limbs reached sharp fingers out to grab at my shirtsleeves. The go bag thumped against my back, soaked with sweat. I ran as fast as I could, with every step sure that I would hear the crack of a gun, the whoosh of an explosion, the shouts of the men who were hunting us.

"STOP."

I stumbled, nearly falling over, my body in such instinctual flight that it couldn't keep up with my mind's obedient response to my father's command. I slowed, turned, braced myself against a pine as my lungs pulled in ragged gulps of freezing night air. My father stood silhouetted in the trees, in no hurry at all. He was smiling, pointing to his wristwatch.

"Four minutes fifty-eight seconds," he said. "That's a record."

I could feel my heart pounding so fast that I thought it might come right up through my throat. The sweat was already cooling against my skin, bringing up goosebumps.

"So it *was* just a drill?" I was still tense, ready to bolt.

"Just a drill. You did fine. A little slow on getting that lighter out. If you were on your own, you'd need to be quicker on the draw with that fire. But overall, not bad."

My heart was slowing to a dull, leaden thump. Why was I always so surprised by this? Twice a year he'd done this, since the tunnel had been completed; this had to be the fifth time, or maybe it was the sixth. And every time, I believed it.

"Seriously, Dad?" I said, suddenly furious. "It's my *birthday*."

"When the feds come, they won't care if it's your birthday or not," he said. "I don't care if you like these drills. This is for *us*. You know that if they come for me, they'll put you in foster care. One of those horrible group homes where kids get shanked or end up addicted to crack. We do these drills so that we can both survive."

My mouth was full of gritty saliva, thick with dust from the tunnel. I spat on the ground, trying to wrap my head around the word *survive*.

My father had an answer to everything. He'd made sure I'd always known that. But that night, for the first time, I realized that the one answer he'd never given me was the answer to the most pivotal question of all: What happens *after* survival? What does it mean to survive, when you're not quite sure what you're living for?

What do you do when you start to realize that you want more than just . . . existence?

8

MY FATHER HAD an old photo of himself from his Harvard days, and it was hard to believe it was the same person I knew: The baby-faced boy, clean-shaven and short-haired and pale in a crisp white shirt, seemed like an utterly different species of human. I couldn't quite fathom how the jagged father I knew had emerged from that soft, malleable face; and yet there was still something about his eyes that hadn't changed, their corvine gaze. In the photo, he was giving the photographer a sharp sideways look, as though about to instruct them to put the camera down. I knew that look.

I asked my father once who the photographer was: I was always desperately curious about details of his life before, his life out *there*. "No one of importance," he replied. "A classmate. They were all the same: striving, greedy, and empty."

This photograph was one of only a handful that my father possessed. When I asked where the rest were—why there weren't albums from his years before—he shook his head in apology. "Lost in a move years ago." Besides the college photo, there was a photograph of him as a little boy, sitting on a brand-new Schwinn five-speed with a red tinsel bow on the handles. Another photo was of eight men, bespectacled and wearing boxy suits, standing on the steps of a glass building—his colleagues, he said, from a job he'd once had. There were names scrawled on the back of this last one, in handwriting that wasn't my father's: *Nick Raymond Baron Peter Ajay Adam Mike Isaac.*

But the photo I was most interested in, of course, was the one of my mother.

My father liked to talk about ideas more than he liked to talk about himself, but over the years he'd dropped tidbits of his biography that I collected like breadcrumbs. I knew that he'd grown up in an anodyne working-class suburb in the San Francisco Bay Area, with unkind parents who didn't understand him. I also knew that he'd attended Harvard, which he'd paid for by waiting tables for his rich classmates. He'd taught mathematics somewhere on the East Coast, before coming to California for some "high-profile job" that he didn't want to tell me about. (The CIA? I could imagine him as a spy; maybe this was why we hid from authorities now? Or maybe he'd been a politician, a businessman, a journalist?)

California was where he met my mother. She was a kindergarten teacher named Jennifer who played the guitar and grew roses. They fell in love after a conversation at a restaurant—he was vague on the details about this, and I was too shy about love to ask how that worked—and quickly got married. There was a house that was painted blue, somewhere on the West Coast—San Pedro? San Jose? San Diego? One of the Sans. And then there was me. Four years later, my mother's convertible Cabriolet was T-boned at an intersection by a speeding bus. She died instantly.

My father found it painful to talk about her: I could tell by the way he winced, and then looked away, whenever I brought her up; the way his words came out haltingly, each one requiring immense effort. "Jennifer was . . . always so . . . joyful. She . . . loved you . . . so much." More often than not, he shut down my questions with a "not now, Jane" or "why do we need to talk about that?" At some point, in my tween years, I just stopped asking. Instead, I stole my father's photograph of her and kept it hidden in my room. He never looked at it anyway.

The photo was a faded snapshot with rounded corners. In it, her hair was long and wavy, with a neat center part that divided her into matching halves. She was wearing a knit vest and a shiny pendant on a long chain around her neck; and even though the snapshot had that regrettable sepia-yellow-brown overtone that characterized so much early-eighties photography, you could still see how poised she was, as graceful as the drawing of Athena in my book of Greek myths. Her smile was lopsided, as if she was trying to communicate with the person behind the camera while simultaneously gazing down at the fair-haired toddler in her arms.

Me. The toddler was me.

I spent so much time studying that photograph, waiting for the moment of recognition—the moment where I would *feel* the truth of myself as that baby in my mother's arms. And all I ever felt was a strange, empty longing: the desire to make that scene real, rather than reliving the memory itself. I couldn't project myself into the body of that chubby, happy kid. I couldn't remember at all what it felt like to be held by my mother.

It's not like I didn't have any memories of her. They would slip in and out sometimes, like momentary shadows: my mother at a sink, peeling carrots while I stood below her with my arms flung around her leg, catching at the orange curls that flew off her paring knife. The memory of her smell, jasmine, as she pulled a blanket up under my chin. A flash of her with a pile of Legos, the clicking of the bricks as she stirred them with a graceful hand.

I read somewhere that explicit memories—the autobiographical memories of moments and experiences—begin when you are two and a half. So if my mother died when I was four I should have had at least eighteen precious months of material to summon; but all I could conjure were these few implicit memories, mere emotional impressions. I had to wonder sometimes: Did I truly remember anything at all or were all these memories just falsehoods, images and stories and feelings that I'd purloined from novels I read or advertisements I saw in newspapers and magazines? How would I even know? How much of our childhoods can anyone *really* remember, anyway; and how much do we just piece together from the photographs in our family albums, the stories that our parents tell us about ourselves, until we have enough detail to color them in in our minds and claim them as our own?

If you don't have any photographs, or any family stories, you're left with nothing but wisps of fog, impossible to grasp.

A FEW DAYS after my birthday, as I was finishing my morning studies, my father came to stand over me in the kitchen. He put his finger on the page, stabbing a sentence with a mud-rimmed fingernail. "*Optimism is the obstinacy of maintaining that everything is best when it is worst,*" he said. "What is Voltaire trying to tell us?"

"That he thinks it's intellectually lazy to say that everything will turn out just fine."

"And whose teaching is this book arguing against?"

"Leibniz. Who believed that because God is inherently good, everything that happens has to be intentional and positive. Voltaire disagreed with his premise."

"And you? What's your position on that?"

I hesitated. It was a trick question. I knew where my father landed on the spectrum of optimism versus pessimism—there was a reason he had me reading *Candide*—and if I didn't agree, we would end up in an endless philosophical debate that I would, inevitably, lose. "I don't believe in God," I said carefully. "Therefore, Leibniz's central thesis is based on a meritless argument. Irrelevant question. Q.E.D."

He laughed. "Well put. Now: What does Candide argue are the three greatest evils?"

"Boredom, vice, and poverty."

My father smiled. "Which can be resolved through the embrace of the pastoral life. Which is what we are doing here, of course." He gave me a half hug, his arm flung around my neck, his chin resting on my head. It was then that I noticed that he had his backpack in the other hand.

"You're leaving again," I observed.

"Just for a day or two. I'll be back before it snows."

"Delivering magazines?" I asked. This was the charade we'd settled upon a few years ago, when he first began self-publishing *Libertaire*. I was perfectly aware that he did not need to hand deliver magazines to the half-dozen bookstores in the Mountain West that carried *Libertaire* on their zine racks. That could have been handled with a few phone calls and a trip to the post office. Besides, these trips predated the magazine's existence.

He'd been leaving me alone at the cabin since I was old enough to cook dinner for myself (and I'd been adept at boiling spaghetti for as long as I could remember). I had never been quite sure what he was doing after he left. I suspected it had something to do with money. My father had never worked an actual job since we'd been in Montana. And while we lived frugally, still, there must have been money coming in somewhere. Did my father have a secret bank account, a trust fund that we were living off of? But that didn't square with the image that I had of his parents and their working-class roots. Perhaps he had an agreement with an old friend and was going to do odd jobs. Perhaps he was selling his plasma, or his semen, or renting out his body for medical experiments.

He sure as hell didn't make much of an income from his writing, I knew that much. Other than the copies that he sold off the zine racks in a half-dozen college-town bookstores, *Libertaire*'s subscription base consisted of roughly four dozen readers, each of whom sent him a self-addressed envelope with a ten-dollar bill for an issue. Many had addresses in Montana and Wyoming, but others lived in cities like New York and Dallas and St. Louis; a few were as far away as Mexico and Canada. I was never quite sure how they had found his writings: Had they plucked an issue off a bookstore shelf during their travels? Had someone handed them a dog-eared copy? Was there a whole underground network of Luddite radicals somewhere out there?

My father corresponded with a few of them, slipping handwritten letters into the envelopes when he mailed off their copies. Letters were returned from a handful of readers—letters that were dense with smeared ink, written with a frenetic intensity that matched my father's. When he found one in our mailbox, he'd brighten, and vanish into his study to read it. I studied the names, wondering who these men (and they were always men) actually were: Malcolm Torino, from North Dakota; Benjamin Fenniway, from Texas; Jim Johnson, from Arkansas. I wondered, when my father left to "deliver magazines" once or twice a year, if he was actually going to visit some of these correspondents. Whether a vein of community ran below our lives, invisible to me, but rich and vital to my father.

"I hear there's a new bookstore in Salt Lake City," he answered, his eyes squinting at a spot just above my head, a tell that he was lying. "Might see if they're interested in *Libertaire*."

"Well, don't worry about me," I said, trying not to sound eager. "I'll be fine."

"That's never in doubt." He squeezed my shoulder once, turned, and was gone. My father was never very big on goodbyes.

I WAITED TWO hours, just to be safe, before breaking into my father's study.

It wasn't large—six feet by six feet—but every square inch of it was jammed with crap. Tangles of fishing wire and scraps of wood and jagged bits of metal, sitting on stacks of books about ethnology and dendrology and ornithology. Old alarm clocks that he picked up at the thrift store in Bozeman, dismantled and spilling their gears. Batteries and rusty pliers and an electronic multimeter whose function I couldn't fathom. Newspapers cut into pieces, crumpled pages from his typewriter, and cups of tea that had been long forgotten and were growing a thick scum of fuzz. Empty oatmeal carton full of bent nails.

My father's desk sat in the middle of this mess, a scarred old beast with ink stains across the top and a brick holding up one missing leg. Its drawers were locked with an old iron key, which I'd never managed to locate, though I'd tried.

The room smelled like my father's sweat and something else I couldn't identify, something chemical and sharp. It was a window into my father's secret mind, one he didn't want me to see; and my presence in the room was like a splinter in the sole of a foot. I would never have gone in there if it weren't for the television.

The television sat on a bookshelf, directly across from my father's desk and on top of an empty milk crate. It was an old black-and-white set that surely dated back at least twenty years. My father had rescued it during a trip to the thrift store, where it had been sitting outside the back door with a *FREE, BROKEN* sign taped to the top.

I'd nearly keeled over when I saw him picking it up. "What are you doing?"

He turned it around so he could study the back. "Going to repair it. These old televisions have pretty simple engineering, assuming it's not a broken cathode-ray tube."

"That's not what I meant," I said. "You said, and I'm quoting here, that television is 'just a conduit for corporations in their quest to control social and political thought. It's an opiate, worse than organized religion.'"

"'The Cathode Wasteland,' right, that was in issue two." For once, he did not look pleased to be quoted back to himself. "But I also need to understand what society is up against if I'm going to write about it in an informed manner. It takes too damn long to get periodicals out to the cabin, and the news shows are the root of society's problems anyway. It's for research only. Don't worry, I'll keep it in the study, so it doesn't poison you, too." He placed the television set in the truck bed and smiled.

It had taken me less than a month to figure out how to pick the lock to my father's study with a rusty paper clip. Whenever he left me alone to go on one of his trips now, I'd binge television to my heart's content, on the three fuzzy channels we managed to pick up. Cartoons, romantic comedies, soap operas, science fiction: the more florid and sentimental and outrageous, the better. *Sabrina the Teenage Witch* and *Star Trek: Voyager* and *Days of Our Lives* and *Friends*. Filled with guilt the whole time; wondering if I was slowly destroying my brain with empty ideas. Quotes from "The Cathode Wasteland" running through my mind: *Modern society uses television as a form of mind control, to blind man to the feelings of stress and dissatisfaction. Rather than absorbing himself in quiet and solitude, and learning how to be at peace in his environment, the modern man requires constant entertainment and stimulation. Thus, society keeps its citizens drugged and listless, sitting on their couches without engaging their minds.*

Yes, yes, right, of course. But holy Christ, I still loved *The X-Files*. Even in grainy black and white, on that tiny twenty-inch screen with a crack in the lower right corner, with muffled sound and terrible reception. My father was right, that shit *was* a drug. The classic fiction my father had fed me—*Anna Karenina* and *The Red and the Black* and *The Scarlet Letter*—hadn't prepared me for these wild flights of imagination. Aliens and mutants and mass murderers, viruses that came from outer space, and kids who were government-built clones. Vulnerable Scully and swoony Mulder, the festering question of whether they would ever have sex just under the surface of every interaction.

No wonder my understanding of the world beyond my window was somewhat warped.

That evening, I made myself a plate of scrambled eggs for dinner and settled in to watch the latest episode. It was about a serial killer who met his female victims by seducing them online. An internet chat room: I'd never heard of such a thing before. According to *The X-Files*, this was an anonymous text-based computer conversation that was conducted late at night in a dark room, lit only by the glow of a computer screen, with ominous music playing in the background. And if you arranged to meet the person who had sent you the messages, they would murder you, liquefy your body fat with digestive enzymes, and drink it.

The serial killer was caught—just in the nick of time—and as they locked him in a jail cell forever, he muttered a line in Italian to Scully: "*I morti non sono più soli.*" The dead are no longer lonely.

As the credits rolled, I stretched and kicked my feet up onto the top of the desk, and that was when I noticed that the top drawer wasn't quite in alignment. When I looked closer, I could see that the catch on the old iron lock was askew; it appeared that my father had turned the key, but not quite far enough, so that it was only hanging on by a thread. I gave the handle a sharp tug, and the drawer immediately popped open.

It was jammed full of paper: yellowing receipts, crumpled letters, handwritten pages that had been torn from a legal pad. There seemed to be no order to it at all, as if it had been yanked out and riffled through, and then shoved back in willy-nilly.

I gingerly lifted the top sheet from the pile, a page that was dense with my father's cramped, spiky hand. The words were complete gibberish—*Ixpde ei bkpwj feayx vqoplit*—but I recognized this as a cipher my father had invented. He'd taught it to me when I was eight, and for a time used to leave notes around the cabin written in code for me to decipher; but that had been years ago, and now I was rusty. I painstakingly translated a random line—*Peter's advances in logic programming and neural networks dovetail neatly with her theories about the future of intelligence*—before giving up. It would take me forever to decode all this, and based on the mystifying sentence I'd just read it didn't seem worth the effort or the subterfuge of putting it in code in the first place. Sometimes my father's thinking was impossible for me to follow.

Disappointed, I put the pages back where I'd found them. I nudged the pile with a fingertip, wondering what else was in this mess. If I disrupted the collection any further, I knew that my father would notice. And yet I couldn't quite resist: I carefully wedged my hand down along the edge of the drawer, feeling for anything of interest.

Paper, paper, more paper. My father had clearly used this drawer as a place to store every stray thought he'd ever jotted down or letter he'd received from a *Libertaire* reader. Why, I wondered, was *this* worth locking up? Surely there had to be something of more value somewhere in here.

Near the bottom of the drawer, my fingers brushed up against something else, a square of paper that was stiff and slick to the touch. A photo? I carefully pinched it out. And then I stared at it, suddenly frozen with shock.

It was a snapshot of my mother and me, one I'd never seen before. I recognized my mother instantly, although she looked a little different in this photo: her hair shorter, brushed back from her face in blond wings; and her dress more conservative, a white blouse with a looped bow tied at the neck. She was sitting in what looked like a big wooden chair, in some sort of office. And I was planted square in her lap, a smirk of delight on my face as I held a coffee mug to my lips, pretending that I was about to drink from it. Above my head, my mother was gazing down at me, her lips parted to say something, a look of bemused pride on her face.

If I was one or two in the earlier photo, I must have been nearly four in this one; my hair long enough to wear in braids, my milk teeth fully grown in. So, close to the end. How many more days would I have with my mother?

Why hadn't my father ever let me see this photo? Had he just forgotten it was there?

A dangerous pressure was building up behind my eye sockets. I pushed a finger into the corner of my eye, holding back an unexpected tear as I flipped the photo over to see if there was anything written on the back. There, in neat black ink, was a caption: *Esme and Theresa. February '83.*

Esme and Theresa?

My heart seemed to stop for a moment; and when it started up again, it was beating twice as fast. I read these three words again and again, willing them to make sense. They did not. I flipped over the photo once more, just to confirm, but there was no question: The photo was definitely of my mother and me. But if these two were *Esme* and *Theresa,* who, then, were *Jennifer* and *Jane*? And, for that matter, which one was Esme, and which was Theresa?

Was *this* why the drawer had been locked?

I examined the photograph more closely. The handwriting was not my father's—it was round and curvy and feminine (my mother's?)— and there were abrasions on the corners of the photo, perhaps from being carelessly extracted from an album. I stuck my hands back down into the drawer and felt around a little more, but if there were more photos down there, I couldn't feel them; and I was afraid to disturb the pile more.

I sat there for a good half hour, just studying the photo. Soaking in every little detail that might offer some clue to my childhood: The scab on my left knee, half covered with a dinosaur Band-Aid. The braids: Were those the ones I thought I remembered my mother combing into my hair? The cartoon on the coffee mug I was pretending to drink from: a fat orange cat with a caption, *I Hate Mondays.*

Finally, I carefully tucked the photo back in the drawer where I'd found it, locked the study back up, and went into the kitchen. I'd seen something I was pretty sure I wasn't supposed to see, and it left me feeling shaky and penitential, as if I'd been punished for going into my father's sacrosanct study. As if this was all *my* fault for bingeing *The X-Files* episodes when I knew it was strictly forbidden.

At loose ends, I picked up the phone and dialed Heidi.

"Guess what? My name's not actually Jane," I said when she answered.

"So what is it, then? Let me guess. Tiffany? Natasha? Oh, no, I got it: Michelle. That sounds like you." I could hear her radio blasting in the background, playing a girl band that sounded like bubbling soda.

"I'm not sure. It's either Esme or Theresa. I found an old photo of me with my mom, one my dad had hidden away, and those were the names written on the back. But it's not clear which one was me."

The music went suddenly quiet, as she snapped it off. "Wait, you're serious?"

"I'm serious."

"But—why? Why would your father hide that from you?"

I'd already come up with an answer, the only one that seemed to make sense. "The obvious explanation is that he changed my name at some point after my mom died because we're hiding from the feds. I've told you how he's always so worried about them. It would explain a lot."

There was a telling silence from the other end of the line. "Is that *really* the most obvious explanation? Your dad's whole spiel about the authorities—you know it's all just a paranoid delusion, right? My mom says his convoluted theories are just an excuse to keep you trapped out there in the woods."

This made me bristle. "Convoluted theories? That's called philosophy, Heidi. Have you even bothered to read *Libertaire*?"

She ignored this, continuing: "Anyway, why would he lie to you about your *mom's* name, if that was the case? She's not in hiding."

"It's probably all part of his cover." Stubbornly, I wanted to believe in this story. It was the one that let my father still be a hero.

"Maybe, but I can think of other, far more logical reasons why he would be hiding your real name." Her voice was breathy with excitement; I felt a sour pulse of annoyance that my shock was her thrill. "I mean, Jane, if he lied to you about that, then you have to ask yourself if he's lied to you about other things, too."

"What do you mean?"

"Think about it. What if your mom isn't even *dead*?"

9

I COULDN'T SLEEP THAT night. The wind had shifted after darkness fell and was now blowing in from the north, cold fingers clawing at the corners of our cabin. I lay in bed listening to the sounds of the woods, just on the other side of the planks: The hooting of the western screech owl that nested in the gnarled ponderosa pine at the bottom of our hill. The scratching of the barn mice that sheltered in our walls during the winter. The squeak of the tree branches rubbing against each other as they swayed. Sounds as familiar to me as a lullaby.

And yet, for the first time since my father had started leaving me alone at the cabin, I felt on edge, anxious about what was out there in the dark. I looked out the window and thought I could see strange shapes, circling just beyond my view. Serial killers from chat rooms. Shadowy government agents. Monsters beyond my imagination.

I knew these fears were irrational, and yet I couldn't shake the sense that something critical was changing. My world had, over the last few days, somehow tilted off its axis: The shift in the wind, the workers pounding at our door, the dead wolf in our road, the doomsday drill. Esme and Theresa. Or maybe it was the passing of another birthday, my growing awareness of the scope of the world beyond my cabin, which was imparting this feeling of doom.

What was it that I was afraid of? The apocalypse my father kept predicting? Or was it something much closer to home, a seismic shift in the only relationship I'd ever known?

Your dad's whole spiel about the authorities—you know it's all just a paranoid delusion, right? My mom says his convoluted theories are just an excuse to keep you trapped out there in the woods.

What if your mom isn't even dead?

I circled this last thought tentatively, as if it were a hot coal that might burn me if I prodded it. Because while it was what I longed for the most—a real live mother!—it was also what I wanted the absolute least. If it was true, how could I ever look my father in the eye again?

It's painful for me, now, to think about the intellectual contortions I went through for so many years in order to accept my father's way of thinking. But at the time, they didn't feel like contortions at all. It was simply what I had been taught, the "way things were." If my father told me that we were living in a cabin in the woods because my mother was dead and shadowy government types were out to get us, of course I believed him. If he lied to me about my real name, well, there had to be a good reason, right? I had no reason to question him.

Except now, for the first time, I did.

THE TEMPERATURE DROPPED below freezing in the night, and when I woke in the morning there was a feathery white crust on the trees, glittering in the sunrise. The light of day had brought everything back into focus; the shadows in the woods resolved themselves into familiar shapes. The western larch that had blown over a few years back. The trellises for our green beans. As I lay in bed, I forced myself to laugh out loud, just to bust a hole through my own panic. Everything was fine. There was a logical explanation for everything. There had to be.

I made myself a coffee, grabbed a book, and took the quilt off my bed to sit on the porch. I was reading *Great Expectations* for the third time and had just gotten to the part where Miss Havisham admits to Pip that she intentionally raised Estella to be cruel and heartless, as her revenge against the men she blamed for her own heartbreak.

I knew not how to answer, or how to comfort her. That she had done a grievous thing in taking an impressionable child to mould into the form that her wild resentment, spurned affection, and wounded pride found vengeance in, I knew full well. But that, in shutting out the light of day, she had shut out infinitely more; that, in seclusion, she had secluded herself from a thou-

*sand natural and healing influences; that, her mind, brooding solitary, had
grown diseased, as all minds do and must and will that reverse the appointed
order of their Maker; I knew equally well.*

There was something about poor, sad Miss Havisham, in her rav-
ished seclusion, that made me profoundly uncomfortable. Maybe it
was because she reminded me, in some dangerous way, of my father;
in which case, did that mean I was Estella, the breaker of hearts? If so,
whose heart was I supposed to break?

I sat wrapped in a blanket, watching the mist rise off the frozen
ground as the sun began to warm the earth below, creating a soft low
fog that clung to the forest like a dream. A family of deer—a mother
and two fawns—tiptoed out of the woods and stepped lightly down
the hill, stopping to sample the moss that grew in the glade below our
cabin. I remained motionless, just watching. I knew I should go check
on the hens in the henhouse and make sure they hadn't frozen to
death overnight, should collect eggs for breakfast and cut some firewood for the stove, but instead I just sat there, as though time had
stopped.

I sat there until the coffee in my mug was as cold as a stone. I sat
there until the frost melted off the trees and I lost all feeling in my
legs. I thought my heart might break from all that beauty, which felt
like a gift just for me.

I sat there as the saws began their work in the cut down the hill,
broadcasting my father's failure. I closed my eyes and saw the fresh
cable lines stretching off into the infinite horizon, encircling the globe
with their electrical currents. Inside them, the buzz of life, the exchange of information, the movement of human existence, all taking
place just beyond my line of sight.

Inside me, I was experiencing an entirely different variety of buzz,
a discontented whir of unanswerable questions. Who were Esme and
Theresa? Why was I living here, in the middle of nowhere in Montana? Where did my father and I come from originally, and what was
he so afraid of? And, most important of all, was it possible I *did* have

a mother out there, somewhere, still? And, if so, why had my father lied? Was *she* the malevolent force that we were hiding from?

I knew that I couldn't confront my father about the photograph. He'd know instantly that I had been breaking into his study and watching the forbidden television; and my fear of my father's disappointment still trumped all other fears. There had to be other ways to piece together the meaning of those names on that photo, ways that didn't involve asking him directly.

I sat there until I finally understood, with knifelike clarity, that I had to find a way out of this cabin. I couldn't let myself be a prisoner here anymore—because yes, I could finally see it, Heidi was right about that. There was something out there I needed to learn about myself. It was time to escape beyond the borders of my claustrophobic world, and find it.

Now I just needed to figure out how.

10

My father came back the next day, when I was dutifully study-ing my partial derivatives. He was carrying a large cardboard box, which he dropped unceremoniously on top of my calculus homework.

"New project," he said.

I reached out and pried open the flaps of the box. In it was a big black slab of a laptop, with *IBM* emblazoned on the cover.

I gave my dad a questioning look. "Keep going," he said. I could feel the excitement zinging off him, a manic energy that I recognized with a faint ping of alarm.

I put the laptop on the table and dug back in the box, this time coming out with a flat, black, plastic device. "Is this a . . . ?"

"It's a modem." He had lost his patience with this game and was fishing around in the bottom of the box. He handed me a book, bright purple and thick: *Teach Yourself Web Publishing with HTML in a Week*.

I stared at it, unsure how I was supposed to respond. Was this some sort of a test?

"I'm finally going to write my manifesto, and put it on the World Wide Web," he announced. "And you're going to help me do it."

I didn't know how to respond. I flipped open the laptop and ran my hands over the keys, with their mysterious symbols and inscrutable labels. I touched a fingertip to the little red trackball and was sur-prised that it felt spongy under my touch. "How did you pay for all this?"

"A friend gave it to me," he said. I looked at the pile of technology, which surely represented thousands of dollars. Who was this friend? One of the letter writers, I assumed. Malcolm or Ben or Jim.

He was extracting more things from the box: instruction manuals, loose cables, a CD with a purple symbol that looked just like the Eye of Providence, as if access to the World Wide Web had been divined by God. *1,000 HOUR FREE TRIAL,* it said, in big yellow letters.

"You know how to use all this?"

He was distractedly studying the manual for the modem. "The computers have gotten faster and smaller since I worked in Silicon Valley, but it's still the same concept."

"Silicon Valley? What's that?"

He looked up, his brows knitting together, realizing he'd just said something he didn't intend to. "Where the computer industry is based. In California."

"So *that's* what your 'high-profile job' was? In computers? Why didn't you tell me that before?"

"I didn't think it mattered to you. Anyway, you see that I have first-hand knowledge of why all this is dangerous."

This is what my father did: He told me something fascinating, then expected me not to be fascinated by it at all, and changed the subject. It was the boring stuff that he wanted me to pay attention to. "If it's so dangerous, then why are we doing this?"

He put the manual down and picked up a wire, plugging it into the back of the laptop like this was something he did every day. "I know it may seem hypocritical. But I've thought about it a lot lately, and it's the logical next step for us. Bookstores are phasing out their zine racks, not just the Country Bookshelf but at least half of the stores that have been selling *Libertaire* tell me that they're paring back their shelves. Print is going to be obsolete soon, they say. It's all going on-line. Christ, what a miserable future, can you even imagine that? No books, no magazines, no newspapers—nothing tactile and intimate. Everyone just staring at screens until their eyes fall out. Someone needs to *stop* this nonsense, before it gets out of control. They call it progress but they're blinkered idiots, the whole world is just going about blithely ignoring how *this*"—he waved the instruction manual in the air, like a priest gesticulating with a religious text—"is going to utterly shift human existence as we know it. They're just ushering in their own obsolescence."

I stared at my father, really seeing him for the first time since he'd arrived home. His eyes were red-rimmed and wild, and I wondered if he hadn't slept since he left two days before. His salt-and-pepper beard was far too long, his hair was stringy, and there was a pungency to him that cut through the woodsmoke smell that perpetually lingered in our cabin at this time of year. Something about him felt off.

"Dad, when was the last time you took a bath?"

He looked down at his chest, as if the answer was to be found in his lap. "Exterior surfaces are irrelevant, squirrel. It's all about the interior."

"Well, the exterior surfaces smell. It's not pleasant to be around. And this cabin is small."

He was frantically plugging and unplugging things now, fishing around in the box for wires. "Here's the conundrum. We have to find readers where they are. If they're truly all going on the internet, well then, we have to go there and shine a klieg light on the whole goddamn charade. Show them what they've bought into. Otherwise, aren't I just preaching to the choir? My current readers, they're already believers. So where do we find more? We need to *convert them.* And we can capture so many more readers online, where you have unlimited reach for free. You know how many issues of the last *Libertaire* I sold? Eighty-nine. On the internet you can get that in one day. One *hour.*"

"Dad, it sounds like you're arguing in favor of technology now."

He whirled around to look at me, wires dangling from his fingers. "Not at all. Don't you see? We make it work for *us,* instead of working for it. We're smarter than them."

"If you say so," I said uneasily.

"Your job is to read that book," he said, gesturing at the bright purple manual. "You learn how to get online and make a website. I'll start working on my manifesto. See, that's another benefit to publishing online. No need to fit everything in twenty-four pages; I can write as long or short as I want, there's unlimited space. I can write a whole goddamn book and I don't even need a publisher."

He must not have been listening to his own words, because if he'd heard himself he would have realized that he sounded more like an evangelist than a critic. I found his self-contradiction alarming: What was I supposed to believe now? Surely, he would wake up in the morning, see his delusions in the clear light of day, and change his mind. Surely, he would wake up to the fact that he had just invited the enemy right into our house, given it a seat at our kitchen table. Surely, he would dump everything right in the trash.

And yet I knew, looking at the wires in his hand, that something vital had already shifted, and was never going to go back. This was so much bigger than a television and a few stealthy viewings of *The X-Files*. My father was opening a direct conduit to the outside world, and what he failed to see—and what I, in some subconscious way, already understood—was that this wasn't just going to be about Saul Williams announcing his presence to the world. Instead, the world was about to come to us.

And that was when it hit me. My father had brought my method of escape straight into our cabin. I wouldn't even have to leave the woods to visit the outside world and get the answers I wanted. I had my portal right here.

I opened up the pages of that purple instruction manual and began to read.

11.

I've LEARNED, OVER the years, that it's impossible to explain the beauty of coding to someone who is not, themselves, a coder. Looking at the source of a website or a game or a piece of software is a lot like turning over an elaborate piece of embroidery and seeing the complicated tangle of the threads beneath: Only a certain kind of mind is interested in the complex logic of that mess, rather than the tidy end result. The cause, rather than the effect.

Learning to code HTML that week made me understand something vital about myself: I may have spent most of my life thus far observing and consuming and regurgitating (my father's thoughts, mostly), but what truly brought me joy was making something *happen*. Learning the secret language that allowed me to speak to the computer, and then using it to create something from nothing. All I had to do was string together a cryptic arrangement of letters and symbols, and there my private world would be on the screen, my vision magically made manifest. For the first time in my life, I felt like a god.

My father, unwittingly, had given me a hobby.

Scratch that—a *vocation*.

Of course, it wasn't so hard to code a website back then. In 1996, Web design was as simple as deciding whether you wanted your background to be black or white or Netscape gray, and whether you wanted your text to blink. You could center your photos, or not; maybe you'd use a "fun" font, like Comic Sans. If you really knew what you were doing, you'd throw in an animated GIF of a silly cat or a dancing baby.

It was, in retrospect, a beautifully egalitarian time to be building websites: The field was wide open to entry because everyone was equally new to the game. We were all still just stabbing in the dark, figuring out this new medium. And you didn't need to be an expert programmer to plant your flag on the internet. All you needed was an *HTML for Dummies* book and a dial-up connection; at the very least, a GeoCities home page.

Elsewhere, more experienced developers were already playing with the tools that would transform the look and feel of the internet as we now know it—Flash and JavaScript and cascading style sheets—but for the rest of us novices, building websites in 1996 was like being handed a Lego set and directed to build a castle. No matter how creative you got, there was only so much you could do with the tools you had.

And that was the beauty of it all: Your Web page was valued less by how it looked than what it contained within. Content truly was king, as the saying went.

I may have been living off the grid for my entire life, but for once I wasn't actually that far behind.

WITH THE ARRIVAL of the internet, the pattern of our days shifted.

Each day, after breakfast, my father would vanish into his study and start banging away at his Smith Corona. He was writing his manifesto, and nothing else existed. Our morning study sessions had been forgotten completely; all pretense of home school had gone out the window. The logs in the pile went unsplit. The vegetable garden needed to be tilled before it started to snow, but that seemed increasingly unlikely to happen. Meals, always a haphazard affair in our house, were downgraded to canned chili and our ubiquitous oatmeal.

There was a new manic intensity to my father, one that wasn't entirely unfamiliar. His moods had always swung with the seasons, the arrival of the mail, the results of an election, or an epiphany about a new invention. He was happiest when he had a new project to fixate on, something that he believed had the potential to change everything. The last time I had seen him like this was when he first noticed the zine rack at the Country Bookshelf and came up with the idea for *Libertaire*.

While he wrote, I worked my way through *Teach Yourself Web Publishing with HTML in a Week*. It took me five days. As soon as the door to my father's study closed, I would sit down at the laptop and stay there—tinkering with source code, test-driving the results, my fingers fumbling across the unfamiliar keyboard—until the cabin grew dark. My father would emerge around dinnertime. We would eat our chili in near silence, my father too wrapped up in his own thoughts to bother being interested in mine; me too absorbed in my own new discoveries to care. After dinner, he'd disappear back into the study again and stay there until long after I'd fallen asleep myself.

"Keep focused, don't surf the internet, it'll rot your brain," my father had warned me, but it was a futile instruction, and surely he knew it. I spent every free moment tumbling down the rabbit holes of this fascinating new wonderland.

Keep in mind that there was hardly anything to do online in late 1996—not in comparison to today's internet. You could read *The New York Times*. Get the weather. Poke around the websites of assorted universities and research institutions. You could shake a virtual Magic 8 Ball or zoom in on maps of the world or visit the home page of some kid in Wisconsin who was really, really into the Grateful Dead. You could hang out in chat rooms or watch a live webcam of coffee dripping into a pot in San Francisco or look at photos of dogs with funny haircuts. Wherever you went, it would be as slow as syrup.

There was a reason that the average time that someone spent on the Web in 1996 was thirty minutes a *month*.

But me? I felt like a dehydrated camel who had just stumbled onto a desert oasis. I drank that shit up, puppy Mohawks and all.

And when I was one hundred percent sure that my father was preoccupied, I would plug terms into search engines, troubling ones that had been nagging at me. *Silicon Valley. Paranoid delusions. Federal agents.*

The most important, of course, were *Esme Williams* and *Theresa Williams*. I had thrown these names at AltaVista at my first opportunity, then watched with a sinking stomach as the search engine spat back an anemic selection of results. A Black pediatrician in Los Angeles, a teenage track star in Iowa, the geriatric winner of a pie-baking contest in Texas. Nothing that pointed to a dead kindergarten teacher from (I had to assume) Silicon Valley or her bereaved toddler daughter. I tried again, this time with different combinations—*Theresa Williams car accident* and *Esme Williams obituary* and *Esme and Saul Williams wedding.* Then, just to be sure, *Saul Williams wanted by federal authorities* and (guiltily) *Saul Williams criminal.* Nothing.

I realized, then, that it was entirely possible that I was still searching for the wrong name. Who was to say that I was even a *Williams?* If my father lied to me about my first name, it was possible he'd also lied to me about my last.

So much for the internet having all the answers.

It had grown clear to me that I needed to somehow get back inside my father's desk drawer. Surely there was something else buried in that pile of papers that would shed light on the mystery of my name. More photos, perhaps. Medical records with my name on them. An obituary for my mother. A wedding certificate. But with my father practically living in his study, frantically typing away at his manifesto at all hours of the day, there was to be no opportunity. Not until he left town again.

And so, as I bided my time, I surfed the Web until my eyes glazed over, filling my brain with all the pop ephemera I could cram inside: cat memes and Justin's Links from the Underground and *Dilbert* cartoons. I pretended that this was almost as good as being in the real world. I pretended that each passing day didn't bring further evidence that I was, as Heidi had warned, living in a prison of my father's making.

12

WolfGirl96 >   Hi, anyone here?

SFWired1 >   . . . I'm here.

WolfGirl96 >   Who are you?

SFWired1 >   Steve. You?

WolfGirl96 >   My name is Jane. Is Steve your real name? Or did you make that up?

SFWired1 >   Does it make a difference?

WolfGirl96 >   To me it does.

SFWired1 >   OK, then. My real name is Lionel. Like the train set. Don't laugh.

WolfGirl96 >   It's a nice name. Better than mine.

SFWired1 >   What's wrong with Jane?

WolfGirl96 >   Plain Jane. Think about it. Books never have heroes named Jane.

SFWired1 >   Jane Eyre. Jane Banks. Jane Marple.

WolfGirl96 >   OK, fine. I stand corrected. You are well read, congratulations. So, are you going to try to lure me into meeting you someplace in order to murder me and eat me?

SFWired1 >   That's . . . dark. No. What gave you that idea?

WolfGirl96 >   *The X-Files.*

SFWired1 >   Sorry to disappoint, but I'm not a serial killer.

WolfGirl96 >   That's a relief.

SFWired1 >   Now that we have that established, what brings you to this chat room?

WolfGirl96 >	Curiosity. I've never been in one before. I wanted to see how they worked. Do you spend a lot of time in chat rooms?
SFWired1 >	I have to. Actually, I'm a programmer here. This is my software. Just doing a routine check to see that everything's working OK.
WolfGirl96 >	Really? That's cool. Where is "here"?
SFWired1 >	San Francisco. I work at Signal.
WolfGirl96 >	Should I know what that is?
SFWired1 >	It's a network of Web publications. We run this chat room. Plus a print magazine, a search engine, and a few other things. You should check it out. We're at the forefront of the digital revolution, blah blah blah. What about you?
WolfGirl96 >	I don't work. I'm still in school.
SFWired1 >	And where do you live?
WolfGirl96 >	In Montana. I live in the woods.
SFWired1 >	Really? Do you have a pet wolf? Hence the name?
WolfGirl96 >	I did, kinda. Someone shot him.
SFWired1 >	Oh fuck. I'm sorry.
WolfGirl96 >	It's OK. We also have a lot of deer. And foxes and raccoons and the occasional bobcat.
SFWired1 >	The only wildlife I see here are the rats that live in the BART stations.
WolfGirl96 >	. . . BART stations?
SFWired1 >	BART is the subway in San Francisco, except it's not as useful as a subway because it doesn't really connect anything with anything.
WolfGirl96 >	I've never been on a subway.
SFWired1 >	You're not missing much. Anyway, it was nice chatting with you.
WolfGirl96 >	Wait!! Don't leave yet.
SFWired1 >	. . . ??
WolfGirl96 >	Sorry, I don't get to talk to strangers very often.

SFWired1 >   Oh. OK. What do you want to talk about?

WolfGirl96 >   I don't know. What do people talk about in chat rooms?

SFWired1 >   Anything you want. Video games. Your favorite movies.

WolfGirl96 >   I've never played a video game. I've never been to the movies.

SFWired1 >   Never?

WolfGirl96 >   Never ever.

SFWired1 >   Damn. Well, you could also just tell me about your life.

WolfGirl96 >   It's not that exciting. Probably not as interesting as yours.

SFWired1 >   You'd be surprised how boring my life is. OK, enlighten me on how you could possibly have never seen a movie or played a video game.

WolfGirl96 >   Sorry, I have to log off, I think my dad's coming.

SFWired1 >   Your dad?

WolfGirl96 >   . . .

SFWired1 >   Jane?

13

I WAS CLICKING AROUND the internet one evening when I realized that I could feel my father's breath on the back of my neck. Could smell it, too, and the hand-rolled cigarette he'd smoked after his dinner. I'd been so absorbed, I hadn't even heard him leave his study.

I turned, with a reddening face, knowing that it was too late to slam the laptop closed to hide what I'd been doing. Not that I was doing anything particularly objectionable. I'd been reading articles on the website of the company that Lionel said he worked for, a sprawling internet destination that offered advice for coding HTML alongside cocktail recipes and articles about adventure sports. It wasn't like I was looking at celebrity gossip or researching bus schedules to New York City. But I still felt like I'd been caught doing something terrible.

"I'm just doing some research," I mumbled.

He peered over my shoulder and read the headline of the article I'd been reading: "'Hypertext, the Web's Unsung Hero.' Computer code is the hero. See how they do that? Personification of technology, pretending it's better than we are. That's how the computers will end up in charge someday, because we've forgotten that we need to be afraid of them."

Usually, I would have nodded and filed this away for future regurgitation, but for some reason his pontificating grated on me. "It's just an article about how to use links on your pages, Dad. It's not a harbinger of the apocalypse."

"Don't kid yourself, that's how it all starts." He remained hovering over my shoulder, staring at my screen as I sat there, frozen, waiting for him to leave. He looked decidedly unhealthy, which wasn't surprising, since he'd barely slept in weeks. "I basically invented this thing," he muttered.

"*You* invented the internet. Got it." Were delusions of grandeur a sign of a mental breakdown? I'd been too distracted to pay attention to him lately, and now I wondered if that had been a mistake.

He ignored this. "OK, let's do it. Show me how this thing is working now."

I turned around to look at him. "Are you sure?"

"I can't write about it if I don't know about it."

I tried to think what my father might be interested in. News seemed like a safe bet. I typed in the URL for *The New York Times* and we sat there watching together as the site resolved, pixel by tedious pixel. He leaned in closer, squinting. "They put the newspaper up for free? You can read the whole damn thing?"

"Every day." I thought of the dog-eared newspapers that Lina saved for us, weeks old by the time we read them. Surely *this* was proof that the internet had something of value.

"*The New York Times* is a liberal rag, read that thing too much and you'll end up a mouthpiece for their left-wing propaganda. What about *Reason,* is that here?" He had already leaned over me to take control of the trackball and was scrolling wildly up and down.

"See, if you click on this underlined word here, it'll take you to a different page—" I offered, but he wasn't listening to me anymore. He nudged me aside with his shoulder, and then sat down in the seat he'd just pushed me out of. I stood watching him as he began to click away at the browser. "How do you see the code behind this thing?"

I showed him how and he studied the source code with curiosity, then clicked back to the Web. The familiarity of his fingers flying across the keyboard made me feel uneasy: It was as if my father had been taken over by a stranger I'd never met. One who clearly knew computers. One who clearly knew code.

"Dad, what were you doing, exactly, in Silicon Valley?"

He turned to look at me, his mouth slightly agape, and I could tell he was working through his memories to recall what, exactly, he'd already told me. "Working for a technology research institute, in a group that was trying to figure out the future of computers. What they might be used for." His response was slow, each word carefully weighed and measured. "And I didn't feel good about what we were hatching up. Felt downright ill about it, actually. I could see what was coming down the pike, the way these things were going to take over our lives. Governments putting them in missiles and spaceships, using them to conduct wars and track civilians. Artificial intelligence, stupidly teaching the computers to be smarter than us, so that they would eventually control *us* instead of the other way around. A society composed of brainwashed keyboard slaves, addicted to their screens. I didn't want to be part of that. So I quit."

"Was that before or after Mom died?" I tried to keep my tone casual, but something about the way I asked this gave him pause. He looked up at me with a sharp, inscrutable gaze, meeting my eyes. I stared right back at him.

In the end, he was the one who caved and looked away. "Around the same time. Went through a crisis of faith after she died, you could say. Suddenly saw what was important in life." He reached out and gripped my hand, squeezing it so hard I could feel my finger bones pressing against his. An urgent smile spread across his tightened lips. "You, squirrel. *You* were what was important. And I wanted you to have all this"—he gestured out the window—"without first being poisoned by *that*." He pointed at the screen.

Something about this sudden burst of affection felt contrived, like a shiny bauble thrown out to distract a wayward child. "And my mother, did she feel that way, too? Was she . . . one of the good guys?"

His smile drooped. "That's a strange question." He turned back to the laptop and went back to typing.

I sat watching him, weighing what I could get away with asking next. "Dad?"

"What?"

"Did you ever change my name?"

His index finger hesitated. Just the slightest hitch, before striking the key. "What do you mean?"

"Just wondered. If we ever had to, you know, disguise ourselves. To throw the feds off."

"To throw them off?"

"You know. Because you were in trouble with the law."

He whipped his head around. "You think I broke the law? Doing what, exactly?"

"I don't know. It's just, you worry about them an awful lot. And you're never exactly clear *why*."

He gave me a long, assessing look. "Thought crimes, squirrel. I commit thought crimes." Then he turned back to the screen. I'd been dismissed.

I stood there a beat longer, watching him click away, and then went to my bedroom to finish *Great Expectations,* which I'd abandoned not long after Miss Havisham died. But I found that I couldn't focus on the words on the page. My eyes ached in an unfamiliar way, dry and throbbing. Too much screen time. It was already damaging me.

Instead, I lay there, trying to imagine my father sitting at a computer in Silicon Valley, surrounded by notebooks full of calculations and prognostications. And my mother, drinking her coffee in that big wooden chair, as I sat in her lap. Where had we been?

I fell asleep to the sounds of our chattering modem, softly clicking and humming as it reached its electronic feelers out across the network, allowing my father to creep his own way around this new frontier.

14

WolfGirl96 >   Lionel, is that you?

SFWired1 >   Fancy running into you again.

WolfGirl96 >   It's not an accident. I was looking for you.

SFWired1 >   Are you a stalker?

WolfGirl96 >   No! . . . Wait, what's a stalker?

SFWired1 >   Someone who obsessively pursues someone else. Forget it. It was a bad joke.

WolfGirl96 >   How about a good joke, then? What's black, white, and green all over?

SFWired1 >   I don't know, what?

WolfGirl96 >   A panda during mealtime.

SFWired1 >   That is not a good joke.

WolfGirl96 >   Don't blame me. I read it on the back of a cereal box.

SFWired1 >   OK, I gotta ask—how old are you?

WolfGirl96 >   Seventeen.

SFWired1 >   Huh. I probably shouldn't be chatting with you.

WolfGirl96 >   Why?

SFWired1 >   You're younger than I thought.

WolfGirl96 >   My dad says that age is just a number, boundaries and limitations should be based on intellectual capacity rather than the date of your birth. Why? How old are you?

SFWired1 >   Your dad sounds like a piece of work. I'm twenty-one.

WolfGirl96 >   Did you go to college?

SFWired1 >   I graduated from Stanford a year and a half ago.

WolfGirl96 >   Isn't that pretty young to be a college graduate?

SFWired1 >   I was kind of a kid prodigy. I started college at 16. Finished
              in 3 years and when I graduated I got recruited for this job.

WolfGirl96 > And do you feel like a tool of the industrial-technological
              system?

SFWired1 >   What???

WolfGirl96 > Having a job. Your personal agency being sacrificed to the
              god of corporate profit. Your life being reduced to routine
              obedience and oppression. Does that ever bother you?

SFWired1 >   Where the hell did you get that idea?

WolfGirl96 > Something I read.

SFWired1 >   Hey, Jane? You're weird.

WolfGirl96 > I know. I'm sorry.

SFWired1 >   That's OK, I kind of like it.

WolfGirl96 > So, here's the reason I was looking for you. I need some
              advice. I want to find information about someone who died
              13 years ago. Is there a place I could do that on the
              internet?

SFWired1 >   Use a search engine.

WolfGirl96 > Tried it. Got nothing.

SFWired1 >   Then try going to a library. If you know where they died,
              the library there will have microfiche of the local
              newspaper, with obituaries.

WolfGirl96 > I think she lived in Silicon Valley. Where is that, exactly?
              Should I go there?

SFWired1 >   Silicon Valley isn't really a place. Well, not a city at least. It's
              kind of the whole metropolitan area between San
              Francisco and San Jose, grouped together by profession. A
              mass delusion, you could say. Anyway, you need
              something more specific than that.

WolfGirl96 > Oh. Another issue is that I only have her first name.

SFWired1 >   All you have is a first name and no place of death? Well,
              you got me there. Sorry.

WolfGirl96 > So there's no secret online database that only insiders
              know about?

SFWired1 >   Ha. Not yet. Maybe someday. The big secret of the
internet is that there is no there, there. It's still more hype
than reality.

WolfGirl96 >   I think it's pretty incredible.

SFWired1 >   You're easily impressed.

WolfGirl96 >   And you're really jaded.

SFWired1 >   You're not wrong, Jane.

15.

I woke up to discover that it had snowed in the night. My breath was visible in clouds above my bed as I lay there, under the quilts, shivering with the cold. The forest was deathly silent—the construction crews had finally moved on, their mission accomplished. When I went out to the kitchen to light the woodstove, I found a stack of papers sitting by the side of the closed laptop. I lifted the first page and read *THE LUDDITE MANIFESTO by Saul Williams.*

In 1812, British workers known as Luddites rose up against the new automated weaving machines that threatened their jobs, a bloody revolt that pitted impoverished artisans against greedy entrepreneurs. Unfortunately, the Luddites did not win their battle against their era's technology, and the resulting industrial revolution led to centuries of inequity and suffering. Today, nearly 200 years later, we find ourselves in a nearly identical position, with new technologies threatening our very way of life. Once again, it's time to take a stand. This time, we cannot lose.

I skimmed further. The material was familiar—he'd covered similar ground in his essays for *Libertaire*—and yet it seemed like he'd finally coalesced his disparate thoughts into one cohesive worldview. A call to arms. But who was he calling?

The world today has lost its mind, and it can all be traced back to the rise of technology. The consequence of the ever-forward march of "progress" has been a society whose citizens are greatly suffering and aren't even aware of it. The more we continue to replace a life of value with the "virtual" life, the less satisfaction we derive from our existence, resulting in a world in which citizens are anesthetized by pharmaceuticals and entertainment, living entirely in their heads rather than in a tangible, physical world.

Reading this, I realized, with a spasm of guilt, that I hadn't read a book since the internet arrived at our house. I hadn't gone on a walk in the woods, or sketched the deer in the meadow, or played a game of chess with my father. I'd abandoned everything that we valued, seduced by the infinite delights of the Web. Photos of strangers' children and webcams that showed the weather in Austin and all the news you could read for free. Less than a month, and it had already turned me into a zombie. I was living proof of my father's prescience.

So maybe *I* was the one that my father was calling. His daughter, so quick to set aside everything he'd spent a lifetime carefully teaching me. I pushed away the laptop with a spasm of self-loathing.

Where was my father, anyway? I walked over to his bedroom, knocked, and then pushed the door open: His bed was neatly made, his slippers set at the end of the bed, a glass of water forgotten on the floor next to the stack of books he was currently reading. I checked the titles: *Fundamentals of Industrial Problem Solving* and *The State and Revolution*.

The truck wasn't in the driveway. The tire impressions in the drive were already filled with snow, which meant that he must have left at some point in the middle of the night. I wondered what might have set him off at such a strange hour. It probably wasn't good, whatever it was.

I wished he'd taken me with him.

I went back to the table and opened the laptop. Inside, I found a note scribbled on a piece of graph paper sitting on top of the keyboard. *Please type up manifesto and put on internet. Back in a few days. Dad.*

The stack of typed pages was dauntingly thick. A week's worth of transcription alone, plus more for formatting for the internet. Why hadn't my father just written it with the damn laptop, instead of his useless typewriter? Maybe this was why he had snuck out in the middle of the night: so that I wouldn't be able to complain.

On the bright side, his departure meant that I would finally have the opportunity to break into his study and dig around in his desk. If

I could just find something else with my mother's name on it—her death certificate, perhaps, with the name of the town where she'd died, and a last name—I could look up her obituary and get more information about her.

With more information to plug into a search engine, I could stop torturing myself with the question of whether she might even be still alive.

I grabbed a paper clip and headed for the study door, then stopped abruptly, my breath sticking in my throat: My father had added a bolt to the door and padlocked it.

I hit the door with the flat of my hand. And again, and again, until my breath came fast and the flesh on my palm began to bleed. Had he figured out that I'd snooped in his desk? Maybe he didn't know how much I knew, but one thing was for certain: I was being punished for *something*.

I picked up the phone and dialed Heidi. We hadn't spoken since our last unsettling conversation, and I wasn't sure if the silence was more about her or me; but I needed someone to talk to. She answered, breathless, on the first ring. "Jocelyn?"

"No. It's Jane. Who's Jocelyn?"

"Oh." Was that disappointment that I heard in her voice? But whatever it was, she recovered with the next breath. "She's a girl I met yesterday when we went in for a tour of Gallatin High. She drives a Mustang, isn't that cool? She invited me to join the debate club when I start school after the new year."

"Debate club?" I felt the gulf between us, already so daunting, opening up even further. "I wouldn't think you'd be into arguing for the sake of arguing. Maybe you can take lessons from my dad."

"I'm *nothing* like your father, Jane. That's not even funny."

The distaste in her words shut my mouth entirely. I could hear her breath, measured and tight, on the other end of the line. "How was your college visit?" I finally asked.

"It was awesome. I'm thinking I might rush when I get there." I had no idea what this meant and was too embarrassed to ask. "Hey—did you ask your dad about the whole name thing?"

"I tried. It didn't go well, and now I think he's mad."

"When *isn't* he mad?" I listened for pity in her words but all I could hear was impatience. "Look, Jane, I have to go. Jocelyn was going to call me and I want to make sure the phone isn't busy, OK? I'll ring you later this week. Promise."

The phone went dead. I thought about flinging the receiver across the room but if it broke I'd have no way to call anyone. Then again, who else was there to call if Heidi wasn't particularly interested in answering? I'd never felt so alone.

With nothing else left to do, I sat down at the computer, pulled the first sheet of my father's manifesto toward me, and dutifully started typing.

16

WolfGirl96 >   Lionel?

SFWired1 >   Hi, Jane.

WolfGirl96 >   What are you doing?

SFWired1 >   Not much, just playing Tomb Raider. You?

WolfGirl96 >   Nothing. Just a little lonely.

SFWired1 >   Yeah, that's usually why people hang out in chat rooms. What's going on?

WolfGirl96 >   My dad's been gone for over a week now. I'm stuck in this cabin because I have no way of going anywhere. It's snowing. I don't have a car. And my only friend is too busy to talk to me.

SFWired1 >   Wait. Your dad left you in a cabin in the woods without a car in a *snowstorm*?

WolfGirl96 >   It's not a big deal. I've got a phone if I need it. And my dad's rifle.

SFWired1 >   It kind of is a big deal. I think it might even be illegal, since you're under eighteen. A rifle? Do you actually know how to use it?

WolfGirl96 >   Of course. I'm very self-sufficient.

SFWired1 >   You're not scared?

WolfGirl96 >   I guess, a little. Just because he's never been gone this long. Five days is usually the limit. I think I'm being punished.

SFWired1 >   Punished? Why?

WolfGirl96 >   Long story. But it's fine, he'll come back eventually. He always does.

SFWired1 >	So he does this on a regular basis? Jesus. I feel like I should be calling Child Protective Services.
WolfGirl96 >	I'm not a child. And it's fine. I'm pretty used to being alone.
SFWired1 >	I have four roommates so I'm almost never alone. We're so jammed in this apartment, there's always someone sleeping on the couch or using the toilet or blasting techno so loud you can't think.
WolfGirl96 >	You're lucky.
SFWired1 >	Just to clarify, just because I'm never alone doesn't mean I'm not ever lonely. What have you been doing by yourself for a week?
WolfGirl96 >	Surfing the Web, mostly. Which I'm technically not supposed to be doing. Maybe that's why I feel so awful.
SFWired1 >	What else are you *supposed* to be doing?
WolfGirl96 >	Reading. Studying. Working on this website I'm making.
SFWired1 >	Just a thought, the reason you feel awful is probably not because you're spending too much time online. It's because you're alone in a cabin in the woods.
WolfGirl96 >	Maybe.
SFWired1 >	Seriously. It's OK if you're angry at your dad, too. I would be.
WolfGirl96 >	Really, I'm fine. I should go.
SFWired1 >	Wait—I just want to say. If you ever need help, you can reach out. Anytime. I know I'm across the country from you, so that's of limited usefulness. But maybe I could do something.
WolfGirl96 >	Thanks, but I don't need help.
SFWired1 >	Everyone needs help sometimes, Jane.

17

THE SNOW THAT had carpeted the forest in white had already melted by the time my father drove back over the ridge, his truck jolting over the mud-stricken potholes. I could hear him coming from a half mile away. I arranged myself at the kitchen table with a book, my back to the front door so that I wouldn't have to look up and greet him when he came in. I didn't want my face to betray my relief that he was home, or my guilt about the hours I had wasted on the internet while he was gone, or my fury that I'd been left for so long in the first place.

And I *was* angry; I'd needed a stranger on the other side of the country to point that out to me. It felt like a curtain had been pulled aside, allowing me to see my life from the outside. And for the first time, instead of being proud of my self-sufficiency, I was righteously furious that my father hadn't taken care of me.

I heard the door swing open, felt a cold draft pierce through the heat of the cabin. My father swore softly under his breath as he scraped the mud off his boots. I didn't turn around as he came up behind me and peered over my shoulder at my book. The outside air clung to him, a damp aura with an undertone of moss and dirty socks.

"You aren't going to say hello?"

"Hello." I turned a page in my book, stuck the pencil nub in my mouth and chewed it thoughtfully, pretending that I was absorbed in vector analysis.

"Are you not talking to me for some reason?"

I flipped another page in my book, not seeing a word. My father stood over my shoulder, waiting for me to turn around and greet him properly. I couldn't make myself do it. Something critical in our dynamic had shifted; I could feel it in the charged air around us. For the first time, I realized that I had the power to piss him off.

Finally, he turned away and began unpacking his bags, methodically removing each item and stacking it on the floor. Books, sacks of beans and rice, a pyramid of cans, a box full of something metallic and rattling. "Well, all I can figure is you're having some kind of hormonal fit. Just let me know when your period is over."

I turned to watch him, my eyes hot and damp with a sudden rage. "Ten days," I shot at him. "You were gone ten *days,* Dad. And it was snowing. What if I had run out of food? Or wood?"

"Did you?"

I remained stubbornly silent.

He came over to me and placed a reassuring hand on my head, ruffling my hair. "You know I checked the food stores before I left. We're stocked. And there's no way you were going to run through all that wood. Don't be silly. There's a phone for emergencies. Nothing was going to happen that doesn't happen every day."

"But what if—" I reached for something, anything, to thrust at him, and landed somewhere I hadn't expected. "What if I was lonely?"

An odd expression passed over my father's face, his brows knitting together with puzzled concern. As if loneliness were an emotion that had never occurred to him. And saying it out loud made me realize that it wasn't an emotion that had ever occurred to me, either. At least not until I had a portal to the world outside, an awareness of everything that was happening that I was not a part of. Life a party to which I had not received an invitation but hadn't missed at all until I was made aware of the event.

"Companionship is a crutch. Learning to be alone is the most critical life skill of all—haven't I taught you that? Because when you rely on other people, for emotional support or intellectual engagement or entertainment or just survival, you are weak. You are *vulnerable.* Because it means that you will suffer when it's taken away—and it inevitably will be. You should never rely on anyone."

"Not even you?" I shot at him.

"Not even me." His face was stony.

I turned away, not wanting him to see how red my face was or the tears collecting in the corners of my eyes. I walked over to the table and opened the laptop, fired up the modem. We sat in silence, listening to it squawk and shriek like some sort of electronic pterodactyl.

"Here," I said and shoved the laptop toward him. "Here's your precious manifesto."

By any standards, the website for *The Luddite Manifesto* was utterly unexceptional. I'd created it as a GeoCities home page, since it was free and foolproof; the address marked me as a newbie, but I *was* a newbie, and didn't know any better yet. GeoCities was broken down into thematic categories, which they called "neighborhoods," though I couldn't imagine we were going to be meeting anyone camped out at the surrounding Web addresses, making small talk or throwing virtual block parties. I'd toyed with the idea of settling into Area 51, just because of Mulder; but ultimately landed on an address in Capitol Hill.

The page itself was as rudimentary as I could make it. Although in my most petulant moments I considered throwing in some blink tags or a few headlines in Comic Sans—just to see how my father might react—I'd ultimately done exactly what I knew he'd like best. Gray background, headlines in 36-point Arial, a front page with an introduction and then hyperlinks to each subsequent section. My father's words, in dense blocks of black text. The only design liberty I'd taken was to slip in an occasional hyperlink to elucidate some of my father's more grandiose terminology. *Corporate overlords* linked to a fan page devoted to Scrooge McDuck. *Apocalyptic future* to a website about the Exxon Valdez oil spill. *Genetic engineering* to a photograph of a square tomato. *Digital pornography* to a *Star Trek* fan fiction page with homoerotic stories featuring Kirk and Spock.

What did I think I was doing, tinkering with my father's text like that? Was I trying to undermine him? It would be convenient to think so now—and it's true, that some of my winking references undermined the serious intent of his manifesto (Scrooge McDuck, I knew, would particularly irk him)—but the truth was that I was still in awe of him. I wanted to believe that this document was the apotheosis of his years of careful study, that he knew something that I did not, and that his philosophy was finally going to be embraced by the world at large. I didn't want to mock him.

Despite the nagging voices in my head, I still wanted him to be right. Because if he wasn't, what had so many years of my life been all about? Why had I just obligingly spent a week of my existence uploading his words to the internet, sentence by painstaking sentence? If he wasn't right, what else did I have to cling to?

And yet. I had never before seen all of my father's ideas strung together quite like this; and reading through the manifesto had filled me with a lingering unease. Parts of it read more like science fiction than plausible reality—*the hubris of technologists is driving us toward a future of artificial intelligence in which humans themselves will become utterly irrelevant, reduced to grunt work while our computer overlords do all the jobs we once held*—and others read, alarmingly, like a call to arms. *We must rise together and fight back against the march of technology, even if it requires violence, to eradicate the voices that are blindly leading us toward our own inevitable destruction.*

Whose voices, exactly, did my father think needed to be "eradicated"? *It's just hyperbole,* I had reassured myself, as I typed up these last few paragraphs. *It's not like he wants technologists to die.*

Did he?

My father skimmed through the pages of the site, clicking on a few of the links to see where they led. He hesitated when he saw that I'd linked *educational system brainwashing* to the home page of Harvard University, and he threw me a look. Then he laughed, almost begrudgingly, and I knew he approved.

"How do we know when people start to read it?" he asked.

I pointed to the lower corner of the website, where I'd installed a hit counter. *You are visitor 0001. Don't forget to sign our guest book!* "That counts the number of visitors. And they can leave a message if they like it."

"Can you tell if it's been seen by government officials? Figure it out from the IP addresses?"

"That's way beyond my skill set, Dad."

"Well. I guess we'll know the feds saw it when they show up at our door to arrest me." This prospect seemed to delight him, although I was pretty sure you couldn't get arrested for what he'd written in the manifesto, no matter how anti-government it was. As far as I was aware, the Constitution still contained the First Amendment.

He patted me on the shoulder. "Good work," he said and picked up the laptop. He walked over to the door to his study and began fiddling with the new padlock. My stomach knotted up as I realized what he was doing.

"Wait, where are you going with the laptop?"

He stopped and turned back to look at me. "I'm putting it in a safe place. No need for you to be messing around with it anymore, is there? Your work here is done."

"But—" I could hear my own voice: needling, whiny, pathetic. I shut up before I could say anything that would further implicate myself. I couldn't exactly tell him about the hours I'd been spending reading feminist Web zines with names like *Maxi* and *Floozy;* or scrolling through fan sites for TV shows I'd never even watched, like *The Smurfs* and *Battlestar Galactica;* or picking my way—titillated and nauseated—through the smutty posts on alt.sex.stories. I couldn't possibly reveal that instead of studying my Marxist theory while he'd been gone, I had instead been killing the hours chatting with a total stranger in San Francisco whose name might or might not be Lionel. I couldn't explain the endorphin hit that I got from just surfing the Web and witnessing the weirdness of human interests in all their myriad forms.

I couldn't explain how much I craved my newly minted connection with the outside world.

From under his wild eyebrows, my father's eyes were coolly studying me, as if I were a mouse who'd crept into his lair and he was waiting to see in which direction I'd run. I realized, with a sudden sinking recognition, that he knew exactly what was going through my mind.

Of course he did. Wasn't that what his manifesto was all about? How technology was enabling our worst, basest impulses; suppressing our intellect; causing our disconnection from nature and the "real world"? *Eliminating our humanity and replacing it with compulsive consumption and empty connection.* Touché, Dad. He'd left me alone with internet access for ten days; he had known from the start *exactly* what would happen. It had been a test, to see if I was strong enough to resist temptation. I failed it.

"You see why I need to take it away, don't you?" His words were soft, girded with empathy and disappointment.

I said nothing. I knew he was right.

And yet, even as he vanished into his study with the laptop under his arm, my next thought was, *He's going to leave again soon.* He always did. And the minute he drove out of the driveway, I would somehow find a way to break into his office and get right back online.

18.

Bᴜᴛ ʜᴇ ᴅɪᴅɴ'ᴛ leave again.

The day after he returned, he took the television set out to the backyard and set it on the mangled stump where we split our logs. Then he went to the shed and came back out with a pickaxe. Before I had time to process what was about to happen, he heaved the axe into the front of the television. Again, and again, and again, he slammed the pickaxe, glass splintering into tiny pieces, metallic shards spraying in every direction, sweat flying off his brow. We would be picking bits of television out of the weeds for years to come, I thought.

I watched him through the window, the knot in my throat making it hard to swallow. I wondered if the modem would be next to go; and then the telephone; and then the toilet; until we were back where we started thirteen years earlier, with just four walls and a woodstove. I saw all the gains of my childhood being clawed back; and I wondered where this all would end.

Who was I kidding? I already knew where it would end. With me trapped in this cabin forever. It was becoming clearer and clearer that my father had no intention of us ever going anywhere again. And maybe, just a few months ago, that might not have seemed so awful; but now it felt like doom. I needed to break out of my jail, but how? Steal his truck? He kept the keys locked in the study. Try to hike out, in the dead of winter? I'd end up dead of hypothermia before I made it to civilization. It made more sense to wait until our next trip to Bozeman, and then slip away when he wasn't paying attention. Maybe Heidi would even let me live with her for a while.

My father threw the television carcass into the trash pile at the bottom of the hill and when he came back inside I was still standing by the window, pale and shaky. He washed his hands in the sink, carefully flicking bits of glass out of his beard, a bright gleam in his eye.

"Don't look so alarmed, squirrel. It was time to get rid of that thing. No good was coming of it. And if I'm not publishing *Libertaire* anymore, there's not such a need to be up on the latest news. Anyway, there's the newspaper if we really need to know what's going on out there."

WITHOUT THE TELEVISION, without the clattering of my father's typewriter, our evenings grew quiet. It was as if the manifesto had been a purge, scraping years of pent-up thoughts out into one towering document, and now my father was lighter, almost giddy. Instead of locking himself away in his study, doing God knows what, he now sat with me in the evenings, rereading books from his shelf—Fourier and Chernyshevsky and Bowles—while I sketched with my new pastels, sulky and angry. Sometimes he would even whistle little tuneless songs that didn't seem to have beginnings or endings.

His pleasure, I was starting to realize, was usually tied to someone else's displeasure; nothing made him happier than imagining that he'd *really taught those fools a lesson.*

"Would you *stop* that?" I barked at him one night.

"Stop what?"

"Whistling."

He looked puzzled. "I was whistling?"

"It's annoying, Dad." I looked at him suspiciously. "Why are you so cheerful, anyway?"

"Oh nothing. I was just remembering." He was gazing across the couch at me, where I sat slumped in the corner with my sketchbook, doodling pointless shapes in my notebook, pushing so hard on the pastels that they left slicks of colors on the page. "The time when I rescued you from the bear."

"The time *what?*" He had my attention now.

"You don't remember? No, you wouldn't. You were probably, oh, six? We'd been here for only a year or two, still figuring everything out. I was out back working on the septic system and you were playing nearby—pressing wildflowers I think—and at some point I looked up and realized that you'd vanished. Probably chasing a butterfly or something along those lines. You knew you weren't supposed to go into the woods on your own, but you were stubborn when you got a notion in your head." He laughed. "Guess you inherited that from me. Anyway. I drop everything and start combing the woods for you, calling your name, and there's nothing. Just *nothing.* Absolute silence, which was the most terrifying thing of all, because you know how sound echoes out here.

"I'm running frantically through the woods, getting more and more panicked. What if you got hurt and we're so far from the hospital? And I'm kicking myself for moving out here. Telling myself that if I find you, I'll move us to someplace safer, a house that has a fence around it. Finally, I walk into a glade—that one with the sideways cedar tree and all the bracken ferns—and there you are, sitting cross-legged in the dirt with your back to me. And just ten feet beyond that, staring straight at you, is this mangy-looking black bear. His snout moving back and forth as he takes a big whiff of you, trying to figure out if you're going to be his lunch.

"And you—you are just as calm as can be, looking straight back at him. My heart is going crazy and I come up right behind you and make myself huge, the way you're supposed to, and start yelling at him to go away. The bear stares at me for a while and finally turns and ambles off. And that's when I look down and realize that you're crying. Not because you're scared but because you're upset. With *me.* And I see that in your hand you are holding out some beef jerky. You were trying to feed the goddamn bear."

"'He was a *nice* bear,' you insisted. 'He wanted me to bring him home.'"

My father started to laugh now, an unlikely giggle, his chest rising and falling as he struggled to catch his breath. "My bold daughter wanted to adopt a bear. God, I was so amazed by you. I remember that was the moment when I finally knew for sure I'd done the right thing, bringing you out here. I had nothing to worry about as long as I kept you close; and while there were so many things I had to teach you, I saw that you could also teach *me*, about how to be fearless. As fearless and open and pure as a child, the most beautiful thing in the world."

I stared at him, tearing through my brain for this memory—my father as a giant, coming to my rescue?—but came up empty-handed. He reached out and gripped my toe in its threadbare sock. "She's still in there, that unpolluted little girl, even as you grow into a woman. And every day that I wake up and see her in your face, I am proud of what I've done. What *we've* done."

I shifted my toe out of his hand and watched the smile slide right off his face.

"Maybe you should have just let the bear eat me," I said. And I stood up and walked away to my room and closed the door behind me—knowing that I'd wounded him in the place where it would do the most damage, and hating myself for how good that felt.

THE REMAINS OF December passed like this, and then January. Winter blew in with a fury, dumping a snowy blanket on our cabin, trapping us there until the plows came, driving us into the numbing dullness of hibernation. We spent the days huddled up by the stove, eating cans of SpaghettiOs and Quaker Oats from the endless boxes in our storeroom, drinking plain hot water because my father had forgotten to stock up on tea. The tedium of our short days was broken up only by the occasional spotting of a coyote in the garden, or the drama of a dead chicken. I'd gone through thirteen long, brutal winters in that cabin, but this one seemed to drag more than any of the ones that had come before. For the first time, I was acutely aware of everything else I was missing.

We hadn't been to Bozeman since late November; and with no *Libertaire* to take to the bookstore—and the roads unplowed—it seemed that our visits to town were over for the foreseeable future. So there would be no slipping away during a visit to town, no chance of moving in with Heidi. Anyway, our friendship seemed to have dried up; she never called anymore. Maybe it was just the chaos of the holidays, and then her starting classes at Gallatin High, but I suspected the real reason for our growing distance was that she just didn't have a use for me anymore. Jocelyn had filled the space that I once occupied, and there was no way I could compete with a friend that was actually part of her day-to-day life. One that wasn't a weird, socially naïve recluse with a pedantic, paranoid father.

I knew she was halfway along the path to forgetting my existence forever; and I couldn't really blame her.

I'd never felt so trapped in my life.

MY FATHER'S GOOD mood came to its inevitable end at the end of January, six weeks after I uploaded *The Luddite Manifesto* to the internet. The sun had finally emerged after five straight days of snow, and my father had sent me out to the henhouse to check on the chickens and see if there were any eggs to be had. When I returned, my pockets empty, I found my father sitting in front of the laptop. He'd connected to the internet without my help and had made his way to the Luddite Manifesto website. He was staring at the home page with a frown on his face.

"I think this thing is broken," he said, stabbing at the screen. "Are you sure you coded it correctly?"

I followed his finger and realized that he was pointing at the hit counter. *You are visitor 0012. Don't forget to sign our guest book!*

No one had signed the guest book.

"It's working. See? Eleven more people have visited since the last time." I wasn't sure why I felt so defensive. "Oh, wait, ten, because it's counting us for a second time."

"*Ten* people? Can we even tell who they are? Or if they read the whole manifesto?"

"I don't think so. I don't really know."

"Christ." He shoved the laptop away with a slap of his palm. "I should have just left a copy in the men's room at the bus station, more people would have read it there."

"I'm sure more people will visit the site," I objected. "They just have to find it. It's only been up for six weeks. That's no time at all."

"How do people usually find websites? There's a directory, somewhere?"

We stared at each other, realizing we'd both neglected to consider this critical piece of the puzzle. I shrugged. "Yahoo, maybe? But I don't know how you get listed on that. I mostly find websites by following links. So, someone needs to link to you."

I could see my father suddenly realizing that his hermit-like existence had its drawbacks. No friends meant no connections. No connections meant you were essentially invisible, even online.

"You could send a letter to your *Libertaire* subscribers? Let them know about it? What about those guys you write to a lot? Malcolm? Benjamin?" He nodded in agreement, but his eyes were far away. I realized—and surely he did, too—that if his *Libertaire* readers were true believers, it wasn't going to be likely that they were also internet early adopters. He'd wanted a broader audience than that; it was the whole point of going online.

"Not a single comment." He shook his head. "Christ, it's worse out there than I thought."

"Just give it time, Dad. Someone who sees how brilliant it is will find it eventually. Word will spread. Even if it's just a small audience, that's something, right?" I knew, even as I said this, that it was the absolute worst thing I could have uttered. It sounded patronizing. It sounded like I didn't trust his genius. The tone in my voice made him look sharply up at me, and the expression on his face was that of a wounded lion: proud and dangerous and unpredictable.

I should have known to be scared.

19

The next morning, when I stumbled into the kitchen, I found my father still sitting at the laptop. Judging by his clothes and the red-rimmed state of his eyes, he'd been there all night.

He barely looked at me as I walked across the room and put on the coffeepot.

"You look terrible," I said.

He grunted in agreement, but didn't lift his head. There was a notebook at his elbow, and I wondered what he'd been writing in it. The silence in the room was as thick as a layer of snow, and just as cold.

When the coffee was done percolating, I handed him a cup. He took a big swallow, and it seemed to thaw him. "Plows came through last night," he said, "so I'm going to head out again soon. Not sure how long I'll be gone this time."

The coffee, too strong, burned my throat. "You're leaving . . . today?"

"In the next few days, before the next storm comes through and shuts down the roads again. Got to put together a few plans first."

"What are you *doing* out there, Dad?"

My question seemed to exhaust him. "Same thing I do here. Trying to make the world a better place. Trying to save humanity from itself."

I hated him, then, for his ability to come and go as he pleased while I remained stuck here in my seven-hundred-square-foot jail. It occurred to me that if I was ever going to get out of here in the dead of winter, the only way it would ever happen was with him. If I could just piggyback on my father's next trip to wherever the hell it was he went, perhaps I would find an opportunity to slip away. I had the two hundred dollars stashed in my go bag; that would surely get me wherever I needed to go.

As for where *that* was, exactly? Well, this remained fuzzy, being as I was working with limited information, the vaguest grasp of geography, and absolutely no real-world experience. But my half-cocked plan went something like this: Go to Silicon Valley. Find a library; go to *all* of them if necessary. Search for my mom's obituary. And if there was no obituary, I'd look for *her*.

"Take me with you." I put my hand on his shoulder, and gave it a tight squeeze, the way he always squeezed mine. "Whatever it is you're doing out there, I can help you."

He shook his head. "Jane. You don't want to get caught up in my business. You're still just a kid."

"You're the one who likes to say that age is just an abstract construct. And haven't I helped you already? With the manifesto. I'm already a part of whatever it is you're doing, whether you like it or not. So you might as well include me in the rest of it."

He flinched, as though I'd just flicked water in his face. The opaque expression in his eyes faded, and was replaced by one that was ruminative, maybe even . . . mournful? He squinted hard at me, apparently seeing something unexpected in my familiar features, and that was when I knew I'd won.

"OK," he said. "You're right."

20

The dress was red and shiny, with puckering threads along the seams from a previous owner who had stretched it out. It had spaghetti straps and lace insets and was made from polyester ineffectually masquerading as satin. It was the kind of thing you'd wear to work in a nightclub, or quite possibly the streets.

The dress was spread out on my bed, a blindingly bright interloper in our realm of browns and grays and greens. A pair of cheap silver sandals sat neatly on the floor in front of it, as if the person wearing the outfit had sat down and then just vanished, leaving their clothes behind. I had no clue what it was doing there, or how it had mysteriously appeared in my bedroom.

I stood in the doorway, contemplating it.

"Dad?"

My father appeared at my shoulder. I pointed at the dress. "What is that?"

"A dress. For you."

"It's a gift?"

"Do you think it will fit?"

I picked it up from the bed. It was so light, it didn't even feel like real clothing. How could you wear this and not feel naked? I wanted desperately to put it on. The longing made me feel weak.

"When am I supposed to wear it? While I'm working in the vegetable garden?"

My father walked past me and sat down on my bed. "Think of it as a costume."

Now I was really confused. "A costume?"

"You said you wanted to help me. I've got a job for you."

"Go on." I stood there watching him. He'd been in a strange state since my offer to help a few days earlier. I'd expected him to be in one of his black funks because of the failure of his manifesto, but instead he'd been preternaturally calm, like something critical had been decided. There was a distance in his eyes when he looked at me, though, his focus boring straight through me to something on the other side. He'd even made a rare solo trip into Bozeman the previous morning; for this dress, I had to assume.

"I need to go talk to an old friend. In Seattle. And the thing is—he isn't an easy person to see." The words came rattling out in a toneless staccato, almost like he was reciting a speech he'd memorized. "He works in a building with a security guard who won't let anyone in to see him. So, I need some assistance getting past the front desk. That's where you're going to come in."

"You can't just call him?"

This gave him pause. He scratched his beard, gazing over my head at a fixed point on the wall. "I don't have his number."

I couldn't quite make this add up. It was the first time I'd ever heard of the existence of a friend, beyond my father's loyal *Libertaire* correspondents. Then again, my father had told me so little of his life before me. "What exactly am I going to have to do?" I asked. I ran a hand across the silky fabric of the dress. It felt like escape.

"Nothing," he said. His smile, toothy and yellow, was not reassuring.

"Nothing?"

"You," he said, pointing at the dress, "are just going to be a distraction."

I was weirdly flattered by this. The idea that anyone could find me interesting enough to be *distracting*. "Is this related to *The Luddite Manifesto*?" I asked.

"*Everything* is about *The Luddite Manifesto*. Oh, and—"

He shoved a hand into the pocket of his jeans. When he pulled it out, there was something wedged in the palm of his hand. A small, pink, plastic cylinder. It took me a minute to recognize it as the lipstick that I'd stolen from Walgreens, the one that had disappeared from my sock drawer a year earlier. The pastel tube was incongruous in his big, calloused palm.

"Go ahead and use this."

21

W E HEADED OUT for Seattle the following morning.

So many aspects of the situation should have been alarming to me. The dress and the plasticky heels and the purloined lipstick. The suit that I'd watched my father pack, gray flannel with thrift-store tags on it. The new Smith & Wesson that he'd tucked into the glove box. The strange leather satchel that he'd shoved behind the driver's seat. The fact that he had, for the first time I could remember, cut his hair short and shaved his beard entirely, leaving only a thick mustache brushing the top of his lip.

Behind the wheel of the truck, my father had been rendered unrecognizable to me: his cheeks pale and vulnerable, scraped raw by the razor. The tender nape of his neck, the exposed skin behind his ears, so naked I had to look away. His new smell, of Castile soap and shaving cream. My intimidating, inviolable father had vanished, replaced by this benign man who looked like he spent his life stapling documents together in an office cubicle.

Maybe I would have been more worried if I hadn't been consumed with an amaurotic eagerness for our road trip. While he was busy hatching his own plan, I was hatching mine. I'd secretly taken the emergency money from my go bag and hidden it in the toe of a rolled-up pair of socks. I'd packed extra clothes in my overnight bag, along with my pastels and a sketchbook, the only possessions I truly cared about. I'd looked up the entry for Seattle in our Oxford world atlas, too, and familiarized myself with a map of downtown. I figured I'd wait until my father had fallen asleep at our motel, and then I would sneak out and walk to the train station and buy a ticket to California.

As we drove away from the cabin and west along the ice-socked roads, my heart felt tight in my chest. Was it excitement, or was it guilt about my betrayal? What was my father going to do if I disappeared? He would be angry, yes, but more to the point, he would be *hurt*. This was harder for me to stomach. My desire to leave wasn't about abandoning my father. I still loved him, despite my wilting worship. No, it was more about finding *me*.

All this is to say that I was too distracted to think much about the fact that the leather satchel, the one my father carefully placed behind the seat before we drove out of town, smelled an awful lot like fertilizer.

WE DROVE STRAIGHT through the day, stopping only to gas up and eat at a greasy roadside stand somewhere in Idaho. By the time we crossed into Washington, the sun had already set. The highway was lined with dense pines, but I knew when we were in the proximity of Seattle because the sky was glowing in the distance, the ambient city lights trapped in a low cloud cover.

We were still in the woodsy fringes of the suburbs when my father abruptly pulled off the road.

"Why are we stopping?"

"We're going to stay here tonight."

"Here? We aren't actually going to stay in Seattle?"

We'd pulled up alongside a shabby motel, crouching in the dark recesses of an empty parking lot. A flickering roadside sign advertised *Rooms $18 TV Fridg No AirCon Pet OK*. An erratic rain had started falling, spattering impotently across the windshield. There would be no walk to the train station from here. I hadn't even seen the city skyline.

"This *is* Seattle; it's just the outskirts. What, did you think we were going to stay at a five-star hotel?"

"Not, it's just—" My disappointment was palpable, and potentially incriminating. I tried to temper my tone. "I wanted to see downtown.

And the Space Needle. I read about that in the atlas. I've never seen a city before."

I don't know why this observation came as a surprise to my father. Something softened in him then and put a nostalgic gleam in his eye. "If all goes well tomorrow, we can go there after. Seattle's not so bad as cities go. There's a pretty good arboretum, if it's not raining. And we'll go to the fish market and eat some oysters. They taste like the ocean. You'll like them."

So, I'd have to wait until tomorrow and slip away when he was distracted. Maybe at the fish market. I told myself that it wouldn't be so bad to wait until *after* we'd already completed my father's project, anyway. I was, after all, still curious about what he had been doing all those times that he'd left me behind. This was my one-and-only chance to find out. Besides, what would it hurt to do this one last thing for him before I headed out on my own? It was the least I could do; it would take the sting out of my departure. And all he was asking me to do was put on a dress and smile. How problematic could that be?

Never underestimate the power of love to lead you down the path toward willful blindness. Faith in the people you adore doesn't disappear slowly, with each tiny disappointment; instead, it collapses all at once, like the final snowfall that triggers an avalanche when the weight suddenly becomes too much to bear. I was nearing that tipping point, but I hadn't quite arrived there yet.

THE MOTEL WAS a dump: The twin beds had comforters that smelled like wet dog; the cottage-cheese ceiling was flaking off in chunks; the television only worked if you put a quarter in a slot. But for someone who had only slept in one room her entire life, it might as well have been the Four Seasons. I opened every drawer and peered in every corner, fascinated by the miniature soaps wrapped in paper and the cups heat-sealed in plastic and the gilt-edged Bible in the nightstand.

My father bought us a dinner of vending machine food, Twinkies and Flamin' Hot Cheetos, Mountain Dew and Slim Jims, and I remember how excited I was by this. (And a hair resentful, too: Was *this* how he ate when he traveled? And why had he never brought any treats home for me?) The sugar high from all the unfamiliar junk food left me so manic that when my father went to take a shower, I turned on the tinny AM/FM clock radio and jumped on the bed to "Sweet Caroline" until I was breathless and sweaty. It felt like all the pieces of my life were suddenly falling into place; all truths about to be unveiled.

And so the last minutes of my childhood ticked away, unnoticed, as I naïvely careened around that shabby room, feeling so very pleased with myself. I didn't know to try to catch those fleeting moments and hold them close, so I let them vanish, just one of so many things I was about to lose.

I SLEPT POORLY. The strange sensations—the rough sheets and the chemicals pulsing through my bloodstream and the sounds of the highway just fifty feet away—kept me tossing for most of the night. My father snored, apparently unbothered, in the other bed. I drifted off just before sunrise and when I woke up again a few hours later my father was standing over me with a paper cup of coffee and a sack of donuts. He was already dressed in the thrift-store suit, his hair carefully slicked back, a plain black baseball cap perched on top.

"Better put the dress on," he said, handing me the coffee. "It's time to go."

He waited outside in the truck while I tugged the dress over my head and wiggled the zipper closed. The dress was so tight that I had to take tiny, birdlike sips of air so that I wouldn't pop the seam. I studied myself in the rust-speckled mirror over the sink. The Jane I knew was still there, with the lank blond hair yanked back in a ponytail, the farmer's tan burned in from a childhood spent without sunscreen, muscled shoulders from years of chopping wood. But that Jane had taken a back seat to this new coquette with her candy-floss lips and her cleavage hefted so high that it threatened to hit her chin. I wanted to slap the girl in the mirror. I wanted to kiss her, too. It was all very confusing.

What was to come hadn't even begun, but I was already starting to split in two, dizzied by my own bifurcation.

Outside, a half-hearted drizzle was still falling, the low clouds a gunmetal gray. My father hadn't thought of getting a nice jacket to go with the dress, so I teetered to the truck in my parka and high heels, the fabric clinging to my goosebumps. He watched me approach through the windshield. The expression on his face looked like he'd just bitten into an unripe plum and was trying to decide whether to swallow it or spit it out.

"Maybe this is a bad idea," he said, his hands gripping the steering wheel so tightly that I could see the outline of every tendon. "I'm thinking we should just go home. You don't need to be here."

And even though my impulse was to flee, too—back to the predictable safety of our cabin—I found myself thinking of the story he'd told me, about the bear that he'd rescued me from, the one I'd tried to feed. I looked deep down inside myself and tried to locate that child, the fearless little girl my father so admired.

"It's fine. I'm fine," I said. I reached up and buckled my seatbelt across the dress, smoothing the fabric over my legs. My father gazed at me for a long minute, doing some invisible calculations, and then sighed and started the truck.

We pulled back onto the freeway.

The roads were quiet, but the parking lots of the churches that we passed were overflowing with station wagons and minivans. As we drove, I let myself imagine that we were a totally different father and daughter, normal ones, headed to Sunday service with everyone else. We'd stand around afterward and eat coffee cake and make small talk—about the weather, or football scores, or our upcoming vacations—like normal families did on television.

Not that a church would let me through the door in the outfit I was wearing.

My father put me in charge of the map, and I mirrored our route with my finger as we drove out of the woods and over a hill and then down through the industrial suburbs. In the distance, the skyscrapers of Seattle finally came into view, silver-faced stalagmites rising up from the horizon. We were headed to an *X* that my father had marked on the map in black ink, across the water from downtown Seattle.

When we finally arrived at our destination, it turned out to be a collection of low-slung, brick-clad office buildings, spread along a tangle of tree-lined streets. Block after block after block: It seemed to go on forever. I turned to read a sign as we passed, and a little jolt of electricity passed through me as I recognized the logo in four-foot-high letters: *MICROSOFT.* I'd seen it on the screen of our laptop, every time we booted it up.

Even though it was a Sunday, the campus wasn't completely deserted; a handful of cars were scattered throughout the parking lots. Fancier cars than I had ever seen before, ones I had no names for but now would identify as Ferraris and BMWs and Mercedes. The sidewalks were totally devoid of pedestrians. No one was out and about who might notice the mud-spattered Chevy S-10 pickup carrying a girl and a man dressed for a night on the town and a business meeting, respectively.

My father pulled over along the road, just past the edge of the campus. "We'll walk in from here," he said. He looked in the rearview mirror and adjusted his tie and baseball cap, then pulled a pair of cheap aviator sunglasses from his pocket and perched them on his nose. When he looked at me, I could see my own image reflected back at me, and I couldn't decide what was more alarming: the cloaking of his eyes or the dolled-up stranger who was reflected in the mirrored lenses.

The drizzle had turned into a fine mist. I didn't particularly want to get out of the warm truck. Neither of us budged from our seats.

Finally, he reached over me and unlatched the glove box, retrieving the Smith & Wesson. He checked the safety latch and then handed it to me.

It was squat and cold in my hand, unlike the wood-barreled rifle we'd always used for hunting. "What am I supposed to do with this?"

"It's just to have in case of an emergency."

"What kind of emergency are you imagining? I thought I was just distracting a security guard."

"Always plan for contingencies, squirrel."

Unease settled over me like an itchy shawl. "How am I supposed to distract the security guard, anyway? You didn't explain that part."

He took off the sunglasses and rubbed the lenses with his sleeve; emitting a throaty little cough as he gave me a sideways look. "Jane. You're a beautiful blonde in a tight dress. It should be easy."

If there's one thing a teenage girl should never have to hear, it's her father describing her sex appeal. I flushed and stared down at my legs. The bare flesh exposed by the dress reminded me of a chicken plucked of its feathers. "You didn't exactly cover this in home school."

His gaze fluttered down from my eyes to rest on the sticky fuchsia gloss that was gluing my lips together, and then flung itself upward again, as if the sight upset him. "I figured some things just come naturally to women."

We both fell silent, thinking. Finally, I spoke: "Do you have any money?"

My father hesitated, taken aback, before slowly extracting a wad of cash from his pocket. It was a fat stack of fresh-from-the-bank twenties, folded in half and held together by an old rubber band. He handed it over, and I waited for him to ask what I planned to do with it, but he said nothing. I shoved the cash in the pocket of the parka, along with the gun. The weight of them was incongruous against my polyester-clad thigh.

"OK," I said. "I'm ready." I didn't move.

"Wait—" My father reached around me with one arm and for one moment I thought he was going to embrace me. But instead he reached behind my head and forked out my ponytail holder, letting my hair spill loose around my shoulders. Haircuts being rare in our house, it had grown almost to my waist.

He fluffed it a little with his fingers, sat back and squinted at me. "Yes. Good. You're going to do just fine." There was an odd hitch in his voice, one I hadn't heard before, throaty and—could it be?—mournful. He cupped my cheek with his palm. "Look. I know I've given you a strange life, and I've been hard on you sometimes. Too hard, maybe. I had the best intentions, you have to believe me; but I've still sometimes wondered whether I did the right thing. And lately, I've been watching you grow up, practically a woman, and I've worried that you're starting to want more than I can give you. I can't fault you for being curious. But the thing is, Jane, deep inside you're just like me. You can *see* things, understand them, the way I do. And that's a gift I'm glad we can share as equals. Because you're my girl."

My girl. I'd never heard him use this phrase before. Maybe it was just that the dress was too tight, but I suddenly felt dizzy, almost euphoric. His belief in me—so clearly articulated, after all these years—was what finally propelled me forward, my hand reaching for the handle of the door, my legs swinging out toward the pavement. And off I marched, wobbly-ankled and pimple-fleshed, like a lamb to the slaughter.

22.

MEMORY IS A fickle beast. So often we choose what we want to remember; but sometimes memories choose us. The memories we most want to forget are the ones that fold themselves into our subconscious, waiting until we least expect them to rise up and pinch us tight in their talons. You'll be walking down the street on an otherwise-normal morning and suddenly there it will be, the thing you most wish you didn't remember, stealing your breath away, leaving you horror-struck and ashamed.

I wish I could forget everything about that day—most of all, my own complicity—but of course it's the one day of my life I will never, ever forget.

I will never forget the look on the security guard's face as he glanced up from the desk in the stone-clad lobby and saw me frantically knocking on the glass-paned door. The way his expression morphed from annoyance to bewilderment to something resembling hunger, like a starving coyote who has just spied a rabbit across a field.

I will never forget the unpleasant feeling of power I experienced when he walked toward me, his jaw slackened, his eyes sliding up and down the tight red dress; and I understood for the first time what it meant to possess control of another human being.

I will never forget the fat meaty fingers of his hand, and the way they felt huge on my upper arm as he steered me toward the far end of the parking lot where I told him I'd just lost my money. The way his grip was protective and paternal—the man was older than my father, quite possibly I reminded him of a daughter or a niece—but also a little too eager, a little too tight, in the way he hooked his elbow around me and used it to press his body against mine.

I will never forget the wiry black hair that grew out of the top of his butt crack, which was exposed when he knelt down to peer underneath the sedan. Or the sight of his pale gut wobbling—the pants of his too-tight uniform having separated from his shirt—when he stretched his arm deep under the chassis of the car, trying to reach the wad of bills that I'd tossed under there, just out of reach.

I will never forget how, as I stood there staring down at the guard's prone, vulnerable body, I watched my own father scurry through the unattended doors of the office building, the leather satchel gripped in one fist. Head down, utterly innocuous, like a middle manager on his way to an important meeting. And how I felt a sense of victory and pride, thinking of the praise I would receive from him later for doing my job so well.

God, I shudder every time I remember *that*.

When the security guard stood up, there were big, damp patches on the knees of his pants from where he'd knelt on the rain-soaked asphalt, and I remember that *this* was what I was suddenly concerned about—that the security guard might get in trouble for the state of his uniform. It never occurred to me that the real terminable offense was the monster who had just slipped through the doors that this man was being paid to guard.

I remember reaching out to grab the fold of money from the security guard's fist, so anxious to get back to the safety of the truck that I didn't even bother to pretend to be thankful. And how the grin on his face, wolfish and self-satisfied, began to collapse when he realized there was no Samaritan reward to be had—no girlish gratitude, no sweet kiss on the cheek.

I remember how, then, as I tried to wrestle the cash out of his fist, he suddenly decided to grip it even harder. There we were, having a tug-of-war out there in the parking lot, me teetering in the stupid heels, panic rising in me along with the realization that he wasn't going to let me go so easily. That perhaps the power in this situation wasn't mine, after all.

I remember his free hand snaking up the leg of my skirt, his rough palm on the inside of my thigh, his hot breath in my ear—*c'mon, don't be coy, I know what you are*—and the horror as it dawned on me exactly what he thought that was. That he'd measured me up—the tight dress, the tattered parka, the wad of cash—and pegged me a prostitute. The reward he'd expected wasn't a kiss on the cheek: It was a trip to the utility closet, buckles undone, me taking my own turn on my knees.

I remember the hot rush of adrenaline that caused me to jerk away, so that I lost my balance entirely and found myself on the ground, looking up at the leering security guard. His hand drifting toward an object on his belt as he started to kneel next me, his crotch perilously close to my head . . .

What I don't remember: how the gun from my pocket suddenly ended up in my hand. Nor do I have any memory at all of making the decision to fire it.

I can play the scene over in my mind, time and time again, but I still can't quite figure out what happened and why. It's quite possible that I overreacted, and he was just leaning over me to help me up. Or maybe he *was* about to yank me into the empty lobby to do unspeakable things to me. I will never know exactly what his intentions were at that moment. All I can say for sure is that, in an instant, all those years of paternal indoctrination—*uniformed authorities are out to get us*—escalated my panic into an instinctive rush of self-preservation.

And so the security guard was suddenly on the ground, my ears were pulsing from the reverberations of the gunshot, and there was a spray of dark red across the Valentine fabric of my dress. The security guard was moaning and clutching at his thigh, calling me a bitch as something viscous pooled onto the storm-slick pavement; and then I had my heels in my hand and the gun in my other hand and I was running, running, running so fast that I split out the sides of that ridiculous dress.

———

I DON'T REMEMBER the long sprint back to the truck, either, just that when I came back to myself I was sitting in the front seat, shivering so hard that my entire body was vibrating. How much time passed before my father returned? I couldn't tell you that, either—just that it seemed to take an eternity even though surely it was just a matter of minutes, and that the whole time I was waiting for the police to show up and surround the car. If they had, I would have been too blind with tears to see them.

What I didn't know, of course, was that the police had been distracted by something else entirely, something that had happened just a few minutes after I raced out of that parking lot.

Did I hear the horrible roar that marked the disaster taking place just a half mile away? I must have, but I don't remember this, either; perhaps it was drowned out by the deafening hammer of my own heart.

When the door to the truck finally flew open, I nearly jumped out of my skin. I was fumbling my way toward an apology—*I screwed everything up*—but something about my father's appearance stole the words while they were still in my throat. His face was red and beaded with sweat. His gelled-back hair had collapsed and was falling in spikes across his forehead; there was a long, gooey scratch across his chin. The leather satchel he'd brought into the building with him had vanished; in its place was a big brown shopping bag, with something heavy tearing at its seams.

He thrust the bag into the truck and then began peeling off his suit jacket. "Listen. You can find your way back to the motel by yourself, right? You were good with that map."

I rubbed at my tearstained face with the back of my hand, feeling the lipstick smear across my cheek. "I can. But, Dad—is everything . . . OK?"

He wadded the jacket into a ball that he shoved under the seat. "Why?"

Was it possible he hadn't noticed the state I was in? "The security guard—" I was at a loss for words.

"You did a fine job, that was some very creative thinking," he said. "But now they'll be looking for me. We need to split up." He replaced the suit jacket with his old blue parka, then extracted the baseball hat from its pocket and tugged it over his hair.

"Looking for you? Not me?"

"You? Why would they be looking for you?" He reached across the seat and shoved the truck keys in my hand. "I need you to pay attention, Jane. You go back to the motel and wait for me. OK? I'll meet you there as soon as I can."

I stared dumbly at the keys in my palm. "But how will you get back, if I have the truck?" I didn't want to be alone right then, not at all.

"I'll take a taxi. It doesn't matter. The important thing is, you stay at the motel until dark. And if I'm still not back by then, you drive back to Montana."

In the distance I could hear the wail of a siren, winding up the speed of my pulse. "Dad. I'm scared. Is he dead?"

My father hesitated. "Peter?"

"The security guard's name is Peter?"

My father shook his head in frustration. "We'll talk about this later. I've got to go. If I don't come home within a day or two—let's say Tuesday—and I haven't called you yet, either, you know what to do, right?"

"Wait. You're not coming home?"

My father turned his head to the road, his ears tuning in to the approaching siren. His words came quicker now: "I'm coming home. Of course I'm coming home. But we always have a contingency plan, just in case, right? So tell me what you do. If I don't come back. Or if they come before I do."

"Get the go bag, light the fuse, run," I recited, trying not to tear up again as I imagined the authorities forming a noose around the cabin while I sat there, alone, unaware. "But run where? Where do I go if you're not with me? We never talked about that."

"You make your way to North Dakota. To Malcolm Torino. We can meet there, it's safe. Bring what's in that bag." His eyes slid to the shopping bag on the floor. "You'll find his address on top of my desk. Look in the bottom drawer of the desk, too; there's more money in there, I'll need it all."

"But the door to the study is locked. So is the desk."

He turned back to look at me then, one last time, his lips twisting into a dark smile. "That didn't stop you before, did it, Jane?" And then he turned on his heel and ran off in the opposite direction of the approaching siren.

I watched as he hitched right, and then changed his mind and veered left, turned a corner, and vanished.

AND HERE'S ONE last thing I remember, one last monster of a memory that claws me awake, pulse pounding, chest convulsed in a cringe: that as I drove away, my fingers white-knuckled on the steering wheel, I still believed that my biggest crime was shooting a potential rapist in an act of self-defense. And that *this* was what was going to get me into trouble with my father, once we made it back to Montana. Even as I passed the fire engines—one, two, three—racing in the direction from which I'd come, I couldn't begin to fathom how much bigger my crisis actually was.

23

I WAITED FOR MY father all afternoon, sitting stiffly on a bed in the motel room with the lamps turned off and the blinds drawn. I finally had the means of freedom in my grasp—the keys to the truck, an afternoon with no supervision—and yet I'd completely abandoned all thoughts of escape. I was nailed in place by guilt and terror. All I wanted was my father to come back and reassure me that the security guard was still alive, that they didn't know that I was the one who shot him, that everything was going to be OK.

Outside, the sun had finally made an appearance, judging by the strip of light that leaked from underneath the curtains. I marked the passing hours by the movement of that little patch of sun along the stained blue carpet, before dusk swept it all away and I was left alone in the dark.

At some point, it dawned on me that my father had given me all his money, and therefore had no way of paying for a taxi back to our motel. He would have to find someone to give him a ride, or hitchhike, or scrounge up some change and figure out the local bus system. Which perhaps explained why it was already sunset and he hadn't yet arrived.

This was reassuring, but not reassuring enough.

The clock radio on the desk marked six, then seven, then eight o'clock—long past the time when my father had ordered me to abandon ship and head back to Montana. I began to realize that I'd been worrying about the wrong thing entirely: The issue wasn't how he was going to get back to the motel, the issue was whether he was going to make it at all. Whether something awful had happened to him.

They'll be looking for me, he'd warned, before running off without me. Why would they be looking for him, and not me?

As I sat parsing through our last conversation, it began to occur to me that perhaps my father wasn't running because of something I'd done. It was possible he'd done something himself. But what? He'd gone to talk to a friend; that's it. And yet there had been that scratch on his face, which suggested an altercation. I imagined an argument and a scuffle with his old friend. It was possible that my father had stolen something, too: The shopping bag, when I'd opened it, held a heavy beige metal box, labeled *IBM Power Series 850.* I was pretty sure it was a computer hard drive.

And who, exactly, was the *they* he had been referring to? *They* had always been his catchall word, encompassing the vast web of government bureaucrats and police state agents and elected officials and corporate overlords; but most of the time, when he used it, what he meant was *the feds.* Was it possible that the feds had finally caught up with him, here? But no matter how much I puzzled over it, I couldn't figure out why the authorities would have chased him all the way to Seattle. Was he right about them coming after him for his manifesto? But only twelve people had even read it. I was pretty sure the police wouldn't come after him for thought crimes of such an insignificant scale.

My imagination hadn't yet expanded to match the size of my father's ambitions.

By the time the clock display flipped over to nine, my fear of getting in trouble with my father won out over my fear of accidentally abandoning him in Seattle with the feds on his heels. I packed up our belongings, threw in the paper-wrapped soaps just because, and crept out to the truck.

I paused at the entrance to the highway. It would be so easy to point the truck south toward California, toward Silicon Valley and a wild shot in the dark. Instead, I settled on the path of least resistance. I headed back east, the way we'd come, alone.

———

THE DRIVE BACK to Montana took almost twice as long as the trip to Seattle. I crept along in the slow lane, terrified by the cars zooming past me, trying to render myself invisible to the highway patrol who would surely arrest me for driving an unregistered truck without a license. At one in the morning, somewhere near Spokane, exhaustion and hunger caught up to me. 1 pulled over at a gas station, bought myself a desiccated hot dog off the spinning racks of doom, and then slept the rest of the night in the truck, my stomach gurgling unhappily.

I hoped that, with morning, everything would feel less ominous. No dice. I woke, stiff and bleary and sick with the knowledge that I'd shot a man, and the only person who could help me make sense of the situation was the father I'd left behind in Seattle. A father who may, himself, have done something bad. As I finally turned onto the familiar roads near Bozeman the following afternoon, my hands aching from my vise-grip on the steering wheel, I couldn't shake the feeling that something was very, very wrong.

And so I disobeyed my father. Instead of heading straight back to the cabin to wait for him, I drove to Gallatin High and parked out front.

At exactly three o'clock, teenagers began pouring out of every orifice of the building, a torrent of pimples and hairspray. I could practically smell the hormones from where I sat, slumped behind the wheel of my father's truck. Throngs of girls, arms tangled together, swarmed past the truck, casting a curious eye at me before immediately deciding I wasn't worth their attention. A boy wearing a sideways WWF baseball hat jumped on my fender and then jumped off again while his friends jeered.

They looked like foreign creatures, these teenagers; so vivid and real and yet also pale copies of the pretty technicolor teenagers I'd seen on television. I'd never before been in such close proximity to my own peer group, and from this perspective it was more obvious than ever that I was a different species altogether. Kids like these didn't worry about the feds showing up at their door; they didn't have to wring a chicken's neck if they wanted meat for dinner; they weren't made to read Hegel's *Philosophy of Nature* at age nine. They certainly didn't shoot strange men with their father's unregistered handgun.

When Heidi finally materialized in the doorway of the high school, my despondency lifted. She was limping her way down the steps, in conversation with a girl in full orthodontic headgear and a sweatshirt that read *MATH: The Only Subject That Counts,* and when her eyes finally rose to the street she immediately clocked my father's truck. Heidi stopped, said something to her friend, and then headed straight toward me. I was relieved to see that she was smiling; though it was a crooked sort of a smile, her brows furrowing even as her lips tugged up.

I rolled down the window and she leaned on the frame, taking the pressure off her bad leg. She looked different from when I'd last seen her in November; less puppy, more hound, her nails painted red instead of pink and her eyes rimmed in dark liner. "I don't believe it. Your dad finally let you borrow his truck?"

"Sort of," I said. "I was wondering—could we go to your house? And watch TV?"

"My house?" She gazed over the top of the truck, reading an invisible clock in the sky. "I mean, sure. I'd love that. But I only have a few minutes because debate team practice is at four. You sure you don't want to do it tomorrow when I'll have more time?"

"No. It has to be today."

Something about my voice made her smile fade. "Is everything OK?"

"I don't know, Heidi," I said, and started to cry.

HER HOUSE WAS exactly as I'd always imagined it, a sweet mint-green bungalow on a quiet block near the south edge of town. It was a study in Librarian Chic: crocheted heirloom blankets that smelled like lavender, a tea cozy shaped like a chicken, and two fluffy cats who had shed enough hair on the furniture to knit a sweater. Books were stacked in piles everywhere, though not the kind of books I was used to: Heidi and Lina preferred self-help and celebrity memoirs and rom-coms with candy-pink covers.

I sat with a cat in my lap, while Heidi brought me a damp wash-cloth for my eyes.

"Maybe you could call the Bozeman police?" she said. "They'd probably be able to help you find him."

"That's a terrible idea. You know how my dad hates the police. What if he got into trouble with them and it was my fault?"

"But for what? I don't get it. You went with him to meet a friend and then he just ran away? What do you think could have happened?"

I shrugged. I had soft-pedaled my problems to her—leaving out the data points that might frighten her, like the fact that I'd shot a man—and focused instead on the marginally less-alarming truth of my father disappearing three states away. But secretly, my mind was going to darker and darker places the longer I had to think about what had happened in Seattle; places I sure as hell wasn't about to go with Heidi.

"Maybe we should ask my mom to help. She might have ideas."

I suspected my father wouldn't like this much, either. Heidi turned on the television with the remote and began scrolling through chan-nels. "So, what are we looking for?"

"I don't know," I said. "The news, I guess."

She rolled her eyes at me. "They don't put grown-ups on the *news* just for going missing, Jane, especially if you haven't even filed a re-port."

Still, she humored me by flipping rapidly through cable channels. (Cable! I'd never seen such a treasure trove of trash.) We cruised past episodes of *Bewitched* and *Judge Judy* and *Blue's Clues;* stopped long enough on MTV to watch five women in nipple-y tops writhe to a song about being best friends *for-ev-ah!*; and finally landed on *The Oprah Winfrey Show.* I would have been more excited, if it weren't for the fact that I was looking for a news segment informing me I'd killed a man.

"I don't think the news is on right now," Heidi offered. "I have to leave for practice, but you could stay for a while and see if it comes on."

"No, I should go home. I should have been home hours ago. He's probably been trying to call me." I seized on this idea, perking up a bit. "Probably, he's worried about *me*. Because I haven't made it home yet. God, I didn't even think of that."

"See? You don't need to freak out. It's going to be fine. But it was nice that you got to come over, for once." Heidi stood as I gathered my keys to the truck. We were hugging goodbye, my face buried in the sticky nest of her hair, when I heard a stentorian voice cut through Oprah's theme music.

"On news at five, our update from Seattle on the explosion on the Microsoft campus. Police have released surveillance footage of two people who are wanted for questioning in the murder of chief scientific officer Peter Carroll by a homemade bomb . . ."

Over Heidi's shoulder, I caught a glimpse of a familiar brick building, caution tape framing a partially collapsed wall, the blackened hole regurgitating mangled office furniture. And then the image cut to two grainy black-and-white video stills, side by side on the screen. A man in a dark suit and mirrored sunglasses, head down, walking through a lobby; and a blonde in a skimpy dress and parka, blurry, on the other side of a plate glass window. The angles were high; the images pixelated and out of focus; it's hard to imagine now that anyone would have recognized my father and me in our unlikely disguises. But to me, the photos were crystal clear.

And of course, I'd just told Heidi enough about my predicament that she might be able to figure out what she was seeing, too.

My self-preservation instinct kicked in. I grabbed the remote control and turned off the television just before Heidi snapped her head around to look at the screen. When she turned back to look at me, her face had corkscrewed into a puzzled twist of confusion.

We were silent for an uncomfortable moment.

"You know you can trust me, right?" Heidi said slowly. "Like, I'm really good at secrets. I swear. No judgment."

"I know," I said. The static buzz in my ears was making it hard to stand upright; I worried that I might pass out right there in her living room. I was still trying to fully absorb what I'd just seen, but I knew one thing for sure: no way was I going to involve Heidi in whatever we had done. "I'm sorry, but I really have to go."

I stumbled blindly out the door and climbed into the truck. Heidi came out to the porch to watch me leave. I lifted a hand and waved at her as I started the engine, hoping that I came off as cheery and unconcerned, even though my insides felt like overheated Jell-O.

I waited for Heidi to wave back, but she just stood there, motionless as a statue, as I drove away.

24.

There are moments, even now, when I think back to the time before I knew anything about the world—when the extent of my awareness began and ended with what I could touch with my fingertips, what I could see from our window—and wonder whether it might have been better to remain that naïve forever. We sentimentalize childhood innocence for a reason: Kids have no reason to fear the world. They believe themselves immortal. They know nothing of evil and decay. They don't know to be afraid of hungry bears.

And don't all adults wish that we could still feel that way, too?

I lived in that liminal place for far longer than most children—lived it deep into my teens—and maybe I would have stayed that way forever, if I hadn't begged to leave the cabin. I'm convinced, even now, that this is what my father wanted for me: for me to stay in that protected bubble, naïve to the feeling of despair, until the day I died.

The irony, of course, is that kids believe that knowledge unlocks happiness. More than anything, they crave access to all the things that they aren't supposed to know yet; as if being privy to the secrets of the world will open up some magical door to adulthood. They believe that if you *know*, you will *understand*. But in fact, the opposite is true. The more you come to know about the world, the less it makes sense; and the more you wish you could just climb right back inside your mother's arms and hide there, an oblivious kid, forever.

Of course, I didn't have a mother, so I was shit out of luck on that front.

As I drove, I found myself wishing that I'd obeyed my father and gone straight back to our cabin to sit by the phone. I realized that if I hadn't gone to Heidi's house—if I hadn't managed to watch the news—I might never have found out what actually happened in Seattle. For a brief, hallucinatory moment, I let myself believe that if I'd just managed to stay ignorant, it would have somehow nullified what happened. My father wouldn't have killed a man; and I wouldn't have been his unwitting accomplice.

But life doesn't come with a Rewind button. There is no convenient amnesia that can undo the damage already done.

HEEDING CAUTION, I parked my father's truck on the old logging road at the edge of the forest and crept in on our secret path, my feet soggy and numb in my frozen boots. But there were no strangers waiting at the cabin, no cars in the drive, or police waiting on our porch. The cabin stood silent, windows dark abysses, the chimney cold.

Inside, nothing had changed at all in the two days that I'd been gone. Newspapers were still strewn across the sofa and my quantum physics textbook was open to the same page and the hens had produced exactly zero eggs. Everything felt bizarrely normal, and for a fleeting moment I almost believed that my father and I could just step back into our lives and resume as we were.

I was cold and starving, and what I really wanted to do was light a fire in the stove and make a plate of pasta; but there was no time for that. Sure, Heidi was my friend; but how good of a friend was she these days, really? What were the odds that she picked up the telephone after I drove away, and made a call to the Bozeman police? I'd fucked up, and I knew it. My father was going to be livid.

Get the go bag, light the fuse, run. My father's voice kept running through my head. I was a fugitive now, wasn't I? It would be stupid of me to stay here and just wait for the cops to show up.

But before I took off, I at least wanted to know more about what I was running from.

The laptop and modem were sitting on the dining room table where my father had left them. Five minutes after I arrived home, I was online and clicking through the pages of *The New York Times*.

My father and I hadn't made the front-page headlines. For one glorious second I let myself believe that this meant that everything was going to be just fine; that whatever had happened, it wasn't *that* bad; that it was possible I'd even misheard the news reporter entirely.

That fantasy blew up the second I clicked to the U.S. News section.

There we were, in an alarmingly large font. *EXPLOSION KILLS AI PIONEER AT MICROSOFT CAMPUS.*

In a smaller font, underneath, an equally chilling subhead: *Suspects leave behind anti-technology screed.*

I read the article, my brain at a boil. An explosion on the Microsoft campus on Sunday had caused significant damage to a research and development building. One person had been killed: Peter Carroll, the chief scientific officer at Microsoft, a pioneer in the study of neural networks and artificial intelligence. There had been no additional casualties, but a security guard had been treated for minor injuries stemming from a gunshot wound.

At this, something inside me unclenched. At least there was this: At least I hadn't killed a man. Though, apparently, my father had. Which made me an accomplice to murder.

No suspects had been identified yet. Video footage from lobby security cameras had pinpointed two unidentified visitors to the building, and they were wanted for questioning. (The footage stills were not available online, photos still being a luxury in those glacial-download days; but of course, I'd already seen them.) Authorities believed the explosion was the result of a homemade incendiary device. Meanwhile, the perpetrator had left behind a URL, scrawled on a hallway wall, which led to a website with a long, anti-technology screed.

The URL was printed in the article. It was, of course, the Luddite Manifesto.

I'm embarrassed now to confess that seeing that URL in print thrilled me, despite myself: that something *I had made* was in the pages of *The New York Times*. But that momentary frisson was accompanied by a rising swell of nausea, as everything else began to sink in. The dead man, the injured security guard, the charred remains of a tech campus office. My father, his face bleeding, running off into the mist. Me, in a red dress, fleeing the scene.

I raced to the front door, leaned over the edge of the porch, and vomited into the snow.

25.

L ook, i know what you're thinking. *How could she not have seen this coming?* It was all right there on the page, from the jump: *We must rise together and fight back against the march of technology, even if it requires violence, to eradicate the voices that are blindly leading us toward our own inevitable destruction.* He wasn't exactly subtle about his intentions. Why didn't I think to question the bag that smelled like fertilizer; the gun in the glove box; the use of a seventeen-year-old girl as a honey-pot decoy? None of it added up to anything good.

I should have seen disaster coming, and found a way out of it; maybe even found a way to *stop* it. Instead, I had volunteered for the job.

If it makes you feel any better about me, I've thought these things, too. I've spent the last twenty-eight years hating myself, wondering whether naïveté is really a valid excuse for blindness. All these years later, I still don't have an answer to that question.

But in my defense, I was just a kid. And I had never really known anyone but my father. How was I to know what was normal and what was sociopathy? How was I to distinguish mental illness from reason, when whatever *he* was was all I'd ever known?

i disconnected the modem in order to free up the phone line. And then I sat there, frozen, for far longer than I knew I should. *Get the go bag, light the fuse, run. Get the go bag, light the fuse, run. Get the go bag, light the fuse, run.* Outside the cabin, I could hear the wind picking up in the pines, a storm blowing in. I listened hard, wondering if I'd be able to pick up the crunch of approaching tires; feet picking their way through the snow.

I sat there, weighing my options. I could do as my father had instructed, and head to North Dakota to meet him. He would surely have a plan to navigate me through this mess. My father, however, was a murderer, which made whatever plan he might have suddenly far less appealing. So perhaps I could head in the other direction, toward California and self-determination, to continue my search for answers about my mother. But then I would be totally on my own, a fugitive without a support system. And what if there still weren't even any insights about my mother to be found; what if she *was* simply a dead schoolteacher, and I was heading off on a wild-goose chase?

Option three: I could stay here and passively await my fate. Either the return of my father, or the arrival of the authorities, or nothing at all.

I wasn't about to decide until I had more information; and the information I needed was in my father's padlocked study.

The axe was out by the firewood pile, half buried in a crust of dirty ice. It was snowing again, tiny pellets hardened almost to hail, blown sideways by the wind. By the time I retrieved the axe and returned to the house, I was soaked to the bone, my skin red and stinging, my boots caked with slush. I stood at the study door, hefting the familiar weight of the axe handle; and then I swung it as hard as I could.

The doorframe splintered open on my third try, and the bolt swung loose.

I dropped the axe and went to my father's desk. As he'd promised, Malcolm Torino's address was sitting right on top, an old envelope with a return address scrawled in the left-hand corner: *4263 26 St. NE, Heimdal, North Dakota.*

I folded the envelope into quarters, and then eighths, and tucked it in the pocket of my jeans. The wad of twenties that I'd taken from my father was still there, warm and slightly damp. I'd counted it in the motel room: exactly five hundred dollars, minus the sixty I'd spent on gas and hot dogs on the road. More money than I'd ever possessed in my life. It finally occurred to me to wonder why, exactly, my father had bank-fresh money. And so much of it, when we were supposedly so broke.

Then I stepped back and studied my father's desk itself: The old wooden beast he'd hauled home from the Salvation Army so many years ago, battle-scarred and ink-stained. The forbidden drawers that locked with the missing key. The bottom drawer contained money, he'd said. And then there was the top drawer, where I'd found the photo: What else was I going to find in there, if I really started to dig?

I grabbed the brass handle of the top drawer and yanked it as hard as I could, just in case the lock was loose again; but all that accomplished was wrenching the muscles in my wrist. Instead, I began methodically ransacking the room, dumping out every can and mason jar and oatmeal carton I could put my hands on; but all I found were bent paper clips and oxidized pennies and caps to pens that had dried up years ago. Teetering piles of crap, stacked almost to the ceiling: Wherever the key was hidden in this chaos, I was never going to find it.

Outside, hail began to clatter against the windows. My breath collected in misty clouds in the unheated cabin; and I thought, again, about building a fire in the stove, making myself a meal. Maybe inertia was the best path after all. To await my fate—father or feds—like an obedient little duckling.

Instead, I went and grabbed the axe.

The desk was made of much sturdier wood than the doorframe. With my first swing, the edge of the desk splintered, but held. I swung the axe again, and again, and again—sweat popping out on my forehead, a scream building up in my chest. It felt like some subterranean geyser of emotion—all the rage and frustration I'd spent so many years sublimating—had finally broken the surface. It stopped only when the front of the desk finally gave way, the drawers disintegrating into slivers.

Panting, I went for the bottom drawer first.

The drawer was stacked to the top with bundles of money in paper bank wrappers. Ones and fives and tens and twenties, mostly; but also some fifties, and even a solitary stack of hundreds. The wrappers were labeled with boggling (at least, to me) sums: $100, $500, $1,000. I picked up the pack of hundreds and thumbed through the stack of bills, just to make sure they were real. They were.

I pushed this aside and pulled out the remains of the top drawer.

I could tell, immediately, that the drawer had been rearranged since I'd last been in it. I dumped it upside down and began sorting through the pile, until I found the photo I'd seen before: *Esme and Theresa.* I put this aside as well and began picking through the rest of the papers. On top was a manila folder I hadn't seen before, with *JANE* written across the front. When I opened it, I found the handwritten cipher pages, now neatly organized into a stack. I riffled through the meaningless pages, recalling the one sentence I'd managed to translate before: *Peter's advances in logic programming and neural networks dovetail neatly with her theories about the future of intelligence.* That name: *Peter.* Maybe it was a wild coincidence that this was also the name of the "friend" he'd just killed in Seattle, or maybe these pages were some sort of blueprint that explained his plans. A memoir, perhaps. Or a letter to me, explaining what he'd done.

Whatever it was, he seemed to have expected me to find it.

I put these with the money and photo, to decode later, and kept digging, not sure what I was looking for but knowing that *something* in here had to shed light on the mystery of my name, my mother, my entire existence. But there was nothing but some yellowing documents: receipts for farm equipment, outdated prescriptions, the deed to the truck. Disappointed, I kicked the mess away from me.

But then, there it was. A plain white envelope, a little crumpled around the edges, perhaps from having once been shoved in someone's pocket. I was about to sweep it up with the rest of the pile when I realized that it was sealed, and two initials had been written on the front in my father's cramped cursive: *E.N.*

I tore it open and extracted a Social Security card and a birth certificate.

CERTIFICATE OF LIVE BIRTH, the document read, *STATE OF CALIFORNIA. COUNTY OF SAN MATEO.*

San Mateo. A name that was curiously familiar, though I couldn't figure out why. But a warning bell was going off, softly, in the back of my brain.

Both the Social Security card and birth certificate belonged to a girl, Esme Sarah Nowak, who had been born to Adam Nowak and Theresa Nowak. The birth certificate included the home address of the parents—a street in a town called Atherton; and the occupation of the father (but only the father, of course, because *patriarchy*)—computer scientist. Esme Nowak had been born seven pounds, eleven ounces, on February 12, 1979. Exactly nine months to the day before me.

I sifted through the pile of documents again, more carefully this time. And now that I knew what to look for, the evidence was everywhere. The deed to the truck? Sold to Adam Nowak, back in 1983. The ancient prescription for Valium? Adam Nowak. Finally, I found incontrovertible proof sandwiched between the pages of an old copy of *Reason:* an expired U.S. passport that had been issued, back in 1975, to Adam Nowak of Boston, Massachusetts. The Adam Nowak in the government photo had short hair and pale, lineless skin, and was squinting at the camera with his teeth slightly bared in annoyance.

It was unmistakably my father.

So there it was. I wasn't seventeen-year-old Jane Williams, daughter of Jennifer and Saul; I was eighteen-year-old Esme Nowak, daughter of Adam and Theresa.

"Fuck you, Dad," I whispered.

On cue, the phone in the other room started to ring.

The sound shot through me. I gripped the birth certificate and froze in place—as if by staying motionless I was somehow rendering myself invisible to the person on the other end of the line. The phone rang and rang and rang until my teeth were vibrating from the racket and I thought I would have to answer it just to make the terrible sound go away.

And then it stopped. Silence descended on the cabin again.

I could feel the passing minutes pressing down now, an anvil hanging just over my head. I'd been back at the cabin at least an hour, maybe more. Maybe no one was coming; but maybe everyone was. Whatever I was going to do, I needed to do it immediately.

The phone started ringing again.

I imagined my father on the other end of the line, perhaps in a phone booth in Seattle, or maybe already at his friend's safe house in North Dakota. I could envision the frustration settling into the furrows of his face with each unanswered ring. (Frustration, or concern, or—even—anger?) I felt a familiar tug of subservience, compelling me toward the receiver. Thinking of my father's words: *Deep inside you're just like me. You can* see *things, understand them, the way I do.* Isn't that what I'd always wanted, to be just like him?

And yet. Something vital had shifted in me, giving birth to something new and electric and terrifying. My father was not the man I'd always thought he was. I didn't know what it meant to be "like him," but I was pretty sure that I didn't want it, whatever it was. Not anymore.

I ran into the living room and yanked the ringing phone out of the wall. It died with a metallic bleat of surprise.

I plugged the modem back in and logged on to the internet one last time. This time, when I clicked over to AltaVista, I plugged in a new, more accurate name: *Theresa Nowak death car accident.*

Exactly one link popped up. *Worst Car Accidents in California History, Ranked.*

The feeling was like when I licked my fingers to snuff out a candle: an acrid sizzle, a dying ember. So there it was: She *was* dead. My father hadn't been lying about that at all.

I scrolled down the page—a macabre fan page of sorts, documenting bus crashes and multicar pileups, a driver who crashed through three entire restaurants and another who drove the wrong way down an interstate, killing fourteen—before I finally landed on a familiar name. And then I paused, surprised, because it wasn't my mother's name linked to the accident.

It was my own.

On September 18, 1983, prominent computer scientist Adam Nowak was driving with his young daughter Esme on the Pacific Coast Highway after a weekend, father-daughter camping trip in Big Sur. It was a foggy night, with incoming storms, and visibility was poor. We can only surmise what drove their Volkswagen convertible off the road—a deer? a slick of oil? or was it intentionally steered off the cliff?—because there were no witnesses. All we know is that the car dropped nearly four hundred feet down a sheer cliff to the rocky shoreline below, and blew up on impact. Theresa Nowak reported her husband and child missing twenty-four hours later, but it took over a week to find the wreck, due to its remote location. By then, powerful waves had already dragged the contents of the car out to sea, leaving only the incinerated chassis. The bodies of the father and child were never recovered.

WAIT—*I WAS DEAD?*

Frantically, I tried a few more searches. *Esme Adam Nowak car accident Big Sur. Theresa Nowak obituary. Theresa Nowak current whereabouts.* But there were no more results to be found. My family's story had, apparently, been relegated to history, and the internet was still too fresh to have any documentation of the world before its invention.

So that was all I had, barely anything at all; but it was enough for me to deduce the rest. The truth about me. The truth about what my father had *done* to me. He had, for some reason, faked our deaths. It was the only logical explanation, wasn't it? But *why?*

I would have thrown up again, but I had nothing left in my stomach except a sour acid stir.

Meanwhile my heart was racing so fast that it felt like my pulse was a blur, because on the flip side of this horrible revelation was the thrilling realization that my mother wasn't dead. There was no longer any question. She was alive, she had to be. And, thanks to the birth certificate, I even had her address.

So now what?

I jumped up and went to grab the world atlas from where I'd placed it on the bookshelf, after looking up the entry for *Seattle*. I flipped through the pages until I found a map of San Mateo County, and then ran my finger down the page until it connected with a dot: Atherton. A small town, south of San Francisco.

San Francisco.

I sat back down at the laptop and clicked over to the chat room where I'd always found Lionel, in what felt like a lifetime ago.

WolfGirl96 >   Lionel? You here?

WolfGirl96 >   It's Jane. The girl with the dead wolf. In Montana.
                Remember me?

WolfGirl96 >   You told me to get in touch if I ever needed help.

WolfGirl96 >   Hello?

The cursor blinked. I waited, longer than I should have, for a reply. But no one was there. Maybe Lionel had moved on to a different chat room. Clearly he wasn't sitting around waiting for me to show up all these months later. Quite possibly he'd forgotten about me altogether.

I was about to log off when one last thought occurred to me. I re-opened my Web browser and directed it to the Luddite Manifesto.

A few days earlier, the counter had stood at 0012.

Now, it was at 33,257.

There were hundreds of comments in the guest book now, too, most of them filled with loathing—*Psychopath. / This is utter garbage. / You deserve to die.* But scattered in there, too, were words of admiration: *Truth. / I'm glad someone had the guts to say these things. / Revolution is here!*

I watched in disbelief as the number ticked up in real time: 33,258 . . . 33,259 . . . 33,262. And it finally dawned on me that this had been my father's endgame from the very beginning; that *this* was what the Seattle trip was all about. A stunt, a statement, a bloody advertise-ment for his belief system. A bid for fame. A bid for *respect*. He wanted *The Luddite Manifesto* to be taken seriously, to be talked about, to be-come gospel.

For that, he had murdered a man.

And I had volunteered to help him do it.

A gust of wind raked against the windows. Was that another spat-ter of hail, or was it the sound of footsteps moving through the rocks in the drive? I peered out the window: The moon was new, the sky dark, everything in shadow. But there was a flicker of light, some-where deep inside the tree line—a faint glow, quickly snuffed out. Like a car door closing. Someone was out there.

Panic kicked in. I grabbed my go bag from where it hung on the back of the door to my bedroom. I emptied out all the survival gear that had been so carefully packed inside: the camp stove, the water purifier, the emergency ponchos, the crank flashlight, and the AM/FM radio. In their place, I shoved the money from my father's desk. I threw in the passport and the birth certificate and the Social Security card, and all the old photos I could find—my mother, my father as a child, the group of men in front of the building. I shoved in the manila folder with my father's hand-scrawled cipher pages. The backpack's zipper strained but managed to close.

Then I pushed aside the coffee table in the living room, threw back the rug, and climbed through the hatch.

There, in the dark, in the damp, in the dust, I extracted the lighter and lit the fuse on the carefully constructed pile of explosives that my father and I had been living on top of for the last four years. The fuse sizzled and sparked, and I turned and scuttled down the tunnel as fast as I could, knowing that this time, it wasn't a drill, and my life was actually on the line.

The dynamite blew up just as I closed the hatch at the far end of the tunnel; the force of the explosion flattened me and filled my mouth with fine particulate. By the time I got to the dusty window of the storage shed, the entire cabin was engulfed in flames. A column of fire shot up at least twenty feet in the air. We'd been living in a tinder-box all along; it was a miracle, really, that we hadn't blown ourselves up years ago.

I watched, hypnotized, panting, as everything I'd believed about myself got burned to a crisp. Bawling like a baby, of course—I couldn't help it. But underneath those tears was a curious new feeling, something thrilling and wild and free. I'd been given a phoenix-like opportunity to reinvent myself from the ashes of a life that had never, it turned out, been mine at all.

If I wasn't Jane Williams, who was I going to be now?

Only then did I realize that, by instinctually following my father's final command—*Get the go bag, light the fuse, run*—I'd just helped him destroy every last shred of evidence that he might have left behind.

And there was this, too: If it was true that I was Esme Nowak and not Jane Williams, it meant that I was *eighteen*, not seventeen. Legally an adult. Eligible for real jail time.

Like it or not, my father and I were still utterly entangled. His fate was doomed to be mine, too.

I could hear voices in the distance now, calling out through the dark. Time had run out. I crept out the back door of the shed, and then raced blindly through the forest, soaked to the bone, listening for footsteps behind me, until I made it out to the old logging road and the truck I'd left parked there. Starting the engine, I set the car on a path west, toward California.

Toward—I hoped—my mother.

Part Two

ESME

26

Her name, she said, was Desi. "Short for Desire—don't ask—my mom was a hippie and things apparently got real weird on the commune. But believe me when I say that you don't want guys to know that your name is a synonym for *horny*. So just *Desi*, OK?"

I noticed her the minute she climbed on the Greyhound bus in Boise. How could I not? She had hair that was bright blue and fell across one eye, elaborate Japanese tattoo sleeves crawling up her arms, and a pair of hoops winking from the fold of one nostril. She wore head-to-toe black, except for the bright pink lace bra that was visible underneath her strategically shredded T-shirt. The backpack that she had slung over her shoulder had been spray-painted with a giant skull whose eyes were ejecting acid green.

Desi stood at the front of the bus, her eyes sweeping across the other riders—a grim-looking lot, faces gray with exhaustion, breath reeking of Wild Turkey—before finally alighting on me. She made a beeline straight for my row, and then plopped down in the seat next to mine, carrying with her a cloud of cigarette smoke and musk.

"Power in numbers," she muttered.

"Sorry?" It was unclear if she was talking to me or to the bag that she was currently jamming under the seat with the toe of her steel-tipped boots.

She sat upright, yanking up the front of her top. "You know. If we sit together, then there's no chance that either of us will get stuck with a creepazoid who's gonna try to put his hand down our pants. Or a nosy old lady who wants to show you her photo album of her grand-kids."

"Oh. OK. Grandmas are bad. Got it."

She gave the seatback in front of her a sharp shove, jarring awake the drunk in army fatigues who had reclined his chair as far as it would go. "Hey, don't be a dick! There are other people sitting here, too. Personal space, yeah?" Then she turned to smile at me. "Anyway, hi! Where you headed? I'm going to San Fran. Oh really, you, too? Coincidence! So what's your story? Don't feel compelled to tell me *everything*, I'm mostly being polite, but if we're going to be smelling each other's BO for the next two days we might as well get to know each other."

I felt like I'd been plowed under by a backhoe. How to respond? I'd had two days to come up with a plausible new life story, but it already felt insufficient. I didn't want to talk to this girl; I didn't want to talk to anyone. My only goal was to be inconspicuous, to hide until I figured out how to become someone new. "I'm moving to California to be with my mom," I said tersely.

"OK, but not your dad? So, what, your parents are divorced? Mine called it quits when I was a baby. I've had two stepdads and *three* stepmoms at this point and they were all total pills."

"My dad's dead," I said.

"No shit." Her eyes grew wide. "Well, *that* was insensitive of me, wasn't it? How'd he die? Or is that rude?"

"No, it's fine," I said. "He died in a car accident. When I was four."

She made an exaggerated sad face that I think was supposed to look sympathetic but mostly just looked like she'd swallowed a gumball by accident. "So why the hell were you living in Idaho, the armpit of America, if your mom is in California?"

"College," I said.

"College? In *Idaho*?"

"They had a good . . . Russian literature department?" My life story was falling apart with only the tiniest poke; this did not bode well.

She didn't seem to notice, though, as she was too busy screwing her face into a grimace of disgust. "Wow. Sounds deadly." I nodded, hoping it would end here, because I wasn't sure how I was going to pretend I knew anything about college life, being as I'd never stepped foot on a campus in my life. I didn't even know the names of any colleges in Idaho. In retrospect, it was a pretty stupid life story to pick.

I pivoted quickly. "What about you?"

"So yeah, I thought I'd go surprise this guy I'd been seeing? Who moved last month, to Twin Falls, of all godforsaken places. Thought I was doing him a solid by visiting him in bum-fucking-nowhere; you know, interstate booty call. But when I got there it turned out he already had *another girlfriend*. Some fakey blond bitch. I had to turn around and head straight back to San Francisco and he wouldn't even pay for my bus ticket. Asshole. You got a boyfriend?"

I felt trapped in the spin cycle of her thoughts, barely able to catch my breath. "Boyfriend? Um, no. Yeah, definitely no."

I was starting to wish I'd gotten the creepazoid.

Exhaustion was stealing over me like an incoming tide. I'd barely slept since driving away from my father's cabin two nights earlier. The first night I'd spent driving in circles around Idaho, completely lost and afraid to stop to ask for a map. And then, when I finally pulled into a truck stop for pancakes and coffee just after dawn, I found myself staring at my own face, in the pages of a *USA Today* that the previous diner had abandoned on the table. *FBI Seeks Pair in Microsoft Murder.* When I looked up, I saw myself again, on the television just over the counter, which was playing CNN on mute.

I left without even touching my pancakes.

By the time I found myself in Boise, later that day, I had worked myself up into a panicked lather. I checked in to a Motel 6, yanked the curtains tight, and then sat there in the dark, hyperventilating—the horror of my own culpability twisting my insides, leaving a coat of bitter bile on my throat. *What have I done what have I done what have I done?*

Sleepless hours passed as I tried to organize my thoughts. The good news, I realized, was that the news media seemed to only have the black-and-white images from the Microsoft surveillance cameras. Nor did the grainy still of the blonde in the tight dress look anything like the Jane Williams I saw in the mirror. And yet it still felt inevitable that I would eventually be recognized by someone eagle-eyed and civic-minded.

What would my father do if he were in my shoes? I kept returning to this question as I sat there in the dark, listening to the other guests pass back and forth just outside my door. My father would not be blindly driving across the country without a plan, just waiting to be stopped and caught. My father would not be hiding in a motel room, cowering and afraid and riddled with guilt. He would think strategically. I needed to do the same.

The truck, I realized, was going to be a problem. If the feds knew exactly who my father and I were—and I had to assume they did—then they would also know about the existence of the truck. Driving it would be like wearing a neon sign that said *HERE I AM*. The truck had to go.

My appearance, too, had to change. And my identity. I needed to become someone else entirely.

In that grim motel room, I decided that instead of thinking of myself as running *away*, I should think of this as running *toward*. Toward *Esme Nowak*, a version of me with far less baggage. Toward my mother, who would surely help me resolve my crisis, because wasn't this what mothers did? Protected their children. Performed magical jiujitsu to make their problems disappear. Her elation about being reunited would surely trump any dismay that her long-lost daughter was a fugitive criminal.

I just needed to make it to San Francisco without getting caught, I told myself. I would sort the rest out when I arrived.

I spent two nights in Boise, coming up with a plan of attack and then executing my reinvention. I drove myself to a Kmart and emerged a few hours later with a new wardrobe of generic-brand jeans, zip-front hoodies, and crisp white tennis shoes. No flannel shirts or utility boots, no flimsy dresses, and definitely nothing red: nothing that might connect me with either my Montana persona or the wanted criminal in the slip dress and the tattered parka.

I took care of the rest in the bathroom of my motel room: the brand-new haircut, dyed muddy brown and cropped to my chin, only a little crooked in the back where it was hard to reach with the scissors.

As for the truck, I scoured every surface with bleach spray to rid it of fingerprints, then left it parked on a grubby-looking side street not far from the motel, unlocked, with the keys in the ignition. I figured, if no one bothered to steal it, it might at least go unnoticed for a few months.

When I was done, I made my way to the local bus station and bought myself a one-way ticket to San Francisco.

IN THE SEAT next to me, Desi had finally stopped talking and now was just studying me, her eyes narrowed in silent judgment. Could she have recognized me? She didn't strike me as the type to watch the news, but how was I to know? I willed myself to disappear, to become invisible, the kind of person you'd have a hard time describing to authorities later.

Her stare went on for so long that I was on the verge of jumping up and making a dash for the bus door. But then Desi's face suddenly lit up, with a toothy smile of delight that unexpectedly shot warmth straight through my veins. "Hey, you're pretty, you know that? Your hair could use some help and you really need some mascara—God, your lashes are almost *white*—but I bet you'd be a hit with guys if you put some effort into it. You kind of look like Liz Phair, with those big blue eyes of yours."

"Who's Liz Phair?"

She looked at me like I was an idiot. "You don't know Liz Phair? Jesus, where have you been living? Under a rock?"

You're not far off, I thought, but I didn't even have to respond because she was already digging in her backpack. She emerged with a Walkman and an enormous pair of headphones, which she clamped over my ears without bothering to ask permission. I flinched as the music began to blast: a cacophony of jangling guitars, a woman whose voice spoke of damage, as though she had been scraped raw by life.

I pried a headphone off. "What kind of music is this?"

Desi raised an eyebrow in disbelief. "Indie rock?"

I replaced the headphone and listened some more. I'd never heard music so intimately; it felt like an invasion of my brain. Especially *this* kind of music, the kind that made my father wince whenever we spun past it on the radio. (*If you want atonality, try Schoenberg, at least that has intellectual merit.*) And yet. Something about the song made my skin tingle, its plaintive minor key opening up something at the center of my chest. A triumphant ache, a determined defiance.

It's cold out there
And rough
And I kept standing six-feet-one
Instead of five-feet-two

I can do this, I found myself thinking, for the very first time since I'd left the cabin. *I can reinvent myself entirely, and no one ever has to know that I used to be Jane Williams. I can be someone I haven't even imagined yet. A girl who listens to indie rock and makes friends with strangers. A girl with a living mom and a new kind of life waiting for her in San Francisco. A girl without a father at all.*

"By the way," I said, realizing too late that I was shouting to hear myself over the music, "I'm Esme."

Desi smiled, squeezed my hand, and returned to digging through her backpack. I turned to look out the window, Liz Phair's voice washing over me as I gazed west, past the frost-ravaged plains and the stone-colored sky, and toward the infinite blue promise of San Francisco.

27

I'D LISTENED TO the album four times already and was halfway through a fifth when the bus finally came shuddering to a stop. Night had fallen; it was past nine o'clock. Desi was asleep next to me, her legs hooked over the armrest so that she was half in the aisle with her body weight pressed against me.

"Salt Lake City," the driver called. "Connect here."

Desi sat upright and ran a hand across the back of her mouth, wiping away the drool that had collected there. "Christ, I'm hungry," she said. "We got a few hours before the next bus, want to see if there's anything to eat around here?"

We collected our bags and descended into the fluorescence of the bus depot. She scanned the buildings around us, then pointed at a pair of yellow arches that jutted up into the sky a few blocks away. "Let's hit up Mickey D's. I could kill a McRib."

I followed her. Walking was a little awkward because of the weight of the duffel, which banged against my thigh with each step I took.

"What's in the bag? Looks heavy."

I looked down at the bag in my hands, which was straining from the weight of the IBM hard drive. The hard drive was large and unwieldy, and more than once in the last few days I'd thought about tossing it in a dumpster. And yet I kept lugging it around, even though the bag was close to dislocating my arm from its socket. The drive was of some value; it had to be, since my father had bothered to steal it. And even though I wasn't planning to deliver it to my father in North Dakota, per his instructions, I also wasn't quite ready to get rid of it. Not until I at least knew what it was.

Instead, I'd purchased a duffel bag at Kmart and shoved it in there, along with the stacks of money that I'd taken from my father's desk and the pages of ciphered writing, which I hadn't yet begun to untangle. I kept all my personal possessions—my new clothes, the handful of family photos—in the backpack. Stashing all the illegal contraband in the duffel made me feel just slightly distant from it: I could drop it and walk away at any time.

"It's textbooks," I said.

"Oh yeah? Why do you need so many textbooks?"

"Because I'm really smart?"

She raised an eyebrow but laughed. We turned a corner and arrived at a desolate strip of fast-food restaurants, mostly empty at this hour. Desi stopped under a streetlamp and dropped her backpack to the ground. She plopped down on the sidewalk next to it and gestured for me to sit down next to her. I looked down at the dirty cement, pebbled with abandoned chewing gum and stained with yellowish shadows that were most likely dried urine. I stayed standing where I was.

"Why are we stopping here?"

"I don't have any money," she said. "We're going to have to panhandle. It always works best if you're sitting down, so that people feel bigger than you and pity you a little. They like to feel superior when they're giving you their pennies."

"Oh." This wasn't appealing to me at all. I thought of the cash in the duffel. "Look, I have money. I'll cover your dinner."

She brightened. "Brilliant," she said, and jumped up.

And so I walked into my first fast-food restaurant. Inside, the lights were so bright they made me wince. Desi ordered a McRib, and a milkshake, and two orders of fries, and a hamburger for good measure; and by the time I ordered my own Happy Meal (I was absurdly excited about the free toy) plus a drink and a sundae, the bill was well over twenty dollars. At which point I realized that I only had a a few singles in the pocket of my stiff new jeans.

There were audible sighs from the line forming behind us as I counted and recounted my money. "Shut it, people," Desi instructed them, then turned to me. "Look, I can send back the fries if that helps."

"No, just give me a second," I said. I reached down into the duffel bag at my feet, opening the zipper just enough to wedge a hand inside. I felt around for a packet of money and then slipped a bill off the top.

It wasn't until I pulled my hand out that I realized I'd managed to grab a hundred-dollar bill. I slid it as discreetly as I could to the cashier, who slapped the crisp bill into the cash register without missing a beat and then handed me back a fistful of crumpled twenties.

If Desi had noticed this interaction, she wasn't letting on. She'd grabbed our tray of food from the counter and was already cramming fries into her mouth, her eyes scanning the room for the best table. "Thanks, doll, I'll get you next time," she offered.

"It's not a big deal," I said; and it truly wasn't, considering that the duffel bag I was carrying was stuffed with nearly $23,000. I may not have had a firm grasp on the value of money yet, but I was pretty sure this would be plenty to start a new life in San Francisco and also cover some fries.

I followed Desi to a table by the window and we sat and wolfed down our meals, surrounded by transients and travelers grimly chewing their McNuggets. Under the unforgiving lighting, I could see that Desi was older than me; maybe even in her late twenties. She had bruised-looking circles under her eyes, and her skin seemed to sag off the bones of her face, making her look gaunt and hungry.

"This food is disgusting," Desi said as she shoved the last bite of McRib in her mouth. Her red lipstick was feathering and faded, her lips slick with grease.

"I think it's possibly the best thing I've ever eaten," I said, not joking at all, though Desi laughed like I was.

"I work part-time at a juice bar in San Francisco, the owners are total health Nazis. I swear they would fire me if they even knew I had stepped foot in a McDonald's. I had to tell them I was a vegetarian just to get a job there."

"Why? Were they worried you were going to put steak in their smoothies?"

Desi slapped the edge of the table with her hand. "Oh my God, Esme, you're hilarious. Weird, but funny. Are we going to hang out when we get to San Francisco?"

Something surged inside me, a little frisson of excitement; that this new persona was already working out in my favor; that I had somehow made a friend. "I'd like that," I said, maybe a little too earnestly.

"Hey. Hey, you."

The voice was coming from behind me and when I turned my head to see who it was, I realized that there was a policeman standing just behind our table. He was a heavyset man with a stubby mustache and broken capillaries across his nose, a greasy paper sack in one hand, and he was staring right at us. I whipped my head around and looked quickly down at the floor, trying to disappear, hoping he wasn't talking to me. But his shiny black shoes crept into my view as he stopped right in front of our table.

"Is something wrong, officer?" Desi's voice was dripping with saccharine. I still wouldn't look up.

"Is this bag yours?"

The shoes were now nudging the edge of my duffel bag. Staring at the floor was not helping my situation. I forced myself to raise my head. "I think so?" It did not sound like the answer of an innocent person.

He had been looking at Desi when I lifted my head, but now he swiveled to look at me. "You think so? It's not your friend's?"

I shook my head and he turned back to Desi, his eyes narrowed to slits, clearly displeased with the look of her. Desi, for her part, seemed utterly bored by the encounter. "It's hers," she said flatly.

He turned back to me one last time, his eyes scanning my features so intently that I was sure he was looking for something specific. I willed myself to smile back at him, trying to conceal the panic that I knew must be written all over my face. But his features went slack, as if what he'd found in mine had been lacking in interest. "OK. Do us all a favor and keep it under your table. It's a hazard sticking out into the walkway like that. I almost tripped over it."

"I'm sorry," I said, "sir."

He continued on, as the blood rushed back into my face. I pushed my fries away, even though they were only half eaten. "Can we get out of here?"

"Good idea." Desi glanced at her watch. "We still have an hour before the bus leaves. Enough time to put back a few shots of tequila. It'll make the next leg of this trip more bearable. Let's find a bar. There's gotta be one nearby."

I hesitated. "I'm eighteen."

Desi raised an eyebrow. "No shit? And no fake ID? I thought every college kid had one." She stood to peer out the window and then turned back to me. "OK, so look, there's a dive bar right across the street, I'm going to hit it up real fast. I'll just meet you back at the bus. Cool?"

I stood to follow her as she headed to the door, struggling to keep up with her under the weight of all my baggage. "Sure," I said. "I'll hold a seat for you."

"Awesome, thanks, but hey, do you mind lending me one of those twenties in your pocket? Actually, let's say two, just to be safe." She lowered her voice, looking suddenly very serious. "So I don't have to panhandle for it. It's probably not safe, you're right about that."

I was pretty sure I hadn't said anything about panhandling not being safe. But I slid two bills out of my pocket anyway, and she plucked it out of my grip with a pinch of her fingers. Then she leaned in and kissed me on my cheek, an unexpected oily smack that made me flinch. "You're a doll. I'll pay you back when we get to San Francisco. Promise."

And then she was off, dashing through the traffic toward a neon sign across the street that read *Pabst on Tap*. An oncoming Toyota braked to avoid hitting her, the driver pressing on its horn in protest. She stopped in its path and stared down the driver, slowly holding up both middle fingers in a gesture that reminded me, jarringly, of my father. And then she flashed a grin at me, winked, and vanished into the bar.

SHE DIDN'T GET back to the depot until a minute after our bus was scheduled to depart, and I was starting to despair that I'd never see her again. The engine had already grumbled into life and the lights had gone off when she was suddenly banging on the bus door. The bus driver, swearing under his breath, opened it to let her in.

"You're lucky I'm feeling generous," he said.

She burped in response and threw herself into the seat next to me. "Oh Jesus, I just did four shots in less than an hour. I hope I don't puke."

Her breath smelled abominable, sour and ashy. "Please don't," I said.

She closed her eyes. "I'm just going to sleep until we get to the next transfer. Where's that?"

"Las Vegas."

"No shit, Vegas. Maybe we should just jump off there and go hit up some casinos. Or go to a rave. They have epic ones, out in the desert, I hear. I'll call my friend Johnny."

I wasn't about to ask her what a rave was. "I really need to get to San Francisco."

"Your mom, right. Sure. God, I'm tired. I think I'm going to pass out." She reached into her bag and pulled out a small orange prescription container. She fumbled with the cap for a minute before shoving it at me. "Childproof. You do it."

I twisted it open and peered inside at the little white pills. "What is that?"

She grabbed the open bottle and tipped a few pills into her palm. Squinting at her hand, she plucked one up and stuck it in her mouth. "Ambien."

"Still don't know what it is."

"Sleeping pills, you ninny. Here, have one." She held her palm out to me.

I veered back. "I don't need one."

"Of course you do. This seat is hellaciously uncomfortable. Trust me, you'll feel way better in the morning if you actually get a decent night's sleep." She pushed the palm with the pills under my nose. She wasn't wrong: I still hadn't slept more than three hours a night since I left Montana. My head felt thick and fuzzy, my faculties dangerously dulled. What would be worse—taking an illicit pill, or going another night without any sleep?

Fuck it, I thought, *maybe Esme takes sleeping pills.* I popped one in my mouth.

"Two is even better. It'll knock you out until we get to Vegas," she said, and then smiled approvingly as I obeyed and swallowed another.

"You'll thank me later," she murmured as she dropped her head to my shoulder and closed her eyes. She was snoring before we'd driven three blocks. Three blocks after that, I, too, slipped into the merciful oblivion of sleep.

I WOKE UP to a hand roughly shaking me awake. The bus driver was leaning over me, his fingers digging into my shoulder. "Wake up, kid. It's time to transfer."

I felt like I'd been hit with a pickaxe. My cheek was flat and sticky from where it had been pressed against the window of the bus while I slept. Rubbing my eyes, I looked out the window and realized that we were parked in another bus station lot, baking under a desert sun. Outside, sunburnt tourists in shorts and fanny packs trudged toward the waiting buses, clutching foot-tall plastic glasses that were still blue with cocktail residue.

"Where are we?"

"Vegas. Where you headed?"

"San Francisco." My eyes drifted closed.

But the bus driver poked me again, harder this time. "Well, you better hurry then, or you'll miss your connection. It leaves in five minutes."

My eyes flew open again. Only then did it occur to me that the seat next to me was empty. In fact, the entire bus seemed to be empty. "Wait. Have you seen my friend? The girl with the blue hair."

The bus driver shrugged. "Everyone got off when we stopped, almost an hour ago. I just noticed you sleeping back here."

That jolted me awake. I pushed myself to standing and looked up and down the aisle in disbelief, then turned to peer out the window. Lots of tourists, no blue hair in sight. Maybe Desi had rushed off to squeeze in another round of drinks before our next connection? I reached under the seat in front of me and fumbled out the backpack that I'd been using as my footrest, and then stood up to grab the duffel that I'd stashed on the overhead rack.

It was gone.

I stared numbly at the empty space where the duffel with all my money had been. Then at the other racks, just in case I'd misremembered. But there were no bags to be seen, anywhere. The bus was eerily silent, except for the hissing of the air-conditioning.

"My bag is missing," I said. I was dangerously close to tears.

The bus driver shrugged again. "Can't take responsibility for that, kid. Sorry. But you gotta get off now. Your connection is over there, look for the number four."

I stumbled my way off the bus, my backpack clutched in my arms. Outside, I was hit in the face by a blast of hot, dry air. Sweat immediately glued my sweatshirt to my back. I shaded my eyes against the blinding morning sun and made my way toward the bus that was waiting in slot number four, my wobbly feet still asleep underneath me. Surely Desi would be waiting for me on the next bus, I told myself; she was probably wondering where I was. Quite possibly she'd grabbed my duffel for safekeeping.

She wasn't on the bus.

I stood at the front of the number four connection, scanning the seats with mounting alarm, but there was no shock of blue hair, no tattooed arms flung out into the aisle. "Dammit," I said, and turned around. Then turned around again. Unsure what to do.

"You gotta pick a seat," the new bus driver offered. "We're about to leave."

I hesitated, considering my options. Maybe Desi *was* sitting at the bar nearest to the depot, my duffel safely stashed beneath her chair, waiting again until the very last second to race for the bus. But I somehow knew, even as the bus's engine shuddered to life and the doors squeaked closed behind me, that Desi wasn't ever coming. She'd seen her opportunity and taken it. (Or had she *made* the opportunity? I thought of the two pills I'd popped so unquestioningly, and felt sick.)

Should I get off the bus and try to track her down? The odds weren't in my favor. If you didn't want to be found in Vegas, you wouldn't be. I didn't even know if it was she who had taken my duffel, or if it had been another opportunistic traveler. Besides, if I got off the bus and *didn't* locate her and all my money, I'd never be able to make it the rest of the way to San Francisco. All I had in my pocket was the thirty-eight dollars in change from our dinner at McDonald's the previous evening. At least if I stayed on the bus, I'd still be on my way to finding my mother.

Besides my money, I suddenly remembered, she also had the in-criminating stolen hard drive. Evidence that could lead to me. *And* she even had my father's cipher pages, the ones he apparently wanted me to read: What if they explained everything about my mother, and me? The information I wanted the most had probably been right in my hands, and now it was gone.

I felt Esme with all her confident potential slowly leaking out of me, leaving me only with lost, naïve, stupid Jane. *My father would never have let his most important possessions get stolen,* I thought. For the first time since I'd driven out of Montana, I felt the urge to give up and head to North Dakota, and just let him take over. To throw myself back into a life as his criminal accomplice.

It's cold out there. And rough.

"Are you going to sit down or what?" the bus driver barked, his patience worn out.

The bus shuddered. The passengers grumbled. My moment of weakness passed.

I sat.

28.

IT WAS 1997 in San Francisco, and society was teetering on a preci-
pice, though no one realized it yet. Underemployed college grads sat
in Mission cafés, grumbling about their McJobs, oblivious to the opportunities that the world was about to fling their way. Pale-faced
bankers scurried along Market Street, unaware of just how stupidly
rich their ilk were about to become. San Francisco was sleepy and
provincial, a town of tattoos and fixed-gear bicycles, techno clubs and
plates of cheap spaghetti and wrinkled society mavens who dressed
like their dogs. San Francisco was a city that was still easy to overlook.

No one could see what was coming. How much everything, *everything*, was about to change. Even the ones who did—the manic-eyed
prognosticators, those Panglossian optimists, clustered on the grass
down in South Park—didn't quite understand the monster they were
unleashing from its chain.

Did my father? I think he did, though even his imagination couldn't
fathom the distance that all *this* was going to go. He just knew that
something cataclysmic was in the wind. He'd caught a whiff of disaster. And he believed he was the only one to stop it.

Meanwhile, I was ready to jump right into the abyss.

BY THE TIME I disembarked at the Greyhound bus depot on Mission
Street on Friday afternoon, I had exactly thirteen dollars left in my
pocket and I smelled like a cheese sandwich that had been left too
long in the sun. I hadn't slept since Las Vegas. Instead, I'd simmered
with paranoia, afraid to close my eyes, my thoughts a toxic stew of fear
and self-recrimination.

I stepped off the bus into a cold fog that frosted my insubstantial sweatshirt with a delicate layer of damp. My hair, greasy and limp from the long bus ride, whipped in a frenzy around my face. I had thrown my old parka in a trash bin in Idaho, figuring I wouldn't need one in sunny California. But there was no sun here. There were no palm trees, or sandy beaches, or convertibles driven by girls in bikini tops. Just a gray marine layer that clung to the tops of the stoney-faced skyscrapers and a piercing wind that sent empty Big Gulp cups skittering along the gutters.

Apparently I looked as overwhelmed as I felt, because one of the other passengers from the bus—a woman with a pet-carrier and leopard-print bifocals—stopped to stare at me. "Honey, you need directions or something?"

"I'm trying to get to Atherton."

Inside the pet-carrier, a cat was mewling plaintively. The woman jiggled the carrier and frowned. "You're still a long way from there."

"Can I walk?"

"It's a forty-five minute drive, so no, I wouldn't advise that."

"How do I get there, then?"

She shushed her cat and then looked at me again. "Without a car? Hmmm. Get yourself down to the train station, if you don't want to walk you can take the Muni, just catch the 30 over on Third. Caltrain will get you to Atherton in an hour or so, make sure you don't take the express or you'll end up in San Jose. You'll probably need to call a taxi once you land in Atherton; it's not very walkable down there in the suburbs and the bus system is spotty."

She smiled at me as I stared blankly back at her, frantically trying to parse the foreign language she had just spoken. "How much will all that cost?" I asked, even though this was hardly my biggest concern, not compared with the fact that I couldn't fathom navigating three or four new transportation systems when I'd only just barely managed one.

"Five or six dollars, not including the taxi. So maybe fifteen or twenty, total."

I considered the handful of bills in my pocket, and thought I might cry—to have made it so far and yet to be seemingly nowhere near where I needed to be. "Do you happen to have some money I could borrow?"

"*Borrow?*" Her laugh was a bark. The cat mewled in response. The woman adjusted her glasses and took a closer look at me. "Is someone actually *expecting* you in Atherton?"

I nodded, but apparently the expression on my face had given me away because the woman leaned in closer and lowered her voice. "Look, honey, it's dangerous for girls like you to be hanging around a bus station. There are predators here." She cast her eyes around us, as if she were looking out for a panther or a shark. "Pimps, you know. Looking for vulnerable girls, who need money and don't know any better."

I nodded soberly, wondering what a pimp was. It wasn't acne-related, presumably.

"There's a shelter for homeless youth over on Market Street, near the Castro," she continued. "They'll help you figure out how to get you in touch with whoever you're trying to find in Atherton."

"I'm not homeless," I objected. Except that I was, wasn't I? I thought of the Montana cabin, reduced to ashes. It felt like I had arrived at the end of the earth and now had nowhere to go back to, even if I wanted to try.

"Well, good luck." She patted me on the shoulder and scurried off, the cat thumping against her thigh.

After she left, I stood there on the street for ten minutes, watching the traffic whiz past. I felt more lost than I had since I'd left Montana. I thought of Desi, prepared to panhandle for her dinner—*she doesn't have to do* that *anymore*, I realized glumly—but couldn't imagine doing that myself. And even if I did manage to scrape together enough money for all those trains and taxis and Munis and whatnot, even if I did manage to make my way to some obscure address in Atherton— did I really want to meet my mother looking like *this*? I hadn't showered in days, my face was sticky with grease and dried sweat, and my clothes were stained with cheese dust and bus station coffee.

The homeless shelter—maybe that *was* my best option. A shower and some logistical assistance, maybe they'd even give me some money. But I wasn't prepared to talk to yet more strangers, to spin my lies for people whose entire job was to identify people's problems. Maybe not feds, but still: authorities. Surely they'd sniff me out. Besides, I hadn't seen a newspaper or watched the news since I boarded the bus back in Idaho. What if they had better photos of me now, and the homeless shelter recognized me and turned me in?

I had one last option, even if it felt like the most desperate choice.

A twenty-something Black kid in a leather jacket was walking past me, headphones clamped over his ears and a messenger bag slung over his shoulder. I lurched forward and tapped his arm. He stopped in his tracks and turned to regard me suspiciously. He slowly slipped his headphones off and tilted his head, waiting.

"Yeah?"

"Can you tell me where Signal is?"

"Signal? No idea what you're talking about."

"It's a website."

He frowned. "I don't know anything about the internet, sorry. I use those stupid AOL discs as beer coasters. Is this some kind of test? Am I on *Candid Camera*?"

"What? No, I don't even own a camera. Signal is a business. I want to go to their office."

"Gotcha." The boy smiled at me, revealing dimples, as I realized (with a delight that now embarrasses me) that this was the first time I'd actually had a conversation with a Black person. "Sorry, still can't help you. But the address is probably in the phone book."

"OK, can you tell me how to find a bookstore, then?"

He gave me a funny look, probably wondering if I was still trying to pull one over on him. "Bookstores don't sell phone books," he said slowly. "You can usually find one attached to a pay phone. Pretty sure there's a phone about three blocks up, on First and Market. It's in the financial district so the phone book might not have been stolen yet."

PERHAPS YOU ARE wondering, at this point, how well I had been navigating my new existence in the Great Big World, considering that my knowledge of how to function was based on nineteenth-century Russian fiction, television sitcoms, extensive newspaper consumption, and aggressively chaperoned visits to small-town Montana.

The answer: not well.

There had been, most egregiously, the loss of my duffel bag. But even before I naïvely let a grifter walk away with all my money, an incriminating stolen hard drive, and my father's personal paperwork, I had already made dozens of rookie mistakes. To wit:

- Asking the clerk at the motel where I spent my first night if he was going to give me the key to my room, just moments after he'd handed me the key card; and then staring, in disbelief, at the square of plastic that he insisted *was* a room key. Then spending five minutes struggling to understand exactly *how* it opened the room, once I got to my door.
- Trying to buy my first bra at the Kmart in Boise, and the saleswoman looking baffled when I told her I didn't know what size I wore, but it was probably a medium.
- Getting lost on my way to that same Kmart, to which I was navigating using oral instructions given to me by the hotel clerk, because he'd told me to "turn left when you see the Subway"; and so I'd driven for a half hour, looking for a subway entrance, before someone at a gas station finally told me there *was* no subway system in Boise, but there was a fast-food sandwich chain by that name.

Everything I understood was outweighed by three things I didn't. And so even this boy's simple directions felt like an inscrutable puzzle to me (why, for example, would anyone steal a phone book?). I wan-

dered around downtown San Francisco for what felt like hours, baffled by streets that didn't connect in parallel lines. So overwhelmed by
awe—at the skyscrapers that loomed overhead, the businessmen with
their overcoats flapping like sails in the wind, the cable cars that
clanged by with tourists hanging off them like monkeys—I kept forgetting the task at hand. Eventually, I stumbled across a pay phone
with a phone book still dangling from its metal cord, and looked up
the address to Signal, an address that of course meant absolutely
nothing to me. By the time I finally screwed up the courage to ask for
directions from yet one more passerby and made my way to a dingy
beige commercial building a half-hour walk from downtown, it was
almost five, and growing dark. My entire body throbbed with exhaustion and hunger.

There were no signs in the elevator, so I pushed all the buttons and
peered out at each floor. The first one opened on a cavernous room full
of Chinese and Latina women, their heads bent over sewing machines. The air was thick with fabric dust and the cacophony of the
machines echoed off the soaped-over windows. Not my destination,
presumably. The next floor was more of the same, and I began to wonder if I'd written down the address incorrectly. But when the elevator
slid open one last time, I was relieved to find myself face-to-face with
a giant, neon-yellow logo that read *SIGNAL*.

I wandered down the hall and found myself in a room similar to
the ones below, except that this one was full of young people who were
huddled over keyboards instead of buttons and zippers; and rather
than the rattle of sewing machines, rock music echoed off the walls.
Pink cable wires snaked along the ceiling and down the room's concrete support pillars, like a venous system pumping life into the computer monitors that sat on every flat surface. The desks—not proper
desks so much as repurposed doors propped up on trestle legs—were
cluttered with junk: printouts and computer manuals, *Star Wars* action
figures and stacks of CDs, empty Odwalla bottles and breakfast cereal
boxes. An inflatable Oscar Mayer wiener hung overhead, like an ab-
surdist dirigible.

The average age in the room was only a few years older than me. There had to be a hundred twenty-somethings, maybe more, jammed into the space, all of them thrumming with intention. I had never been in an office before, but based on what I'd seen in the Business section of *The Wall Street Journal*—images of men in suits taking conference calls and being served coffee by be-skirted secretaries—I sensed this scene was not typical. The energy in the room was jittery, irreverent, more like what I imagined a house party to be than a place of serious business. I itched with a curious desire to be part of whatever *this* was, even though it wasn't quite clear from where I stood what anyone was actually doing. It looked . . . fun?

Once upon a time, the world economy was built on concrete *things*, objects with longevity that could be held in your hand. But that day I was witnessing the beginning of the era of ephemerality, a whole new kind of existence based on little more than zeros and ones, ideas and information. The kids in this room were igniting the fire that was about to immolate everything that had come before. They were revolutionaries who couldn't anticipate the scale of their victory, or the devastation it would leave in its wake.

There was no receptionist standing guard at the entrance. So I walked over to the closest desk, where a girl with short platinum hair and a butterfly tattoo on the back of her neck was flying her fingers across the keyboard, impossibly fast. She looked up, saw me staring at her hands, and stopped abruptly.

"I gotta get this debugged before six or we'll have to push launch, and we're already three days late," she said, accusingly.

"I'm sorry," I said. "I'm looking for Lionel?"

She was already back to her work, clacking at her keys. "Lionel Sung? Yeah. Back corner, the desk under the Bart Simpson piñata," she said, and jerked her chin toward the wall of windows.

"Bart Simpson?"

She looked at me like I was an idiot. "Hello? The cartoon?"

"Right." I looked around the room until I saw something that seemed to fit the bill, and I headed toward it. I had to maneuver my way through the maze of desks, tripping over bicycles parked in the pathways, edging around a woman doing yoga on the carpet. No one seemed to notice me as I stumbled apologetically past their desks.

When I'd imagined Lionel, I'd envisioned someone who looked like a younger Mulder (I was short on other comparison points): floppy-haired, furrow-browed, tall and cerebrally masculine. But the boy who was working in the corner was slight and pale, with neatly combed black hair; smudgy thick-framed glasses slid down a nose that was peppered with freckles. Unlike the rest of the kids in the room, attired in sweats and jeans, he wore a white button-down shirt tucked neatly into khakis, and a skinny black tie that had fallen askew. He looked up to see me standing by his desk and blinked a few times, his eyes needing a moment to adjust to a view that wasn't a screen.

"You're Asian," I blurted.

He let out a startled cough. "And you're rude."

"Why is that rude?"

He spun in his chair, studying me. "Did Janus put you up to this? OK, I'll play. I'm half Asian, actually. Dad is Chinese, Mom is Irish. That answer your question?"

"Interesting. You're not how I imagined you."

"I'm sorry, do I *know* you?"

"I'm Jane." I smiled hopefully.

He smiled back, blankly polite. "Are you . . . the new college intern?"

"Jane, from the internet," I said.

"Jane . . . from the internet . . ." he repeated, clearly churning through a mental Rolodex. I suddenly wondered just how many girls Lionel had been talking to in chat rooms. Probably I wasn't the only one; maybe there were a dozen other Janes out there. How stupid of me to imagine that he'd remember someone he'd spent all of an hour or two chatting with, months ago. How stupid of me to imagine that he would be my savior.

"Jane with the dead wolf," I tried, one last time.

His eyes lit up with recognition. I watched as his face subsequently convulsed through a parade of emotions: delight, and then shock, ending in a twist of confusion. "Holy shit," he said, his voice gone husky. "*Holy shit.* Jane, from Montana? WolfGirl96?"

"Actually," I offered, "my real name is Esme."

"Esme? You mean, after all that grief you gave me about being a serial killer, you were the one who was trolling *me*?" He'd spun his chair fully around and was now looking me up and down. "Huh," he said. "For some reason I envisioned you as some kind of farmer girl, in overalls and hiking boots. You look so . . . normal."

"See, I'm not how you imagined me, either," I said. "But not Asian."

He laughed. "Touché. So, *Esme.* What the hell are you doing here? Are you visiting with your dad?"

"Not exactly. You could say that I ran away."

The smile wobbled. "Oh shit. Really? I mean, that's good, right? The way he was treating you—leaving you alone in the woods— I didn't like that. It was weird. But wait—why are you *here*?" He shifted in his chair, gripping his armrests with a death vise. "Um. Wait. Did you come all the way here because of . . . me?"

"You mean, am I a stalker?"

He coughed. His eyes darted behind me and around the room, as if seeking assistance. "I mean, no offense, I'm flattered; but you're seventeen, which makes you a minor, and . . ."

"Eighteen, actually. And no, I'm in San Francisco because of my mom, not because of you. Although technically speaking, yes, I'm here—as in, here in this office—for you. Not in a creepy way, though. Promise. It's just"—a piteous inflection had slipped into my voice— "you said you would help me, if I needed it. Remember?"

He slowly unclenched his fingers, releasing the chair. "I do. I did."

"Yeah, well, I need it." Phlegm was clogging my throat. I realized that I was on the verge of tears.

He rolled his chair a hair closer as his eyes crinkled with concern. "Hey. Hey! Don't cry, OK? I'll help you, of course I'll help. What do you need?"

I wobbled in my shoes. I was so lightheaded that I thought I might pass out onto his lap. "For starters, a place to sleep tonight? And I'll explain the rest over a meal. It's kind of a long story."

"Not a problem," he said. "Want to go grab a burger? I'm buying."

"Good, because I can't," I replied.

29

He took me to Burger Island, a graffiti-tagged diner just down the street, at the end of a run-down strip of old industrial buildings; it was a dive, but considering that I could count the number of restaurants I'd eaten at on one hand, I still found it magical. We sat at a chipped Formica table eating baskets of burgers oozing with cheese as I laid out the rough outline of how I'd found my real birth certificate and the story about the car crash that "killed" me; how I'd stolen money and some personal papers from my father and run away to San Francisco to look for my mother, but had been robbed of everything on a Greyhound bus by a girl with blue hair. I left out any inconveniently self-incriminating details. For example: that I'd shot a security guard, that I'd unknowingly helped my father murder someone, and that the police were looking for me; or that I'd burned down the cabin I'd grown up in; or that the purloined duffel had contained $23,000 and a stolen hard drive. He didn't need to know any of *that*.

By the time I was done, his jaw was practically in his fry basket. "That's the craziest story I've ever heard. Are you . . . OK?"

"Depends how you define *OK*. That's a pretty vague and nondescriptive word, don't you think? My idea of *OK* is probably completely contextual, compared to yours. Do you mean, am I going to have a nervous breakdown?" He gave a tentative nod. "Probably not. But I would say that I've had better months."

We were silent for a long time, Lionel frowning as he tried to piece together the puzzle I'd just thrown at him. "So," he said slowly, "it's pretty clear you were kidnapped by your dad, right? And that's why he changed your names, because he was in hiding from the authorities."

I nodded; realizing, as I did, that this was probably why my father had always been so cagey about why he thought the feds were after him. It wasn't for his thought crimes; it was because he'd faked our deaths and then absconded with me. *This* was why we had lived so thoroughly off the grid, in a libertarian state where we could exist without much scrutiny. Where no one would ask for his ID, or mine.

God, I'd been so blind.

"OK, so, it also stands to reason that your mom has probably been thinking about you all this time. I mean, she thinks you're dead; how excited will she be to learn you're actually *alive*? And the accident sounds like it was a big deal, surely there's a police report and all that. So all you need to do is go straight to the police, and they'll help you figure it all out and take you to your mom." He smiled, pleased to have solved the puzzle so easily.

"No."

"No?" He looked confused.

I toyed with the fries left in my basket. "I just . . . don't like police."

"OK . . ." He frowned. "I guess you could visit city hall and ask for the records department, see if you can dig up a marriage certificate with her maiden name or something? You might need to visit a bunch of city halls, though, if you don't know where they got married."

"City hall. That's a government building, right?"

He nodded. I shook my head. He sighed.

"Not sure how else to tackle your problem, in that case."

"But see, I already know where she is. I have her address," I explained. "She lives not far from here, in a town called Atherton. So there's no reason to talk to the authorities."

"The address from the birth certificate?" He frowned again. "You really think she's still living there?"

"Why wouldn't she be?"

"That address is eighteen years old. Most people move houses, a lot. I think I read that the average American moves, like, 11.7 times during their life."

Oh. Having lived in the same cabin for my entire existence, this had not occurred to me. "But maybe she didn't want to move. She's my mother, aren't mothers supposed to just *know* things about their kids?" I didn't know where I'd gotten this idea—from watching the unspoken intimacy between Lina and Heidi, perhaps—but suddenly I felt it very deeply. "Maybe she suspected what really happened. Maybe she never believed I was dead and has been waiting this whole time for me to come back to her. They never found our bodies, right? So maybe she held out hope. Maybe in her heart, she *knew*."

"God, if one person in this world truly knows nothing about me, it's my mom." He took his glasses off and examined them, then wiped them on the end of his shirt. When he put them back on, they were just as smudged as they'd been before. "Sorry, that was harsh. I mean, I don't know your mom, so who am I to say? It's possible. I'm just not usually a glass-half-full kind of guy, so feel free to ignore me if I'm being a downer."

I shrugged. *"I'm a pessimist because of intelligence, but an optimist because of will."*

"What?"

"It's a quote from Antonio Gramsci."

"Should I know who that is?"

Was it fair of me to be frustrated that I knew so many things that other people did not? Especially when they knew so many more *practical* things of which I was completely unaware. "He was a Marxist theorist. Italian. My father loved him. Gramsci came up with the idea of cultural hegemony. How the ruling class manipulates ideology to oppress the common man through cultural institutions they control. Government. Education. The media."

Lionel nodded thoughtfully. The neon *OPEN* sign in the window above us lit our faces with a surreal yellow glow. "See, that's why the internet is cool. It can't be controlled by the ruling class. It's the ultimate equalizer."

"You think?"

"It's totally decentralized, totally neutral. Free information, for everyone. I mean, if anything, the internet is a socialist medium. Something your dad might like."

I opted not to correct him. Instead, I tipped my head back, tugging at this thought, reeling the thread back toward my father's writings. My father had spent the last decade teaching me that technology was oppressing society. What if he had gotten it all wrong, and it was actually our liberator? The notion lodged in me, a warm glow in my chest. If it was true, it certainly validated my decision to come to California instead of fleeing to North Dakota to be his Luddite sidekick. I hoped like hell that Lionel was right.

"Anyway. I assume you need a ride to Atherton?"

"Why? Do you have a car?"

"Sure. I mean, it's a piece of crap but it works. I can drive you, no problem. Tomorrow? It's Saturday. I don't have anything else going on." I smiled at him, a lump in my throat suddenly rendering me mute. "Also—you said you need somewhere to sleep. This is going to sound weird but . . . you can sleep at the office."

"Where? Under your desk?"

"No, there's a little room in the corner, we put a bunk bed in it. When the programmers have to pull all-nighters, we'll sometimes crash in there. But it's the weekend, no big deadlines coming up, so no one will be sleeping there. You can stay there tonight."

"Is there a reason I can't just stay at your apartment?"

The freckles on his nose flushed pink. "The thing is . . . my bedroom is basically a converted closet with a twin mattress on the floor. I mean, you *could* take my room and I'd sleep on the living room couch. Except that it's a Friday, which means my roommates will be partying until the sun rises. It's always a zoo on the weekends. Believe me, the office will be quieter than my apartment." He hesitated. "I'll stay there, too, if you want. So you're not alone. And then we can drive to see your mom in the morning."

I'd spent the previous night sleeping upright in a bus seat with a window as my pillow. *Anything* sounded better than that. And honestly, I was intrigued by the idea of spending more time in that office. It felt like a place where I might be able to get lost, on my way to finding myself.

"Thank you," I said. "It's so nice of you to do all this for a complete stranger."

"Well, we're all strangers to each other, when you get down to it. It's just that we sometimes choose not to be." He shrugged. "I'm choosing not."

BY THE TIME we wandered back to Signal, it was past eight o'clock. As we exited the elevator, a group was getting on. They smiled glassily at us as we crossed paths, a miasma of skunk clinging to their clothes. A gangly red-haired boy wearing carpenter pants and a sweatshirt with an alien head looped around to call after us. "Hey, we're headed down to the Eagle's Drift-In to play some pool. You wanna join?"

"We're good, Janus, thanks."

The redheaded boy cocked his head at me and raised an eyebrow before the elevator doors slid closed.

The office that had been such a buzzing hub a few hours earlier was now mostly empty. The music had been turned off, along with most of the lights. But a scattering of people still sat at their desks in the semi-dark, their faces ghoulishly illuminated by the glow of their computer screens.

"There are still people here," I whispered.

"There are almost always people here," he said. "It's kinda nice, if you don't like to be alone."

"Are you going to get in trouble for bringing someone into the office?"

He shook his head. "Frank's hiring people so fast that no one knows who everyone is anymore. Most people will probably figure you just started."

"Even though I'm only eighteen?"

He shrugged. "You wouldn't be the first. They'll hire anyone who knows HTML."

I know HTML, I thought, with a little surge of pride; feeling, for the first time, that I might not be *so* woefully behind.

The sleeping quarters were just as he'd promised, a room taken up entirely by a bunk bed and a green corduroy couch that looked like it might have been dragged off the street. A case of some kind of drink called Zima sat in the corner, one bottle missing, the rest gathering dust. I changed into a clean T-shirt and sweats, brushed my teeth in the bathroom sink and washed my face with pink hand soap. Lionel hovered stiffly in the doorway, seemingly unsure what to do with himself, as I settled into the bottom bunk. I had a sudden memory of my father tucking me into bed when I was very young. He used to read to me, poems by Yeats and Wordsworth, tangles of old-fashioned verse whose effect on seven-year-old me was mostly soporific. When had he stopped doing that?

"I'm just going to work for a while, OK?" Lionel offered. "I'm not really tired yet. I'll be quiet when I come in."

"That's fine." We stared at each other, strangers-turned-unlikely-roommates. "You didn't have to be so nice to me, you know. Just because you talked to me for a few minutes online."

He shrugged. "I have a thing for underdogs and outcasts," he said.

"Why? Are you an underdog, too?"

"Honestly, everyone here is. This is where you land when you don't fit in anywhere else. It's a wonderland of weirdos."

And maybe he meant this dismissively, but all I could think as I slipped under those dirty sheets, was that it sounded like my kind of heaven.

DESPITE MY EXHAUSTION, I couldn't sleep. Instead, I lay awake in the bottom bunk for hours, listening to the rasp of Lionel's breathing. City noises—so foreign to me—drifted up from the street, breaking the night: boisterous drunks stumbling out from the bars and clubs, a cacophony of honking car horns, a woman's plaintive wail. And then, every time I drifted close to sleep, my brain would seize on an image that would jolt me awake again. The terror in the face of the security guard as the blood pulsed out from his thigh. Flames, outlined against the night sky. My father's eyes, welling up as he called me *my girl.* The blackened hole in the side of the Microsoft building.

I finally drifted off near dawn. When I woke up, thanks to the sun that blazed through the wall of windows, Lionel was gone. I found a note at the end of my mattress that explained that he was going home to change and retrieve his car. *Back in an hour,* it read, though I had no idea what time it was or had been.

While I waited for him to return, I wandered through the empty office, studying objects left behind on the desks as if they were archeological artifacts. A collection of miniature Lego toys, dressed like medieval knights. A collage of printed-out photographs of Celtic knots. A glowing lamp with bubbles that floated in pink oil. Books everywhere, none that I had ever read before, with titles like *Neuromancer* and *Infinite Jest* and *Society of the Spectacle* and *Stolen Lightning: The Social Theory of Magic.* I riffled through a few and then decided to borrow one of the more interesting-sounding novels, a fat book called *Snow Crash.* It would be my first science fiction, but not my last.

Even empty, the room seemed to hum with an electric static, like a high-pitched wind; and as I walked through the office I finally realized it was the sound of a hundred whirring hard drives. I imagined them connecting to the outside world through those hot pink cables, like a particularly elaborate spiderweb unfurling its strands out toward a million anchor points.

Halfway through the room, I stopped abruptly. There, on a desk piled high with newspapers and magazines, was a copy of the most recent *New York Times.* I scanned the front page with a sense of dread, already anticipating what I was going to see.

There it was, in the lower corner of the front page: *Authorities Identify Suspects in Microsoft Bombing.*

The story didn't have any photos of me—and how would it? I couldn't recall ever having had my photo taken. We didn't even own a camera. But that was only a small consolation because there I was in the first paragraph anyway:

Authorities have identified a Montana man, Saul Williams, and his teenage daughter (a minor whose name is being withheld), as suspects in the Microsoft bombing last weekend. Authorities were able to trace the IP address of Williams's website, called the Luddite Manifesto, to a cabin outside Bozeman, Montana. An explosion at the cabin, as agents arrived at the scene, is suspected to have been triggered by their arrival. Authorities are currently combing through the ruins for clues.

Little is known about the father and daughter, who are described by locals as "recluses" who lived mostly off the grid in the woods and had few ties to the community. Their current whereabouts are unknown, although authorities are offering a $100,000 reward to anyone who can provide information that leads to their arrest.

There was a black-and-white photo of the smoking ruins of our cabin, with police caution tape threaded around it. I stared at this, a pixelated heap of burnt wood and corrugated tin and fire-scarred stones. Was that the blackened cushion from the chair on our porch, leaking its innards? The only thing that remained truly recognizable among the ruins was our cast-iron woodstove, which still stood sentry over the ashes of my childhood.

My mind whirred. The authorities knew who we were. They knew, and yet they didn't know that Saul Williams wasn't actually Saul Williams, nor was I Jane. No one was looking for Esme Nowak—and why would they? I was dead. For that small mercy, I was begrudgingly thankful. I was lucky, too, that the authorities believed I was still a minor—who had told them I was seventeen? Presumably Heidi, or her mother. Regardless, even if Lionel happened to be following the news, he wouldn't necessarily connect his Internet Jane from Montana with this unnamed fugitive from the same state. I hoped.

As I scanned the story, I realized that the authorities had identified us not because Heidi turned us in, or because of evidence somehow left behind at Microsoft, or even by the images in the surveillance cameras. They'd found us because of the Luddite Manifesto. Technology had led them straight to us. My father clearly hadn't thought that part through; or maybe he just didn't know what he was doing; or maybe, just maybe, he did know and didn't really care. Maybe he wanted to be found, and made a martyr.

How long would I be safe as Esme Nowak? Would the feds find anything in those ashes that would point them toward my current (and past) identity? I put my nose close to the photo, studied it as if it were a rune that might reveal its secrets. But my father's incendiary had done its job, hastened along by the massive stacks of brittle books and newspapers and magazines that had lined our rooms. There wasn't much left to see.

And yet. It was hard to breathe; it felt like someone had slipped a noose around my neck and was pulling it tighter and tighter. I felt incapable of navigating this alone; but who was there to help me? I certainly couldn't lay all this on poor unsuspecting Lionel; it was bad enough that I'd asked him to unknowingly harbor a fugitive.

My mother. We would find her, and she would help me. Wasn't that what mothers did? Make all your problems go away? I thought of Lina, gently tucking away the loose strands of Heidi's hair, always watchful, always ready with a solution.

The elevator in the hallway pinged, announcing Lionel's arrival. I dropped the newspaper back on the desk, racing back to the bunk room with my cheeks aflame. By the time he appeared in the doorway with a paper bag in his hands, I was sitting on the bed, tying my sneakers, my face hot and my fingers shaky.

Lionel looked pinkly scrubbed. His straight dark hair, freshly washed, still had comb marks in it. Even on a Saturday morning, he was wearing a shirt and tie. I found it oddly endearing; for some reason I couldn't quite identify, he made me feel safe.

"You're up! I bought bagels. Do you need coffee? There's a pot in the lunchroom, I can make you some if you need it."

I smiled at him, my face a bland mask of eagerness that hid the panic thumping through my veins. "No, I'm good," I said. "Let's go. I just want to meet my mom."

30.

LIONEL'S CAR WAS a boxy gray Volvo with cracked leather seats and a vague smell of spoiled milk, despite being spotlessly clean. It gave off the impression of a hand-me-down from his mother, perhaps because of the girls preparatory school sticker that was peeling off the bumper. He drove with his hands fixed firmly at ten and two, perched up on the edge of his seat in order to get a good perspective over the dashboard.

The roads were quiet, the city still rubbing sleep from its eyes. As we drove south on Highway 101, the clouds began to break, revealing a milky blue sky. To the east, the chop of the San Francisco Bay was clotted with sailboats and windsurfers, tilting against the wind. To the west, pine-covered hills blockaded the coastal fog.

Lionel handed me a stack of printouts. "Here, tell me what to do. I mapquested it."

"Mapquested?"

"New website, just launched. Searchable digitized maps of *everything*. You type in your destination and it gives you turn-by-turn directions that you can print out." He looked genuinely happy for the first time since I met him. "It's a game-changer. The kind of thing the internet was made for, you know? Thomas Guides are so fucked."

After forty minutes, we turned off the freeway. Lionel's directions wove us left and right and finally landed us in a neighborhood where the streets were shaded by oak trees and there were no sidewalks. The homes were mostly low and sprawling, single-story ranch homes surrounded by tangles of bushes and leaf-strewn lawns; but these were interspersed with looming new builds that stretched into the corners of their lots, imposing houses that looked like they belonged in the Italian countryside. I'd never seen anything like them.

Every time we passed a house that had been painted blue, my pulse would accelerate, wondering if *this* was where I'd been born. I imagined climbing the steps to one of these houses, knocking at the door, and the woman with wavy blond hair who would open it, her face crumpled with shock. Pulling me into her jasmine-scented arms, crying *my baby is alive*, ushering me into a kitchen to feed me oven-fresh chocolate chip cookies. A reunion that would somehow make everything else—the guilt of what I'd done that was eating away at me, the horror of my name on the front page of *The New York Times*—dwindle away into insignificance. Having a mother again would somehow fix everything.

"This is where Silicon Valley money lives," Lionel offered, filling the silence. "Computer industry, VC, that kind of thing. I actually grew up in Los Altos, a few towns over. Steve Jobs's garage was six blocks away."

"Steve Jobs?" I realized I was coming off like a particularly clueless parrot.

"You know . . . Apple?" I nodded tentatively. The computers, yes, I'd seen them all over the Signal office. "The founder. He's kind of my hero."

I looked out at the houses, their driveways filled with understated European station wagons, shiny bikes left lying on their sides and rope swings dangling from the gnarled limbs of the oaks. My father had worked in tech, too, I realized. If we'd stayed in the place where I'd been born, would my life have been similar to Lionel's? A Swedish sedan to drive, an all-girls private school, a post-collegiate shared apartment in San Francisco. For the first time since I'd found my birth certificate, I realized that I'd been robbed of not just a mother but a whole different life.

Maybe it isn't too late to get it back, I thought. Maybe I'd move right back in with my mother and begin to rebuild my life. I could start fresh, abandoning everything that had come before. Become *Esme*

Nowak for real, rather than feeling like an imposter trying on some-one else's skin.

The line between hope and delusion can be awfully narrow some-times.

Lionel was craning to see the directions in my hand. "Oh shit, number fifty-three. We're here."

He veered over to the side of the road and stopped.

"This can't be it," I said.

There was no blue-painted house at this address. There was no house at all. All that remained of whatever had once stood at 53 Catalpa Drive was a mailbox and a vast brown swath of dirt. Two bull-dozers sat idle in a pitted asphalt driveway that currently led to nowhere, next to a dumpster and a dusty blue Porta Potty. It looked like a giant had wandered by and scraped the lot clean with his trowel.

"Oh man," Lionel whispered.

We got out of the car and stood there, staring at the construction site, as if expecting a house to suddenly materialize out of the dirt.

After a few minutes, an older woman in a lemon-yellow sweatsuit appeared at the end of the street, half stumbling after a Labrador retriever that strained at its leash. When she got close, Lionel flagged her down.

"Hey, do you know how we could find the woman who lived here?"

The dog lunged toward us, its tail wagging so hard that its entire back half wiggled. The woman came to a stop several feet away, reeling her dog in like a fish on a line. "You mean, the Trevantes? You're upset about this, too? They're building some modern monstrosity, totally out of character with the neighborhood. Believe me, I complained."

Lionel shot me a questioning look. "Not the Trevantes," I said firmly. "Nowak."

The dog whined to be let free. The woman shook her head. "No, sorry. That's not who owns this place. You've got it wrong." She began to walk again, giving us a wide berth.

"What happened to the people who lived here before?" I called after her.

She shrugged. "As long as I've lived here, it's been Trevante. And I've been here a decade."

She vanished and Lionel turned to me. "I'm really sorry."

I kicked at a clod of dirt, sending it flying into the empty lot. "I really thought she'd be waiting for me."

"Probably she is." Lionel's eyes had gone soft and introspective behind his glasses. "She must have moved sometime after you were born. Probably your mom is still waiting for you wherever *that* is."

"But *that* could be anywhere," I realized helplessly. "My father never told me anything about where we moved from. I just assumed it was Silicon Valley because he said he worked there. All I really know is that when I 'died' we were living somewhere within driving distance of Big Sur. But that could be so many places."

"Most of California." Lionel exhaled softly. He looked up and down the street, nervously turning his keys in his hands. "So . . . now what? Do you want to go ring doorbells or something?"

"And see if people know the current whereabouts of someone who lived here eighteen years ago? Seems unlikely."

The denuded lot was as naked as a blank notebook page. I breathed in deeply, smelling nothing except a faint chemical tang from the Porta Potty and a whiff of diesel engine fuel. Now that I was standing in front of the address, it seemed stupidly childish to have believed that my mother might be still waiting there, frozen in time, after all these years. Waiting for a dead child to miraculously return. Only a fool would do that.

I kicked another clod of dirt, so violently that Lionel's eyes popped with alarm. "Let's just go," I said.

31.

THE MOOD IN Lionel's car as we drove back to the city was one of abject gloom. Traffic was now clogging the highway, the fog closing back in overhead. As we inched our way toward downtown San Francisco, Lionel glanced sideways at me. "Mind if we go back to my place for a while? I forgot something."

I shrugged, still mired in despair. I hadn't thought past finding my mother; now that this fantasy had popped like a soap bubble, I had no plans at all.

But as we pulled off the freeway and began to drive through Hayes Valley, my mood began to shift. Here, finally, was a San Francisco that felt familiar from reading Steinbeck and London: Victorian homes in candy colors, pressed tightly together like books on a library shelf. Hilly streets that climbed at implausible angles, vertiginous stairways ascending into parks where moisture dripped from wind-beaten cypress. Quirky little stores and restaurants with names that sounded more like baby babble than businesses: *Noc Noc* and *Zam Zam* and *Cha Cha Cha*.

Lionel parked in front of a three-story Queen Anne with an octagonal turret and gables that had been painted bubblegum pink. Inside, he led me up a set of carpeted stairs that smelled like cat pee, to a dimly lit landing, where he battled with the front door in the gloom.

He hesitated before ushering me in. "If it's a madhouse, I'm sorry."

I liked his apartment immediately: the foyer with its worn-smooth wooden banister. The long hallway papered in sweet knots of green flowers (faded paper that I would much later recognize as a William Morris print). Ceilings of pressed tin from which dangled milk-glass fixtures that were missing half their bulbs. Overlaid across these original features were the leavings of a half-dozen twenty-something boys: a tangle of bikes leaning up against the balustrade, a bong sitting on a fireplace mantel, a spilled bag of Cheetos ground into nuclear-orange dust on the original hardwood floors.

In the living room, two of Lionel's roommates sat on a sagging leather couch, playing video games. They lifted their eyes to us as we passed by the doorway and then shot their attention straight back to the carnage on their TV screen. I lingered in the doorway for a moment, fascinated. "What's that?"

"Duke Nukem." Lionel made a face.

"You don't like it?"

One of the boys piped up, his eyes still fixed on the screen. "Not cerebral enough for him. Too much gore."

Lionel shrugged. "What can I say, I'm a pacifist."

The roommates seemed radically uninterested in me, which suited me just fine. Lionel grabbed my elbow, tugging me farther down the hallway, until we reached the last doorway.

"It's a mess," he warned me.

It was neat as a pin. A twin-size futon took up most of the floor space, made up with an old, crocheted blanket and two perfectly stacked pillows. A row of science fiction novels, arranged by size, marched along the floorboards. A fish tank burbled away on top of a milk crate, with a lone betta fish swimming in surly circles. A framed family portrait—a chubby teenage Lionel, his face peppered with acne, flanked by two younger sisters in identical pinafore dresses, empyrean parents looming behind.

What the room lacked in size and furnishings, it made up for with technology. Whatever space wasn't used by the futon had been taken up by a battered metal desk, on top of which sat a hard drive and a printer and two separate monitors. Animated toasters flew slowly across the screens, in hypnotic syncopation.

Lionel reached across the futon and grabbed a pill bottle that was sitting by the bed. He popped a pill in his mouth and swallowed it down with the remains of a glass of water, grimacing. His eyes met mine, over the glass. "Prozac," he mumbled.

Prozac had been a perennial subject of my father's. *The technological age has triggered widespread chronic depression, but instead of addressing the root causes of society's unhappiness—feelings of uselessness, the awareness of impending doom—we drug people into oblivion.* "You're depressed," I realized, surprised.

"Not as much as I used to be."

"Why were you depressed?"

He looked taken aback by my question. "You're not supposed to ask that."

"Why not?"

"Because depression is the result of a chemical imbalance, your brain's inability to regulate moods. So it's hard to explain *why*, it's not like some situation caused it."

"So you can't pinpoint *anything* that contributed to your depression? Like, feelings of uselessness or worries about the apocalypse?"

He coughed, dribbling water. "What? No. Not those. But yes, sure, I can think of things that exacerbated it. I was a weird kid, didn't have any friends, so I got into computers instead and became a programming whiz and escaped off to college early. Which also wasn't very helpful in the end because I was still the oddball, but now I was also a few years younger than everyone else to boot. Plus, a little OCD. So. Yeah." He had grown quiet. "It's taken a while to find my people, you could say."

"I could say the same, about finding my people. Quite possibly I was depressed, too, living in the middle of nowhere without any real friends, except my dad. But how would I even have known if I was? My dad and I never talked about emotions. Only ideas."

"You'd know," Lionel said. "Plus, I know we only just met, but you don't strike me as a depressive. You seem to be pretty good at dealing with your problems without spiraling into a black hole of despair. It's nice to see, to be honest." He put the pill bottle back down and then we stood there, side by side, looking around his room. He smiled apologetically. "Anyway. I told you my bedroom was small."

"What do you do with all that computer equipment?"

"Mostly play PC games. I'm trying to write one myself, a kind of puzzle fantasy thing, like Myst, but everything I come up with is stupid."

We were standing so close in that tiny room that I could feel the heat coming off his body. The moment had crossed from curiosity into awkwardness: The longer I stood there taking in his monklike existence, the more it reminded me of my own life back in Montana, which made me feel oddly sad for him, and then equally sad for myself. "Do you mind if I use your computer?" I finally asked, breaking the silence.

He waved a hand at his desk with an expression of relief. "Oh yeah, of course. You need to check your email or something?"

"I actually don't have an email address."

"Seriously?" He looked horrified. "I can help you sign up for Hotmail, if you want."

I had no idea who I was supposed to email, but I nodded, pretending that I was equally concerned. I sat at the desk chair and jiggled the mouse until the flying toasters disappeared. Lionel hovered over my shoulder, ready to help, until I finally turned around. "I'm just going to read some things online."

He flushed. "Oh, right. Sorry." He flopped down on the bed and grabbed the novel that was closest to it, turning so that he was facing away from me.

Once I was sure that he wasn't watching, I opened up his browser and typed in the address of the Luddite Manifesto. I stared at the front page as it loaded, fear bitter on my tongue. I don't know what I was expecting—that my father might have updated it himself? that the government might have pulled it down?—but it was exactly as it had looked the week before. The only thing that had changed was the visitor counter, which was now hovering just shy of two hundred thousand views.

Two hundred thousand people had read his manifesto.

I wondered if my father had seen this number. Surely he had, wherever he was. And my heart sank as I understood the message that it would have telegraphed to him: that the murder of his friend had been worth it for the fame. That people were finally listening.

"Have you read that thing?"

I whipped around to see Lionel gazing up at me from where he lay on the bed, his eyes impossible to read behind the reflection in his glasses. I tried to keep my face still. "Sure. Have you?"

"We all did," he said. "Apparently it's the most visited page on the internet, *ever*. And that guy he killed? Peter Carroll? Ross knew him." Off my blank face, he added, "Ross Marinetti? He founded Signal. You could say that he is my boss's boss. Anyway, Ross brought him in to Signal last month, as part of the futurism lecture series that he's making us all attend, and he gave a talk about AI and machine learning. Everyone freaked out when we heard what happened to him." He hesitated. "That *thing* you're reading, that so-called manifesto, it was written specifically about us, wasn't it? My industry, and everyone working in it. What a pile of bullshit."

I bristled despite myself. "I mean, some of it makes sense, don't you think? Technological progress as the opiate of the people, making us obedient to corporations, disconnecting us from what's most vital about human nature. That we should be scared about where this is all going." I knew, even as the words came out of my mouth, that saying this was a mistake.

He stared at me, his jaw slightly agape. "The guy's a psychopath, Esme. You can't possibly take any of it seriously."

Hearing that word—*psychopath*—did something to my innards, and my eyes involuntarily filled up with tears. "Of course I don't. Just thought I'd take the contrarian view."

"Hey. Don't cry." He fumbled around and grabbed a tissue box and offered it to me. "What's wrong?"

"It's just . . ." The totality of my problems came crashing down on me suddenly, a tidal wave of woe. "I'm not sure what to do now. I have no other leads to find my mom. And the thing I keep kicking myself about is that if I hadn't so stupidly let that girl on the bus steal that bag with my money and all those pages my father wrote, I might actually have some information to go on. Who knows what I would have found out if I'd had a chance to read them? Maybe where else they lived, or the name of the school where my mom taught, or her maiden name and where she grew up so I could at least reach out to my grandparents. Instead, I'm left with nothing, other than going to the police, which I can't bring myself to do. Meanwhile I'm broke, and I'm homeless, and I don't know what the hell to do."

Lionel looked a little shell-shocked by my barrage. "We'll figure something out," he offered. "You can stay at the office a few more days, if you need time to sort through your options."

I chewed over his offer, which seemed at once supremely generous and utterly insufficient. "I don't exactly *have* options. I mean, what would you do if you were me?" Then, as a cautious look crept over his face, I added, "And don't say go back to my dad. That's not an option."

"I wasn't going to say that," he said quickly.

"Then, what?" I demanded.

"Live your own life. Get a job, find an apartment. That's what people do."

He might as well have been telling me to build a rocket ship, that's how little I understood about how to go about those kinds of things. Find an apartment? Where did you even start with that? Get a job? Who would hire someone without any experience or school transcripts or skill sets, whose existence could be boiled down to a Social Security card and a fishy-sounding life story?

"I'm too tired to think about any of this," I said. "Can we pick up some food and head back to the office?"

He leaned across me to shut down the computer, his body so close that I could smell the spicy deodorant he wore. From this vantage point, I could see how long his eyelashes were behind his glasses. I felt a curious impulse to lift the frames off his nose in order to touch the delicate freckles underneath. I wondered if he still thought of himself as the chubby, pimply misfit in the photo; I wondered if he took Pro-zac partly because he did.

Electronic dance music started up in the other room, fast and thumping and frenetic. Lionel turned and blinked at me, his face inches from mine. We stared at each other until he tore his gaze away, and snapped the monitor off.

"Let's go," he said.

32

THAT NIGHT, I climbed into bed, pulled the covers over my head, and let myself cry until exhaustion finally took pity on me and knocked me out. When I woke up nine hours later—groggy and disoriented—there was a strange man standing at the end of the bed.

I sat up so fast that my head slammed into the underside of the upper bunk. My vision went fuzzy.

"Ouch," I complained.

"What?" Above me, I could hear Lionel rustling awake. And then— "Oh shit."

Lionel's legs appeared over the edge of the bunk as he jumped down to the floor. He stood there in flannel pajama pants and a baggy T-shirt that read *D.A.R.E.*, myopic and so naked-looking without his glasses on.

"Hey, Frank," he said.

"Good morning, Lionel," the man said. He was probably in his thirties, a sandy blond with a scruffy beard that failed to compensate for his prematurely receding hairline. "Didn't expect to find you here on a Sunday morning. Don't you have a perfectly adequate apartment?"

"I didn't know you came in on weekends." Lionel was patting around for his glasses. He located them on the edge of the couch and shoved them crookedly on his face.

"Thought I'd get a jump on the week." Frank glanced at me and then looked quickly away, uncomfortable with the sight of me in my pajamas. "Please tell me you're not having sex in here. You promised no one would be screwing in the office if we gave you guys the beds."

"No!" Lionel lifted his hands in protest. "She's a . . . friend, in need. I figured it wasn't going to hurt anyone to let her crash here for a night or two."

Frank's eyebrows shot up. "Seriously? I'm trying to run a website here, Lionel. Not a homeless shelter. Ross will lose his shit if he finds her here. He already thinks digital is a lunatic asylum."

"No, I get it. Sorry. We'll figure something else out." Fumbling, Lionel snatched up a dirty sock that I'd tossed on the floor. He picked up my backpack with his other hand, and shoved these toward me, his face slack with apology.

I didn't take them from him. "I know HTML," I blurted.

Frank's head swiveled. His eyes met mine with an expression of vague puzzlement. "I'm sorry?"

"Lionel told me that you're hiring anyone who knows HTML. I know HTML." I climbed out of bed and stood in front of him, arms crossed over my chest.

He cocked his head. A tiny smiled tugged at the edges of his beard. "Is this your way of saying that you want me to *hire* you? A vagrant who has been squatting in our office?"

"*Vagrant*'s kind of a strong word," Lionel muttered. "She's more of an itinerant intellectual."

I smiled. I liked this.

Frank looked me up and down. "How do I know you really know HTML? You have a website I could see?"

Yes, I thought, but I wasn't about to pull up the Luddite Manifesto to show him. "It's not online anymore. But I can mock up one for you now, if you want? You can watch me do it."

"Christ, no, that sounds tedious." He sighed. "You a college dropout? Stanford kick you out for smoking pot in the dorms?"

"Homeschooled. No college. But I can recite Baudrillard's theories on hyperreality, if you like, or lecture you on Keynesian economics."

Frank tugged at a particularly wiry tuft of beard. "CV?"

"What's that?"

He sighed. "You're killing me."

"You'll kill me if you kick me out." It didn't feel that far from the truth, and I was too desperate not to work every angle I had.

He raised an eyebrow at this. "Spare me the melodrama." He turned to Lionel. "You can vouch for her?"

Lionel nodded. The nod was a little tentative for my liking, but I couldn't blame him.

"OK, look, we were supposed to get a new production intern this week but she just bailed on us to do a project with Survival Research Labs. So you caught me on a good day. Plus I have a soft spot for Lionel here; he's probably the straightest arrow we have in this office, keeps the trains running on time. So here's the deal: I'm giving you a trial period of two weeks. It's minimum wage. No benefits, no over-time. You'll probably end up working sixty hours a week but we're only going to pay you for forty. And you have to find somewhere else to sleep, OK?"

I breathed out, finally. "OK."

"You got a name?"

"Esme Nowak."

"*Esme.* Welcome to the revolution, Esme." He turned to leave but pivoted at the door. "And seriously, no fucking in the office!"

Once he was gone, I turned to Lionel, rumpled and shell-shocked, his glasses still askew. My head was still throbbing where it had con-nected with the underside of the bunk bed; I was a little dizzy, but that might have been excitement rather than a concussion.

"So," I said. "What's 'minimum wage'?"

33

And so, life began anew.

For the first time in my existence, I was part of a collective "we." And yes, I was just a tiny cog in a big machine—the lowliest code monkey in the room—but still, I was part of something new, something that was being invented all around me. Every week, it seemed, there was a new product launch, a new website, a redesign using new programming breakthroughs. At Signal, it was impossible to feel small, when what *we* were building felt so expansive.

And I loved it.

I could delve into the minutiae of my job for you, and how in my first weeks in San Francisco I was thrown into the deep end and had to learn to swim fast. How I quickly learned to mark up HTML and navigate online scheduling calendars and parse an entirely new set of computer terms. How I spun a quasi-truthful story for my new co-workers about how I'd moved from rural Montana in order to get a job in tech after meeting Lionel online; and how I gave my employers my very real Social Security number and birth certificate as identification, cementing my new identity as my original self. How I ended up working directly with the girl with the butterfly tattoo—Brianna, who ran the feminist Web zine *Floozy* on the side and was delighted to hear that I'd read it—but who had grown up in rural Tennessee and was therefore patient with my ignorance. How I was thrillingly given my own desk, and my own Power Mac computer, thus anchoring my tiny toehold in this brave new world. How I found myself spending far more than sixty hours a week at the office, because what else could

I possibly be doing that was more interesting than what was happening in the office anyway?

But that isn't the part of the story anyone is ever interested in, so I might as well elide a bit.

Needless to say, I spent so much time at Signal that Brianna began to joke that I must be sleeping under my desk. I wasn't. Lionel had found me a sublet in his roommate's ex-girlfriend's cousin's apartment, two blocks away from his own apartment in the Lower Haight. I slept under the eyelet coverlet of a medical student named Megan, who was currently spending a semester in Africa, doing research with AIDS patients. Her room still smelled like her—laundry soap and dried rose petals—and the mirror was barely visible because there were so many photographs shoved into the frame, mostly of Megan with her arms flung around women whose smiles revealed perfect teeth. It felt like I was squatting inside someone else's existence. But! She had cable TV in her bedroom, which was my definition of nirvana. My temporary roommates were also med students, both a decade older than me and both named Heather; we mumbled greetings at each other in the kitchen when I was making my spaghetti and scrambled eggs, and that was about the extent of our interaction.

The number of things I actually knew began to grow; and although they were still vastly outnumbered by the things I didn't yet understand, I at least didn't feel *quite* as clueless as I had when I got off that Greyhound bus. I was a sponge, ready to soak up every possible drop of modern life. I lifted a notebook from Signal's supply closet in order to jot down every reference my new coworkers made—JenniCam, *Mystery Science Theater 3000,* Wu-Tang Clan, Beanie Babies, Baz Luhrmann, JonBenét Ramsey, *Bridget Jones's Diary,* Orbitz—and then spent every spare minute watching television and listening to the radio and surfing the internet, giving myself a crash course in modern pop culture.

There was so much to learn, and I wanted to know it all, immediately. The more I filled my brain with fresh information, the less space there was to think about the mother I'd failed to find, and the father

I'd run away from, and the horrors of Seattle, and the authorities that were out there looking for Jane Williams. Already, just a month after my departure from Montana, my entire life there was starting to feel like a slowly fading dream, foggy and ephemeral compared to the sharp-edged glitter of my new San Francisco existence.

If I felt pangs of homesickness on occasion—for the frozen dew dancing, diamond-like, on the tips of the wild grass; for the tawny spring fawns, tripping down to our pond; for the smell of woodsmoke in my father's hair, his hand on my shoulder—I buried these feelings under an avalanche of pop culture. *Toy Story.* "Macarena." Smashing Pumpkins. *Scream.* SimCity. O. J. Simpson. Frappuccino. Paul Frank. "Wannabe." *People*'s Sexiest Man Alive. As if becoming an avid pupil of this fascinating new world would help me forget that I wasn't quite sure exactly who I was anymore.

In my free time, I walked the streets of San Francisco until the treads of my tennis shoes were slick from wear and my thigh muscles grew taut from climbing the hills. Seven square miles: It sounded like such a small city to master and yet I had barely seen a thing. And so I'd walk up through the damp paths of Golden Gate Park and out to Pacific Heights to ogle the grand Beaux Arts mansions, and then turn down to the fish-scented streets of Chinatown and out through the taquerias and nightclubs of the Mission District and then back up to my home in the Lower Haight. Staring at every person I passed, trying to take in all the iterations of human existence I'd never before imagined.

I absorbed all this overwhelming stimuli until it felt like I'd shot magma into my veins—a hot and itchy sensation, but not an entirely unpleasant one. I tried to ignore the insistent voice in the back of my head that warned me that something bad could happen at any moment: that, if not diligent, I might get hit by a bus / robbed / identified by a police officer / kidnapped and sold into slavery / raped. That voice, I knew, belonged to my father—*cities are cesspools for criminals and drug addicts and the insane*—and I was done listening to him. So I defiantly wandered the streets alone even at night, stepping over the drunks passed out in the doorways as casually as someone who had been doing this their entire life.

It's a miracle I wasn't ever mugged.

As I walked, I would keep an eye out for juice bars, remembering what Desi had told me that night at McDonald's. *I work part-time at a juice bar in San Francisco, the owners are total health Nazis.* Eventually, I figured, I would find Desi, cramming celery into a machine. But this was California in the nineties, when it was your civic duty to drink at least one carrot-apple-ginger juice a week, ideally with a wheatgrass booster. There were shops with punny names in every neighborhood— *The Juice Box, Feeling Smoothie, The Green Goddess, Juicy Lucy's*—but Desi was never behind the counter. As the days passed, my hope of finding her—and with her, all those critical possessions—dwindled.

Meanwhile, the Microsoft bombing story slipped from the front pages of the newspapers to the back; and then, after a few weeks, the story vanished altogether, supplanted by more pressing news. An earthquake in Pakistan. A gunman at the Empire State Building. The murder of a rap star called The Notorious B.I.G. If the authorities had made any headway on the case, it certainly wasn't enough to make the news.

The page visits to the Luddite Manifesto had also stalled out, I noticed. People had moved on to shinier new things; and it was easy for me to imagine that this meant that I could, too. That the danger was over, and I could finally stop worrying.

Maybe I really *was* living my own life, as Lionel had instructed me to, and this could be forever. Maybe it wasn't just wishful thinking.

I didn't stop to think what it might mean to my father to be relegated to the recycling bin.

ABOUT A MONTH after I started working at Signal, a film crew began to creep around the office. You'd look up and there a camera would be, the black void of the lens pointed at you. They were like safari hunters, trying to capture the exotic creatures living in the wild.

Frank had sent out an email about the camera crew earlier in the week. *CBS will be at the office all week, featuring Signal as part of a docu-series they are putting together about the digital revolution. Please play nice. No funny business. Unless you tell us otherwise we will assume you are OK with being filmed.*

I had my reasons for not wanting to be featured on the news; number one being that I was a fugitive hiding behind a subpar makeover and a dead girl's name. But neither did I want to bring attention to myself by going to Frank and trying to explain exactly *why* I didn't want to be filmed. Instead, I just pivoted on my heels whenever the cameras approached me; and once I even dived below my desk, pretending I was hunting for something I'd dropped, until Brianna finally yelled at me to stop rolling around down there because I was in danger of unplugging her monitor.

A few days into their arrival, I looked up to see the show's producer—a man with a horrible case of eczema, his skin peeling and raw—heading straight for my desk. I jumped up and took off in the opposite direction. The producer picked up his pace, chasing me down the hallway, his loafers slapping against the industrial carpet, a clipboard wedged under his arm.

"Hey, kid! Got a few minutes? I want to get your perspective on how cyberspace is—"

I dashed into the bathroom and slammed the door before he could finish his sentence; then I sat there, heaving with my back against the door, until I heard his footsteps receding down the hall. When I emerged again, I found Lionel standing there with a cup of coffee, waiting for me.

"I was wondering how long you'd hide in there."

"I don't know why they keep following me."

"Frank told them you're our youngest employee and so they're kind of obsessed with you," Lionel said. "They think that you're the face of the next generation."

"I'm not the face of anything."

"You're *a* face."

"Not one that anyone should want to look at."

"*I* want to look at it." As soon as the words had fallen from his mouth he turned scarlet, then yanked the glasses off his face and rubbed them against his shirt. "I mean, on a scale of one to twenty, you're definitely cracking double digits."

"Gee, thanks." The intention was sarcasm, but the result sounded needy. I flushed, too.

He put his glasses back on. "Anyway, we need to go down to the futurism lecture now. They say it's optional but, honestly, they'll notice if you don't go and decide you're not a team player. Especially if you're a new employee."

"The *what* lecture?"

He shook his head. "You'll see."

TWO HUNDRED EMPLOYEES converged in a space on the second floor, another capacious room that I'd heard was about to be transformed into a studio for a new television endeavor. The floor had only recently been vacated by one of the sewing shops, and it still smelled like fish sauce and cotton fiber. Rows of folding chairs had been set up facing a screen and a podium, and before these stood a tall man in a rumpled linen shirt, his silvering hair flopped over his forehead.

I slid into a seat between Lionel and Brianna. "What's a futurist, exactly?" I whispered.

"Someone who is trying to predict the future, like, social upheaval, economic change, political trends, all that," Brianna said. "They bring in thinkers every month who are supposed to inspire us."

"So that guy is a futurist?"

Lionel shot me a look of utter disbelief. "That's *Ross*. Ross Marinetti. Your boss."

"I've never seen him before," I said.

"That's because he doesn't come over to digital often. He prefers the magazine side of the office. Less chaotic."

I eyed him. Ross looked laconic, half asleep even, except that if you really looked at him you could see that his hooded eyes were darting across the room, eagle-like, absorbing. "What's his story?" I asked.

Brianna leaned in. "He came up out of MIT Media Lab, used to be a professor there, and he knows, like, *everyone* in technology. He was already kind of legendary even before he launched Signal; he was in with the *Whole Earth Catalog* crowd and all that. And now he's, like, a *prophet.*"

I wasn't sure what half of this meant, but I nodded as the lights dimmed and the room went suddenly silent. Ross cleared his throat and began.

"Signal started as a groundbreaking magazine about the new technologies that were changing the world as we knew it. But at a certain point, I had to ask myself: Why were we just *writing* about the new digital age, instead of *being* the new digital age?" Ross's voice was low and smooth and sticky, like maple syrup pooling on a plate. I looked around and realized that almost everyone was leaning forward in their seats, to better catch what he was saying. "Four years later, here we are. Not just a magazine but a media *destination* both online and off. We've got a network of the most innovative websites around, covering a whole gamut of topics, from sports to travel to technology. We've got a network of chat rooms. We're hosting the very first live online events, interviews and gatherings of the greatest minds around. We're launching our very own search engine that's going to be so much better than AltaVista! And soon, we'll even have Signal TV, which you'll be able to—get this—*stream* online. We're a goddamn digital conglomerate, guys."

The room broke out into applause. Next to me, Lionel muttered under his breath. "After all, why let everyone *else* profit off the dot-com boom? Why just *write* about it, when you can get that IPO, make those millions." The man sitting in front of us turned around and hushed Lionel, a finger pressed to his lips, but Lionel just shrugged. "It's true, isn't it?"

At the front of the room, Ross was still talking. "But what most people don't realize is that Signal isn't *just* a business. What Signal is—and you guys should really see this by now—is nothing less than a revolution. The future is now, and it's a future that so few people have had the foresight to see. But you"—he lifted his eyes to scan the audience, and when his eyes briefly met mine it felt that, somehow, he had shined straight into me, seen something inside me that I hadn't even seen in myself—"*you* know what's ahead for society. You are the harbingers of change. You guys all know how exciting this is. That's why you're here. That's why we are all here together. We *found* each other."

The crowd had started clapping halfway through this little speech and now they broke out into cheers. I felt myself lifted up by their excitement, an unfamiliar hot sensation bubbling up inside me. Mild hysteria? The wildness of hope? The infectious madness of a crowd? I was on the verge of tears and I didn't know why.

I thought of how the internet had so swiftly shifted my life; how, thanks to a modem and a chat room, I had landed here, in a room full of new friends, with a job that was helping me usher in *the future,* in a city that glimmered with promise. I was a living example of the marvels of the internet.

"We are shifting the axis of power, guys. The old political systems are soon going to be obsolete. Corporate culture is going the way of the dodo bird. And religion! Forget it. All our institutions are going to radically shift, and that's a *good* thing. Because what we are doing here on the World Wide Web is empowering people. The common man, the one currently without a voice. Giving him—and her!—the tools to create the change he wants to see in the world. It's absolute decentralization."

Was that me, screaming with excitement? I didn't even remember standing up, but there I was, with the rest of the group, giving Ross an ovation. *My father was so very wrong about all this,* I thought. How could he object to empowering the common man? I wished he were there with me, listening; surely he would hear what I was hearing, and change his tune. Maybe it wasn't too late. Maybe he could still be saved.

I missed him more than I wanted to admit to myself; because who wants to admit that they miss a man the entire world thinks is a psychotic murderer?

In the chair next to me, Lionel was still sitting down in his seat, lids at half-mast. I kicked his shin and he looked up at me with a surprised expression.

"Aren't you listening to this?" I asked.

"I was up all night, debugging the 3.0 chat program. My NoDoz just wore off." He rubbed his eyes. "Anyway, I've heard this speech four times already. He does it every time."

On my other side, Brianna poked me; and when I looked at her, she rolled her eyes at Lionel. "He thinks we're drinking the Kool-Aid."

"Oh, I *like* Kool-Aid. What's wrong with drinking Kool-Aid?" But Brianna had shifted her attention back to the podium. I didn't know what to make of Lionel's cynicism. How could he possibly *not* find this uplifting? Maybe it was the depression.

Up at the front of the room, Ross had pulled another man onstage with him, a blandly bespectacled man with a flannel vest zipped over his button-down. "So, today, furthering our conversation about all this, we are so fortunate to have George Gilder with us. He's going to talk to us about the concept of techno-utopianism and our post-scarcity future. A world where no one is in need of anything: We're so close, guys! The internet is going to take us all the way there in a decade, maybe two." Ross clapped George on the back as the man beamed, absently shuffling through a stack of note cards.

"Buckle up, kids," Lionel groaned, slumping even farther down in his seat. "Hope you remembered to use the bathroom first."

When I looked around, I realized that the television crew had parked itself on the edge of the room, just ten feet away from me. The eye of the camera was firmly fixed on me, capturing my cheers and applause. I dropped back into my chair and put my hand over my face to shield it from view, but the damage had already been done.

34

Six weeks and two days after my arrival in San Francisco, I turned on Megan's television set and learned that my father had murdered another man.

I wish I could say that I was surprised, but in my heart, I think I knew that he would do it again.

This time, the victim was a man named Baron Macomber, who was killed when he opened a mail bomb that had been sent to his office in Virginia. According to news reports, Macomber was a physicist who had been developing nanotechnology for military use. No evidence had yet been found that tied the bombing to my father—the package it came in had been obliterated—but already the conjecture had begun. Two prominent technology researchers killed within weeks by homemade explosives: It wasn't much of a leap.

I watched the evening news sitting cross-legged on Megan's eyelet coverlet, my legs gone numb beneath me. Was it possible they were wrong, and it wasn't my father at all, just a wild coincidence, or even a copycat? I wanted, desperately, to believe this. But the newscasters seemed to take his complicity as a given, and the sick pit in my stomach was a sign that I knew they were right.

"A nationwide manhunt is on for Saul Williams, the man already being nicknamed *The Bombaster*, and his teenage daughter," intoned the helmet-haired newscaster in a dutifully sober voice. "Although their last confirmed location was Montana, federal authorities are asking citizens everywhere to be on the lookout for this pair, possibly traveling under assumed names."

At this, the screen filled with black-and-white police sketches of my father and me.

I couldn't help it: I laughed out loud. The portrait of my father made him look like a small-time thug: the short hair jammed under his baseball cap, the Tom Selleck mustache, the disarming mirrored reflections of those sunglasses. His mouth was curled into a sneer, his chin pointed down as he glowered menacingly. The sketch looked nothing like him. I wondered if anyone in Bozeman had contributed to the portrait; or if the police had rejected the locals' descriptions of the hermit Saul Williams—grizzled and bearded and slightly feral—and opted instead to draw the far more telegenic criminal from the security camera.

The sketch of me was just as unrecognizable. The coquettish girl in the portrait was bow-lipped and arch-eyebrowed, with a heart-shaped face and long fringed lashes. She gazed sleepily at the artist from behind thick hanks of long blond hair, a look of mild invitation in her eyes. The woman in the sketch looked at least a decade older than me, like she'd been around the block a few times but wasn't about to tell you what she'd seen. (Was this how the security guard had described me? It couldn't have come from Heidi or Lina.)

I should have felt relieved by this, but instead regret and self-recrimination surged through me, a bitter chew. Even though I hadn't had anything to do with this second murder, I couldn't help blaming myself. If I'd just stuck with my father, could I have stopped him? Been the positive influence he needed to temper his murderous impulses? Then again, my presence hadn't exactly given him pause in Seattle, so what hubris made me think I could have prevented it this time?

Was my father still in North Dakota? There was a tip line listed at the end of the news segment, the FBI asking for information, promising anonymity and a cash reward. It would be so easy to call, to give them Malcolm Torino's address and send them after my father. Megan's phone, a modern cordless number, was sitting there. All I had to do was dial.

I didn't.

———

AT THIS POINT you might be asking yourself why I hadn't gone to
the police from the very first minute that I arrived in San Francisco.
My father had killed a man. The ethically and morally correct move
would have been to turn him in before he could do any further damage.

Looking back, I can clearly see three reasons for my fatal hesitation.

First: Because I believed that by walking away from my Montana
life—by reinventing myself as Esme Nowak—I was somehow wiping
the slate clean. That by pretending I was a whole new person (or, technically, stepping back into my original identity) I had washed my
hands of everything that Jane Williams had done. That by closing my
eyes, it would mean there was nothing to see; that Peter Carroll's murder would magically vanish. A terrible act, of course, but one that had
been relegated to the past.

Second: Fourteen years of listening to my father rail on about how
the authorities could not be trusted had left me deeply skeptical of the
legal system. What I knew about "justice" was based entirely on his
paranoid mutterings about the feds. Could you blame me for believing that the minute I'd become a fugitive, there was no turning back?
That if I walked into a police station, my life would be over? That the
system was so rigged against me there was no true justice to be had?

Even if I made an anonymous call, I knew I would be turning myself in, too. After all, if the authorities found my father, it would surely
be just a matter of time before they figured out his real name—*Adam
Nowak*—and then *Esme Nowak* would be next. I would be right there
in San Francisco, a sitting duck, waiting for them to catch up to me.
And after that: a lifetime in prison, I figured.

Third, and perhaps the most weighty reason of all: I loved my father.
Despite it all, he was the only safe haven I'd ever known, the person
who'd nurtured me, the person I admired most in the world. I may have
been horrified by his actions, but I certainly didn't want him to suffer.
What kind of a daughter would turn her father in to the *enemy*?

Do you see why, if it came down to choosing my father or choosing justice, I was always going to choose my father?

What I *didn't* choose: to see that this made me complicit. To imagine that my father might do it again.

But consider this: I was barely eighteen, and just experiencing the real world for the first time. I was like a baby fawn, taking my first wobbly steps into the world. I still couldn't see past my own feet.

Decide for yourself whether that's a valid excuse.

AND SO I turned off the television without writing down the tip line number, without picking up my phone. Something was bothering me. Something about the latest victim's name, a faint ping of familiarity. *Baron Macomber.*

And that's when it dawned on me.

I ran to my backpack and pulled out the photographs that I'd shoved in the pocket before I left the cabin. My father's childhood photos; his college portrait; the two snapshots of me and my mom; and—finally—the image of my father in a suit and tie on the steps of a glass building, surrounded by work colleagues. I turned this last photo over and examined the names on the back. *Nick Raymond Baron Peter Ajay Adam Mike Isaac.*

Baron and *Peter.*

My father was targeting his former colleagues.

Why them? Was it something to do with his old job? Where had they worked? In Silicon Valley, presumably; but what had he said he was doing? *Working for a technology research institute, in a group that was trying to figure out the future of computers. What they might be used for.*

I looked at the photo more closely, and then—realizing—pulled out the *I Hate Mondays* photo, and the one of me in my mother's arms. The three photographs had the same shape and size, the same yellowish tint, the same black fleck in an upper right corner, perhaps the result of a flawed lens: They had clearly been taken by the same camera. I flipped them over and compared the two that had captions. *Esme and Theresa. Nick Raymond Baron Peter Ajay Adam Mike Isaac.* The handwriting on both was the same, loopy and feminine, definitely not my father's. The natural assumption, then, was that it was my mother's. Who else would be so carefully labeling our family photos?

If that was the case, was it possible that my mother was there, too, on the steps of that office building? The ninth person, the person *behind* the camera; someone who clearly knew everyone in the photo by their first names.

In a rush, I understood two things: that if I could somehow figure out who the rest of the people in that photo were—if I could go find them and talk to them—maybe *they* would know my mother's current whereabouts. And that somehow, in the process, I'd have to find a way to warn them that they were in danger.

So now I just needed to find someone who knew everyone—or, at least, everyone who worked in the tech world—to name some of the other people in that photo. The good news was that I happened to be working for just that someone.

Ross Marinetti.

35

THE MAGAZINE AND digital sides of Signal used the same kitchen and bathrooms; but beyond the sharing of urinals and coffeepots, the two divisions barely mixed at all. I'd never ventured beyond the central kitchen, a domain ruled by a tattooed chef who doled out portions of vegetarian chili and eggplant paninis; and featuring a refrigerator of Odwalla juices that you could buy using the two-dollar honor box, but that everyone mostly stole.

Beyond the kitchen, a hallway opened up into another cavernous room that roughly mirrored the size and shape of ours, and yet couldn't have felt more different. Here, on the magazine side, there was no music blasting through the office or inflatable toys hanging from the exposed air ducts. Instead of open-plan chaos, the space was portioned out by a neat maze of cubicles; desks were clutter free, and shades blocked out the glare of the afternoon light. The average age was a decade older, and no one was barefoot—unlike digital, where staffers often didn't bother with shoes, and digging industrial rug staples out of the sole of your foot was a hazard of the job.

I'd heard that this disparity was because Ross had his office on the magazine side, where he kept a tight leash on his orderly, firstborn child. Whereas digital was the precocious bastard that he'd accidentally birthed but didn't know quite what to do with, so he'd abandoned it to the zookeepers on the other side of aisle, hoping for the best.

It was easy enough to find Ross's office: It was the glassed-in box in the corner, with a view that looked down over the entrance of South Park so that he could monitor the steady growth of the neighborhood that everyone had started calling Multimedia Gulch. As I approached,

I could see him through the windows of his office, puzzling over a set of magazine layouts with a red wax pencil.

I stopped at the open doorway and waited for him to notice me standing there. When he didn't, I knocked tentatively on the frame. "Mr. Marinetti?"

"No one calls me that. What's up with the formality?" He didn't even bother to lift his head.

"I was raised to believe that it was a sign of respect, to honor the intellect and experience of my elders."

He frowned, finally looking up at me. "*Elders*. Christ. I'm only forty-two. Let's leave outmoded ways of thinking behind us, shall we?" He put down his pencil on his desk, aligning it carefully with the edge of his layouts. "And who are you?"

"Esme," I said. "I'm a new production assistant over in digital."

"And I'm pretty busy here. Issue closes tomorrow. Did you come by just to introduce yourself or is there a reason for your presence in my office? Because if every new hire over there drops by to say hi, I'm never going to get anything done."

I held out the photograph. "I've been asked to do some research. For a story someone is working on." This was the most plausible cover I'd been able to come up with; it seemed pretty thin, but then again, this *was* a magazine, and it seemed like a task that he'd warm up to. "I need to identify the people in this photo and someone said you might be able to help me. They said you know everyone in tech."

He unleashed a tight, bemused smile, seemingly less for my sake and more as if he'd just remembered an inside joke. He put a hand out for the photo, and I gingerly placed it between his fingers. The smile vanished the minute he gazed down at the snapshot. "Oh. That's Peter." He looked up at me sharply. "Is digital working on a story about his murder? I heard the same guy might have killed someone else yesterday, is that right? I've been too busy closing the issue to turn on the news."

"I don't know," I said, hedging. "I'm just helping assemble some biographical details. Where he worked before Microsoft, for example."

He squinted at the photo. "Well, I'm going to guess this is Peninsula Research Institute."

"What's that?"

"A nonprofit that does scientific R & D. Computing, environmental technology, biomedicine, nanotech, space travel, all kinds of future-forward stuff. A lot of their research goes to the government, some gets sold to commercial businesses and foundations. Peter worked there all throughout the seventies and eighties, researching neural networks, developing the AI algorithm that he ended up taking to Microsoft. Died before he finished it, though. What a goddamn travesty. That was going to be the future, right there."

I nodded, remembering my father's words. *The future of computers. What they might be used for.* So this was what he was talking about. "Do you recognize anyone else in this photo?"

Ross peered at the photo again, running a hand through his floppy hair. "Hard to tell, this photo has to be fifteen, twenty years old, right? And I don't know *everyone,* despite what you might have heard. A few look familiar, though, I think one of them's that VC guy, I forget his name." Then he stabbed a finger toward a man on the edge of the group, a skinny man with shaggy brown hair that didn't quite conceal his ears, which stuck out like jug handles from the sides of his head. "OK, this one definitely has to be Nicholas Redkin. Those ears haven't changed a bit. He went bald, though. Gained a lot of weight, too."

"Nicholas Redkin. Who is he?"

He gave me a slightly withering look. "He was on the cover of issue 3.2. Founded the e-commerce site Kaboom, he's one of the first true innovators of the new Web economy. You don't read our magazine?"

"Kaboom. Is it based in San Francisco, too?"

He sighed as he handed the photograph back to me. "Three blocks over. Why don't you do your own homework? That's why we invented the internet, so the information would all be there and free and no one would have to bother me with silly questions."

I was pretty sure that Ross hadn't invented the internet, any more than my dad had, but I let him lay claim to it anyway. "Yes sir." He rolled his eyes at this, as I tucked the photograph in my pocket and backed, slowly, out of the office.

HAPPY HOUR BEGAN early on Fridays. The work itself didn't stop midafternoon; it was just that the staffers started drinking at their desks—first surreptitiously, and then brazenly—and no one bothered to stop them. Six-packs of beer and bottles of tequila materialized out of drawers, and a coalition of potheads made their way to the roof, returning with red-rimmed eyes and a wildly inflated sense of humor. Often, Monday mornings were spent surreptitiously undoing the coding that happened on Friday evenings, after shots and joints were consumed. It was just part of the routine.

When I got back to my desk after visiting Ross, still giddy with excitement about my new lead, I found Brianna sipping from one of the dusty bottles of Zima that had been abandoned in the bunk room. "I didn't know people actually drank that," I said.

She grimaced. "We're out of everything else and no one felt like going on a booze run. Want to try one? They're actually not terrible if you close your eyes." She pushed one toward me.

My father never kept alcohol in the cabin, so I had no comparison point. But I thought it didn't taste bad at all; in fact, it was rather pleasantly sweet and malty, despite the chemical tang and the hint of artificial lemon. And so I drank it quickly, enjoying the way the bubbles fizzed at my nose, enjoying even more the way it made my brain fizz. And when it was gone, and Brianna silently pushed another one toward me, I drank that one, too. I silently toasted Ross, who really did seem to know everyone, and who just had slid me one square closer to finding my mother.

By the time Lionel wandered over to where we were sitting, it was dark and much of the staff had departed for other adventures; the ones that remained were playing basketball with a trash can and someone's collection of Beanie Babies. I was supposed to be proofing the HTML of a new batch of stories—an interview with Neal Stephenson, an article about a feud between two hackers—but the Zima had left me feeling loose and floppy, and I kept forgetting to close my tags.

Lionel and Brianna were conferring, and I was drinking yet another Zima, and then somehow a collective decision had been made by the basketball crew that we all needed to pile into the van belonging to Janus, the redheaded news editor, and drive out to Baker Beach, where there was a Full Moon dance party happening. And so I found myself shoved in the back of a VW that was normally used to transport Janus's bass cello to his string quartet performances, sharing a square of Astroturf with two girls from the art department named Amy and Jamie. And we were talking about . . . I honestly couldn't tell you what we were talking about. It was nothing important at all— maybe it was office gossip, maybe it was something we'd all watched on television that week—but the point was that I felt for the first time like I fit in easily with them all. Like I'd finally achieved some semblance of normalcy, despite myself.

The van deposited us on a beach that was freezing cold and very dark, and we followed the muffled throb of a bass line that sounded like it had been trapped inside the fog that pressed down from above. A few hundred people had gathered at the far end of the cove, in front of a DJ table and a stack of speakers and a strobe that illuminated intermittent snapshots of the shoreline. The Golden Gate Bridge loomed overhead, a copper-hued sentinel piercing the cloud cover.

Lionel and Brianna flanked me as we picked our way across the sand, and Brianna leaned across me to talk to Lionel. "I have some E. Would it be considered child endangerment if I gave Esme some?"

"I dunno. Do you think she would like it?" The strobe flashed white in Lionel's glasses.

"*Everyone* likes it. I'm asking: Is she ready for it, you think? Our country girl."

"We don't want to overload her. We don't want her to go all *Go Ask Alice* on us."

"Hey. I'm standing right here, you two. And I'm a legal adult and perfectly capable of making my own decisions; and I don't need to ask

Alice, whoever she is, what I can do." I had only the dimmest grasp on what was being debated—wasn't there a *Beverly Hills, 90210* episode I'd watched about club drugs? I seemed to remember things hadn't ended well, that police raided the party and people had to flee; I *really* didn't want to think too much about that part of it—and I also knew that my father would be horrified by this entire scenario. *Narcotics are just another tool of institutional oppression, blunting the minds of the common man rather than freeing them, turning them into addicts who are incapable of intellectual autonomy.*

But I was Esme Nowak now, not Jane Williams. And Esme wanted to be part of everything in this new life; she didn't want to have to think so hard all the time; she didn't want to worry about what her father would say or the consequences of every action. After a life of having nothing and doing nothing, she wanted to have and do it all. She wanted to just say *yes*.

Yes yes yes.

And so I said *yes* to the little white capsule that Brianna handed me. And then, when something warm began to build inside me just a short time later—a crescendo of elation that felt like a volcano erupting inside my heart—I said *yes* to dancing on the sand. And when I said *yes* to that, I discovered that I could actually dance—me, who had never been on a dance floor before, who had always been embarrassed not to know how my feet were supposed to move or what I was supposed to do with my hands, out there stomping to the beat. And maybe I wasn't a particularly good dancer, but I was surrounded by my new Signal friends who all looked just as blissfully uncoordinated as I felt and so we were all *yes* together. *Yes* to the hammer of the bass line and *yes* to the lift of the chords and *yes* to the peak and the drop, over and over again, a tension and release so exquisite it almost hurt.

And sometime after the full moon revealed itself from behind the parting clouds, and everyone cheered in unison—*yes!*—I turned to find Lionel beside me. His pale face was like a reflection of the moon above us, his hair falling in damp hanks, his tie undone and wrapped around his forehead like a sweatband. He'd shoved his glasses in his pocket, and with his eyes closed he looked like he'd found his own personal oblivion. But then he opened his eyes and saw me, and he leaned in and said something. I couldn't hear him so he shouted it again, his mouth so close to my face that I could feel the heat of his breath in my ear: "You look happy."

"I am. I think I figured out how to find my mother. I found someone who can help tell me who she is."

His face was pure empathic joy. "That's so *fantastic*, Esme."

And so I pushed my own mouth close to his ear and shouted back. "You look happy, too."

"Life is *amazing*. Right? It's easy to forget it, but then you have these moments that remind you how incredible it is that we even fucking exist. The rest of it—all the crap we worry about, the cerebral contortions we go through to try to make meaning of existence—is nothing at all compared to the miracle that we can do *this*. Just being together with other human beings. Dancing. *Alive*."

"*Yes*," I said, because what else was there to say?

And then he was smiling at me and I was smiling back at him, and we were dancing together with our hands entwined, sparks lighting up in every nerve, and he was leaning in, and then we were kissing and I was saying *yes* to that, too. *Yes yes* a million times *yes*.

THE NIGHT VANISHED. I remember it only as fragments now, emotional impressions like the flash of that strobe. Kissing Lionel on the sand; and then sitting on the edge of the beach by a bonfire someone had started, still kissing with swollen lips but also talking about *feelings;* and later yet, piling in a heap on the sand with the rest of our Signal friends. I remember Brianna kissing a strange girl—a sight I'd never seen before, and it seemed amazingly normal—and Art Department Amy massaging my scalp, and the taste of the watermelon lollipop someone stuck in my mouth. I remember Janus pontificating earnestly about the concept of karma, arguing that perfect nights like this were a cosmic reward for all of our previous good deeds.

And I remember wondering what good deeds *I'd* done; and realizing, with the thunderbolt clarity of intoxication, that I'd sidestepped the most important good deed of all, and that if I wanted my karma to remain balanced I needed to turn in my father. And then—earnestly, so earnestly—promising myself that I would make that call to the FBI tip line, I *would*, just so I could have more nights like this, with these wonderful people, the best ones I'd ever known. Whatever happened after that would be fine, it would all be fine, *yes yes yes*.

And then light was dawning in the east and suddenly we could see the other people out there on the beach with us, sandy and sweat-stricken, their baggy jeans puddling around their legs, their jaws chewing at the air, eyes like pinpricks. Beautiful zombies.

And I gazed over my new life and felt like an overripe fruit, about to burst out of my skin. This was a happiness I'd never experienced before. Joy is always sweetest when loss lurks just below it. Like that orchestra on the *Titanic*, playing their final arrangements while knowing that everything would be gone by daylight. You fiddle as hard as you can, close your eyes to what's to come, obliterate yourself in *now* because it may be all you ever have.

Even then, I must have known that the new world I had found wouldn't last forever, but in that moment, I deluded myself into believing that it could.

36

I slept off my very first hangover on Lionel's futon bed, the two of us curled like spoons. The dust in his crocheted blanket made me sneeze. When I woke up, the afternoon had already tiptoed away and evening was settling into its place. Every part of my body felt like it had been put through a blender and rearranged in an alarmingly unfamiliar way.

Lionel was propped up on his elbow, looking at me. When I smiled at him, he turned a guilty pink.

"Were you watching me sleep?"

"I was afraid if I moved I'd wake you up." He touched a finger to the part in my hair. "You dye your hair? You're actually blond?"

Suddenly wide-awake, I put my palm over my head, although it was too late to conceal the fact that I had waited too long to touch up my roots. A lazy mistake. "No one takes blondes seriously."

"Oh. Well, I guess you do seem more like a brunette to me." He sat up and stretched. "You hungry?"

"I don't know if I can eat anything. My mouth feels like I chewed on walnut shells."

"Same. We could walk down to the store and get ice cream?"

I didn't really want to get out of his bed. I wanted to kiss him again and see what that felt like when I was sober, but I'd lost my grasp on the previous night's boldness. In the thinning light, I was crushingly insecure: What if he thought the whole interlude had been a regrettable mistake? I had no experience whatsoever in reading body language. And so, reluctantly, I crawled out from under the blanket and grabbed my sweatshirt. The fabric smelled like bonfire and had stains across the front that looked suspiciously like spilled Zima. I studied it with dismay.

"Here, you can wear this, it's clean." He handed me a scarlet hoodie with *Stanford* across the chest. When I pulled it over my head, it smelled like him—faintly spicy, almost cinnamon—even though I'd never seen him in it. He was wearing his plaid pajama pants and a pilled gray sweater, and without his usual uniform of shirt and tie he looked so much more vulnerable to me.

Together we walked into the evening, hollowed out and shy. The closest market was six blocks away and we walked in near silence, our bodies bumping against each other occasionally, unsure how much space we were supposed to be sharing. When a bus pulled up to the curb next to me, a little too close for comfort, Lionel grabbed my hand and tugged me back. After the bus passed, he didn't let go.

"Can I ask you a question?" I asked.

"I have a feeling you're going to ask anyway, so go for it."

"Have you ever had a girlfriend?"

"Not really," he said. Then he seemed to reconsider. "Sorry, let me amend that. The answer is no. No I have not."

He didn't ask me the reciprocal question, but I assumed that was because the answer was already obvious. I gripped his hand back and we continued to walk in silence.

"Brianna invited everyone over on Monday to watch the Signal docuseries. It's airing on TV," Lionel finally said.

"Are you going to go?"

"I guess so, though I don't have high hopes. They treated us like a bunch of circus freaks. I don't think they understood the fundamentally flipped nature of this whole medium."

"What do you mean?"

"That online, the misfits *are* the cool kids."

I squeezed his hand, warm against my palm. "Hey, speak for yourself, misfit."

"I mean, look at us, and our freakish childhoods. Brianna, a lesbian growing up in conservative Tennessee? Janus, a kid prodigy at the stand-up bass who spent his childhood being dragged around to international competitions? And me, an obese sixteeen-year-old college student at Stanford. And you, homeschooled out in the woods of Montana. That applies to most everyone who works at Signal: We all grew up weird in some way, the kids who stood on the edges of things and just watched the other people who seemed to have life all figured out. And then the internet comes along, and it's for *us*—the freaks, not the normals; the kids who got into computers because we had nothing else to hang on to—and we are suddenly the ones in charge. It's our world. Our rules. We get to build it the way we want it to be. And it's going to be so, so much better than the way the rest of the world is. We're going to create utopia for people like us."

This was the longest string of words I'd ever heard him say. His speech made me feel strange and teary. "I thought you weren't an optimist."

He shrugged. "Maybe it's still the Ecstasy talking."

"Well, you should have said all these things to the documentary team."

He shook his head. "They still wouldn't get it."

And they wouldn't; nobody outside our bubble ever really would. And by the time they did, that moment in time would have passed entirely. We had no idea, Lionel and I, how fast everything was about to be wrenched from our grasp. How naïve we were, to believe that we could build the world's coolest toy and keep it all for ourselves. We should have known that the playground bullies—the alpha dogs and the mean girls—would come sniffing around and claim it for themselves. That they would see the ugly potential within our utopia, and exploit that in ways we hadn't imagined. That for every nerd victory—the online communities for lonely LGBTQ kids, the social media networks that fueled the Arab Spring, the fringe artists finally able to connect with an audience—there would be a far greater number of tech bros undermining everything we loved in their pursuit of a unicorn IPO. Art and movies and music, small businesses and local bookstores, courteous civil discourse itself. All would be eroded until they were shells of what they'd been.

But that was still decades away.

At the store we bought two pints of Ben & Jerry's and a quart of lime Gatorade, and then turned to head back up the hill. As we walked, we passed a juice bar I'd never seen before, a tiny little storefront called Infini-Teas and Elixirs. I stopped abruptly.

"Mind if we go in?"

Lionel looked confused. "You want a smoothie, too?"

"No," I said. "Remember the blue-haired girl who stole my bag on the bus? She said she worked at a juice bar. So I'm going into all the ones I find, to check if she works there."

The juice bar was painted pink and orange, bisected by a shiny white counter where an enormous metal juicer hulked like a piece of industrial machinery. The woman shoving carrots down its maw was definitely not Desi: She had long gray hair and wore a tie-dye shirt, and she was not pleased to discover that we hadn't come in for her juice.

"I'm just wondering if Desi works here," I asked her.

"Desi? Like Desirée?"

"Like Desire."

She brandished a carrot at us. "That's a terrible name."

"Yeah, but does she work here?" Lionel asked.

"She most definitely does not."

"Are you sure?"

"I own this place so I'm pretty sure I'd know."

We bought a carrot-apple-ginger juice as an apology and wandered back up the street toward Lionel's house. The ginger stung my raw tongue, so I threw it away.

"You know, there's a more efficient way to figure out which juice bar Desi works for," Lionel mused. "Get the yellow pages and just *call* them. All of them."

"The yellow pages?"

"The phone book."

"Oh yeah, I know what that is!" It was possible I sounded a little too excited about this. "Should we go look for a pay phone?"

He gave me a funny look. "I have a phone book at home we can use. One gets dumped on our doorstep every year and my roommates use the cover for rolling joints."

We arrived back at Lionel's apartment to find it empty, for once: His roommates had left a note on the kitchen table that read *GONE FOR PIZZA COME IF U WANT.* We did not want. We found the yellow pages under the leather couch and flipped through it as we sucked on spoonfuls of Chunky Monkey. The phone book's cover had mostly been torn off and the pages underneath were peppered with tobacco and splattered salsa, but the Juice Bars section was intact. There were a manageable forty-seven listings, a clutch of which I had already visited in person.

Lionel handed me a cordless phone. "Go for it," he said.

"What should I say? Just ask if she works there?"

He thought about this. "No, ask them what time her shift starts. That'll sound less suspicious, like you already know she's an employee."

I dialed the first listing, Beta Juice. When a man answered I immediately asked, "Hi, I'm checking to see what time Desi's shift starts." I glanced over at Lionel, and he gave me the thumbs-up.

"Sorry, you must have it wrong," the man said. "No one by that name works here."

I hung up and put a line through Beta Juice. "You're right," I said. "A much more time-efficient system than visiting them all in person."

Nineteen listings later, we had ruled out nearly half the juice bars in the city. It occurred to me that it was perfectly possible that Desi had been fired a long time ago and no longer worked at a juice bar at all. After all, she wasn't exactly Employee of the Month material. Or perhaps she'd decided to use her financial windfall to quit working entirely. Perhaps she was now living a life of leisure on my dime.

But call twenty was to a store called The Smoothie Factory. And this time, when I asked my standard question—*what time does Desi's shift start?*—the girl on the other end didn't even hesitate before answering. "She's already here."

My eyes shot to Lionel's. "What time is she off?"

"We close at eight. Hang on, I can get her for you." I heard the sound of the receiver being dropped, a muffled conversation taking place in the background, and then a familiar voice suddenly came on the line. "Yeah, who's this?"

I hung up as fast as I could. I turned to Lionel. "She's there until eight," I said.

He'd been lying prone on the couch, half asleep while I made my calls, but now he was wide-awake again. "Let's go confront her!"

I shook my head. "I know what she's like. She'll lie and pretend she doesn't know what I'm talking about. We need to find out where she lives and somehow get into her apartment and see if she's still got my bag."

"So we watch and follow her after she gets off work," he said.

"Exactly. Like a stakeout." And we smiled at each other like giddy children about to climb on their very first roller coaster, which was when I finally screwed up the courage to kiss him again, and he kissed me back; and it was just as nice as it had been the night before, maybe even better, because I knew it was *him* kissing me this time, and not just the intoxicants.

37

THE SMOOTHIE FACTORY was in a neighborhood of San Francisco I'd never walked through before, an upscale waterfront enclave that Lionel told me was called the Marina. We found the juice bar sandwiched between a beauty supply store and a Mexican restaurant in a busy shopping strip. Lionel had to drive in circles around the block for nearly twenty minutes before a parking spot finally opened up within eyeshot of the store. We parked just minutes before eight o'clock.

It was a Saturday night and so the sidewalks were crowded, the women in heels that made their ankles wobble and the men in variations of the same striped rugby shirt. They milled from bar to restaurant, coats flung open despite the chilly night. I thought of what Lionel had said about misfits. These were not them.

At eight o'clock, the lights inside The Smoothie Factory flickered off. A few minutes later, two women appeared in the doorway. One turned to lock the door behind her. The other scanned the street and then stepped out into the pool of light being cast by a streetlamp.

It was Desi.

She had changed the color of her hair—it was purple now, not blue—and she was wearing an expensive-looking leather motorcycle jacket (a jacket that I suspected *I* had paid for), but other than that she looked exactly the same. Same pink bra, same torn black jeans and tiny little top.

I poked Lionel. "That's her."

He peered over the steering wheel at her. "Oh, so she's a punk?"

"Is that what you call it?"

He threw me a look. "Do they not have punks in Montana, either?"

"Not where I lived."

He shook his head in disbelief. "I guess now we wait and see where she goes."

But where she went was immediately next door, to the Mexican restaurant, where she remained for nearly an hour as we sat in Lionel's car, which still smelled awful. ("I let my sister borrow my car and she spilled a latte in the back seat and didn't tell me and it hasn't been the same since," Lionel explained.) When she finally exited, she was staggering.

"Now she's a drunk punk," I observed.

Lionel's laugh was disarmingly horselike, it convulsed his whole body, which put us in danger of losing track of Desi as she weaved her way down the sidewalk in the opposite direction. I hit his arm. "Drive!"

If Desi had bothered to look behind her as she walked, she would have noticed that a geriatric Volvo was following her as she turned right and then left and suddenly bolted to catch a crosstown Muni bus. She also might have noticed that this very same Volvo was there when she disembarked twenty minutes later, in a neighborhood of shabby apartment buildings just north of Fillmore Street. But presumably she was too inebriated to notice, because when she finally turned to climb the steps of a peeling converted Victorian, she didn't even turn her head to see our car pulling up beside her. Instead, she just staggered her way up the stairs to her door, fumbling her keys out of her pocket.

We caught up with Desi right before the door swung closed behind her, wedging our way into the entrance of her apartment. She turned, swaying in her Doc Martens, and regarded us in the dim light of the hallway. Our presence seemed to register on time delay.

"Oh. Fuck. It's you. Where'd you come from?"

"I want my bag back." The adrenaline had worn off during the drive, and my hangover had returned. My voice sounded like it was coming from somewhere far away.

"I don't know what you're talking about." She looked glassily from me to Lionel. "Who's this? Your boyfriend or something? I thought you said you were here to visit your mom."

"Don't be an asshole, just give it to her," Lionel said. His expression was bright and defiant. I got the distinct impression that he was enjoying playing savior. Standing next to him, his hip just grazing mine, I felt pleasantly inviolable.

"I don't have it anymore." She drew the leather jacket tighter around her.

"Bullshit," Lionel said. "You're lying."

She pivoted to glare at me, almost losing her balance in the process, her eyes struggling to focus. "I'm not the liar, *you* are. You're not a college student, are you? What kind of college student carries around *that* much money? I mean, twenty-three-thousand fucking dollars? What are you, like, a drug dealer or something?"

Lionel froze at this and cast a sideways glance at me; but then he recovered quickly from this momentary hitch and turned and stalked with purpose down the hallway. Desi lived in a railroad apartment that smelled of moldy carpet and stale beer, the hallway littered with unidentifiable flotsam. I followed him, and together we threw open one door and then another as Desi stumbled along behind us mewling protest. Two of the doors revealed her roommates' bedrooms—one occupied by a couple passed out on a bed, naked limbs flung out from under limp sheets, another by a girl in underwear who swore at us when the door was opened—and one was a filthy bathroom, but behind the last door we finally found Desi's bedroom.

A bare mattress sat on the floor surrounded by piles of clothing, like an iceberg drifting among its floes. CD jewel cases were haphazardly stacked against the walls, and an old-fashioned decorative mirror was set up in front of a stool covered with crusty makeup palettes. In the middle of the room, a pyramid of brand-new electronics—a stereo system, a mini fridge, a television—were spilling out of their boxes.

In the middle of this mess, ineffectively concealed behind the mirror—as if Desi had made a half-hearted attempt to hide it before losing interest entirely—sat my duffel bag.

I walked over and unzipped it as she lunged at me from the doorway. Lionel grabbed her arm to stop her, and she swayed in his grip like a broken swing.

"Everything's still there?" Lionel asked.

I riffled through the contents. "I think so," I said. The bag still contained stacks of paper-wrapped bills, though considerably fewer than before. The folder with my father's handwritten pages was still there, too, crumpled at the bottom of the duffel. As for the IBM hard drive, it was sitting right out in the open, next to the bag, and I hastily jammed this back into the duffel as they both watched.

"I was trying to sell that computer thingy on Craigslist," Desi mumbled. "But no one responded to my ad. Maybe I was charging too much."

The triumphant expression on Lionel's face was slowly fading, like a deflating party balloon, as he watched me wrestle with the unwieldy drive. Now he mostly seemed watchful and wary. He edged toward the door. "You got what you need, Esme?"

I hefted the duffel over my shoulder. "Yes. Let's go."

We walked quickly back down the hallway toward the front door, Lionel a few steps in front of me. He seemed distracted, his eyes fixed on the filthy carpet; he didn't even react when Desi let out a wail of frustration behind us.

"Lying bitch! You better watch out!" Desi called, her voice high-pitched and quavering, until we slammed the door behind us and couldn't hear her scream anymore.

Outside on the sidewalk, we paused and looked at each other. The street was dark, the only light coming from an anemic streetlamp a half block away. I couldn't quite see Lionel's face. I stood there with the heavy duffel bag hanging awkwardly from one hand, unsure what to do next.

Lionel had his hands shoved deep in his pockets. When he spoke, his voice was soft and unsure. "Esme? Where did all that money come from? And why are you carrying around a giant hard drive?"

I looked down at the bag, realizing I'd made a critical mistake. I let go of the handle and it fell to the ground with an alarming *thunk.* "It's all my father's. I took it when I left."

"Why?"

I tried to think fast. "I was mad at him." It was technically the truth, I told myself, even if it wasn't the whole story.

"Is there something important on the hard drive?"

"I honestly don't know."

"Oh." I could tell that my answer was unsatisfying. Then, "Is there ... anything that you want to tell me?"

My smile felt unconvincing. "About what?"

"I don't know. It just feels like maybe you haven't told me everything."

There was so much I wanted to tell him. The traces of the MDMA still in my system strained toward radical honesty, a compulsion to tell him all my darkest secrets and have them met and returned with love and understanding. The previous night, when we were still kissing in the dark, it might have been possible. But twenty-four hours later, both of us depleted and sour-stomached—with only the chemical edge of the drug remaining in our bloodstream—I couldn't muster the courage. What would he think of me if he knew who I really was, and what I had done? It wouldn't be good. It wouldn't be good at all.

"You know everything important about me," I said. "Everything that truly matters about who I am. The rest is just autobiography. Details I can fill in as we go."

And then, because it seemed the best way to stop this conversation in its tracks, I wrapped my arms around him, a move that still felt more awkward and contrived than natural to me. But his arms slid around my back, and he pulled me in so that my chest was pressed against his and my face was nestled into the crook of his shoulder. He sighed. "That's cryptic. But OK."

I melted into him with relief, feeling the faint pulse of his heart, his breath in my hair; I was glad I didn't have to look him in the eyes. "You're unlike anyone I've ever met," he said, almost to himself. "It kind of freaks me out."

"You like me," I said into his shirt.

"I do like you."

"I like you, too. And I know that I haven't actually met that many people, so I'm lacking comparison points, but I think that even if I had I would still think you were special."

"Wow, that's a ringing endorsement." But I could hear the smile in his voice. He pulled back and yawned. "Look, let's get out of here before that crazy girl comes outside."

I clutched the duffel bag as we drove back across town, the weight of its secrets heavy in my lap, my head hollowed out with exhaustion. I couldn't help wondering if this was a Pyrrhic victory, whether the retrieval of my bag might have caused more problems than it solved. Lionel was too smart to be satisfied for long by my nonanswers. But there were so many more auspicious things to think about—the fact that I appeared to be in my first relationship, even if I didn't yet understand the rules; the growing proximity of my mother, assuming Nicholas Redkin would be able help me; and, most of all, the return of my father's pages, and the answers they might contain—and so I closed the door to my fears.

Better to believe that luck might last forever; better to hope that I might decide my own fate.

38

BACK AT HOME, I spread the cipher pages across the top of Megan's vanity, my father's smudged and cramped handwriting incongruous against the creamy white paint. When I put my nose close to the paper, I thought I could catch a faint whiff of our cabin, of the woodsmoke that seeped into everything we owned. My ciphering abilities were rusty, at best—translating all these pages was going to take weeks—but it was clear even in the first few laborious minutes that I had no choice in the matter.

I bent my head and went to work.

Jane -

If you are reading this, it means that things have not gone as planned; presumably, I'm no longer with you. As much as it pains me to imagine this being the case, I take some solace in the knowledge that you will be fine on your own. I've been preparing you for this all your life, and I'm sure you're ready. Your intellect and self-sufficiency are a source of great pride for me.

Judging by the questions you've been asking me lately, I've surmised that you suspect that I haven't told you the whole truth about us. These pages are my way of remedying this. I hope that, by reading them, you will be able to step into my shoes and see how and why I made the decisions that I did. And I hope that when we find each other again—and I have faith that we will—we can move forward from a place of mutual understanding.

I have coded these pages with our cipher so that no one but you can read them; when you are done reading, burn them.

The most important thing to know is this: Everything I did was for your sake.

Love,
Your father

*   *   *   *

You grow up in the suburban sprawl of San Lorenzo. Your home, beige stucco, sits in a field of concrete, surrounded by homes so identical that you sometimes can't figure out which one is your own. The garages empty out early in the mornings, as parents commute to their jobs, and fill again after dark; in the hours in between, the streets are empty except for the occasional child on a dirt bike, doing wheelies in the abandoned driveways. Just a few generations back, this land was apricot farms. Now, the only trees visible for miles are the solitary hackberries planted at precise hundred-foot intervals along the main thoroughfares.

The ocean is forty-five minutes away and the forest is ninety; you never visit either.

Your father is a floor manager at a frozen meal factory, in one of the thousands of new postwar industrial buildings that populate the eastern edges of the Bay. His extremities—fingers, nostrils, ears—are blasted by chilblains, and his demeanor is just as cold. Your mother was a secretary, once upon a time, but quit after her diabetes diagnosis. She now spends her days in her room, with the curtains drawn, watching *Guiding Light* and *As the World Turns*. She is like the figurehead on the prow of a ship, a silhouette in bed, divorced from the world that she ostensibly oversees.

You are seven years old when your father decides to teach you how to play baseball. He buys you a glove and takes you out to a field and spends an hour throwing a ball to you. You fail to catch it even once; you flinch when it comes your way; you do not understand the mechanics of the too-big glove that keeps slipping off your hand. After a while you realize that your father is not throwing the ball to you anymore, he is throwing it *at* you, as hard as he can. And when it finally connects with your face, and you start to cry, he walks away in disgust.

After that, you are left to your own devices. You spend most of your time at the library, since your own home doesn't have anything to read besides your mother's old copies of *Reader's Digest*. Besides, at the library you can avoid your father, who has started drinking heavily. When he does, he isn't cold anymore: He is hot and loud and full of disdain, calling you boring and weak, calling your mother pointless and a leech. He doesn't hit you—he mostly hits the walls—but you're still afraid of what he might break.

It is 1962 and you are ten years old when your teachers start to realize that you are not a normal kid. (*Normal* denoting the average intellect at your school, which is populated primarily by Neolithic boys who roll cigarettes in their sleeves and torture frogs for fun.) You score 167 on an IQ test; you win the chess tournament at the San Lorenzo community center, where you are the only person under the age of twenty-six; you read Plato and solve math puzzles for fun.

Your father is summoned to a meeting with the principal—your mother, sickly, won't attend—where it is suggested that you skip ahead a grade or two. Your father resists this idea. "He'll get bullied for being younger than everyone else," he informs the principal, unaware that you are, already, being bullied, not for your age but for your general disdain for the mouth breathers with whom you are forced to share a classroom. They jump you a grade anyway.

Socially ostracized, you soldier through middle school, then high school, and when college applications come around you bypass the practical suggestions of the guidance counselor—inexpensive state colleges an hour or two away, Hayward and Sacramento and San Jose— and apply to every Ivy League you know of. You get into most of them, on the merits of your perfect SAT scores and 4.2 GPA, and choose Harvard, of course.

Your parents did not go to college. They do not understand why you feel compelled to fly across the country to a school where a year's tuition is the equivalent of your father's entire salary. He arrives home drunk after work one night and comes up to your room, where you are studying calculus. His breath in your face smells like gasoline. "Think you're better than me, think that reading books somehow makes you smarter, but let me tell you . . ." He peters out then, coughing bile, unable to finish his thought. His hand, calloused and meaty, waves uselessly in the air, his eyes are damp and red; and you wonder if he planned to hit you.

"I *am* better than you," you reply.

The one thing you can say about your education at Harvard is that it is thorough. You double major in applied mathematics and engineering, and then add one more in philosophy just to prove you can. It is 1969 now and you manage to avoid Vietnam because of your college studies; instead, you somehow find yourself involved in the development of ARPAnet, the Department of Defense–funded computer network protocol that is the genesis of the internet. (No one needs you killing gooks in Southeast Asia when you could be building the future of the military.) You toil in the windowless basement of the engineering department, surrounded by humming computers the size of refrigerators, enormous air conditioners blasting to keep all those electronics from overheating. Your classmates on the project are bespectacled and pocket-protected and cerebral, and you feel like yourself in their company for the first time in your life.

Sometimes, in that freezing basement—a peacoat thrown over your button-down and tie—you think of your father in his fingerless gloves, heading off every morning to his refrigerated warehouse. His cold room, slowly killing him; yours, launching you into the future. You wonder if what you feel for him is pity; but if you are honest, you mostly feel contempt.

Inside that space, you are part of a team of peers, but outside of it you don't fit into Harvard at all. Even with a scholarship, you can't fully cover tuition, and you have to wait tables at one of the final clubs in order to make up the shortfall. You come to loathe the inside of those halls. The future titans of industry with their side-slicked hair and marble-mouth elocution and cashmere sweaters with moth holes, who look straight through you as they demand that you bring them polished cutlery and chilled butter. The objects they claim as their own: So many objects! Tennis rackets and silver cigarette cases and leather valises and tweed sport coats. Varsity rings studded with jewels. Sports cars with removable tops. When you look at them—you, who own almost nothing, you, who know that what is truly valuable is what is between your ears and not what is in your wallet—you see nothing but waste.

Between the hours spent in the claustrophobic computer room and the hours spent in the even more stuffy final club, you start to crave fresh air. And so, in the little free time that you have, you start hiking. First, the trails on the edge of Cambridge, heavily trafficked parks with paved paths; and then, once you buy a thirdhand Ford, the quieter forests farther out of town. A two-hour drive from campus gets you to a swath of old-growth forest, and you are soon intimately familiar with its trails. You befriend a grizzled old conservationist there, and he teaches you basic forestry and survival skills. How to identify plants. How to build a shelter. Which mushrooms make a meal; which will kill you. Something about nature—how untamed and uncontrolled and unpredictable it can be— appeals to you. It's the antidote to the ordered precision of computers, the laddered logic of philosophy. There is no *quod erat demonstrandum* in the woods.

By the time you finish your master's, you have been profiled in *Harvard Magazine* as a pioneer in networked computing; and you also know how to trap and skin a rabbit.

After graduation, you get work as an adjunct professor in mathematics at Boston College, a job you soon discover that you loathe: the laziness of the students, their dulled minds incapable of grasping concepts that you find so obvious, the way they flirt in class instead of paying attention to your lecture. So when your former Harvard classmate reaches out and tells you about an opening at Peninsula Research Institute, you don't hesitate.

Soon, you are back on the West Coast, working in the heart of nascent Silicon Valley.

Your parents are less than an hour away. You do not go to see them. You have failed to impress them, and so you cannot forgive them for being so small. Your mother will die before you turn twenty-four, and you will not go to her funeral.

Peninsula is an enormous research facility, and you find yourself part of a group of researchers who are prognosticating the utility of emerging new technologies. A few miles away, in Menlo Park, the hackers and hobbyists of the Homebrew Computer Club are inventing the new personal computers—including Steve Jobs and Steve Wozniak's Apple's I and II—and so your group is tasked with figuring out what these things will be good for. It is the late seventies, the computers are still massive beasts capable of very little, and yet you are able see where it is all going. You are a firm believer in Moore's Law: the prediction that the number of transistors on a microchip will double and the cost of computers will halve every two years. And so you can see what's coming, sooner than anyone expects: exponential growth of computer power, and an equal reduction in size. Palm-sized computers that will make humans look like morons in comparison.

Your clients are the government, military, big business. You haven't yet learned that these are the very last organizations who should be privy to this kind of power.

You love your job. Your working group comes from all over the States, from different backgrounds, and yet there's an unmistakable mind meld that happens when you are together: as if you yourselves are a networked computer, everyone making their own contribution to the collective wisdom. It's wildly exciting. You are part of the elite, one of the prophets, the tiny fraction of mankind who can see not just what is obvious but what is next. Finally, you are appreciated for being special, in the way you always suspected you were.

You still spend time in the woods when you can, but—consumed by your work—you find yourself doing this less and less. You try to compensate by buying yourself a convertible, so that when you drive to work in the mornings you can smell the trees and feel the wind against your skin. You aren't completely divorced from the natural world—not yet.

And then, a year into your new life in the Bay Area, you meet someone. She is coolly beautiful, utterly composed, with a mind as sharp and brilliant as a diamond. She rarely smiles, but when she does, you fall in love with her instantly.

Her name is Theresa.

39

THERE WAS A picture of my father staring at me when I got to work on Monday morning. Someone had printed out the Bombaster police sketch and pinned it to a dartboard hanging on a wall directly across from my desk. Above his face, the word *BOMBASTARD* was scrawled in thick black Sharpie.

I tried to circumnavigate the group that had congregated by the dartboard, but Janus caught me by my arm, and pulled me over. "Here," he said, and handed me a dart. "Give it a go. George in Engineering is giving a buck to everyone who gets him right between the eyes."

Art Department Amy impaled my father's chin and turned with her fingers parted in victorious *V*'s. "I saw on the news that they're offering a hundred grand reward for information leading to his capture," she said. "I'm sure it's just a matter of time before someone gives him up."

Janus closed one eye and let a dart sail. It hit my father's earlobe and then hung there, like a particularly dangerous earring. "I hope they give that asshole the electric chair."

"The electric chair?" I echoed faintly.

"Lethal injection is fine by me, too." He flung another dart, catching my father dead center in his forehead, and let out a *whoop*.

I stared at my father's portrait, his sunglass lenses peppered with tiny holes. The image looked so little like my father and yet, behind those mirrored lenses, I could still somehow feel his presence. His eyes on me, judging me. His traitorous daughter.

My father had taught me how to throw a hunting knife when I was nine years old. I could knock a chipmunk out of a tree, if I wanted to.

Instead, I flung my dart with a feeble flop of the wrist. It hit the edge of the paper and clattered impotently to the floor as the group around the dartboard groaned in dismay.

"Give it another go?" Janus said, holding out the dart. I shook my head as I made my way to my chair.

I booted up my computer and sat there as the monitor flickered to life, my mood soured. I hadn't considered the fact that my father might be killed if I turned him in. I recalled, queasily, the promise that I'd made to myself in the throes of my Friday night high. If this was what karma was going to demand of me, it didn't seem in the least bit fair. Anyway, what a silly notion—that goodness and virtue would be rewarded by some invisible spirit force? My father would have mocked me for even considering the idea.

I stared at my screen, trying to reconcile the monster in the police sketch with the man in the cipher pages that I'd taken from my father's desk. I'd spent all Sunday parsing my way through my father's coded scribblings, letter by tedious letter, and I'd barely made a dent. The pages were a memoir of some sort, apparently written expressly for me, and I read them with a pit in my stomach. Here, in this strange second-person voice, I found the insights into my father that I'd always craved, the stories he'd avoided telling me. The genesis of his pathologies opened up for me like a flower exposing its stamen, revealing the unloved little boy who would become my father.

I couldn't possibly betray him, not now that I was finally understanding him.

I shifted my chair so that my father's face was no longer in my line of sight.

"I got you a muffin." I looked up and saw Lionel standing at my desk, a paper pastry bag in his hands. His breath was labored, his glasses fogged, as if he'd just run up four flights of stairs.

"Blueberry?"

"I pegged you as a chocolate chip girl. Was I wrong?"

"Not at all."

I took the bag and bit into the muffin. We smiled at each other, in

the awkward way you do when you have too much to say and no particular words to articulate any of it. "Hi," Lionel said softly.

"Hi," I said back, through chocolate teeth.

Brianna, sitting a few feet away from us, lifted her eyes from her
screen. "Lionel, I need Esme to finish some production scheduling for
me so can you please take your puppy dog eyes somewhere else? If you
guys want to moon over each other, do it on your own time."

Lionel turned even redder than he already was. "Sorry. How about
lunch?"

I shook my head. "Not today. I've got an errand to run."

TO GET TO the Kaboom offices, I had to first walk through South
Park, an ovoid patch of lawn where the local tech workers spent their
lunch hours eating burritos and smoking cigarettes by a play structure
that children never seemed to use. On a rare warm day, it was hard to
spot the grass amid the sprawl of pale-faced programmers, who looked
like they'd been bleached by the sun.

Kaboom took up most of a new office tower near the on-ramp to
the Bay Bridge. The lobby was full of amoeba-shaped plastic furniture
that didn't look particularly comfortable. A young male receptionist
was manning the front desk, but since I didn't have an appointment—
and it seemed unlikely that I'd be allowed to meet Nicholas Redkin
without one—I decided that my best bet was to walk right in like I
belonged there. Signal wasn't the only dot-com hiring people faster
than anyone could track.

I cruised left past the receptionist and down the hall, and found
myself in some sort of rec room, with foosball and Ping-Pong tables,
a row of vintage arcade games, and a wall full of candy in glass jars.
The room was mostly empty, except for a group of twenty-somethings
with bleary eyes who were sitting in beanbags in the corner, huddled
over their laptops. None of them were Nicholas Redkin, so I continued on.

I wandered left and right, down one hallway and into a room with
a maze of cubicles; and then down another into another with disori-

entingly identical cubicles. Big neon signs lit up the walls with comic book slogans: *KABOOM!* but also *BLAM!* and *ZONK!* and *POW!* What did Kaboom do? Its website had said something about peer-to-peer e-commerce systems, which meant absolutely nothing to me. But apparently it was quite profitable—or had, at least, generated a lot of investor excitement—because all the furniture was brand-new and there were hundreds of young people spread throughout the halls.

I must have wandered for twenty minutes, growing more and more anxious that someone would notice that I'd been walking circuits around their office. With each lap, the likelihood that I would somehow encounter Nicholas Redkin seemed more remote. Who was to say that he was even in the building?

But then, as I was walking down an otherwise quiet hallway, I ran straight into a jug-eared man in his forties, head shaved to disguise his male-pattern baldness, the tails of his button-down shirt flapping over his belly. He was stabbing at the buttons of the tiny cellphone in his hand, which was probably why he didn't notice me planted like a boulder in his path.

"Mr. Redkin," I blurted. "Can I have a moment of your time?"

He looked up at me and squinted, trying to place me. "Hi, sorry, I'm on my way out to see Marc at Netscape, go talk to Sabine and she can set up a time." He kept walking with a sideways step, trying to edge past me.

I moved again, blocking him. "I just need a minute." I held out the photograph. "This is you, right?"

He glanced down at the photo in my hand, and then came to an abrupt halt. The irritated expression on his face softened into one of surprise. "Jesus. That's a walk down memory lane. Our research group at Peninsula. Where did you get this?"

"I found it," I said. "It's a long story. I'm wondering if you can tell me about someone from this photo."

His eyes were riveted on the image; the phone in his hand, half dialed, hung limply in his grip as he peered down at his own youthful face. "Dead," he said suddenly. "Three of them are dead. Christ, I hadn't put that together. What a tragedy." He put a finger out and put it on my father's picture—it was jarring to me, to see him identified like that—and then Peter's and Baron's. Finally he pulled himself out of his reverie and looked up at me. "Which one do you want to know about?"

"My question isn't actually about anyone in the photo," I said. "I'm wondering if you might have an idea of who *took* the photo?"

He lifted his head and scratched one protruding ear, looking baffled. "How would I know that?"

"Could it have been . . . a woman? Someone's wife?"

His eyes lit up. "Oh. Of course. That's why she's not in the photo with us."

I hesitated. This was not the answer I expected. "She would have been *in* the photo?"

"Of course. She was in our working group at Peninsula, the only woman. She was smarter than any of us. Of course some of the guys still asked her to fetch them coffee, which pissed her off to no end. And look at her now. Officially a *genius,* who else could say that?"

I still hadn't gotten the answer I was looking for. "Is her name . . . Theresa?"

He nodded. "Tess. Tess Trevante."

Tess. I hadn't considered nicknames. "Trevante? Not Nowak?"

"Both. She remarried a few years after Adam died, now she's Trevante."

This name—*Trevante*—ricocheted through my mind in a strangely familiar way, and then I remembered: the missing blue house in Atherton, the modern monstrosity about to be built in its place. The dog walker had insisted the home belonged to the Trevantes.

My mother had kept the property where I'd been born. She hadn't given up on my return. I'd been right all along.

Nicholas Redkin was still staring down at the photo, a wistful look in his eyes. I now had the information I needed, but I couldn't resist the impulse to press my luck. "How did Adam die?"

"A car accident. Their kid died, too. Car went off a cliff into the ocean. It was awful." The green neon sign in the hallway—*KAPOW!*—was flickering, giving his face a ghoulish cast. "We always thought . . ."

A blade inside me twisted. "Thought what?"

"That it was probably suicide. They'd been fighting quite a bit. Adam had been acting unstable, had just quit his job at Peninsula and was talking absolute nonsense about the end of the world. We were all worried about him. There were rumors, too, about her and . . ." He shook his head. "So the way the accident happened, convertible top down and no seatbelts, at *night* for God's sake, almost like he didn't want his body to be found, like he was sparing Tess something, you know?" He swallowed. "But the kid . . . I mean. He adored that little girl. So it's hard to wrap your head around."

"What did Tess say about it?" Had she held out hope that I was still alive? Did she miss me? Did she keep me front of mind, even now? These were the questions I wanted to ask, but didn't know how.

"Nothing." A noisy cluster of twenty-somethings pushed past us in the hallway, but Redkin was still caught up in his memories and didn't register their presence. "She never talked about them again. She quit Peninsula and went to work for the MIT Media Lab in Boston and was gone for years. Like she'd shut the door on that chapter of her life and was moving on. But that was always just how she was. If you knew her, you'd understand."

My heart sank. "So she's on the East Coast?"

"She goes back and forth these days, not sure where she is at this exact moment. We haven't really stayed in touch. But she's easy enough to find online. You don't know who she is?" He looked at me quizzically, finally remembering that he was talking to a stranger. "These are some very specific questions you're asking, young lady. What was your name again?"

I shook my head, realizing that I couldn't give him either of my names—Jane Williams or Esme Nowak—without potentially getting myself in trouble. I began slowly backing down the hallway. "I'm sorry to interrupt you," I said.

"Wait." He was staring at me now, hard, squinting as if he was trying to identify something in my features. "You look familiar. Do I know you?"

"I don't think so." A flicker of panic—was it possible he recognized me from the news? I ducked my head, let my hair swing over my face.

"Do you work here?" He turned to a woman who was walking past us. "Do you know this girl? Does she work here?" The woman glanced at me and shrugged, continuing on.

But I was already halfway down the hall by then. It wasn't until I got to the doorway that I remembered the other part of my agenda. I turned around, to see him watching me with a strange expression on his face, the phone still sagging, forgotten, in his slack hand. "Peter and Baron were both murdered," I said. "Did it occur to you that maybe you should be watching out, too? Maybe you should be careful for a while. Don't open any packages."

He stared at me, his mouth slightly agape, and I wondered how someone presumably so smart could have missed what felt to me to be so obvious.

"Who *are* you?" he asked once more, and now there was menace in his voice.

"No one," I said, and fled.

40

IN THE END, it was remarkably simple to find my mother once I knew her current name. Back at my desk, I typed it into AltaVista with jittery fingers—*Tess Trevante*—and this time a flood of results came back.

> *Futurist Tess Trevante interviewed by* The Economist.
> Yale Daily News *profile of alumna Tess Trevante.*
> *Tess Trevante to be guest speaker at the Commonwealth Club.*
> *"We are all cyborgs," says author Tess Trevante.*

She had a Web page of course, with her very own domain name: http://www.tesstrevante.com. When I clicked on it, her photo filled my screen. It was an artsy black-and-white portrait, like something you'd find on the back cover of a fat autobiography. She wore a black turtleneck under a blazer and she had one hand pressed up against her cheek as she gazed intently at the camera, really considering the person who might be looking back at her. Her blond hair didn't resemble the long waves from my childhood snapshot, nor the eighties coif from the *I Hate Mondays* photo. Now it was short and slick, cut tight to her head like armor, its blond threaded with defiant silver.

She'd been there all along, my mother, just a click away, if I'd only known how to search for her.

Sometimes I wonder what would have happened if I'd waited a year or two before starting my journey. In 1997, the internet was still a present-tense medium: Information was wide but not deep, going back only a few years in history, as if nothing had existed before the world started to go online in the mid-nineties. Within a few years, though—as archives and databases everywhere were digitized and up-loaded and made searchable—it would have taken only a few clicks to connect the Theresa Nowak of a tragic accident in 1983 to the Tess Trevante of current internet fame.

How much trauma would I have saved myself if, during my very first search in my father's desk, I'd been able to identify my mother and her current location? If I had discovered my father's deception and confronted him; if I had fled months earlier? Certainly I would have avoided my own involvement in my father's first crime. But could I have stopped the Bombaster altogether? Would my departure have disrupted his agenda entirely?

But speculation is a fool's game, like pressing on a bruise to see if it still hurts. Imagining how things might have been, had you made a different chess move, simply perpetuates the pain of how things actu-ally *are*. Better to move on and accept the inevitable now.

After staring at my mother's photo for a long time, I scrolled down to read her bio.

Tess Trevante is a world-renowned sociologist, computer scientist, and the author of CodeBrain *and* Digital Selves 1.0: How to Exist in the New Computer Age. *A faculty member of the MIT Media Lab, founder of the Transhumanist Project, and a recipient of the MacArthur Fellowship "genius grant," she is one of the first futurists to explore how emerging tech-nology is changing human potential, and how new social movements will be unlocked by the embrace of our digital future.*

So. It was true. My mother wasn't a kindergarten teacher who my father had met at a restaurant. She was my father's peer. She'd come out of the same world as him but had apparently not turned her back on it. I recalled, now, the conversation we had when my father first came home with the modem, when he explained to me why he'd left the tech industry. *And my mother, did she feel that way, too? Was she . . . one of the good guys?* I'd asked him. Only now did I realize that he never actually answered my question.

Only now did I wonder who the "good guys" actually were.

I clicked on every link on that website. I skimmed a scholarly article she'd written for the *American Sociological Review* and an interview with CNET and even an essay she'd contributed to Signal, but the words blew right through me because what she *thought* wasn't nearly as interesting to me as who she *was*. I hunted for any tiny detail that might reveal the person my mother had become: What did she like? Did she have a family? How did she live? What did she do for fun?

Did she ever talk about *me*?

But there was nothing. Her website was strictly professional, and the interviews with her never delved into her personal life at all, just her ideas—a motley collection of science fiction statements like *we have no choice but to embrace our machine future* and *human potential is about to be fully unleashed thanks to digital enhancement*. The only telling personal detail I could glean came from a line at the end of a profile in *The New York Times*: *Tess Trevante is married to the investment banker Frederick Trevante, and splits her time between Silicon Valley and Boston*.

That was it. No mention of children, past or present; no mention of a former husband; no mention of the tragedy that must have reshaped her entire life, fourteen years earlier.

"Tess Trevante?" I jolted, realizing that Brianna was standing behind me. "She's an icon. A pioneer. One of the first respected female thinkers in this stupidly sexist industry. I went into tech because of her. I read her first book, *CodeBrain*, when I was in college, and it changed my life. Convinced me to major in computer science."

It pleased me to hear my mother spoken of like this. *My* mother, an icon and a pioneer and a genius? "Do you know her?"

Brianna laughed. "Hardly. She came through here last year, gave one of the futurist lectures, all about how computers are evolving the human brain. I introduced myself afterward and told her how much she inspired me. I wanted to interview her for *Floozy*, but I think the name of the site put her off because she said she was too busy. I guess it's not surprising that she had more important things to do than chitchat with some nobody zine editor."

"I want to meet her," I blurted. "Do you know how I'd do that?"

Brianna pointed to a link on the top corner of my mother's website. *BOOK TOUR SCHEDULE OF EVENTS*, it read.

"Seems like you could start there," she said.

MY MOTHER HAD embarked on an eighteen-city tour for her new book, *Digital Selves 1.0*. According to her events page, she was currently on the East Coast, but in just seven days, she would be back in the Bay Area, reading from her new book at Kepler's in Menlo Park. *An Intimate Evening with Tess Trevante,* the bookstore's website promised. *Come meet this compelling tech guru.*

I would, I told myself, my throat growing tight, my chest cavity aflutter with flowers and butterflies. In just one week I would finally meet her. I would I would I would.

I looked up from my computer and found myself staring at my father's image on the wall just across from me, the feathered dart still dangling from one ear. *BOMBASTARD*. Behind those mirrored sunglasses, I could have sworn he was smirking at me. Like he knew something that I didn't yet.

Like he knew something that I was about to learn, the hard way.

I stood and walked over to the dartboard. Quickly, furtively, I tugged the mangled portrait from the wall. I folded it into quarters and shoved it into the pocket of my jeans, hoping that no one had noticed me doing it.

But when I turned around, and my eyes naturally drifted over to the same spot they had gravitated to all day, I found someone looking straight back. Lionel was peering over his monitor at me, his face a mask of confused consternation, the smile slowly fading from his lips.

41

The CBS DOCUSERIES about Signal aired that night, and I decided to take Brianna up on her invitation to watch it at her apartment in Hayes Valley. Communal television viewing: This was new to me. I still thought of television as a furtive thing, a guilty pleasure to be consumed in secret, where no one could see your brain cells winking out, one by one, like dying stars. A television-watching party sounded like an exercise in collective obsolescence.

Of course I said I'd come.

Brianna had put out a plate of fancy French cheese and miniature hot dogs wrapped in pastry and bottles of sour wine that made everyone's tongues turn purple. At least a dozen of my coworkers were crammed into her tiny apartment, getting increasingly drunk as they waited for the 10:00 P.M. hour to roll around.

The show was about to start when Lionel finally arrived; and it wasn't until I saw him in the doorway and felt that little kick in my chest, that I understood this was the real reason I'd said yes to Brianna's invitation. I needed to do damage control. He'd avoided me all afternoon, ever since he caught me tearing down my father's portrait: Barely leaving his workstation, plugged into his headphones, his hands flying over his keyboard. His hunched form a warning to me not to approach.

At one point, Janus had wandered past my desk and noticed me staring across the room at Lionel. "Just go talk to him," he offered.

"I'm not sure he wants me to," I said.

"Really? Well, it's possible his circuits got a bit overloaded on Friday night. It happens," he whispered, patting my back. "But don't worry. He's not exactly a player, if you know what I mean."

"A player? Like, chess player?"

He laughed. "Sure, chess, that's kind of an apt metaphor. My point is, don't take it personally if he's acting hot and cold. I'm sure he'll come around."

But I *did* take it personally. I knew it was personal. That I'd revealed something about myself that I hadn't intended. I'd told myself that I'd go talk to Lionel again before the end of the day, just to feel things out; but then he left work early, before I could muster up the nerve to do it.

It didn't escape me that he hadn't stopped by my desk to say good-bye.

As the credits began to roll, Lionel settled in near the door, as far as humanly possible from where I sat wedged into a corner of Brianna's corduroy couch. I felt his presence like a magnet, pulling my attention from what was happening on the screen. Around me, my coworkers were shouting at Brianna's television, cheering so loudly whenever one of us showed up on camera that it was hard to take in what the newscasters were actually saying. *This new media Mecca is ground zero for . . .* and a shout as Janus walked past the camera . . . *industry growing at a breakneck pace despite a lack of business model . . .* and more cheers at the sight of Brianna drinking a mango Odwalla . . . *these modern Bohemians see themselves as artists with the capability of changing the entire direction of modern society . . .* and groans as Frank appeared on the screen, bags under his eyes . . . *despite doubts about the longevity of this still-fringe cyberspace medium . . .* and shrieks as the camera pulled wide to show the entire staff, sitting raptly in chairs listening to Ross talk . . . *many still believe is just a fad.*

Everyone was so animated, the atmosphere in the room so manic, that it was easy to keep sneaking glances at Lionel, who didn't seem nearly as amused as everyone else to see himself on TV. He sat with his hands shoved in the pockets of his khakis, his tie a little too tight, looking glum.

And then suddenly there was an elbow in my side and I was jolted back to the television set, where my own face filled the screen. The futurist lecture, of course. I was standing and applauding at Ross's speech, clapping my hands like my very life depended on it. How had the camera gotten so close to me? You could see every pore of my skin, the tears that sprang to my eyes as I cheered, my wonky upper incisors (my father had, unsurprisingly, neglected my dental work) as I cupped my hands around my mouth and let out a shriek.

. . . A movement of idealistic youth, many still in their teens, which begs the question, who is really in charge here, and do we need to be concerned?

My face was still frozen on the screen as the end credits began to scroll, as if the producers wanted to make extra sure that I'd been captured on film. I tried to keep my smile steady as my coworkers patted my back in congratulations. "Esme Nowak, the face of idealistic youth," Brianna said, laughing, and handed me a glass of wine, which I drank quickly, to take the edge off my sudden panic. What a nincompoop I'd been not to call in sick as soon as I'd heard a camera crew was going to be in the office. My new haircut wouldn't fool anyone who knew me back in Bozeman. I might as well have sent a map of my current whereabouts to the police.

I tried to reassure myself that the police didn't really know what I looked like; nor would they ever imagine finding me at Signal, the belly of the beast. And the handful of people back in Montana who did actually know me—Heidi and Lina, our curmudgeonly neighbor Shirley, maybe the cashiers at the Seed & Feed and the Salvation Army?—were unlikely to be watching a late-night docuseries about technology start-ups. Who else would possibly recognize me like this, out of context and with a whole new look?

And yet, when I glanced once more across the room at Lionel, I saw him gazing straight back at me. He quickly looked away, but not before I had time to register the curious expression on his face. It looked distressingly like concern.

As the party began to disband, I unfolded myself from the couch and tripped my way across the room, grabbing Lionel's sleeve just as he was about to slip out the front door.

"I found my mother," I told him. "I went to see Nicholas Redkin at lunch today and he told me her name. It's Tess Trevante. She *did* live in that house we went to! She's an author and a tech guru and I'm going to go to her reading on Monday and introduce myself."

His eyes fired up for a second, and then died just as fast, a spark flaming out. "I know who Tess Trevante is," he said. "That's great. I'm happy for you." He didn't sound happy at all.

A weighted silence fell like a veil between us. "Why are you acting so weird?" I finally asked.

"I'm not acting weird." His eyes, lowered, darted left and right, as if he were trying to pinpoint the location of an object he'd dropped. When they finally lifted to mine, I could see that there was something in them that I hadn't ever seen before: a storm cloud, gray and opaque and full of sorrow. I wanted to be angry with him, but instead I felt like crying.

"I may be naïve, but I'm not stupid. You're upset about something."

He fixed his gaze on his sneakers, which were so white it looked like he had cleaned them with a toothbrush. "I guess I'm just processing everything from the weekend."

"Is this because you regret what happened? With me?"

Pain pinched his brow. His voice was low. "No, that's not it."

"OK, then what?" I threw up my hands. "And don't tell me that I'm just being paranoid. Because I lived with a paranoiac my entire life and I know that what I'm feeling here is justified. You're upset, for some reason that you won't tell me."

At the mention of my father, Lionel's face had sharpened, and his gaze shifted even farther away. "I don't really want to talk about it here," he said.

I reached for the door handle. "Then let's go sit in the park."

He glanced at Brianna's window, rattling in its casement from the wind. "It's late. It's cold."

"You'll survive," I said.

Brianna's apartment was a few blocks away from Alamo Square, a pristine green hill with postcard views of the city and a bustling population of dog walkers and heroin addicts. Lionel and I headed there in silence, our hands shoved deep in our pockets, collars turned up against the night.

At that hour the park was empty, except for a group of teens drinking beer under a towering stand of Monterey cypress and a solitary man walking his geriatric dachshund in circles, urging him to pee. A picnic table sat at the crest of the hill, positioned for optimal views. We sat on top of this, legs dangling over the side, looking down past the candy-box Victorians to the glittering city skyline beyond.

The fog was blowing in from the west, wrapping me in cold tendrils. Our breath formed clouds in the dark. Going by thermometer alone, the weather in San Francisco was warmer than in Montana; and yet I felt the cold here in a way I never had back home. It was a creeping damp that pressed through my clothes, penetrated deep into my skin; the kind of cold that made you feel like you might never be warm again.

I waited for Lionel to speak but he just sat glumly next to me, looking out at the city lights.

"So?"

He opened his mouth, and then closed it again. Finally, he said. "I don't really want to talk about this because verbalizing it will make it real and until then, it could just be *me* who is being paranoid. And I'd much rather have it be that than what I think it is."

"You're not making any sense," I protested. Inside my sweatshirt my heart was beating twice as fast, my armpits sticky and damp. "Just tell me what's going on."

"Don't make me say it," he said.

I could have walked away then. He was warning me. He wanted to not know, to be permitted his ignorance, in order to blindly salvage whatever vestiges of our relationship he could. But I just couldn't let him do it. After working so hard to shed *Jane Williams*—after so many weeks of wearing this strange new skin—I found myself suddenly missing Jane despite myself. I wanted to be seen by someone: not just as Esme, this freshly birthed stranger, but as *all* of the different versions of me, with all the confusing contradictions that would entail. Maybe he could tell me who I actually was now.

I was tired of being alone.

"Just say it," I said. My body drooped with fatigue.

In the silence that followed, I could hear the low moan of a foghorn in the distance, the hiss of car tires on damp pavement. I waited, as he seemed to be trying to formulate words, until finally he just spat it out, like a cat regurgitating a hair ball.

"You're the Bombaster's daughter."

He looked at me then, and even in the dark I could see the anguish in his eyes, and the tiny flash of hope that I might somehow still convince him that he was wrong.

And the strange thing is that instead of feeling panicked that I'd finally been discovered, I felt a painful sort of release. Because whatever happened next, *this* was always going to be the worst part. Going to jail wasn't going to feel as viscerally awful as knowing I'd blown up the only important relationship I had in San Francisco, just by virtue of being me.

"Are you going to turn me in?" My voice sounded very, very small.

He flinched. "You really think I'm an asshole?"

My arms were wrapped painfully tight around my waist—for warmth, but also because I suspected that if I let go of myself, I might fly into a thousand fragments that I would never be able to reassemble again. "Was it because you saw me tearing down his portrait?" I asked.

He kicked his sneaker nervously against the leg of the table, a dull repetitive thump that vibrated straight through my bones. "Yes. No. I guess I've been wondering for a while. That first day at my house, when you had such a defensive reaction to *The Luddite Manifesto*—it kind of stayed with me. And over time I began to piece things together—that you were from Montana, that you'd grown up in a cabin in the woods, just like the people in the news. The way you didn't want to talk to the police, even if it was going to be the easiest way to find your mom. And your weird father, of course. The things you told me he said—the way *you* talk, sometimes—it just sounded so much like the manifesto. But still I thought, *OK, maybe it's just a coincidence. Maybe that's just what people are like in Montana.* I just couldn't square the whole Microsoft bombing story with *you,* as a person. And you didn't look anything like the blond girl in that police sketch. Plus the second bomb went off after you were already working at Signal, so I figured, I had to be wrong." *Thump. Thump.* "But it wasn't until we went to Desi's house and I saw what was in that bag that it became really clear that you'd been keeping a lot of things from me. That you weren't exactly who you said you were. And then, today, with the picture—that kind of cemented it."

"I *am* who I said I was," I objected. "Nothing I've told you was a lie. I just . . . omitted some things."

"Those are some pretty big omissions, don't you think?" His foot drummed faster against the table. *Thumpthumpthumpthump.*

I sat huddled in my parka, my body jolting with every kick. "You're angry," I said. "I don't blame you."

"The thing I'm upset about isn't who you are. I mean, yes, it's a pretty upsetting realization that a girl I'm"—he paused, apparently flummoxed by the thought of defining our relationship—"that she's a fugitive who is wanted by the FBI. I mean, they're saying you *shot* someone." He was silent for a moment, giving me an opportunity to deny it, but of course I couldn't. "What upsets me the most, though, is that you didn't trust me enough to tell me. To ask for my help."

"It wasn't that I didn't trust you. It's that I didn't want to implicate you in my mess. Because I liked you too much for that." I rubbed my hands together, trying to warm them up. "Plus, I knew that you'd never look at me the same way again. And I was right, wasn't I?"

And it was true, he wasn't looking at me at all. He gazed down the hill, still kicking his foot, and I noticed that his pristine white tennis shoes were now covered with black scuffs. "I just ..." He sighed. "I don't even know what to say. This is really hard to wrap my head around."

"You can ask me anything," I said. "I'll tell you the truth. What do you want to know?"

"Everything would be a start."

And so I told him all the sordid facts I'd been afraid to tell him before. About helping my father with *The Luddite Manifesto;* and my creeping concerns about his state of mind and my future; and how I'd only managed to escape from the cabin by offering to be my father's accomplice; and how I'd shot a man but really it was self-defense; and how I truly didn't know what my father had done until I saw the news later. How I'd stolen evidence and destroyed even more by burning down my childhood home, and how I'd escaped when the authorities arrived. I talked and talked, as the park leaked its few remaining occupants, until it was well past midnight and we were the only people left out there in the cold.

Lionel listened in silence; and the quieter he grew the more I felt compelled to reveal every quivery detail—my feelings of complicity in my father's propaganda machine, the withered friendship with Heidi, the way the tight red dress felt so creamy against my skin, the security guard's rough hand on my thigh, the heady mix of panic and power that I felt that day. And this purge felt *good,* like I was emptying my heart of the toxins that had been poisoning it for so long.

When I was done, he let out a long sigh, the cloud from his breath a wraith in the dark. I sat there, watching the trees sway in the wind, sure that at any moment he would stand up and walk away. Instead, I felt something brush along the side of my jacket; and when I looked down I realized it was his hand, seeking mine. I curled my cold palm inside his and we sat there wordlessly, as I felt the heat of his body seeping into mine.

"And here I thought my childhood sucked," he said. "You win."

"It wasn't all bad," I said. "It's more complicated than that."

He turned to study my face. "But you're still going to turn your father in, right?"

I felt my guts twist themselves into a knot. "Would *you* turn your father in, if you knew it would mean he'd probably get the death penalty? And what about me—what if they throw me in jail, too?"

"I see your point," he said. "Still. It's your moral obligation to do *something*. People are dying."

"I know." The knot tightened, making it hard to sit upright. "But there's got to be some other way to stop him that doesn't involve me betraying him. At least until I can talk to my mom and see if she can help me. I was thinking—what if I reach out to the people he's targeting, so they can protect themselves? I already warned Nicholas Redkin."

"You sure you know who he's targeting?"

"The people in that photo, people he used to work with. Both of his victims were former coworkers. But I only know their first names."

He digested this. "OK. We figure out who the rest of the people in the photo are—that shouldn't be too hard. We can send them anonymous emails or something."

"*We* figure it out," I repeated, just to make sure I'd heard correctly. "You sure you want to be part of this mess? What if this makes you an accessory of some sort?"

He hesitated, then reiterated, "We."

I looked out at the city as the meaning of his word sank in. The lights from the skyscrapers refracted through the mist, a lustrous vibration. It all still felt so painfully new to me, this urban beauty; I found it impossible to fully grasp its scope.

"What about the hard drive?" he asked. "What's on it?"

"I don't know. I'm not sure how to hook it up."

"I can help you with that, too."

There was something tickling my face and when I lifted my hand to my cheek I realized that I was crying, tears that had gone cold in the wind. Was it gratitude, or relief, or just months of pent-up fear finally being purged? *Thank you,* I said to Lionel, *thank you for not run-*

ning away from me, or maybe I just thought it, because I was too choked up to speak.

He jumped off the table then, and held out his hand to help me down. I stepped down and took it, and we walked down the hill—our sneakers squeaking in the dew-soaked grass, our bodies enveloped by the swirling fog—together.

42

My father took me to the library in Bozeman only a handful of times. Free reading material was a draw, yes; but the part where we needed to register for a library card was a deal-breaker. (*Don't need the feds tracking what we read, do we?*) And so our visits were limited to the rare occasions when my father wanted to dig up something that wasn't in stock at the Country Bookshelf. Then, we would temporarily camp out at a library table, speed-reading while the librarian warily eyed us from the checkout desk.

The Bozeman library was an eighties-era brick box, featureless and anodyne, a study in harsh fluorescence. And so, when Lionel told me we were going to the library, this is what I imagined, down to the stained blue carpet and the metal shelves that swayed precariously when you replaced a book too hard.

I should have anticipated that the San Francisco public library would outstrip what Bozeman had to offer, and yet the scale of the place still came as a surprise. The main branch—newly remodeled—featured a five-story atrium topped by a windowed rotunda that filled the building with soft afternoon light. Above my head, glassed-in balconies crisscrossed the open space, and an imposing staircase navigated to the top. My sneakers squeaked on the polished stone floors.

I stopped just inside the doors, taken aback by all that grandeur. "This is all books?"

Lionel turned to see me staring up at the rotunda. "And magazines, I guess. Computers, too."

"It's the most beautiful building I've ever seen."

"You haven't seen many buildings, have you?" But he looked up, too, taking it in with fresh eyes. "You're right, it's very pretty. I guess I never stopped to think about it. C'mon, let's go hit up the research desk."

An hour or two later, after several dead ends with a database of periodicals, some fumbling with microfiche and assistance from a helpful librarian, we found ourselves leafing through a book called *The Genesis of Progress: Five Decades of Innovation from the Peninsula Research Institute*. This was a slim volume, full of dry jargon and meaningless names that we flipped through quickly, on the hunt for one thing in particular. And suddenly there it was, in a collection of black-and-white photos bound into the center of the book: a picture of my parents.

A strangled sound came out of my throat that caused the people sitting at the tables near us to look up. Lionel glanced around nervously and then scooted in closer to me. "That's your mom and dad?"

I nodded, studying the photo. They stood next to each other, on the edge of a group of men with familiar faces—faces I recognized from the picture that I'd stolen from my father. This photograph was a formal portrait of some sort, with everyone arranged in a semicircle in front of a whiteboard covered with diagrams and formulas. *PRI's Computing Research Group circa 1981*, the caption read.

My parents weren't touching, and yet there was something about the way my father's body curved toward my mother's, the way her hand hovered near the thigh of his trousers, that made it clear that they were together. 1981—I had been born by then, I realized, probably still in diapers.

Lionel put his face close to the photo, his fingertips tentatively tracing their faces. "He doesn't look much like that police sketch, does he?" he finally said.

I could have studied the picture all day, the only true evidence I had that my parents had ever been in the same room together (besides, of course, my own existence), but we had a more pressing agenda. Lionel had brought a notebook with him and in this we jotted down the names in the captions: *Nicholas Raymond Baron Peter Ajay Mike*

Isaac, all the names I already knew, but this time their last names were included, too.

"Baron and Peter are dead," I said. "I already warned Nicholas. So that leaves Raymond, Ajay, Mike, and Isaac. How do we find them?"

"If they still work in tech, they're probably easy to find online. Let's go see what we can dig up with an internet search."

It didn't take long to figure out that my father's former cohorts were all technology industry leaders, most meriting multiple pages of search engine results. Had my father known that, too? He must have. When had he learned what Peter and Baron were doing now? Was it those few nights when he was surfing the internet without me, or did it come before then? Did he come across the *Fortune* magazine profile of Ajay Chawla, now the founder of a cybersecurity software company? Did he read a *Wall Street Journal* article about Mike Swanson, who ran a technology venture capital fund in Palo Alto? Did he somehow see Isaac Cohen get interviewed on *60 Minutes* about the launch of his palm-sized personal digital assistant? What about Raymond Starr, did my father know that he had stuck it out at PRI and was now its executive director?

I sat there, watching with fascination while Lionel tinkered with increasingly arcane searches, digging his way into interfaces that crawled below the graphical surface of the Web, trying to hunt down their email addresses. He was capable of talking to computers in a way that felt magical to me, as if his brain was fluent in an alien language. "What is that?" I asked at one point.

"This? Just a Unix terminal," he said.

"How do you know how to do that? Are you a hacker?"

He laughed. "No. Just your standard programmer. A real hacker would have been able to get into that encrypted hard drive your father stole." We'd set the drive up the previous evening, connecting it to one of Lionel's computer monitors, but had immediately been stymied by its demand for a password. Lionel had tinkered and tinkered, but eventually gave up. The hard drive went back under my bed, its contents still a mystery.

A bell softly chimed, warning that the library would be closing soon. "OK, that's it," Lionel finally said. "I have email addresses for all four of them." He glanced at the clock and then quickly loaded up Hotmail. "If we're going to email them anonymously, we should do it from here, a Hotmail account on a public internet terminal, so no one can track our IP address," he explained. When he was done setting up a new account, he turned to me. "So what does the email say?"

I leaned across him and typed: *Pay attention, the Bombaster is targeting people from your group at PRI. Baron and Peter already. You may be next. Protect yourself.*

I clicked Send, and then turned to Lionel with an unsteady smile. It felt as though an anvil had just been lifted off my chest; only now did I realize that I hadn't been able to breathe since I'd understood my father's plan. "OK, now they can reach out to the authorities themselves and get help. Right?"

But Lionel was still staring at the computer monitor, even though the email was already working its way through the wires and toward its destinations. A librarian was walking in our direction, prodding the last stragglers to leave, but Lionel didn't move. He blinked at me when I put my hand over his. "What?" he asked.

"That'll work, won't it? They'll know what to do to protect themselves?"

"I think so," he said. "I hope so."

And, God bless him, he was able to muster a smile that was brave with his belief in me. Just because you're smart and rational doesn't mean you're immune to the myriad ways that infatuation can fry a person's logic circuits. And I was young and green enough not to wonder whether I'd just led him blindly into the dark. No, I was just happy that I was no longer alone.

WHEN I WAS a child, one of my favorite books was a dog-eared collection of Greek myths that I plucked off the dollar rack at the thrift store. The book's illustrations were baroque and particularly grisly—Medusa's severed head dripping blood, an eagle snacking on Prometheus's guts—and the previous owner had embellished many of the pages with purple crayon, but I loved the stories nonetheless. I was perfectly capable of reading them myself, but I still preferred my father to read them to me out loud.

One of our favorites was the tale of Alcyone, the daughter of the god of the winds, and her mortal husband, King Ceyx. They were beautiful and just and admired by all, but they doomed themselves when they started idly comparing themselves to Zeus and Hera. Hubris, of course, was an unforgivable sin in Greek mythology, and so a vengeful Zeus decided to wreck Ceyx's boat during a sea voyage. When Alcyone found Ceyx's body washed up on the beach, she threw herself into the waves and drowned. Impressed by this macabre devotion, Zeus changed his mind and turned Alcyone and Ceyx into kingfisher birds so they could be together again.

Perverse and capricious, yes—but hey, that was the gods.

As the myth goes, the god of the winds now calms the seas for two weeks every winter solstice, so that the kingfishers can mate and hatch their eggs by the shore, without the waves washing away their nests. *Halcyon days,* then, are this beatific window of time: peaceful and calm, pure and happy, before the winter storms return.

You and I, we're living our very own halcyon days, my father would say every time we finished reading this myth. Sitting on the porch beside him, listening to the birdsong lifting out of our meadow, I could see exactly what he meant: what kind of paradise we inhabited, the utopia he so desperately wanted our world to be.

But what he didn't seem to absorb (besides the fable's dire warnings about pride and ego) was the fact that halcyon days are always doomed to come to an end. They're just a lull before a coming storm.

Maybe those childhood days in the woods *were* my halcyon days; but my memory of them now is tainted by the edifice of falsehoods that our peace and tranquility was built upon. How can you be nostalgic about a façade? My father poisoned my memories with his lies, and so I no longer recall them in the same pure way that I once lived them.

But if those weren't my true halcyon days, then what were?

When I ask myself this question now, all these years later, I some-times find myself thinking of the days that followed that visit to the San Francisco library: After I clicked Send on that email, we went back to Lionel's apartment and immediately climbed into his bed.

By some measures, that was a week just like the weeks that had come before. Every day I woke up and went to work. I sat at my desk and corrected meta tags and studied JavaScript tutorials, clicked Send and Save and Publish. I watched Brianna tinker with her zine when she should have been working; and I accompanied Janus on his coffee runs to Caffe Centro; and I sat dutifully through another futurist lec-ture and applauded Ross's speech (noting that Lionel had been right: Ross *was* repetitive).

Evenings were different, though. Instead of going home alone and gorging myself on sitcoms until I fell asleep over my spaghetti, I boarded the J Church line with Lionel and went back to his apart-ment. We'd pick up a falafel on Haight Street and rent a video, the latter of which never got consumed because we were otherwise oc-cupied. (Yes, I lost my virginity that week. No, I'm not sharing the details. Needless to say, it was sweet and awkward and earnest and not particularly skillful on either of our parts.) And then we'd stay up late, wrapped in limp and fragrant sheets, trying to find ourselves within each other.

Was it love? Looking back now, I see no reason to believe that it wasn't, for either of us. Sometimes love manifests itself as a kind of amazed awe, as potent a feeling as any other form of connection: the shock of knowing that you are desired just as you are, no matter how broken you might feel.

I remember these few days now as an emotional smear, a warm pulse of pink, the color of my heart. In this bucolic window of time, I let myself believe that all my problems had been resolved. I'd done the *right thing* and foiled my father's plans, but without betraying him. I'd located my mother and would be meeting her in person in a matter of days. I had a job I believed in, and real friends, and my very first boyfriend—things that I couldn't even have fathomed just a few months before.

The winds had finally stopped blowing, and I believed that, like the kingfishers on their beach, it was safe to build my nest and lay my eggs.

I didn't stop to consider the fact that it might just be the eye of the storm.

43

Ross announced that Signal was going to have an IPO, and everyone on the digital side was buzzing with excitement. I was vague on the concept of "going public"—Frank hadn't exactly offered me stock options with my minimum wage position, and I hadn't known to ask—but around me, my coworkers were busily calculating how rich they might become.

"I'm going to buy a condo in the Mission," Brianna announced. "I want to live inside my money. Like a warm, cozy blanket of cash."

We were sitting on the damp grass in South Park, eating pizza slices as fast as we could before our fingers got numb. That was the night I was going to go meet my mother at her reading—our reunion no longer days away, but hours—and I was feeling manic and shaky, as though I'd drunk way too much coffee.

"I hate to break it to you, but five hundred stock options are not going to buy you a condo," Lionel replied. "Signal is not Yahoo, don't let Ross's smoke and mirrors delude you. This IPO isn't going to blow up. Whatever money we make isn't going to be fuck-you money."

"OK, then, just a small condo," Brianna said. "An itty-bitty one. I don't even need a parking space."

My grasp on the value of objects was still tenuous. The duffel I'd retrieved from Desi still had eleven thousand dollars in it, which I hadn't yet touched, and mostly thought of in terms of burritos. As in, *I can eat 2,300 burritos with my remaining money*. I had no idea what a condo might cost, but I was pretty sure it was more than what was in the bag. "What are you going to do with yours?" I asked Lionel.

"Gold bars," he said dryly.

"The safe choice. But maybe you could also invest in a car that doesn't smell like rotten milk?"

"Hey. Don't complain, unless you don't want me to drive you to Kepler's tonight."

"I'm not complaining. Believe me, I've smelled worse." We smiled at each other and Brianna rolled her eyes.

Janus was approaching from the other end of the park, lunch bag clutched in a fist, his hair wild. He stopped where we were sitting. "You guys hear?"

Brianna shook her head. "Hear what?"

"A mail bomb went off at Harvard; it got some professor. They think it's the Bombaster again."

I could feel Lionel, sitting next to me, go rigid. "Got him? As in, he's dead?"

Janus nodded. "Apparently a few others were injured, too. That's all I know. I overhead someone talking about it just now when I was in line for my tacos. I'm headed back to the office; I figure they'll need me to write something up about it."

"Shit." Brianna stood up, dusting off her jeans. "I'll go with you."

And with that, they were gone. Lionel turned to me. "Harvard? We didn't reach out to anyone at Harvard, did we?"

"No." I stared back at him, aghast. My father wasn't targeting his former colleagues after all. Or maybe he was, but that wasn't the extent of his ambitions. His former alma mater was clearly on the list, too; who else had we missed? *We must rise together and fight back against the march of technology, even if it requires violence, to eradicate the voices that are blindly leading us toward our own inevitable destruction.* There must be thousands of "voices" that fit this criterion, I belatedly realized.

Lionel pulled a fistful of grass from the lawn and stared at it in the palm of his hand. "Shit. This is awful." He flung the grass shreds and they fluttered impotently to the ground. He turned to look at me, with red and anguished eyes. "You need to go to the police. You need to tell them how to find your dad."

The excitement I'd been feeling earlier had dissipated entirely, like dandelion fluff in a stiff wind. "I don't know how to find him. All I have is an address for some guy in North Dakota. He's probably not even there anymore, if he ever even was."

"Then give them that."

"I don't know." Panic was making it hard to think straight. "Don't I need to be smart about this? I mean, I'm in trouble, too."

"All I know is that what we did before didn't work. And I know you hate this, but the fact is that your father needs to be stopped and you're the only one with information that might help them do that."

I closed my eyes and saw my father sitting in an electric chair, a metal helmet clamped to his head, wires snaking back to a machine, like something I'd seen once in a Bugs Bunny cartoon. "I'm meeting my mom in a few hours," I demurred. "I want to wait and talk to her first. She must know people. She'll have a better plan than just marching into a police station and giving myself up."

Lionel clawed his fingers into the grass again and pulled out another tuft. I knew how much he hated to be dirty. I knew how upset he was. I wanted to pluck the grass from his hands, wipe the dirt from his fingers, but I was suddenly afraid to touch him.

"And what if she doesn't? What's it going to take before you do what needs to be done? How many more people are you going to let your dad kill?"

I felt ill thinking of this. He was right. I *knew* he was right, that this liminal existence couldn't go on for much longer, that too many people had already died. It was up to me to pull the brakes on this train. And yet I was paralyzed.

"Just give me a few hours," I whispered.

He shrugged, not looking at me. "It's your decision, not mine."

We sat there for a long minute, each of us apparently waiting for the other person to say something that would make everything better, but nothing came. His silence was terrifying. Finally, I ventured: "Do you hate me?"

He gazed across the park, out toward the street, where the lunchtime traffic was cruising past. "No. I mostly feel sorry for you," he said.

This almost hurt more. I had thought that maybe he loved me. But apparently I was a pathetic creature now, only worthy of his sympathy. "*Pity is the most agreeable feeling among those who have little pride and no prospects of great conquests,*" I muttered, a bitter lemon taste in my mouth.

"What?"

"Nothing," I said quickly.

Even though he was looking away from me, I could still see the flash of white as he rolled his eyes. "Let me guess. Another nihilistic philosophy your dad made you memorize? All about how the world is bad and empathy is a sign of weakness?"

I flushed. "It's Nietzsche."

"Don't confuse what you read in books with real life, Esme."

"Books *were* my real life until just recently. Can you blame me for getting confused sometimes?"

He flung the grass aside and stood up, wiping his fingers on the napkin from his lunch. "I'm going back," he announced.

I stood up and followed as he trudged across the lawn and out to the mouth of the park. When we finally made it to the sidewalk, he stopped abruptly and turned around to face me. "I can't do this," he said. "I thought I could, but I can't. I like you, Esme. A lot. But this is too much for me."

"Wait," I said. Lunchtime stragglers navigated around us; they gave us a wide berth, sensing disaster. "Are you breaking up with me?"

"I don't know." He stared down at his hands, at the mud caked around his nail beds. "I guess I just need some space to think."

Then he pivoted and walked straight out into the street, barely bothering to get out of the way of a bus that was pulling away from the curb. I watched him walk with stiff, despondent steps toward the corner, in the opposite direction from our office.

"Does this mean you're not coming with me to meet my mom tonight?" I called after him. But my question was drowned out by the growl of the bus; and by the time it passed, he'd already disappeared around the corner.

My heart still breaks, looking back at that girl standing there, forlorn and confused, on the gum-speckled sidewalk. Overcome by experiencing, all at once, the myriad joys and disappointments of emerging adulthood: love and longing and rejection, emotional connections and risky decisions, the bridges we usually cross bit by bit as we come of age. But for me, emerging as a fully formed adult from my protective cocoon with none of those youthful experiences under my belt, feeling all these things at once was like jumping out of a plane without a parachute. I had no understanding of what lay below me, only that the fall was utterly disorienting and I'd never felt this particular kind of awfulness.

BACK AT MY desk, I opened the website of *The New York Times* and read the cover story. My father had sent a mail bomb to the engineering department of Harvard University. A computer science professor had died, one whose name I didn't recognize, and two students had been hospitalized. It was true: I'd failed.

Almost instinctively, I clicked over to the Luddite Manifesto, which I hadn't looked at in weeks. The visitor counter had shot up again, and now stood just shy of a half-million views. What percentage of that number were people who had actually been converted by my father's rhetoric? I wondered. It couldn't have been high; but even a few acolytes felt like too many.

I thought of all the hours I'd spent meticulously transcribing my father's words, cleaning up his grammar, uploading it all to the Web, and I was filled with burning hatred. At my father, yes; but mostly at myself. For allowing myself to be indoctrinated. For abetting him in his mad pursuit of prophecy. For letting him spend eighteen years filling my mind with ideas—*nihilistic philosophies,* as Lionel had so aptly put it—rather than anything that might be relevant to real life. For being too weak to stop him.

Before I could think much about what I was doing, I found myself logging into my GeoCities account. Three clicks later, and I was staring at a button on the lower-right-hand side of the screen: *DELETE SITE.*

I clicked the button. A window popped up. *ARE YOU SURE YOU WANT TO DELETE YOUR SITE? THIS ACTION CANNOT BE UNDONE.*

I clicked *YES.*

Just like that, *The Luddite Manifesto* was gone.

44.

T HAT NIGHT, I took the train down to Menlo Park alone.

As I sat in the plastic seat, watching the landscape fly past—sterile office parks that crouched alongside the salt flats and brackish marshes of the Bay; rows of commuter homes in various shades of beige; a horse racing track floating in a sea of empty parking spaces—I was suffused with a sense of pride that I had learned so much so fast. Just two months earlier, I had been too intimidated to attempt the train at all; and now here I was, looking like any other Bay Area local with a bodega sandwich in a bag and a novel on my lap, casually gazing out the window.

I wasn't feeling casual at all, of course. The sandwich was like cardboard in my mouth, and so I'd left it uneaten; and my mind couldn't fix on a single sentence of the William Gibson novel I'd nicked from the office. As each stop brought me closer to Menlo Park my pulse accelerated, a staccato drumbeat of a single word. *Mother mother mother.*

Unclear, until it was too late, that there were two kinds of trains—"local" and "express"—I arrived at my mother's reading twenty minutes after it started. I slid into a seat in the back row, next to a sweaty man in a misbuttoned shirt who was scribbling frantically in a Moleskine notebook. He smelled like egg salad.

My mother, on the other hand, was glorious. I had never seen a woman so imposing, so self-possessed. She stood at the front of the room in a beautifully fitted suit the color of an eggplant, hands braced on either side of the lectern as she spoke. Her hair, a trim golden cap, was tucked behind ears that were the size and shape of nautilidae. A luminous pearl gleamed from each earlobe, matching the strand that rested on the neckline of her pale silk blouse. She was smaller than I'd imagined—without the stiletto heels she was wearing, she was at least a half foot shorter than me—and yet somehow she came across as much taller. Maybe this was because of her posture, square and upright, as if she had shoved a wire hanger inside the back of her suit jacket.

She read aloud from her book in a voice that was brisk but slightly affectless, and it was clear that these words were so familiar to her that she didn't even have to think about them anymore.

"We are all cyborgs now, thanks to computers and cellphones and digital cameras," she intoned. "Technology has already given us the capacity to grow exponentially beyond our mundane human capabilities, and it's only going to get more astonishing from here. We can externalize our functioning, outsource our memories and archives, let the computers mediate and collate information so that we don't have to do that busywork ourselves. Once computers become small enough to be handheld"—there was a guffaw from a man sitting in front of me, and she fixed him with a look of disdain—"Oh, it *will* happen, in a decade, probably less. Computers the size of a deck of cards. And when it does, humans will essentially become walking libraries, constantly connected to the internet brain, tributaries of its knowledge, nothing ever forgotten. From there we will figure out how to wire our brains directly to the internet and at that point we will become part of the computer consciousness, and it will become part of us. And we will never, ever die."

I was hypnotized, only half listening to her, waiting instead for her eyes to snag on me, like a burr in a sweater. Would she recognize me, sitting there in the audience? Would her voice falter and die, as she suddenly realized that her long-dead daughter was staring back at her from the very last row? A ghost somehow made corporal?

But it wasn't until she finished her reading and began taking questions from the audience that her gaze came anywhere near me. Next to me, egg-salad man's hand shot straight up into the air. She pointed at him—a little reluctantly, I thought—and as she did, I could have sworn I saw her eyes slide to my face, catch there for a moment, and then dance away again.

"Can it be *dangerous* to have access to all this information?" The man's tone was accusatory. "Like, do we really want to have access to every single memory we've ever had? Won't that be exhausting? Aren't we *supposed* to screw up and forget things, especially the traumatic things we'd rather *not* remember? Isn't that what makes us human, and interesting—our fallibility?"

She frowned. "Fallibility isn't a particularly efficient mode of existence, is it? The human race is ripe for improvement; I think we can all agree about that. And having a personal knowledge archive at our fingertips allows us to constantly work on perfecting ourselves. Computer-assisted existence will allow us to make decisions based not on *emotion*—which is reactive and illogical—but on rationality and reason and shared experience. Artificial intelligence will help us calculate the most efficient response to any scenario. We will optimize our way in the world, eliminating the mistakes that only cause us distress. How is that a bad thing?"

Even as she rebuked my neighbor, I noticed that her gaze had again skipped sideways toward me. There was a tight wrinkle between her brows, as if she'd seen something that she couldn't quite identify. I smiled encouragingly at her, which was apparently the wrong move, because she looked quite startled and immediately flung her eyes away, calling on another person three rows up.

For the next twenty minutes, she didn't look at me once. I listened to the audience questions without hearing a thing—buzzwords like *external brains* and *transcending mortality*, concepts that I couldn't yet wrap my head around (and yet, I somehow knew, would enrage my father)—until finally she stepped back from the lectern, indicating that she was done. The bookstore manager—a stout gray-haired woman in a purple turtleneck and quilted vest—stepped in to take the microphone.

"Let's give a big round of applause for Dr. Trevante and that *fasci-*

nating glimpse into our future. Dr. Trevante will be signing now, so let's be sure to support her by buying a copy of her book."

A line of fans began to form at a table near the door, where my mother had ensconced herself with a Sharpie and a stack of books. I wandered to the front counter and bought a copy of the book, then went to linger near the children's section. I watched the dwindling line with impatience, waiting for the last of my mother's fans to get out of my way. Seated behind the signing table, Tess looked like a queen greeting her court; each supplicant tried vainly to forge some moment of connection with a question or an extempore comment, but she briskly signed each book with only a polite reply and sent them on their way.

When the line was almost gone, I slipped in to take my place at the end. I had no plan. What was I supposed to say when I was in front of her? *Hi, Tess, I'm your dead daughter? Hi, Mom, I've been looking for you. Hi, Dr. Trevante, this is going to sound strange but—* Before I could organize my thoughts into a coherent course of action, I was suddenly standing in front of her. Up close, I could see that she looked far frailer than she'd seemed at the lectern: Her blue eyes were ringed with a delicate circuitry of wrinkles and soft pouches of sagging skin. Her pupils were the size of sesame seeds, suggesting that she'd hardly slept in weeks. (An eighteen-stop book tour—it was quite possible she hadn't.)

Words failed me. Panicked, I simply slid the book on the table in front of her, open to the title page.

"Who should I sign this to?" Her voice was crisp, her pen poised dutifully over the page.

"Esme Nowak?" I didn't mean to put the question mark at the end of the name, but that's how it came out, as though I wasn't even sure of my own identity.

She looked up sharply. Her pinprick pupils bored holes into mine. "That's not funny."

"I wasn't joking. It's my name."

At this, she swiveled in her seat and gesticulated for the bookstore owner. "Can I have some help over here? I think this girl is a stalker." She stood and began to matter-of-factly gather her things. "I don't know where you dug up that name, but I find it very cruel."

My eyes stung. This was not the reception I'd anticipated. "I'm not a stalker," I insisted.

"I don't have time for this." She tried to fumble the Sharpie into her purse but dropped it. Her hands, I noticed, were trembling.

"Honestly. I'm sure that I'm your daughter." I reached into the pocket of my backpack and tugged out the *I Hate Mondays* photo, placing it on the table before her. "See? That's you, right? And me."

She glanced cursorily down at the photo; and then she froze. "Where did you get this?"

"My father. He had it hidden in a drawer. I just found it a few months ago."

She gingerly touched a tip of a finger to the photo, shaking her head as she did. *No no no.* By now the bookstore owner had materialized by my side to grip my biceps. She was starting to tug me away and it felt like the whole thing was going to be over just like that, when Tess finally spoke.

"I'm sorry. I made a mistake. You can let her go." It sounded like there were rocks in her throat.

The bookstore owner released my arm but stood there, hovering. Tess was still shaking her head. "I'm fine. Thank you." She studied me for a long minute; then tucked her bag to her side. "Come with me, please."

"Where are we going?"

But she was already walking toward the door of the bookstore, ignoring the last stragglers waiting to steal a moment with her. The bookstore owner called after us—"Are you sure we can't get you to sign some stock before you go?"—but Tess simply held up the back of her hand, blocking the words midair. She wobbled as she walked, taking small steps; it looked like she had lost a critical sense of balance.

I followed a few feet behind her, still confused by my reception. What was happening?

Next door to the bookstore was an outdoor café, where clusters of well-groomed women sat with plates of salad and sweating goblets of white wine. My mother walked to an empty table and gingerly settled herself in a green plastic chair, pointing me to the seat across from her.

Once we were seated, she closed her eyes, steeling herself, then opened them again and gazed fixedly at me. I flushed, hoping that she'd find what she was looking for in my face. After a moment she sat back in her chair and looked away again, and I wondered if something had been decided. Her face had loosened, and yet I still sensed a wariness to her, similar to the deer in our meadow, as they approached the pond where the wolf liked to sleep.

"You'll have to forgive me if I'm having a hard time believing you," she said. "Logically speaking, this makes no sense, you understand. Esme did not survive; it was not possible. At the time of the accident, I had a friend who was a statistician and we calculated the odds together; that she'd been washed out to sea, for example, but had managed to survive. It was implausible. Just as I'm calculating the odds, right now, that you might be an imposter of some sort, out to get something from me. Which is also implausible—I don't know what you think you would gain—but then again, human behavior is very strange."

She was holding the photo in one hand, though, and her grip on it was so tight that the tips of her fingers had gone white. I noticed that her nails were short, chewed to the quick.

I reached into my backpack and pulled out the rest of the things I'd brought with me: the birth certificate and Social Security card, the remaining photos. My father as a child, me in her arms, the men on the steps. I spread these out in front of her.

A strangled sound erupted from her as she looked at them. "My God. My God. My God." She put a finger in her mouth and tore at the side of her nail. "If this is a prank it's a very convincing one." She gingerly pushed through the other photos with the tip of the other pinkie, seemingly afraid to touch them. "I never knew where these went."

"My father had them," I said.

She looked up from the photos and stared hard at me. "You *do* look like Adam, the nose in particular, the set of your jaw; your coloring was always me, though . . ." Her words drifted off as she stared at me. "You'll understand if I still ask for a DNA test? But for now I'm inclined to take you at your word, as unlikely as this all seems—" Her voice was clipped and tight, as if a rubber ball was lodged in her cheek. She smiled faintly, then, and though I expected her to be delighted— her long-lost daughter returned from the dead!—the expression on her face was one of pure torture. "I don't understand how this could happen. It defies logic. You're dead. You've been dead for fourteen years. Where have you been? How could I not have *known*?"

"Dad and I were living off the grid, in the woods, in Montana," I said. "He told me you were dead, but the truth was that *we* were the ones who were dead. And it wasn't until I found that photo and saw the names on the back and realized that my name wasn't actually Jane, that I began to suspect he'd lied to me about other things, too. He told me he used to work in Silicon Valley and so I ran away and came here. And that's how I found you."

This synopsis, while woefully abbreviated, seemed to appease her. She nodded slowly, then seized on a detail: "Adam." She said his name as an exhale. "Where is he? Does he know you're here?"

"I don't know where he is," I said. "And no, I don't know how he would."

"Did he tell you *anything*? About what he did and how he did it? The car . . . I thought . . . suicide." Her body was tilting slightly in her seat, like she'd been knocked askew. I shook my head. "*Really*. And you don't remember what happened?"

"No. Nothing. I was too young." I hesitated. "Do you know why he would have kidnapped me?"

"No." And then she shook her head, rebuking herself. "Yes. He wanted to leave Silicon Valley, go live in the woods somewhere, a rejection of everything we'd been working toward. I said no, of course. He had become irrational. We were arguing. But I never imagined . . ."

Her voice trailed off. "Jesus, I should call the police immediately. Sue him to oblivion."

"No!" It burst out of me.

She gave me a funny look. "Well, he shouldn't get away with this."

I looked across the table at her, at this imposing woman in her expensive suit, her forehead tugged into a downward arrow as she tried to rewrite the story of her last fourteen years. She seemed so very far away from the mother I'd spent so long imagining, vanilla-scented and soft, a variation on Lina and her woolly warmth. "Do you grow roses?" I asked. "Or play the guitar? Were you ever a kindergarten teacher?"

I suppose I still held out hope that *some* aspects of my father's story were true, but she shook her head. "I learned the clarinet in high school, but I haven't touched one since."

"Can I . . . hug you?" I blurted.

She looked startled by this. She gave a little shake of her head, dispelling herself of whatever impulse she'd just felt. "Yes," she said firmly. "Yes. That would be nice." She stood, teetering just a little in her heels, and then held her arms out as if she was about to catch a beach ball. I stepped into her embrace, and we wrapped our arms around each other. The smell of her summoned up an old familiar memory—*jasmine*—that made my eyes sting. It was electric, to feel her body touching mine, but it also wasn't terribly cozy, nothing like sinking into a down comforter or cuddling with a kitten. Instead, it felt like a simulacrum of a hug, prickly and tentative, similar to embracing a cactus.

I couldn't blame her, though: She was hugging a corpse. There was no normal for that.

Finally, she disentangled herself and sat down again. "I'm sorry, I should have done that sooner, but you caught me off guard," she said. "I imagine this is not the grand reunion you have been imagining."

"Not really. I thought you'd be happier to find me."

She dabbed at the torn cuticle, which had started to bleed. "Happy isn't a word I use much, it's too abstract to be meaningful. And you have to understand—to me, you are dead. I spent many years adapting to this truth, learning to let it live outside me. I did not like how I initially reacted to your death—yours *and* your father's. I fell apart. I had to go away for a long time. And when I came back, I worked very hard to put you both in a locked box, so to speak, so that I could get back into a nondestructive pattern that allowed me to go on with my life." She looked down at her hands. "And that's how I've existed for well over a decade, so forgive me if I don't immediately shift back to the other mode of being."

"Mode of being?"

"Hope." The word came out so sharply that it sounded like an epithet. "I lived without it for fourteen years. This . . . *reunion* . . . is not something I ever imagined. So when a stranger comes to me and says she is my daughter—and I'm sorry, but you *are* a stranger, at least for the moment—I need a minute to wrap my head around it. Understand that you bear little physical resemblance to the toddler I knew."

"And loved?"

She seemed taken aback by the pleading note in my voice. "Yes," she said softly. "Of course I loved you. You were my child."

"*Am* your child."

At this, her eyes went damp and far away. "Right," she said. "And I *am* very glad to be reunited with you. More than I might be showing. This is just . . . overwhelming. But I'm going to give you my private phone number and you can call me to arrange a time to come over for dinner, in a day or two. And we can figure out a path forward for us." She pulled a business card out of her purse and scribbled on the back of it, before pushing it across the table at me.

She smiled at me, then, a lopsided toothy smile that lit up her face like sunshine breaking through the clouds, loosening her features and taking the tension out of her body. "We will not lose any more time, I promise," she said. "The things I have to teach you, Esme. The things we will do together."

There she is, I thought. *There is my mother, the one in the photo.* And in that moment, it did seem like everything might be OK after all. That I might have finally found my home, my real self.

I tucked the card in my pocket, swallowing back the lump in my throat. My mother was still rummaging around in her purse, and when she pulled her hand out again she had keys clutched in her fist, preparing to leave; and I realized then that I hadn't even gotten to the most important part yet. "Unfortunately, there's a lot more I need to tell you," I began. "Things that are going to be hard to hear."

"Harder than *this*?" She barked out a laugh. I noticed a tremble begin in her hands and move through her torso, until her whole body was quivering tightly, like a wind-up toy whose key had been twisted and was desperate to be released.

"I'm sorry, I know, but I could really use your—"

My words died in my mouth as she held up a palm, cutting me off: *Stop.* "No," she said firmly. "No more. I'm already at my capacity for the day. I need to process all this before you throw anything else at me."

"No?" I faltered in my convictions, surprised.

She was standing up now, clutching the purse to her chest like a shield. "Not *no* forever. But *no* for now. Just—call me. We'll talk about whatever it is later." She hesitated. "It was nice to meet you, Esme."

And with that, she fled.

WE ARE UNDONE by the specificity of our dreams. Reality can never live up to the shining edifices we forge inside our fantasies: Life, in all its confusing complexity, is destined to be a disappointment in comparison. The lottery winner discovers that the riches don't equal happiness; the longed-for baby is colicky and sour; losing fifty pounds still doesn't bring you love; winning the election doesn't trigger societal change.

Life is a constant emotional calibration, then: the tiny adjustments we make every day as we come up against our discontents. We ride this seesaw, between hope and disenchantment, seeking some sort of equilibrium.

Was Tess the mother I'd spent so many years dreaming about? Not at all. But motherhood comes in so many forms; the quintessential mom with her apple pies and apron strings and fathomless virtue is just a construct that no real woman could possibly live up to. I was aware of this, at least. And so I pushed away that prickly hug and the awkward conversation, and the fact that she'd walked away when it started to get hard, and focused instead on the bigger picture: That I had a mother, finally. We were going to *figure out a path forward* and *do things together.* And no, I hadn't yet told her the whole truth or asked for her help with stopping my father, but I would do it next time we spoke. Which would be soon, *so so soon,* now that I had her phone number in my pocket.

And so I floated through the next twelve hours on a cloud of euphoria, through the train ride home and the long, damp walk across the city to my sublet; through a night of restless sleep, drifting in and out of maternal scenarios that were half waking, half dream, impossible to disentangle from each other; and on through my morning commute on the crowded bus, windows dripping with condensation, air smelling of damp wool. In my state of limerence, nothing quite registered as real: not the persistent drizzle that soaked my sneakers as I scurried down Third Street, not the faint scent of urine from the pavement outside the shuttered bars, not the horns blaring their grievances from the congested Bay Bridge on-ramp.

Nor was I quite conscious of the man who was standing in the mouth of the alley where Signal parked its dumpsters—a motionless figure set back from the bustling sidewalk traffic of South Park—until he spoke my name.

"Jane."

Even then, I was still in my dream state, too distracted to sound the alarm bells that should have been going off at this use of my old name. I turned, surprised, toward the figure that was now approaching me from the gloom of the alley. My fists curled, ready to defend myself if necessary; the muscles in my calves coiled, instinctively ready to run. The man wore a too-big peacoat over a hoodie that he'd pulled forward to protect his face from the rain, and yet there was something immediately familiar about the way he moved toward me. I knew that loping gait. I knew that voice.

Still, it wasn't until he tugged his hood back that I was forced to finally acknowledge who was standing there, just steps away from me.

"Hi, Dad," I said.

45

Theresa is a Ph.D. grad from MIT, the first female hire in your group. She is blond and pretty, and she has spent her entire life working to get beyond this. You meet her when she materializes in the doorway of your office and then just stands there watching you type.

"C or Pascal?" she asks.

Taken aback—you had assumed that she was a new secretary—you look at your monitor to double-check what you've been doing. "Pascal," you say. "Of course."

"Of course?" She tilts her head.

"It's the more reliable programming language of the two."

"It's also far less flexible and creative." She taps her hand on the edge of the doorjamb. "Believe me, C will be here long after Pascal is gone." And with that, she smiles brightly—pleased to have proven that she knows more than you do—and walks away.

Never before have you been shown up by a woman. (Frankly, you haven't had much interaction with women at all.) Of course you are smitten.

For happy hour on Fridays, the men in your group decamp to the Dutch Goose, a dive bar with peanut shells on the floor and graffiti carved into its wooden booths. You spend these evenings drinking tepid Budweiser and listening to your coworkers brag about their plans for the future: the start-up ideas they are hatching, the venture capital money they are working to line up, the features they're going to get in *Byte* magazine. It bothers you to realize that, while what excites you most about computer technology is the purity of its mathematical logic, what excites *them* is the money to be made. They are monitoring the riches that are starting to pour into Silicon Valley, and they spend their free time wondering how they will siphon off that stream themselves.

In this way, it dawns on you, your new friends aren't so very different from your classmates at Harvard. Is *everyone* out to become a titan of industry? you wonder. Is it wrong to think that there's more to existence than money and power?

A few weeks into her employment at PRI, Theresa is coaxed into showing up for one of these Friday happy hours. The men—unused to female company—buy her drink after drink, which she leaves untouched on the table while she nurses a club soda. The volume of their conversation is twice as loud as usual; they brag about their programming prowess and their open architecture hacks and how much they hate those starched shirts over at IBM. The evening culminates with Nick and Baron and Peter drunkenly arguing about the merits of German versus Italian automotive engineering, an argument that ends with Peter dragging everyone out to the parking lot so that he can fling open the hood of his new cherry-red Mercedes 280SL.

You find yourself standing next to Theresa, who watches this spectacle with her arms crossed, one eyebrow canted in judgment.

"The male peacock displays his plumage in an attempt to woo the female of the species," you say, sotto voce, to her.

"The female of the species is wise enough to see past the feathers and the posturing," she replies, a smile flickering across her face. "Frankly, the female of the species doesn't really need the male at all."

"But surely the female doesn't want to be *totally* alone. Perhaps she just wants someone to spar with, rather than mate with."

She tips her head in your direction, looks at you with an assessing gaze that makes you suddenly self-conscious. "Oh, so you *don't* want to mate with me?" And then laughs when you start to stammer. "Oh hush, I won't hold you to your answer. Let's go back inside and let these boys fight over who is the biggest cock. I think I'm ready for a drink now."

Your connection with Theresa is cerebral and intense. You stay up all night talking about philosophy and technology, Marshall McLuhan and Walter

Benjamin, all these new ways of looking at the world. You drink viscous black coffee at Peet's on Santa Cruz Avenue, listen to her collection of Richard Wagner opera records, and go for weekend drives up to the forests of La Honda. (She begs out of your monthly camping trips, preferring the tidy comfort of a bed to a sleeping bag perched on rocks.) Together, you delight in being part of the future, even as the dying hippie movement is exhaling its last breath thirty miles north in San Francisco.

She, too, comes from a family that didn't believe in her. She is the only person you know who works as hard as you; who feels like she has as much to prove. "My family," she tells you one night, in a postcoital confession, "believes that women are inferior to men in all ways, except for their ability to produce babies." Her baffled parents did not understand why teenage Theresa preferred calculus to cheerleading; they sent her to college only because they thought she'd meet a successful husband there, and still disapprove of her "unladylike" career: *Technology is a man's job; who will want to marry you?*

You fall in love in part because you see yourselves mirrored in each other: sharp-edged loners, chips on your shoulders from being underestimated, brains that work faster than everyone around you. But your relationship is more than just a meeting of like minds. In her arms, you feel seen and understood and admired. In *your* arms, she takes off the armor she's worn her whole life and allows herself to be unapologetically honest about who she is, and what she wants: esteem, accolades, and—yes, amazingly—you.

And yes, it's possible she also marries you to prove her parents wrong. But you wouldn't know, because they aren't invited to your city hall wedding. You don't invite your parents, either.

Four months later, Theresa is pregnant, entirely by accident.

She delivers you a carefully prepared speech along with the positive pregnancy test: She does not plan to have the baby.

"I have to work twice as hard as any man to be given the same kind of career opportunities. How am I going to find that time if I have a child? No one at the office will respect me if I'm lugging around a stomach the size of a watermelon. And the minute I ask for a day off to take the kid to a doctor's appointment, they will fire me. My career will essentially be over. I've worked this hard so that I could do something *besides* have babies."

But you plead with her. You never realized how very much you wanted a child until she told you she was pregnant. You see this as your opportunity to correct all the mistakes that were made in your own childhood: Unlike your parents, you will see your child for the brilliant creature that they are, you will help them become their best selves, you will not burden them with your own inadequacies! And so you make promises to Theresa, so many promises. You swear that you will be in charge of childcare. You will hire help. You will change all the diapers, deliver all the bottles, rock the baby to sleep!

When Theresa finally confesses that the *real* issue is that she doesn't think she will be a very good mother—"I am not entirely sure that I am capable of being maternal," she says—you disagree with her vehemently. Motherhood is innate—look at the animals in the forest, it is an instinct! (You decide not to mention the snake, which abandons its young immediately after giving birth.) Anyway, she doesn't need to be a *good* mother, she will be a *unique* mother, a role model for your unconventional child. Together, you will set a new paradigm: the child of the future, ready for the exciting new world that awaits the human race.

And so, beaten down, Theresa agrees to have the baby. When she is born, you name her Esme, which means *beloved*. You are ecstatically happy and spend hours staring at your mewling little red-faced raisin, marveling at the miracle of human creation.

Theresa takes a three-day maternity leave before returning to her desk.

It turns out that she was correct about not being very motherly. You are not sure why you doubted her own self-awareness. In the first few years, she expends only the most basic efforts on Esme, and seems interested more in the abstract process of parenting than in her daughter herself. Rather than rocking the baby to sleep, she will read five sleep-training books and then present you with a multipage analysis of the best methods for you to use. Rather than spoon-feeding your baby in her high chair, Theresa will analyze the nutritional benefits of assorted vegetables and instruct you on which ones to buy.

That is not to say that Theresa is devoid of maternal instincts. There are moments when you see Theresa sweetly holding Esme, or pulling her blanket over her in her crib, or popping a raspberry in her mouth, and you have a sudden burst of hope that she will grow into her role of mother. She loves your child in her own way, it's clear. Maybe it's just a matter of time.

But instead, as Esme becomes a prickly toddler, rather than a compliant infant, things grow harder. The noises Esme makes drive Theresa crazy. She can't handle the smell of a diaper. She simply walks away whenever Esme has a tantrum. A toddler is not logical, and so Esme flummoxes her.

It breaks your heart to see Esme clinging to her mother's legs, ignored, as Theresa cooks your dinner.

You compensate in every way you can. You are not particularly adept at fatherhood, either—what kind of role model did you have?—but you are good enough. You provide hugs and Band-Aids and wipe away snot. You take Esme to the San Francisco Zoo and Marine World Africa USA. You read endless books aloud; and if those books are maybe not entirely age-appropriate (why bother with *Pat the Bunny* when you can introduce your child to the moral fables of O. Henry?), Esme doesn't seem to mind. By the time she is four, you are taking Esme camping with you almost every month, teaching her how to identify fungi and build a fire.

Theresa spends those weekends at home, working.

Things at Peninsula Research Institute have started to change. It is 1983 now, and Reagan is in charge and the military has commissioned your research division to model doomsday scenarios: things that might happen if computers are put in complete control of modern warfare, the economy, the power grid, and it all goes wrong instead of right. (It is the era of *War Games* and the government-sponsored SDI defense system against nuclear attacks.) You are forced to think about nuclear warfare, whole countries being eradicated; AI triggering mass unemployment, leading to the collapse of the economic system; robot soldiers and global apocalypse. You learn that there are so many ways for a civilization to disintegrate.

All through the tools that *you* have helped create.

You start to sink into melancholy and self-doubt. You dread going to work each day. And as you drop Esme off at daycare—a pinch in your heart as you watch her toddle away from you—you ask yourself why you are still doing this job. Is it for *her*? Because you're no longer sure that you're doing it for you, when there are things that bring you so much more pleasure. The smell of your daughter's scalp; the way she furrows her brow as she puzzles through the books you're teaching her to read. Watching a fern slowly unfurl together or showing her a yellow banana slug beneath a rotting redwood tree. Smaller pleasures that feel so much more critical than the supposedly paradigm-changing technologies you're chasing.

You go to Baron—who is now your boss; your peers are avidly climbing their career ladders in a way you are not—with an idea for a new study. Your hypothesis: Computers are a valuable resource that shouldn't be controlled by government or industry; instead, all source code should be made public, enabling innovation and a redistribution of power. Rather than allowing technology titans like IBM and Microsoft to hold their intellectual property close, you propose studying the effect of eliminating *all* IP. Making technology, essentially, a socialist resource that society at large can hold in check.

Baron stares blankly at you, then turns to check the wall calendar behind him. "April fools, right?"

"It's worth investigating, don't you think?"

He looks at you like you're a squashed bug on the sole of his shoe. "You *do* understand where our funding comes from, don't you, Nowak? That's the craziest idea I've ever heard. Eliminating patents? I mean, even the Commies believe in IP. You don't take the most powerful tool in existence and put it in the hands of the hoi polloi instead of the people who have the intelligence and reasoning to manage it."

"That's awfully elitist, Baron," you say.

"Yeah, well, that's reality." He shakes his head. "For someone who thinks he's smarter than the rest of us, sometimes you're awfully dumb."

You go back to your office and stare at the computer for a long time, quelling the urge to smash it to bits.

Meanwhile, Theresa and Peter are working together on a robotics project and she is deliriously happy. Peter's advances in logic programming and neural networks dovetail neatly with her theories about the future of intelligence; together, they have a far more propitious perspective about what is coming our way. At home, Theresa goes on and on about how the miniaturization of computers is going to turn us all into superhumans, and intelligent robots are going to resolve all the inefficiencies in our systems. A new society, ushered in by AI, and human beings are going to have to adapt up to machine thinking. This horrifies you, but Theresa sees no reason for concern: Humans are dreadfully flawed, she argues, so why not encourage them to be more like computers?

A schism is opening up between the two of you. More and more nights, you find yourself sleeping in Esme's room instead of with Theresa; more and more nights, Theresa stays at work until long after midnight. (You wonder, grimly, if she is having an affair with Peter, he of the cherry-red 280SL.) Some days, you only see her at work. Your marriage is falling apart; and yet even though something seems fundamentally broken between you now, you still miss the Theresa you fell in love with. Maybe you need to get the family out of Silicon Valley—out to the curative openness of nature—in order to see each other clearly again.

Finally, one rare night when you find yourselves alone together, you confess to Theresa that you are going to quit Peninsula; and you think she should, too. "I want to get away from Silicon Valley and back out to the things that really matter," you tell her. "It's not healthy for either of us here, and especially not Esme. I've decided that we should move out to the country."

She stares uncomprehendingly back at you. She is silent for so long that you know she must be furious. You made a mistake, you realize, in presenting this as a done deal; you should have coaxed her, more slowly, to come around to your position. Made it seem like it was *her* idea. She needs to be in charge, even more than you do.

You can see her mind doing its own calculations, and her response—typical Theresa—is a strategically placed bullet. She wants to stay here not for her own sake, of course, but for *Esme's*! "There are award-winning schools here," she responds. "Innovative teachers. Organic food! Museums! She has access to the best of *everything*. We agreed, remember? We were going to set *a new paradigm: the child of the future, ready for the exciting new world that awaits the human race.*"

"I'm not so sure anymore that the new world is going to be that exciting," you say.

The conversation ends at that. And things go back to the way they were; except for one, not-insignificant change. Theresa starts to show a lot more interest in Esme. Maybe it's because Esme has finally emerged into a fully formed human, capable of conversation, capable of logic; or maybe it's simply Theresa's attempt to wrest her away from *you*. (You assume the latter.) She takes her to try on new clothes at Stanford Shopping Center. She buys two tickets to *Carmen* at the San Francisco Opera, dresses Esme in a velvet coat, and bundles her into her Volvo. She takes over reading to Esme at bedtime. She comes home from work early enough for dinner, not just once a week but every night.

Esme, for her part, is radiantly happy. After years of longing for her mother's attention, here it finally is! You can do nothing but watch as you are slowly replaced in your daughter's affections.

You try to bury yourself in work to compensate for this loss, but you find it is making you feel a little bit crazy. Mired in melancholy, you can't be bothered to shave, or shower, or expend any effort at all on your appearance. You spend less time at work actually *working*, and more time with your office door closed reading classic texts that bring you a modicum of relief. Thoreau, Emerson, Wendell Berry. You dream of the woods, the lush silence of a world with no thrumming computers, no static buzz of wires: just you and your daughter basking in the glory of nature.

Your coworkers, you realize, are starting to avoid you.

Finally, there is a night when you come home from work, utterly depleted from a day in which you've been modeling yet more doom and gloom, and find Theresa and Esme sitting in the living room. Strewn about them is a massive pile of Legos, as well as gears and wires and electronics. It's like the living room has been turned into a laboratory. It takes you a minute to recognize what they are building, and then with a rush of panic, you realize: They are building a robot. As big as Esme herself.

Esme turns to see you standing in the doorway. She lights up and shouts with alarming enthusiasm: "Look, Daddy! Mama is building me my best friend!"

Theresa turns to look at you, too; and in her tight, viperous smile, you read: *victory.*

In that instant you see where all this is going. Theresa plans to raise Esme now, not as a child but as a science project. Her cyborg. She sees Esme as a lump of clay that she can model into her vision of the ideal being: a person who is less *human* than computer.

And you know that things have become untenable. You and Esme need to leave.

Divorce, you quickly decide, is not an option. In the same manner that Theresa will always have to work twice as hard to get half the respect in the workplace, you will also never get granted full—or even partial—custody. Traditional gender roles still reign supreme in the early 1980s. And you know that, in a best-case scenario, you'll get a measly weekend or two a month. Probably less, because Theresa does not seem inclined to play nice. She will likely haul your coworkers in front of a judge to testify about how *unstable* and *unpredictable* you've been lately—how you've been talking about apocalypse, quitting, uprooting the family—even though you know you are the only sane one around Peninsula anymore!

A few hours a month with Esme: You would rather kill yourself.

And what would become of Esme? What would *she* become, in her mother's hands? You shudder to think of it.

And so, instead of divorce, you decide that your only option is to die.

Not to *actually* die, of course, but to pretend that you have. After all, it is impossible to just leave with Esme: You would be caught as soon as you used a credit card, and then charged with kidnapping. Esme would end up back with her mom, and you'd end up in jail. No, the far more logical conclusion is that you need to leave and make sure that no one comes looking for you. If Theresa thinks you are dead, she will grieve for a heartbeat and then immediately go back to work.

If this seems like a harsh conclusion about the woman who you ostensibly love, you just keep reminding yourself that she never wanted a kid in the first place. She only wanted Esme when it was a way to hurt *you.*

You know that your window to leave is small: You have to do this while Esme is still malleable, before she is old enough to ask unanswerable questions, and when she still believes that your truth is the whole truth.

Planning doesn't take very long. You already know exactly where to drive your Volkswagen off the cliff in Big Sur. For years, on your camping trips, you've been navigating that perilous turn in the road, the dented metal barrier with a gap in it, the two-hundred-foot drop to the jagged rocks below. You consult the *Farmers' Almanac,* study tide patterns, cross-reference that with incoming storms. You sell a trunkful of electronics to members of the Homebrew Computer Club—mostly older computers rescued from the office archive that no one will miss—and walk away with a neat bundle of cash. With some of it, you buy a secondhand truck, which you leave in the parking lot of a Big Sur trailhead just a half mile away from that turn.

The hardest part of your plan, it turns out, is convincing Theresa to let you take Esme camping. She has a vise-grip on your daughter these days, even drags her to the office for PRI's first "Bring Your Children to Work Day." She sits Esme in her chair and when Peter comes by and makes a joke about PRI's "newest employee," Theresa just smiles and says, "Go ahead and joke about it, but I'm planning to have her programming before she turns six."

"I'd expect no less from you, Tess," Peter replies, with a secret smile so full of knowing admiration that you realize, with a sour punch in your gut, that this alpha male asshole has indeed been screwing your wife.

Just another reason to go, and fast.

Soon a weekend arrives when Theresa is speaking at a computer conference and she relinquishes control of Esme back to you for a few days. You pick a camping spot where no one will see your comings and goings and spend your first night roasting marshmallows and reading the Brothers Grimm aloud. The owls hoot their approval; the raccoons forage in your garbage for treats. The second night, you put Benadryl in Esme's cocoa and she passes out just after dinner. You leave her there, sleeping a dreamless sleep, when you drive out to the turn in the road well after midnight. You put the convertible top down, disconnect the wire that enables it to be put back up, and hit the gas.

You'd expect it to be somewhat dangerous to leap out of a car that's about to drive off a cliff, but it turns out to be fairly easy. You make it out with several feet to spare, sporting a few bruises and scratches, but nothing anyone will notice. The rain begins on your walk back to the truck, which buoys your spirits: You imagine the story they will tell. How a father decided to leave the campsite early because of the rain and was trying to put up the broken convertible top when he accidentally drove off a cliff on the slick roads. Or maybe they'll believe it was suicide, and that you did all this intentionally. Regardless, you pray that the rain and the tides work in your favor, and the car isn't found until it's plausible that the bodies have been washed away.

By the time you retrieve the truck and make it back to the campsite, it's almost dawn. Esme wakes up when you start disassembling the tent, yawning blindly in the dark.

"We have to go quickly, squirrel," you whisper to her. "Something terrible has happened to Mama and so we're going to have to go on a trip for a while."

She wraps her hands around your neck and cries sticky tears, hiccuping her night-sweet breath into your ear. You should feel worse than you do, and maybe you would, if you didn't know this was for her own good. You are saving her from a life that would dismantle everything that is precious and human about her.

You take almost nothing with you, other than a handful of photos you have nudged out of the album that Theresa meticulously keeps—answers to the questions Esme will someday inevitably ask. Other than these, all you need is *her*, and your convictions. With those things, you can survive anything.

46.

The first thing I noticed about my father was how small he'd become. Standing before him, I could look him almost straight in the eyes; and he had lost weight since I'd last seen him, so that the jeans he was wearing were staying up only because they had snagged on the sharp edges of his hip bones. Had I grown that much, that fast, or had I simply taken him down off his pedestal to finally see him at the size he had always been?

Monster, hero, the looming figure of my childhood, the determined rebel of his memoir: No matter who he really was, it suggested someone far more substantial. This man, soaked to the bone, nervously hunched in the gloom of an alley, looked like he might get blown over by a strong breeze.

He wore a plain black hoodie that I did not recognize, underneath a shapeless wool overcoat, and tennis shoes instead of the work boots I was used to seeing on his feet. His face was clean-shaven—even the mustache was gone—and he was wearing wire-rimmed glasses that I was sure must be part of his disguise. My father had his issues, but myopia was not one of them. I had to assume he'd also seen the Wanted image of him that had been all over the news and was doing the best he could to distance himself from it.

I was so startled by his appearance that I didn't see the hug coming. Before I had time to prepare my thoughts, I found myself wrapped in his arms. "Oh, Jane, I've missed you," he said into my ear, his voice low and choked. It triggered something liquid inside me.

I hung limply inside his familiar embrace, as stunned and compliant as a cow on its way to slaughter. Finally, he released me and stepped back. "We need to talk," he said. Rain dripped off his nose, and he wiped it away with the back of his hand. "Where can we go?"

My thoughts spun in eddies; nothing made sense. I should have anticipated this, should have prepared so I'd know how to behave, but he'd caught me off guard. I glanced down the sidewalk, toward the glass-plated door of Signal, where a cluster of my coworkers were shaking out their umbrellas. "Not my office."

"No." His voice dripped with disdain. "Not *your office*, obviously."

I wasn't about to take him into South Park, where we'd have to face a steady stream of Signal employees stopping in for their bagels and lattes. "Do you want to get a coffee?" I asked.

The drizzle had turned into a stinging rain. He tugged his hood back over his head. "I don't care. But we can't stand out here on the street."

"There's a Starbucks up on Market Street," I said. "Let's go there."

I pivoted, expecting him to follow; we'd only walked a few feet when somehow I found myself walking behind him, struggling to keep up as he loped, waterlogged, up the street. Cursing myself for the fact that I was already trying to keep up with him, on my own home turf. How had he destabilized me so fast?

It was 9:00 A.M. and the Starbucks was crowded with morning commuters impatiently waiting on line to fuel their addictions. The floor was papered with a spill of soggy paper napkins; muffin crumbs and abandoned cups littered the tables. The walls reverberated with the grind of coffee beans, the hiss of the espresso machine, the generically jazzy music blasting over the speakers, a cacophony that made it an ideal place for us to talk without having to worry about strangers listening in.

I bought a coffee and a croissant for myself—and then, after deliberating, bought the same for my father—and brought them to the table in the corner where my father sat, his eyes darting across the crowded room. I placed the croissant in front of him, an offering, and he looked down at it with a curl of his lip. "You eat this crap now?"

"It's pastry, Dad. Not poison."

"It's hardly a pastry. It's a preservative-filled facsimile that's made in a factory somewhere and sealed in plastic and shipped down here in giant trucks that spew diesel fumes the whole way, just so you can have a subpar breakfast because you're too lazy to prepare one yourself."

"Well, *I* think it's delicious." I picked up mine and took a big bite, gamely ignoring the fact that it was, unfortunately, rather gummy and stale; then washed it down with a scalding gulp of acrid coffee. He offered me a baleful gaze.

We stared at each other across the table. My father, for once, seemed to be at a loss for what to say—or, more likely, he had *so many* things to say, none of them complimentary, that he didn't know where to start. So I jumped in first. "How did you find me?"

He rolled his eyes, as if this was the stupidest question I could have begun with. "You were on national television, squirrel. Apparently you are the dot-com industry's most enthusiastic employee." He shook his head. "Was that a wise decision, you think?"

I flushed, despite myself. I wasn't sure what decision he was referring to: my choice to let myself be filmed for a national television show when I was wanted for a crime; or my choice to work at Signal in the first place. Possibly the latter was the more objectionable one.

"I like my job," I said.

"I'm sure it's not worthy of your intellect," he said. "Do they have you making their coffee? Taking out their trash? Cleaning their computer screens?"

I refused to take the bait. "Why are you here, Dad? Shouldn't you be in hiding somewhere?"

"No," he said. "That's not the question, Jane. Do you know what the correct question is?"

"My name isn't Jane. It never was. Jane doesn't exist."

He ignored this. "The question is why are *you* here? Here, of all places. It's like you didn't absorb a single thing I taught you." He managed to sound both wounded and disappointed at the same time, and it plucked at something deep inside me. I hated that my impulse was to try to apologize.

"I think you can guess why I'm here. And please, call me *Esme*. That's my real name, although it's also the name of a dead girl. Can you imagine what a strange position that is to find yourself in, Dad? To discover who you really are at the same time that you discover you are also legally dead?"

He didn't seem surprised to hear that I knew everything. He drew the paper cup to him and took a sip of his coffee. "You want me to say I'm sorry?"

"That would be a start. My whole life was a lie, Dad. You hid me in the woods for fourteen years and lied to me about why we were there and kept me away from my mother." I regretted having brought him here, to such a public place; I was finding it difficult to keep my voice neutral and low.

My father glanced around us and leaned in closer, dropping his own voice. "I told you—I *always* told you—that I did that to protect you. All of that was true."

"You needed to protect me from my *mother*?" I shook my head. "I've met her, Dad. She's hardly dangerous."

"So you found your mother."

"Yes."

An uncharacteristic hesitation on his part. Was that nervousness? "Did you tell her about—"

I cut him off. "Not yet."

"Ah." The corners of his lips twitched up into a ghost of a smile, and I knew he had taken this as a sign of my ongoing fealty to him, rather than what it really was: cowardice. "And? Did you see?"

"See what?"

"What she is like. Why I needed to get you away."

I bristled. "There was nothing wrong with her. She's a famous writer and technologist. She won a genius grant. Everyone admires her." I had made a conscious decision to overlook the disappointing aspects of our reunion. Her coolly rational response to meeting her dead daughter was not what I'd expected, it was true. But how much did I really know about the spectrum of human behavior? The number of people with whom I had ever held a prolonged conversation still numbered in the dozens. This was hardly a comprehensive survey of the magnificent diversity of the human mind. How was I to say what was "normal" and what was not, especially when that baseline had previously been set for me by a hermitic zealot?

I'd almost forgotten how it felt to be fixed in my father's hawkish gaze, the way I could feel his disappointment crawling down into my guts and settling there. "So you didn't find the pages I left for you," he said.

"But I did."

This wasn't the answer he'd expected. He turned the coffee cup in his hand, frowning. "If you read them, you should understand what I was doing by taking you away from her. I was trying to protect you from becoming some test case of how technology can mold a child."

I thought of the pages I'd deciphered just last night, pages where he described my mother as a monster; pages I'd read with a knot in my stomach, unsure who to believe. "That's your perspective. Not a neutral one. Colored by your own biases and personal agenda. What you wrote, it reads like you're trying to justify your actions, blaming her for what *you* did. The use of the second-person voice. As if trying to implicate me, your audience, in your actions; making me complicit, too."

He gripped the edge of the table. "You have to trust me on this. The situation wasn't healthy. She saw you as her experiment, a child she could model into her vision of the ideal human."

"Like you did."

This gave him pause. He tilted his head, gazing down his beakish nose at me. "Like I did?"

"You tried to turn me into you."

"No," he objected. "I just gave you all the knowledge that I had at my disposal. It was up to you to decide your own path."

"How was I to take any path at all when I wasn't even allowed to leave the cabin?"

"I was protecting you from outside influences, at least until you became an adult and had a fully formed brain."

"I *am* an adult. I turned eighteen, months ago. Or did you forget my real birthday, too?"

He shook his head, as if trying to disentangle himself from a noose I'd just flung around his neck. "You're missing the point, Jane."

"*Esme.*"

He groaned. "Fine, *Esme.*"

"*The point* is that you kidnapped me in order to prevent me from becoming her science project, and you made me yours instead. You *killed* me, Dad. I don't really exist, because of you."

He blanched. "I know that may seem extreme. But what was the other option? Staying in Silicon Valley, in the belly of the beast, helplessly watching you get indoctrinated by your mother? I wanted you to have more than that. I wanted you to see what was beautiful about the real world. And you did, didn't you? I gave you that gift."

I thought of the tracks of the deer through the silver dew, the smell of moss growing on pines, the color of the sunrise lifting over our forest. As interesting and unpredictable as life was in San Francisco, there was still part of me that felt untethered here, on edge, in a way I never had in the woods. "Yes," I said reluctantly. "But you also turned me into a criminal."

He released his grip on the table. "Well. I didn't plan for that to happen. You volunteered to come with me. I shouldn't have let you. It didn't go the way I'd intended."

"But, Dad—why? Why are you doing this? You're"—I leaned in and whispered urgently—"killing people. Killing your *friends.*"

"They're not my friends. They stopped being my friends a long time ago. They are the horsemen of the apocalypse. The work they are doing threatens humanity's survival. They need to be stopped, and the world needs to understand *why* they should be stopped, and this was the only way to get everyone to pay attention." He threw his hands up in frustration. "You read my manifesto. You know all this. I thought you understood."

"I didn't know you were going to *murder* people. It's awful . . . It's"—I struggled for a word he might relate to—"immoral."

The morning commute crowd was thinning out and the rain outside was slowing to a drizzle. The café windows were fogged with steam, condensation dripping down the inside of the glass in fitful tears. My father took another sip of his coffee and then looked at me coolly. "Morality is just a construct, squirrel. An abstract idea," he said. "There are six billion people in the world; what's one less? Especially when that one person could potentially lead to the eradication of human existence. You could say I'm not killing people, I'm killing principles."

"Like Raskolnikov. *Crime and Punishment*."

He lit up. "Yes. Exactly. Smart girl."

I hated the warmth that spread through my chest at his smile of approval. "Yeah, well, he ends up realizing that he's not that special after all and confesses his crimes and is exiled to Siberia."

He frowned. "It's just a novel. What's your point?"

"You need to stop. Now. No more bombs. No more killing. You've done enough."

He made a sound, deep in his throat, that sounded like a cross between a grunt and a cough. "Was it you who took down my manifesto?"

"It was."

He shook his head. "You think that really matters? You don't think it's already been copied and disseminated hundreds of times, thousands? People are listening to me. You can't stop the spread of knowledge, now that it's finally begun. I taught you all this."

A man in a dripping trench coat sat down at the table next to us and shook out his umbrella. Tiny droplets flew into my father's face and he flinched. I could see him fight the impulse to turn and glare at the man, making himself visible. Instead he took off the fake glasses and dabbed at his face with a paper napkin.

"You really think that getting rid of a few people is going to bring a halt to the forward progression of technology? That's unrealistic, Dad."

"Revolutions aren't built on rational thinking. They are built on strength of conviction."

"And anyway, technology isn't *all* bad, Dad. I *like* the internet. The way it connects people. The way it gives you access to so much information you couldn't get before. It makes life easier. And it's so egalitarian." I was trying to summon Ross's rousing speech, but knew I'd fallen far short. "You *like* egalitarianism!"

His lips were a tight, white line. "Oh, Jane. You've been brainwashed. You've been working at that place, what, two months? Apparently swallowing any bullshit they feed you. Meanwhile, I have spent *decades* thinking about all this. I was on the front lines. I can see things you can't."

I sat back in my chair. Something about the way he was looking at me made me feel like a trapped bug running circles in a sink, unable to find my way back to the path I'd once been on. "But," I said. And then I petered out. What did I really know, other than what Ross and the other futurists had been spouting? How was I to know that they were right, and my father was wrong?

"It's not too late to redeem yourself," he said suddenly.

"What do you mean?"

"You took the money from the drawer in my office?"

"Yes. Where did it come from?"

"I liberated it," he said. "Trust me, no one missed it. Anyway, I need that money. And the hard drive that I took from Peter."

Something dawned on me. "Wait. Is *that* why you came looking for me? To get your stuff back?"

He frowned. "No. I came for you. But—you still have it, right?"

I picked at the crumbs from my croissant. "Why is the hard drive so important? What's on it?"

"All Peter's research. His AI algorithm." He offered a twisted smile. "I will admit it, that is the one thing the internet *is* good for. Research. I brought that modem home to our cabin, thinking only about distributing my writing online. But then I discovered"—he cocked his head at me—"sorry, yes, you *showed me*—how much access it could give me to the current work that was being done in technology. All those university computer science research departments, all those academic accomplishments, all those start-up business plans and white papers and interviews, all posted online for anyone to read. I began to look up my old colleagues, one by one. And I was *horrified*. The things they were doing. The technology leaders they'd become over the last decade, marching us all toward our doom. I found a paper my co-worker Peter had written, talking about the so-called groundbreaking new AI algorithm he was on the verge of releasing. What it was going to be capable of. And it was the same kind of stuff that I'd predicted would destroy us all, years ago. It wasn't just an idea for the future, anymore; the future was *now*. That's why I knew I had to stop him, that something had to be done. And so I did."

He sat back in his chair, pleased with himself. "And now he's gone, and I'm going to destroy his hard drive with all his work, too, so no one else can expand on it. Think of it—it's the equivalent of having killed Oppenheimer during World War II, destroying all his research. The world would have been a better place if someone had done that, right? So many lives preserved. Well, I could be that person."

I considered this. He had a point about Oppenheimer. What if he was right about Peter Carroll, and the research that his hard drive contained was going to usher in the eventual collapse of society? I felt a familiar flood of fear. So many years of his teachings, so many essays of his I'd read and regurgitated, about man's impending doom. I had been so sure he was right, for so long. And now that he was sitting right here in front of me again, I suddenly couldn't remember why I had stopped listening.

Maybe it wouldn't be so bad to at least give my father the hard drive to destroy, I thought. After all, its owner was already dead. He didn't need it back.

My father was still talking. "...And also, you know where I can find your mother."

I startled back to attention. "Sorry. What?"

"Her address," he said impatiently. "Where she lives now. It's not easy to figure out, she doesn't keep an office and the old house in Atherton is apparently gone. I assume she gave it to you?"

I shook my head. "Why?" I suspected I already knew the answer to this question. It was too horrible to consider.

The air between us felt uncomfortably static, an imbalance in the electricity passing between our bodies. "I just want to talk to her," he said. His eyes squinted at a spot just above my head. I recognized his tell.

"Well, I can't help you," I said flatly. "I don't know her address."

At the table next to us, the man in the trench coat had shifted in his chair and was now sitting uncomfortably close. My father noticed this and stood up. "Let's go."

We made our way to the door. Out on the street, the rain had stopped, and everything was the color of old nickels. My father gazed up Market Street to where a streetcar was approaching. It was a vintage tram in cheery yellow, like something from an old movie. He looked over his shoulder at me, and I wondered if he wanted me to go with him; and if so, where he planned for us to go. Where was he staying, anyway? How had he even gotten here?

I didn't want to follow him to find out.

"I have to go to work," I said. "I'm late."

"Get your mother's address; if you're in touch with her I'm sure this will be simple," he said. "I'll meet you back here, at this Starbucks, let's say three o'clock tomorrow. Bring the money and the hard drive. And after that, if you really want to be done with me, you can be. I'll leave you alone, let you navigate life by yourself, make your own mistakes. Or you can come with me, and we can build a better world together." He put his arms out then and pulled me into another embrace. I let myself lean against his chest, inhaled the familiar, faintly sour smell of him, a sensation that sent me dizzyingly back to my childhood. His arms, around me in the dark when I woke up from a bad dream, his voice in my ear whispering that everything was OK, he would protect me from the monsters in the night.

Despite it all, he was still a part of me that I could never excise, the way an amputee lives forever with their phantom limb.

He put his mouth to my ear, and whispered so softly that only I could hear it. "I know you're still one of the good guys, squirrel. You may have gone a little astray, but I understand, and I forgive. I know that in your heart you still understand what I taught you: that the end of life as we know it is coming, and you and I are the only ones who can stop it. I won't lie to you. When the revolution starts, even more blood will be shed, and society is going to break down. But only by doing that can we stop the extent of the disaster to come."

I jerked backward, out of my father's arms. The tram had stopped just in front of us and my father stepped toward it. "I want you to be with me when it happens," he continued. "But you are going to have to choose for yourself. Naïveté, or reality."

The bell on the streetcar clanged, discordantly cheery. My father lifted a hand in farewell, and then turned around and disappeared.

47

No one commented when I slipped in to work two hours late, bedraggled and tearstained. Brianna wasn't at her desk. Across the room, I thought I saw Lionel tracking my arrival, his head angled toward the door; but I was afraid to look his way, lest he note the culpability in my every movement. As if he might somehow see my father's face reflected in mine.

I booted up my computer and stared blankly at the project on my screen for a long time. For once, I could feel the tediousness of my entry-level job. Checking for broken links, adding missing hashtags, closing parentheses: It wasn't making coffee, but it also wasn't exactly rocket science. Between the grunt work and the massive quantities of pop culture on which I'd been gorging myself, I had barely tapped into my intellect in months. I hadn't even picked up a pencil to sketch since I got to San Francisco. My father wasn't wrong.

And yet I loved it here, despite all that.

The latest issue of the Signal magazine was sitting on Brianna's desk and I picked it up to read the cover. *Perpetual Prosperity: The Future Coming Our Way in the Next 25 Years,* it said, emblazoned over an image of a smiling child holding a daisy with a microchip nestled in its center. I flipped it open and scanned some of the writer's predictions. *An economic boom due to new technological breakthroughs will enable everyone to join the middle class, so that there are no more working poor. The proliferation of new media will allow truth to disseminate in new ways, through new voices, bringing an end to widespread ignorance. A rise of liberalism due to a connected global citizenry will usher in the New Enlightenment and the end of fascism and authoritarianism.*

This didn't sound much like an apocalypse to me. It was all very confusing. I wanted to stop fretting about the future and just think about the now, but I was quickly learning that this was a luxury that the modern world wouldn't allow. Today lives in the shadow of tomorrow. And the shape of that shadow is circumscribed entirely by your willingness to hope.

Naïveté, or reality? I sat there, numbed by the horror of the choice my father had placed before me. Did he really just ask me to pick between him and my mother? With the implicit threat of violence just underneath his request? Surely it had just been some sort of harmless test; but if it was, I couldn't figure out what was benign about it.

"Esme?"

I looked up and saw a Black woman standing by my desk, a Bic pen shoved behind her ear. Her braids ended in beads that rattled when she moved, and they were still vibrating from her walk over from the magazine side of the office.

"I'm Marcie, from HR," she said.

"HR?"

"Human Resources."

"Oh. Right. Hi." I tried to muster a smile. "Can I help you with something?"

"Yes," she said. "I've been looking for you all morning. Something strange came back with your Social Security number. According to government records . . . well, you're deceased."

"Deceased?" I parroted this dully.

"Dead," she said, as if I might not have understood the word. "The Social Security database says that Esme Nowak has been dead since 1983. Any idea why that might be?"

"But I am Esme Nowak," I said, relieved that I could say at least *this* with utter conviction. "And I'm not dead. Clearly."

She laughed, a sharp snort, and the beads chattered softly around her chin. "Yes, I can see that you are not dead. Well, it's possible that it was a clerical error of some sort. These things happen. God knows the government is due for a technology upgrade, their databases are a disaster. Assuming it's a mistake, you should really talk to the Social Security Administration because this issue will just keep popping up. But in the meantime, in order to continue your employment with us, we'll need you to show us some proof that you are who you say you are."

"I have a birth certificate. And a Social Security card."

"That's great. But we'll also need a government ID with your name and photo on it. It's just a formality, of course, but we need to make sure you aren't assuming someone else's identity."

"Why would I want to assume the identity of someone who was dead?" I hoped that I sounded indignantly outraged, rather than panicked.

"I honestly couldn't tell you why, but you understand we need to check all the boxes. Don't want to get us all in trouble for Social Security fraud, do you?"

"And you're going to fire me if I can't prove to you that I'm alive?"

She laughed. "That sounds pretty strange, doesn't it? Again, we can clear all this up with a passport or current driver's license. Do you have one of those on you?"

"Not here," I said. "I'll bring something in tomorrow."

"Great," she said. "Because without it, we'll have to terminate your employment immediately. I'm sorry, but my hands are tied."

I watched her walk away, my mind racing. Now what? Was it possible to get a fake ID in twenty-four hours? I had no clue. It struck me that my father might know how—he'd changed my identity once, hadn't he?—and then it struck me again that asking him for assistance would be a terrible idea. And even if I did manage to scare up a fake driver's license, who was to say that Marcie from HR wouldn't start asking some harder questions about why a dead person had suddenly been resurrected?

Barring some miracle, I was going to be out of a job, starting tomorrow. How many more ways could everything fall apart?

As I sat at my desk, feeling my carefully constructed edifice crumbling to pieces around me, I realized that something about the tenor of the office had abruptly changed. An almost imperceptible shift in the familiar pitch of the room. When I looked up, I saw that Ross was making one of his rare visits to our side of the building.

His appearance in the doorway was an electric pulse that swept across the room. As the staff became aware of his presence, people grew rigid in their seats, trash was abruptly swept into garbage cans, the images on computer monitors switched from gaming news back to programming code. The errant children suddenly on their best behavior for daddy.

Ross wasn't alone, which was even more unusual. He was flanked by two men in gray suits, their hair gelled stiffly into place, eyes narrowly scanning the room as they wove their way between our desks. They did not carry laptop bags or leather portfolios; they were not tech, or even finance guys. Who were they?

Someone turned down the Wu-Tang Clan that was blasting over the stereo. The buzz of the office muted as the threesome worked its way through the zoo to where Frank sat by the window; and then rose again as the foursome adjourned to a conference room in the corner. Once the door was closed, staffers began to congregate in small clots throughout the room, heads tipped together, as they tried to guess what this was all about. The impending IPO? An acquisition?

Brianna returned from the other side of the building, carrying a bran muffin, her face shining. "Oh my God, this is crazy," she whispered to me as she plopped down at her desk, already summoning over Janus and Lionel with wild gesticulations of her hands. Janus was by her side in an instant. Lionel drifted our way more reluctantly, like an iron filing being inexorably tugged by a magnet, against its will. He came to a stop on the other side of Brianna, as far from me as he could be.

"Those guys? They're FBI," Brianna told us. "I was just in the kitchen and I overheard some of the people from the magazine side talking. You know how the Luddite Manifesto went offline yesterday? Well, they traced the IP address of the computer that deleted it. And guess what?"

An iceberg dread was threatening to sink me. Lionel was trying assiduously not to look at me. Janus was practically in Brianna's lap, his voice hoarse with excitement. "What?"

"They traced it *here*. To our office."

Janus laughed. "No way. Has to be a mistake."

I tried to laugh, too, but my pitch was a little too shrill, and I knew that my face had to be frozen in a rictus of terror. Of *course* they'd traced it here. What an idiot I had been, a Gretel laying out a trail of digital breadcrumbs that led straight to me. I was trying to form a question that wouldn't give me away when Lionel's voice cut in, asking exactly what I was afraid to ask. "They traced it to a specific computer?"

Brianna shook her head. "Just our general server, apparently. But seriously, what do you think it means? That someone who works here is working *with* the Bombaster?"

"Whoever it is deleted the manifesto, though." Janus crouched down next to Brianna, the two of them wide-eyed with excitement. "So, not an accomplice, but someone who has it out for him. Right?"

As the two of them debated their theories I looked over at Lionel and saw that his skin was the color of sour milk. His eyes slid over Brianna's head to meet mine and lodged there. We stared at each other in complicit silence. I wanted so badly to know what he was thinking, but the glare on his glasses made him impossible to read.

Without saying a word, he turned and began to walk back across the room, his hands tight against his sides, his shoulders a rigid square. I watched as he passed the engineering cluster, and then his own desk below the Bart Simpson piñata; and then my breath seized in my throat as I realized where he was headed.

The conference room.

Brianna and Janus, their conjecture finally running out of steam, noticed that Lionel had vanished. "Where'd he go?" Brianna asked.

I couldn't answer. I was watching Lionel knocking on the door of the conference room and I felt perilously close to cardiac arrest.

"He's been acting really down the last few days, barely leaves his desk," Janus observed. He gave me a sideways look. "Did something go wrong with you guys? He's really fucking fragile sometimes." I danced away from his gaze, thinking, *You have no idea.* And yet even as I was trapped in a maelstrom of panic—*Is Lionel turning me in right now? What should I do?*—I still felt an unexpected pang of sympathy for Lionel. How could he possibly be more broken than I was? And yet I somehow knew that he was. I hated that I was responsible for breaking him; I couldn't blame him for wanting to finally rid himself of me.

I still wanted to tuck him into my arms and hold him there until his sadness vanished.

Lionel disappeared into the conference room, and it was impossible for me to remain in that office for a single moment longer.

I bolted out of my chair and grabbed my backpack. "I'm feeling a little sick," I announced. "I think I'm going to go home early."

Brianna and Janus stared at me as I stumbled past them toward the exit. Down the hall, careening off the walls as I went; my thumb pressing the elevator button frantically; the bright yellow *SIGNAL* sign pulsing painfully against the back of my eyes. Terrified that at any second I would feel a hand on my shoulder, handcuffs snaking around my wrists.

It wasn't until I got down to the street, and began walking as fast as I could in the direction of downtown, that I let myself cry. How the promise of yesterday could so quickly give way to the disaster of today. How I could have gotten so close to having everything I wanted, only to have it all yanked away.

I wanted so badly to blame someone else for the situation I found myself in, but in my heart I knew that this was all my fault. Yes, my father was the domestic terrorist—but *I* was the one who hadn't gone straight to the police back in Montana. And if Lionel had just turned me in to the authorities, it was only because I'd put him in the untenable position of having to choose between his own sense of morality and me—a girl he barely knew.

I could think of only one place remaining to me. I tugged my mother's business card out of the pocket in my backpack, where I'd carefully zipped it for safekeeping. I walked until I found a working pay phone—I was so adept at pay phones now!—and then dialed the number she'd written on it in neatly round handwriting.

48

My mother was renting an apartment in San Francisco while her new house was being built. "I prefer the suburbs usually, it's so *dirty* in the city, but it's a nice change of pace to be up near the dot-coms right now, to see what's actually happening at the bleeding edge of the industry," she'd told me on the phone. "San Francisco is evolving terribly fast. There's so much moaning about all the artists being pushed out, but you have to think about all the exciting things coming in their place. And honestly, I *welcome* a few more decent restaurants and a few less burritos."

Her temporary home was an open-plan condo on the top floor of a modern glass tower in Nob Hill. When she opened the door, I found myself facing a wall of floor-to-ceiling windows, beyond which I could see the illuminated towers of Grace Cathedral, glowing ghost-like against the night sky.

She leaned in and hugged me lightly, a much warmer hug than the previous day's, if still a little tentative. Jasmine perfume wafted off her; her bones felt as small as a sparrow's. I couldn't help comparing her hug to my father's of that morning, sour-smelling and almost painfully tight. "It's so *good* to see you again," she murmured.

"You smell nice," I blurted. "I remember that, from when I was little."

She looked startled, but happily so. "Chanel No. 5," she said. "Yes, I've been wearing it my whole life. You really remember that, but you don't remember your father kidnapping you? Selective memory, so fascinating. Anyway, come in! I just took dinner out of the oven."

I took a few steps inside. My mother was wearing liquid satin pants and a long cashmere cardigan, both of them the color of fresh December snow. In my Kmart uniform of jeans and hoodie—a little worse for wear after two straight months of heavy rotation in my wardrobe—I felt woefully underdressed. Empty-handed, too. Should I have brought flowers or candy? Was one supposed to bring a gift for dinner with your long-lost mother? If tonight was a test, I felt like I was already failing.

She had her hand on the small of my back now, and was pressing me toward a dinner table that was set with candles and an orchid centerpiece, as if we were on some sort of date. We crossed through the living room, where everything had also been rendered in white—furniture, rugs, pillows, even the cat that slept on the couch—and I wondered if my mother turned invisible when she sat inside this monochromatic tableau. The only color in the room came from the shelves that stretched along one wall, where a collection of delicate glass vases was on display, each one illuminated by a perfect puddle of light. It was all very austere, and it struck me that my mother must be quite rich in order to own so little.

I wondered what she would have made of the cluttered cabin where I was raised, with its towering stacks of newspapers and collections of bent nails in oatmeal cartons. It was hard to imagine that this spare woman had ever been married to my father. How radically their roads had diverged the minute my father drove his convertible off a cliff.

As we passed through the apartment, she gestured to a glass coffee table, where a handful of dusty-looking albums sat incongruously next to an Andreas Gursky art book. "I stopped by the storage unit this morning and found all the old photos. I thought you might like to look at them," she said. "I haven't opened those albums in years. It was just too hard. I'm sure you can understand. So it will be a revelation for both of us. After dinner, I think, since the food is hot."

The apartment was stuffy, the heat cranked luxuriously high. I could feel a staticky buzz coming off my mother as she busied herself at the dining room table, straightening silverware and adjusting the dishes. Gone was the coolly detached woman from the reading the night before. This Tess seemed nervous—rattled, even—as though she had found herself trapped in a cage with a wild animal that might not be particularly friendly.

She looked up at me suddenly, studying me hard. "You were so blond as a child," she said. "Flaxen, like me."

"I still am," I said. "I dyed it."

"Oh. If you want to dye it back, I can take you to my hairdresser." She reached out and tentatively touched a strand of my hair, sending a shiver of pleasure up and down my spine.

"Did you braid it for me? When I was little?" I blurted.

She nodded. "It would get so knotted if we didn't."

"I remember that," I said, delighted that this was an authentic memory, after all, and not just something that Marmee did for Jo.

She gave me that funny lopsided smile again, sad and happy at the same time, then picked up a glass of wine that was sitting, already half empty, on the table. "I'm sorry Freddy isn't here to meet you, unfortunately he's wrapping up some financing in Beijing, but I told him all about you and he is very excited to meet you when he returns. He's officially your stepfather, isn't that strange? All this is going to take some getting used to, isn't it? Anyway, dinner isn't anything fancy. I should confess that I'm not a very enthusiastic cook. I find it mostly a waste of valuable time when the food I could buy is so much better. But I certainly can manage a decent roast chicken. So that's what we're having tonight." She stopped suddenly. "Oh. You're not a vegetarian, are you?"

I laughed. "I've been known to kill my own dinner, so no."

The wineglass paused halfway to her mouth. "You *hunt?*"

"I grew up in Montana. Everyone hunts."

She winced. "Well, I suppose you at least know the meat's organic." She gestured at the table. "Sit, please."

I sat. There was an elegantly folded linen napkin on my plate and I picked this up and placed it carefully in my lap without unfolding it, as it was far too pretty to disassemble. My mother pushed the platter of chicken and potatoes toward me and watched closely as I served myself a breast and a heaping pile of potatoes. She served herself a portion that was a fraction of the size of mine, and then refilled her wineglass. She leaned over her plate without touching her food.

"I am so sorry about yesterday. You must have thought I was a terrible human being. So distant. To my own daughter."

"Not at all," I demurred.

"I was. And I feel terrible about it. I talked to my therapist about it this morning and he said that I was exhibiting classic signs of PTSD. Which makes sense, you know."

The chicken was so salty that I was finding it hard to eat. I decided to focus on the potatoes instead. "I'm sorry, but I don't know what PTSD is."

"*Really.*" This seemed to fascinate her. "Post-traumatic stress disorder, from when you and Adam died. It can linger for a lifetime. And emotional numbing is a common symptom. If you think about it, it was inevitable that I would be so shell-shocked at meeting you again. Disbelieving and cool—" I started to object and she held up a hand, silencing me. "I *was*. And maybe it was understandable, but it certainly wasn't very welcoming to *you*. I hope you don't think I'm awful."

"I don't," I insisted.

"Honestly, I wouldn't be surprised if your father tried to poison you against me. We weren't in a good place when he left. He was very . . . judgmental of me." The wine wobbled in her glass as she spun the stem of her goblet between her thumb and forefinger. I noticed that the torn cuticles had been patched over with Band-Aids.

"He told me almost nothing about you." I decided not to mention the damning memoir pages that I'd worked through the previous evening. I didn't think I should believe them anyway: The woman sitting with me was hardly the villain he'd described. I smiled at her, ready to jettison my father entirely. If I had her, I didn't need him.

Relief flooded her face. "Nothing? Well, I'm glad for that, I suppose. It gives us a clean slate, to start fresh."

"To be honest it's hard for me to imagine the two of you together. You're very . . . different."

"We weren't always." Wine splashed over the rim of her glass, and she dabbed at it with a napkin. "In the beginning we liked each other because we both thought of ourselves as outsiders. I liked that he looked at the world in a different way from everyone else, so passionate about the things he cared about; and he was certainly one of the only men I'd known who seemed interested in what was going on in my mind." She went silent. "Well. Things change; you start out thinking you know everything about someone and eventually you realize you know nothing at all." She picked up the wine and drank it, then leaned in. "Anyway, I'd much rather talk about you."

"What do you want to know?" I needed to wipe the grease from my lips, but I was afraid to soil the napkin, which was quite possibly the most beautiful thing I'd ever held in my hands. I dabbed at the corner of my mouth with the very edge of one fold.

"Oh, *everything*." I could see about a hundred shiny white teeth when she smiled, each one as perfect as the vases on the display shelves.

I thought, guiltily, about the most pressing *everything*—my father, what he'd done (what *we'd* done), how to stop him, I needed to ask her for help. But the truth was that I was enjoying this delicate moment too much to break it; I wanted just a few more minutes of being her unsullied daughter before she knew who I really was.

"I've been living in a cabin with Dad," I began. "Studying, a lot. Drawing, I like to draw for fun. And a lot of chores, you know, chopping firewood and taking care of the chickens."

"Chickens?" Her eyes dropped to the carcass sitting on the table between us.

"I had to kill those, too."

She shook her head. "No wonder you ran away to find me. And you've been in San Francisco how long?"

"About two months. I have a job at Signal."

Her face lit up. "At *Signal*? My God, are you a programmer? I always thought you'd be a programmer! You had such a logic-oriented mind even as a toddler. The things you made with Legos. I was teaching you times tables when you die—" She course-corrected halfway through this last word. "Disappeared."

"No," I said, a little embarrassed. "I'm not a programmer. Just a production assistant. A glorified intern, really. I proof a lot of HTML."

"Oh," she said. "Well, still, Signal, that's something. But . . . no college?"

She seemed to still not understand how we'd been living. And maybe this was my fault, that I hadn't explained our circumstances clearly. "Dad homeschooled me," I said slowly. "Technically I haven't even graduated high school yet. But Dad always said he was teaching me as well as he'd been taught at Harvard, and at a fraction of the price."

Her mouth twisted itself into a tight pretzel. "He always did have a high regard for himself," she muttered. "Listen to me, Esme, you're my daughter now and you *must* get a college degree. Ideally a master's, too, though in my opinion a Ph.D. is just too time-consuming these days, there are too many opportunities you'd be missing out on in the current marketplace. I'll pull some strings and find you a spot for the fall. There's MIT, of course, but maybe you'd prefer something a little closer to home? Stanford's going to be a challenge, but the chancellor of UC Berkeley is a good friend of mine."

Closer to home. Closer to *her.* My heart popped. "That would be amazing. Thank you."

"Yes, the Berkeley engineering department is certainly adequate." She shot a look of sudden concern at me. "Please tell me you're not a liberal arts type? If I know your father, he was probably filling your head with all those philosophers he loved. Not that philosophy doesn't have its place in a balanced society, but it's not exactly a driving force in the new economy."

Oh, I was such a fickle creature, so ready to abandon everything I'd learned if it meant I might get a pat on the head from her. "I completely agree, Theresa."

"*Theresa.*" She looked surprised. "So formal. No one calls me that anymore."

"What did I call you when I was little?"

She smiled, a little rueful. "Mama. But that sounds so childish. How about . . . Mom?"

"*Mom.*" The word tumbled off my tongue, I was so eager to use it. We grinned at each other. I hated to disrupt this moment, but the longer I went without confessing, the longer it felt like everything so far had been a lie.

"So, Mom, there's something really important that I need to talk to you about. It's what I was trying to talk to you about yesterday—"

She picked up the salad bowl and proffered it to me. "Have some salad. I got this balsamic in Modena, it's amazing." I shook my head, and she set it back down so soundlessly that I worried I'd somehow insulted her. "Sorry, please go on. I didn't mean to change the subject."

The room had grown unbearably hot. Sweat was gathering in beads on my forehead and I reluctantly sacrificed the napkin to dab at them. "It's about Dad."

"Yes, we need to discuss him. What to do about that. I know you won't like this, but I am going to have to consider legal recourse. It's truly unforgivable, what he did to us."

"Yes. OK. I understand. But wait—no. No, that's not what I was trying to—" I gave up on finding a graceful way in, and instead just dropped my confession in her lap, a grenade with the pin already pulled out. "Mom, listen. Dad—he's the Bombaster."

"He's—what?" Her chin shot up. Her mouth began to form a shape, as if she was about to object, and then it froze. "The . . . from the—"

"Yes."

"Oh my God," she croaked. She set down the wineglass on the table with a horrible crystalline finality. The room went so silent that

I could hear the sound of a cable car clanging its bell ten stories below. "Tell me this is the punch line to a joke I'm supposed to get."

"I wish it were."

She closed her eyes. I could see the slash of her eyeliner, trembling along the edge of her lids. Her voice dropped, until it was a nearly inaudible whisper: "Would he do that? Of course he would. Oh God, it does make sense—Peter, and Baron, and Harvard. And that manifesto, it sounds just like the garbage he was spewing at the end. I should have put it all together the minute you said he was still alive." She didn't appear to be talking to me, so I let her puzzle everything through on her own. Then her eyes flew open again and she fixed them on me. "Then that means . . . you're the one in the red dress. The girl who shot the security guard."

"That was self-defense, a mistake really. I swear. And I didn't know what Dad was up to. He asked me to come with him to Seattle and distract the security guard. It wasn't until afterward, when I saw the news about the explosion, that I found out what I'd been involved with; and that's when I ran away—" The flood of my words suddenly stopped as I registered the look of horror on her face. She had pushed herself back in her chair, as far away from me as she could get, and was staring at me as if *I* were the monster, not my father.

Her forefinger moved to the edge of the torn cuticle, found the Band-Aid, and began to fiddle with it. "Esme—this is—this is . . ." Her thoughts kept dying in her throat.

"I'm so sorry." I felt like I'd just done something terrible to her. Had I?

She jumped up and began to pace back and forth behind the table, her palms on either side of her head. "What a nightmare. I can't—" She stopped pacing and looked at me again. "Your father, you *really* don't know where he is? Is he in San Francisco, too?"

I realized that my answer was going to make me sound like I'd lied the previous day, but it couldn't be helped. Reluctantly, I nodded my head.

"My God, he's going to come after me, too, isn't he?" Her voice had grown high-pitched and panicky. "Picking off the old gang, one by one. He's lost his mind. We need to call the police immediately. I'm going to need protection." She walked across the room to where a small leather purse was sitting on a side table and began to rummage through it.

"OK," I said. My voice sounded very small. Of course she was going to be scared for her life; I'd anticipated that. But somehow this wasn't the response I'd expected. There was no *you poor thing* or *what do you need* or *how terrible this must have been for you.* "But—what about me? Can you help me, Mom?"

This time, the word *Mom* made her visibly flinch. "Help you?"

"I think the FBI might know who I am," I said. "I think someone at Signal told the authorities about me today, and now I'm not sure what to do. I know I need to stop Dad. But what will happen if I go to the police? I'm wanted, too, aren't I? They'll put me in jail. Or worse."

She had extricated a phone from her purse but she was just staring at it now, not dialing. "Right. I see. OK. Let me think this through."

"Maybe if you go with me, to talk to the police. Or make a public statement, or something, explaining that I wasn't really his accomplice, but his victim? You're famous. People will listen to you."

She slowly tucked the phone back into her purse. "I think you're overestimating my influence."

It was beginning to dawn on me that my mother wasn't going to magically solve everything with a wave of her hand. "But I need help." I could hear my voice go high, on the verge of hysteria. "None of what's happened is my fault, I swear." Would anyone believe that? I wasn't sure my own mother did. Even *I* didn't believe it. After all, I had uploaded the manifesto to the internet. I had helped my father murder Peter. I had destroyed and hidden evidence. I'd had two months to turn my father in; the fact that I hadn't was utterly damning.

I hadn't driven the train, but I had gone along for the ride. Of course I was complicit.

What I wanted was for Theresa to soothe my fears with a fistful of motherly platitudes. *You're right, it's not your fault, you were a child, you didn't know any better.* But she just stood there, staring blankly out toward the Gothic filigree of Grace Cathedral, solving a puzzle inside her head.

"All right, I know how we proceed," she finally said. She pivoted to regard me. The woman before me was once again the severe woman behind the lectern on Monday: Cool and collected and a little bit terrifying. Like a warrior, but *my* warrior. "I am going to connect you with a very good lawyer. I'm thinking Rhona Silverberg, she owes me some favors. Her fees will be astronomical, but I'll cover that, don't worry. You'll go the authorities with Rhona first thing tomorrow and you will tell them everything. Including how they can locate your father."

Relief coursed through me—*a plan, finally a cogent plan*—and I thought of Lionel, and how I'd insisted to him that I needed to confer with my mother first. I had been right, hadn't I? "OK. You'll come with us, too, right?"

A look of faint apology washed over her face. "I'm so sorry, but that's not going to be possible," she said. "I'm going to leave town. Tonight. Just to be safe."

"Where are you going?"

She shook her head. "That has to be a secret. The whole point of leaving is so that Adam won't know where I am."

It took a minute for the implications of this to sink in. "You think I'd tell him," I said slowly. "You think I'd help him murder you."

She tugged the edges of her cashmere cardigan tightly together, across her chest. "No, I'm not saying that. But why take unnecessary risks?"

And maybe I shouldn't have blamed her for this. I *was* a stranger to her, tied though we were by blood and a very distant past. She didn't know a thing about my loyalties or motivations. She had no real proof that my presence in her living room meant that I'd decided to turn my back on all that. But it broke me in pieces to realize that even after I'd finally found what I'd been hunting for so hard, I still didn't have the mother I'd wanted to find. One who believed in me, unquestioningly.

She continued. "Now. When the press comes to you—and they *will* come; they will figure out the whole story as soon as your father's real identity is released, and it will be quite the media frenzy—don't tell them that we were in touch this week. And you shouldn't tell them that I'm paying your legal bills, either. As far as the world is concerned, I didn't know you'd survived until the authorities came to me to let me know that you'd turned yourself in, and that you and Adam were still alive."

I tried to wrap my head around this, and failed. "But why?"

She laughed, a little wanly. "You don't want me to get in trouble, too, do you? What if they think I helped you and your father hide out? Or worse? The media is sensationalistic, and it can influence the authorities, like it or not. No, better to keep me out of it, I think."

I gazed down at the plate in front of me, at the unappealing wreckage of my meal, limp lettuce swimming in congealing meat juices, chicken bones gone waxy. I looked away, and over to the glass table, where the faded photo albums sat forgotten in a stack. There would be no convivial stroll down memory lane this evening.

"So when will I see you again?"

"I couldn't say. But don't worry. I'll make sure that Rhona is helping you with everything you need. She's a bulldog and if anyone can get you out of this, she can." The expression on my face must have given away my hurt. "Esme, I'm sure you understand how complicated this is. But it's just for now. When all this is over, and everything has been sorted out by the legal system, I'm sure we can reconnect and start over." She tried for the lopsided smile again, but this time only managed a painful-looking grimace.

And that was when I realized, with a blinding burst of clarity, what her evasions were all about: She wanted to see if I was going to be convicted of murder before she decided to claim me as her daughter. Until then, she could profess to be just another one of my father's victims; not an abettor of any kind. After all, her reputation as a tech guru and futurist might be sullied if she was somehow associated with the Luddite Bombaster and his criminal daughter. She was more worried about her credibility than she was about me.

"So you're saying, as far as you're concerned, I don't exist," I said slowly. "I died fourteen years ago, and that's it, until you decide otherwise."

She frowned, and smoothed the blond cap of her hair, where not a single strand had gone astray. "That's not what I said," she said. "I promise, I'll be in touch eventually."

I stood up from the table. The napkin, still in its meticulous folds, fell from my lap and onto the floor. I didn't bother to pick it up. I staggered toward the door on stiff legs, as if I were a zombie; which was what I really was to my mother, wasn't I? A dead person, thrust back into being, but with little resemblance to the person I once was. It would have been easier for her if I'd just stayed in my grave.

"Don't feel obliged," I said before I shut the door.

49

You have been living as Saul Williams for two years when you first rob a bank.

The decision is not made lightly; it is a result of long seasons of desperation. When you first relocated to Montana, you thought you would be able to live mostly off the land, like a homesteader. You read up on farming methods, kitchen gardens, the most practical vegetables to grow in your new climate zone. For material goods, there was the Salvation Army in Bozeman, where you would scour the dumpster bins for donations that they had rejected. You have always been good at building and fixing—you assembled your own computer in 1978, just for fun—and you found that most trash could easily be brought back to life with a little wire or solder and some rudimentary grasp of engineering. Clothes with holes could be patched. Clocks could be made to tick again. Pots with broken handles could be glued back together.

People waste so much: Our shortsighted consumer culture believes in replacement rather than repair, values cheap Chinese crap over quality materials. You take full advantage of that, scooping up perfectly good discards with only minor flaws. You delight in how Jane doesn't seem to miss owning new things; already, she has forgotten the consumerist mindset of *more more more*.

You figured you could cobble together enough odd jobs to cover the rest of your needs: chopping wood, washing cars, cleaning houses, honest labor for which you could be paid in cash. But you've quickly learned that there aren't that many under-the-table jobs after all, not when you live an hour out of town, and you also have to balance the childcare requirements of a little girl. And meanwhile there is too much, you're discovering, that you *have* to pay for: Sturdy shoes for Jane's ever-growing feet, gas for the truck, sacks of rice. Suitable books, rather than the bodice rippers that tend to land at the thrift stores. Rent.

As for food, your ability to farm has also proven to be rather limited: Although you've planted two bumper crops of potatoes and your tomato plants are impressive by any measure, you've utterly failed to grow a carrot and the squirrels eat your squash before it even ripens. It pains you to look at Jane and see the outline of her tiny rib cage, the bulge of malnutrition in her belly from living mostly on Quaker oatmeal.

By the end of year two, you have run out of money and are starting to feel panicked. In your darkest moments, you wonder if this whole project was a terrible mistake. If it was just *you*, you could leave and start again, someplace where it might be easier to scratch a living together. But Jane is the problem: Jane, for whom this whole endeavor was intended. She is thriving here, it's so obvious to you. She spends contented hours weaving dandelions into crowns and watching the ants deliver sustenance to their queen. She soaks in everything you teach her, her mind clear and undistracted, an avid pupil. The minute you leave the safety of your cabin, you know this will come to an end. Worse: You'll run the risk of being discovered, and separated entirely.

It's clear that you have to find *some* way to survive.

You and Jane are reading aloud *Sherlock Holmes: The Red-Headed League*, about a group of thieves who tunnel into a bank vault, when it occurs to you: Why *not* rob a bank? You don't need to steal a million dollars; the contents of one teller's till will get you through most of the year. A few thousand dollars, more or less.

A week later, you march into a Farmers State Bank in Missoula wearing a wig and a pair of gas station sunglasses, select the youngest-looking teller, and hand her a note that reads *Give me all the money in your till and no one gets hurt*. Three minutes later, you walk out the door with $5,327.

Over the next dozen years, you will repeat this interaction nineteen times.

It turns out that it's remarkably easy to rob a bank. Multinational financial institutions—in their attempt to lay claim to every pocketbook in America—have been opening neighborhood branch offices as fast as they can. And because they want to hide their true vampiric nature behind a "friendly" mien, they no longer bother to hire security guards for these branches. Suburban moms don't like guns.

And so you discover that you can waltz right into any neighborhood bank branch, slide a note to the teller, and no one will bat an eye. The teller, usually an underpaid twenty-something, is not going to cry out an alarm. Why would they? It's not their money to protect. There's no reason to play the hero when their efforts won't ever be rewarded.

You rarely have to actually converse with the teller; when you are forced to speak, it's only to tell them that you have a gun in your pocket if they don't comply with the note's instructions. (You do not have a gun in your pocket, of course; this would only be asking for trouble.) Typically, the teller will obey immediately, sliding over the money without raising an alarm until after you've departed. You are always long gone by the time the police show up.

There are still risks, of course. In the absence of security guards, the banks now rely on dye packs and electronic transmitters shoved in among the bills. But removing these is child's play for you: They are easily identified by using a simple RF radio receiver, which you have built yourself, and you hand these right back to the teller before you walk out the door. Banks all now have CCTV surveillance cameras, but you simply wear a rotation of eyewear and wigs to render yourself unrecognizable. You conduct most of your robberies in the winter, when scarves and hats and gloves aren't considered suspicious. And you vary the banks and locations you target, typically driving beyond Montana's borders, so that authorities won't link the robberies to one person.

In the beginning, you bring Jane with you on these expeditions. You have no choice: She is too young to stay at home alone. You leave her in the car with a book and when you return, five minutes later, with a much heavier backpack, you drive straight to the closest ice cream shop. There, licking your mint-chip cones, you are just a sweetly innocuous father-daughter pair spending the day together. No one looks twice at you, not even the police cars racing past you toward the bank.

You frame these excursions as "day trips." She loves them, of course. There are no ice cream cones in your normal routine.

You stop bringing her along around the time she turns eight and her powers of observation start to amaze you. By then, she is capable of spending a night at home by herself. You are driving farther and farther afield to scout suitable bank branches—ones that are near a highway on-ramp, that have an affluent customer base, that hire easily intimidated teenage tellers rather than jaded adult professionals. These trips take time. When the phone company comes through the area, installing lines for a new luxury hunting lodge ten miles past your cabin, you convince them to also run a line to your cabin; and so you are able to check in with Jane daily while you are gone. It proves unnecessary. Your daughter is supremely self-sufficient—a sign, you think, that your decision to leave California was a wise one.

You soon find that you have more money than you need. You are still living like you have nothing at all, and dip into the money only when necessary. You keep the rest hidden in a locked drawer of your desk, and think of it as your "go cash." The likelihood, you are beginning to realize, is that you will not be able to stay hidden in the woods forever. At some point, your cover will be broken, the police will come looking for you, and you and Jane will need to make a quick escape. So you add to your nest egg bit by bit, until the money in the drawer adds up to more than five figures.

After a time, you come to realize that you aren't robbing banks now because you need to. You are doing it because you *like* to. Because it feels good to stick it to these big multinational financial institutions, the fat-cat bankers, who represent everything you loathe. Because it reinforces your conviction that *you are smarter than they are.* And even though you are aware that what you are doing is nothing at all to them—not even a blip on their radar—you like to think that you are sending a message, however small.

You just wish there was a better way of making your point, one that the rest of the world might hear. An audience of one—even if Jane remains the most curious, willing listener—can sometimes feel quite small. Sometimes you can't help but wonder: What kind of impact could you have on the shape of humankind, if humankind were only to listen?

50.

THE LONGING FOR love is a flawed piece of human coding. It scrambles every circuit in your brain, fries your logic boards, makes it impossible to compute. Seized by our need to be loved, we are unable to see anything clearly, even how we might save our own skin. It's only much later, with the clarity of distance, that we can see how blind we were. How needy. How desperate.

How stupid.

After I left my mother's apartment, I began the long walk back home in a daze. The people that I passed on the street gave me pitying looks, quite likely because I was a volcano of woe, bubbling snot and tears from every facial orifice, sobs erupting at unlikely intervals. By the time I got halfway back to the Haight, the sleeve of my sweatshirt was unspeakable.

Spring had snuck in when I was looking the other way, and the evening was windless and comparably balmy. Pedestrians sauntered down the sidewalks with unzipped jackets and naked fingers. For once, the night sky was clear, and I looked up reflexively, hoping for a familiar glimpse of the galaxy; but the city lights had dimmed the sky, and all I could see was Orion, the most pedestrian of constellations. I thought of my father, who had taught me astronomy by having me draw a map of the stars visible above our cabin every night for a year—*the way Copernicus did it*—so that I could understand the heliocentric movement of the planets.

Thinking of my father set off the waterworks again. In a matter of hours, he would be waiting for me at Starbucks; believing—despite all the ways I'd failed him so far, despite how I'd just been so ready to throw him under the bus to win over my mother—that I was going to show up with his money and the hard drive. *I know you're still one of the good guys, squirrel.* Was I? I had less clarity than ever about who the "good guys" actually were.

But at least one of my parents still loved me; wasn't that better than having no love at all?

A police car blew past me as I was trudging through Hayes Valley, its siren interrupting the night, its lights illuminating the apartment building façades like a demented disco ball. I stepped into the shadowy entranceway of a closed shoe store, a fillip in my heart. But the car raced up the hill without stopping.

As I watched the police vanish in the general direction of my apartment, it suddenly dawned on me that I couldn't possibly go home. Lionel had turned me in. The FBI would be trying to locate me—I was, after all, one of the targets of the nation's biggest manhunt—and my sublet would be the first place they'd go. By now they surely had the hard drive and the money that I'd hidden under my bed, along with the incriminating pages of my father's memoir that I'd painstakingly deciphered (and all the ones I had yet to tackle). I imagined a SWAT team, hidden just behind the door of the apartment, guns drawn and ready to start firing the minute my key hit the lock.

The feds, coming for me, just as my father had always warned they would.

As I stood there outside the shoe store, staring at a display of four-hundred-dollar lug-sole boots—not dissimilar to what I'd always worn in Montana, but ten times the price—I could come up with only three possible choices that remained for me.

I could go back to the apartment anyway, and let myself get arrested, quite possibly in a violent spectacle that would result in my death.

Or: I could do what my mother suggested and turn myself in to the police in the morning, and hope they would be more sympathetic to me because I'd come in on my own accord.

Or: I could go with my father tomorrow, say *screw you* to San Francisco and the mother who failed to live up to my hopes and the industry that I'd let myself believe in despite everything I'd been taught. I could become the herald of change, railing against inevitability, leaving destruction in my wake. A murderer, a criminal, yes, but at least one who was beloved by her father.

Option A felt impossible. Options B and C at least gave me more time to decide, but I would need to find a place to spend the night while I did.

I thought of the bunk beds at Signal—could I hunker down there for the night?—but if the feds were at my apartment, they were surely also swarming all over my place of employment. For that matter, I technically didn't even *have* a job anymore, based on what Marcie from HR had told me. Even if my employers at Signal weren't yet aware that I was a fugitive, they still believed that I was an identity thief. My key card had probably been disabled the minute I walked out the door.

Maybe I could stay in a hotel? I tugged the fold of money out of my pocket and counted: twenty-six dollars, not enough for even the sketchiest Tenderloin motel.

I was debating whether I was tough enough to try to make a go of sleeping rough in Golden Gate Park—my father had taught me how to build a pine-bough lean-to, but it had been years since I'd attempted one—when I heard a familiar voice behind me.

"Esme?"

I pivoted where I stood, coiling like a cat, ready to leap away. Brianna was approaching from down Hayes Street, carrying a greasy paper bag. If she'd learned who I was in the hours since I'd walked out the door of our office, it wasn't evident on her face. In fact, she was *smiling,* as if happy to run into me.

She stopped in front of me. "Hi! You look like crap. Still sick?"

I glanced in the plate glass window of the shoe store, trying to compose myself. I couldn't figure out what she was talking about, and then I remembered the hasty excuse I'd given her when I ran out the door of Signal that morning. (Had it only been nine hours earlier?) "Oh. No. I'm feeling better."

"We wondered if maybe you had the stomach flu. It's going around." She reached into the paper bag, which smelled suspiciously like burrito, and withdrew a tortilla chip. She tossed it in her mouth, then passed the bag to me. "Chip? They always give you too many and then I eat them all and feel ill."

I shook my head. The smell made me queasy, my mother's chicken sitting uneasily in my stomach. "I'm not hungry."

She popped another chip in her mouth. "You picked a bad day to leave early, huh? So nuts."

Her blasé demeanor perplexed me. Clearly, she hadn't yet been informed who I was. Was it possible that Lionel's conversation with the FBI hadn't immediately turned the office upside down? But wouldn't the feds have marched straight over to my desk, looking for me? Maybe they were keeping everything under wraps until they investigated Lionel's claims. Or maybe they hadn't believed him?

"What was nuts?" I finally managed.

"You don't know? Oh shit, I don't know how you would, come to think of it. You don't even have a cellphone so I couldn't call you. You should really get one, you know. Join the twenty-first century, get one of those new Nokias."

I was about to lose my cool completely. "Brianna, *what happened?*"

She leaned in, so close I could smell the chips on her breath. "Check this out: Lionel turned himself in."

"Turned himself in?" My insides collapsed. Her words weren't making any sense. She meant *me*, Lionel had turned *me* in, right? But she'd said *himself*.

"For what?" I managed.

"For deleting the Luddite Manifesto, remember?"

Now I was really confused. "But that doesn't make any sense."

"I know, right? Janus and I were shocked. But it's really not that surprising when you think about it. Lionel was really worked up about that website. I mean, we all were, of course. All the attention that psychopath was getting for his paranoid fearmongering. And the feds just left it sitting there online for anyone to read, God knows why." She was squeezing the paper sack in her fist, mangling the top. "But I guess Lionel decided to do something about it. Apparently, he confessed to hacking into the GeoCities server and deleting it."

I put out a hand and pressed it against the cool glass of the shop window, afraid that if I didn't, I might fall down. "Oh my God."

"Honestly, I can't believe he told them." Brianna was still talking, unaware that I was on the verge of fainting. "I mean, would they ever have figured it out? And now he's in a world of trouble. Hacking—yes, I know everyone does it these days, but it's still a federal offense. Plus GeoCities is going to be *pissed.* And it sounds like the FBI considered that website evidence for the case they're building against the Bombastard. Whenever they catch him. So yeah, everyone is mad. Not such a smart move, Lionel."

Now I felt genuinely sick to my stomach. "What's going to happen to him?"

She extracted one more tortilla chip from the bag and nibbled at the edge like a distracted chipmunk. "We think he was arrested. The two FBI agents who came in—they didn't cuff him or anything, but he was marched out of the office between them. Perp-walk style. I sure hope he has a good lawyer."

"Poor Lionel," I whispered. I imagined him sitting on a metal shelf in a jail cell, his tie askew and glasses smudged, surrounded by drug addicts and murderers and domestic abusers. I couldn't understand why he lied. But the answer was obvious, wasn't it? He did it for me. For *me,* who didn't even deserve it. I wanted to cry. "We have to help him. He's not even a hacker!"

Brianna folded the bag closed and was gazing down at it with an expression of faint revulsion. "Not much we can do, I don't think. Look, Esme, don't take this the wrong way, but—please don't mess with Lionel's head anymore. I don't know exactly what happened between the two of you, but you clearly did something to upset him.

He's not been himself lately and I have to wonder if this stunt is somehow related. Lionel . . . he's vulnerable. He needs stability, OK?"

"I'll stay away from him," I promised.

She rolled her eyes. "That's not really what I meant."

"Oh." I wasn't sure what she meant, then, but it seemed like a moot point anyway. He was in jail, for something I'd done. And no matter what I decided to do tomorrow, nothing was ever going to go back to the status quo between us.

"Not trying to be rude but I taped last night's *Buffy* and I really want to get home to watch it. See you at work tomorrow?"

Unlikely, I thought. *You'll probably never see me again, except on the ten o'clock news.* I was about to continue in the opposite direction when something caused me to pivot. "Brianna, can I stay with you tonight? I got locked out of my apartment."

She hesitated, then shrugged. "Sure," she said. "As long as you don't mind *Buffy*."

AND SO THE final night of my sojourn in San Francisco was spent on Brianna's corduroy couch, watching a blond cheerleader vanquish vampires with a sharpened stake.

After Brianna finally yawned and excused herself, I lay sleepless on that couch for hours. This last night in the city felt like a parallel to my first few nights here: equally homeless, equally guilt-ridden, equally lost. And yet it was so much worse this time around, because the person who was suffering the most because of me right now was the one person who had done the least to deserve it.

I regretted ever going to look for Lionel in that chat room, regretted even more that he'd offered to help me. I wanted to wish myself back to the previous November, before the internet arrived at our cabin, before I found the photo of my mother, before my life slid sideways. Back to the recliner on our porch and the mist drifting across the rain-kissed meadow, to Samson skulking by the pond and the smell of pine needles on the crisp forest air. Back to when I had my books and my father, and that was all I thought I needed.

Now that I knew how much else there was to need, I couldn't help wanting it all.

But there was never any going back.

I rose when the sun was just starting to tint the sky pink. I left a note on the kitchen table—*Thank you, for everything*—and let myself out without saying goodbye. I made my way back to the Haight, bought a cup of coffee, and then sat on the stoop of the apartment building across from mine, watching and waiting.

The city was waking up. Arriving shop owners threw open their gates and roused the junkies that lay asleep on their steps. Buses grumbled past, weighed down with bleary commuters. The smell of blueberry muffins from the diner down the street lingered in the air, with a whiff of stale garbage just below.

There was no sign of a police presence at my apartment. Still, I didn't move until one of the Heathers finally materialized in the entrance of the building around 7:00 A.M. I ran across to intercept her, holding the door open as she tussled with her bike helmet.

"Good morning," I said.

"You're up early." She stood aside to let me in.

I hovered at the door, reluctant to go upstairs. "Just checking—is everything OK up there?"

She gave me a funny look. "Why wouldn't it be?"

So it was true. Lionel really hadn't turned me in, not even after his own arrest. The feds hadn't come by. I was still free, even if it didn't particularly feel that way.

I trudged up the stairs for the last time, the ancient carpet soft under my sneakers. Inside the apartment, I collected the duffel bag from where I'd stuffed it under the bed, still half full of cash, the hard drive bulging through the nylon fabric. I stacked my father's pages on top, along with my own half-finished transcriptions. Everything else I possessed went back into the backpack, where it had started two months earlier.

I took one last look around Megan's bedroom—at the eyelet coverlet and the college diplomas framed on the wall, the giant television and the photographs of friends I would never meet. This room wasn't mine; it never had been. Nothing actually belonged to me in San Francisco—not my job, not my friends, not even my name. I had spent two months as a trespasser, living a stranger's life, based on a scaffold of lies. I could finally see it now.

I just wish I knew the way back to me, whoever I was.

I shouldered the backpack and the duffel bag and headed out.

51

Two months of gloom had culminated in a glorious day of sunshine, and it felt like the universe was sending me a postcard from a future I would not be around to enjoy. *See this? See what you are going to miss?* When I tilted my head back to gaze up at the sky that was visible between the towers of downtown, I was slapped in the eye by a brilliant cerulean slice.

The climate inside Starbucks, however, remained the same as the day before. The bright spring light had been dulled flat by the brown glaze on the windows. The room was still a temperature-controlled 68 degrees, the same inoffensive jazz standards played on the stereo system. The store was emptier this afternoon, but a smattering of bored-looking customers sat hunched over their drinks, flipping through abandoned sections of the *Chronicle*.

My father was perched at the same table in the corner, as far as possible from the bored barista who was rearranging the display of chocolate-covered coffee beans. He hadn't changed clothes—it was possible this was the only outfit he currently owned—and he looked even more rumpled, his coat limp and his hair flat on one side. I wondered where he'd spent the night; if *he* had been the one to sleep rough in Golden Gate Park. I wouldn't put it past him.

I could feel his eyes on me as I stopped at the counter and bought myself a Frappuccino. It had occurred to me that this might be my last chance to taste one. Whatever was about to happen from this point on, it wouldn't involve a lot of three-dollar blended coffee drinks.

Straw wedged between my teeth, sugar coating my tongue, I walked slowly over to my father, and took the chair across from him.

"You came," he said. He knuckled the side of his nose, where a raw patch of skin was erupting.

"You thought I wouldn't?"

He shook his head, a sideways cant to his smile. "No, I knew you would. You're my girl, like it or not. That's never going to change."

A knot inside my chest was making it difficult to breathe. I tried to find words that wouldn't come.

My father pointed at the backpack that I'd dropped at my feet. "That's it? Everything's in there?"

"Everything important."

"The money?"

"No," I conceded. "That's in a safe place."

"We'll need that money. I've been living off the generosity of some of my readers but that won't last forever. Things in North Dakota were getting dicey when I left, Malcolm isn't as rational as I hoped he'd be; turns out he's part of the militia movement, which is a hornet's nest I really don't want to poke. So I think it might be time to head to Texas, Ben's offered shelter, but we'll need supplies." He prodded the backpack with the toe of his sneaker. "The hard drive, it can't possibly be in there, either. Where is it?"

"The hard drive doesn't matter, Dad."

"Of course it matters. We need to destroy it so it doesn't get into the wrong hands. I was thinking—we'll make a movie of it. With one of those little camcorders I've been seeing around. Blow it up, a very symbolic act, and then you can put the video online. You can put video on the World Wide Web, right?"

The knot had risen from my chest to my throat. I was finding it hard to swallow. "But, Dad, Peter Carroll surely backed it up."

A distant expression came into my father's eyes, as if he was trying to dig up something that was lodged in the rear of his brain. "Backed what up?"

"Backed up his hard drive—as in, made a copy? You know what a backup is, right? They back up my computer every week at Signal. I'm sure they did the same at Microsoft." His brow crumpled as the portent of my words dawned on him. He picked up a napkin that was sitting on the table between us and began to twist it into a knot. I couldn't decide if the frustration darkening his face was directed at himself, for forgetting something so fundamental, or at me, for surpassing his understanding of technology.

"Point is, I realized that destroying that hard drive achieves nothing. I'm sure Peter Carroll's bosses at Microsoft have already passed all his research on to someone else." My father opened his mouth to object, but I cut him off. "Dad, Oppenheimer didn't build the atomic bomb himself; it was a team effort. Even without him, the bomb would have happened eventually. Maybe not as fast, but he wasn't the only one working on the concept."

He was silent for a moment, twisting and untwisting the napkin. "All right. I concede your point about the hard drive."

"Don't you think it's the point of *everything,* though? How many people do you think you need to kill to halt the march of progress? For every person you take out of the equation, a hundred more are coming up behind them. It would be a Sisyphean task to try to stop it."

"*Technological progress has merely provided us with more efficient means for going backward.* That was Aldous Huxley, writing in *Ends and Means.* His point being—"

"Dad. Stop. No more lectures."

He opened his mouth, about to persist, but something about the tone of my voice stopped him. Instead, he unfolded the twisted napkin and carefully spread it out on the table between us, running a palm over the wrinkles in a futile effort to restore it to its previous condition. "You know. I thought about it and let's leave your mother out of all this," he said, his tone going unexpectedly tender. "I shouldn't have asked that of you. It wasn't fair. I'm still angry at her, and I let that color my judgment. But I can see now that it was a mistake to ask you to choose between us. Jane, why are you crying? Don't cry."

On the other side of the windows, a cluster of shadows moved past, temporarily blocking out the light. I'd lost my appetite for the Frap-

puccino, too sweet, that was melting into slush in the cup in front of
me. I pushed it away and used the back of my hand to wipe away the
tears that were falling, unwelcome, down my face. My father was silent, for once, watching me; and I could tell that it was dawning on
him that his plan for us had gone awry.

And then there was a clatter at the door of the café, stiff-heeled
shoes scuffing against the floor tiles, a squeak of rubber. The jazz music
suddenly seemed painfully loud, but that was only because the rest of
the café had gone so quiet. I was afraid to turn around, and so it was
only through the changing weather of my father's face that I could
read what was transpiring behind me. First, a sudden wariness, his
eyes shifting down and to the side, perhaps an attempt to render himself invisible; and then a stiffening of his spine, hands braced against
the tabletop, jaw set; and finally, just as I felt the presence of the bodies behind my chair, a sudden slackness in his cheeks, followed by a
long exhale.

"Squirrel," he said softly, a warning, and it broke my heart.

I turned slowly in my seat and there they were, a half-dozen uniformed officers, two more in suits with *FBI* tags clipped to their la-
pels. The bogeymen of my childhood, blocking our path to the door,
hands hovering over the guns at their waists. This time, there was no
escape hatch, no secret tunnel to save us.

My head buzzed so loudly that the words being shouted over my
head registered only as an indiscernible roar. The room seemed to spin
in desultory circles around us; the Frappuccino, somehow, was on its
side and oozing brown sludge across the table. My only anchor amid
the chaos was my father's face, his eyes still latched tightly on mine.
And so, gazing back into this abyss, I could mark the exact moment
when it dawned on him that I was not surprised, and I was not scared;
that, in fact, I had known who would be standing behind me before I
even turned around. That the feds had not tracked us here of their
own accord—but that I had led them here, on purpose.

I watched my colossus of a father break apart when he finally understood that I had turned him in, and it tore me in pieces, too.

But what I didn't expect was the strange light in his eyes, something like wonder, as he stared at me with his jaw slightly agape. As if, instead of betraying him, I had managed to impress him. As if only now—now that it was too late—did he see that his worthy adversary had been sitting there, right in front of him, all along.

52

The Anarchist Cookbook is what sets you on your path.

You find it at the bottom of the dollar bin at the used bookstore in Bozeman, where you often go to find reading material for Jane, now a teenager. The University of Montana students sell their old books here, and you have located a surprising number of useful texts on the shelves. But today, you find something else entirely, something that turns out to be far more important to you than a dog-eared copy of *Organic Chemistry 1.*

The book has a torn cover and is so flimsy that you almost disregard it, until your eye catches on a word that you find intriguing. *Anarchist.* You hesitate: You have heard of this book, a glorified pamphlet that was deemed "subversive" by the FBI and CIA when it was first published in the early seventies. "One of the crudest, low-brow, paranoiac writing efforts ever attempted," the FBI called it. Written as a kind of political stunt, *The Anarchist Cookbook* had the whole computer community buzzing about it back when you worked at PRI because it contained instructions for rudimentary early telephone hacking, the "phreaking" that Woz and Steve used to employ to make long-distance calls for free.

Of course, you buy it.

Inside, you discover instructions for all kinds of illegal activities. How to engage in hand-to-hand combat, make your own LSD, conduct surveillance, sabotage a car. It's all written in the most colloquial language, with guidelines easy enough for a teenager to follow. *Making tear gas is so simple that anyone can do it*, it reads, and then proves itself correct.

But the part that intrigues you the most is Chapter 4: Explosives and

Booby Traps. The chapter is illustrated with a drawing of a grizzled anarchist, setting off a cartoon bomb. At first you are fascinated simply by the engineering aspect of bomb-making, the logical mechanics of it appealing to you in the same way that the innards of a computer once did. You assemble a few explosives of your own, because you can; but you aren't quite sure what to do with them, other than to booby-trap your own escape hatch.

It takes some time for you to return to the introduction of this chapter and realize that there's a bigger message to be gleaned from this little book. *The most heroic word in all languages is Revolution,* the section begins. *Explosives are one of the greatest tools any liberation movement can have . . . An explosion can take the shape of hope for a nation of oppressed people.*

You know exactly what the people need to be liberated from.

Just because you've been away from Silicon Valley for more than a decade doesn't mean you haven't been paying attention to what's happening in the world. You've watched from the sidelines as computers and their miraculous wonders take up more and more of the real estate in the newspapers and magazines that you read (and later, once you realize it's a necessary evil, the television news you consume). The same hackers and programmers and engineering Ph.D.s that you once considered your peers are now on the front page of every periodical, lauded as prophets, rich beyond belief. *Time* magazine declares the computer "Machine of the Year"!

In 1994, you read that nearly a quarter of all households now have personal computers.

Life in the outside world is moving too fast. You feel the upward curve of technology's progression ascending off the chart—Moore's Law, that terrifying accelerating equation—and all your alarm bells are going off. You have so much knowledge about where this is all going—you have the counterpoint to the hype that the world seems to currently lack—and it no longer feels right to hide away and let it all happen without you. You need to speak up. To be the Cassandra to everyone else's Pollyanna.

You try to ignite your revolution with a magazine, *Libertaire,* only to discover that it's hard to get people to listen to you if no one is aware that you exist. A pseudonym and a typewriter will only take you so far. Two years in, you have to admit to yourself that you've failed.

Meanwhile, the internet has arrived with a bang. The latest iteration of what you were working on so many years ago at Harvard with ARPAnet, but shinier and slicker and more user-friendly. So much more compelling, so much more addictive. It is an immediate sensation. You can feel the doomsday clock ticking off the minutes of humanity's demise. How is it possible that you are the only person who sees this? Why is everyone so willing to step smilingly off a cliff, never bothering to look down to see what's below?

And then there's this:

Jane is nearly a woman now, growing curious about the world beyond your cabin. You had naïvely hoped that she would choose to stay with you here in the woods, protected, safe forever; but the older she gets, the more you come to understand that this was always just a fantasy. One day, you find a cheap pink lipstick hidden inside her sock drawer and you realize that it's not long before she will try to leave you. And what will happen to her then? The world out there will eat her alive. It will take everything that is pure and beautiful and mindful about her and strip it away, replace it with pop culture and disposable ephemera, infotainment and beauty tips and laugh tracks that telegraph ersatz emotion.

You think of Jane's eyes, staring blankly at screens, reflecting back only pixels, and you shudder.

And how will she look at *you* then, after her mind has been poisoned? Once she leaves the cabin, it's just a matter of time before she finds out everything you've hidden from her. And when she does, she will not think that you saved her; she will think that you *denied* her. You must find a way to make her see, once and for all, why you took her away from all that.

There is only one logical path forward. You have to change the world that she is about to enter, and force it to become the world you know it should be. If no one is paying attention to you now, you have to do something so big that it can't be ignored.

And that's when you remember *The Anarchist Cookbook*. *An explosion can take the shape of hope.*

You begin to plan to kill people. If the world refuses to wake up to the horrors coming its way, then horror is going to be the only way to jolt it alert. You know that if you succeed with your plan, people will wonder why you did what you did. You'll need to make it abundantly clear that this was not a sick whim, the act of a psychopath, but a moral necessity for the betterment of mankind. A sacrifice you are making for the greater good. For Jane, yes. But also the children of the future—the Janes yet to come.

And so you begin to imagine a manifesto that will make this all clear.

There is one more quote in *The Anarchist Cookbook* that you think about a lot: *Madness creates its own fatal hubris, and will destroy itself; but sometimes it does need a push in the right direction.*

The world is mad, you tell yourself.

It's the world that's mad, not you.

Part Three

ME

53

Anon2993 >   Lionel?

SFWired1 >   Who's this? Do I know you? I don't recognize the
              username.

Anon2993 >   It's Jane. Or Esme. Whatever you want to call me.

SFWired1 >   . . .

Anon2993 >   Hello? Lionel? Are you still there?

SFWired1 >   Yes. Sorry. Just a little shell-shocked. I didn't expect to see
              you here again.

Anon2993 >   I haven't been online much lately.

SFWired1 >   Where the hell *have* you been?

Anon2993 >   Um, haven't you been reading the papers?

SFWired1 >   Well, yes, obviously I know about the trial. It's all over the
              news. I read that you're going to be the prosecution's key
              witness?

Anon2993 >   It was part of the immunity deal that my lawyer negotiated
              when I turned myself in. I had to give them all the evidence
              I had and take them to my father. And then I had to agree
              to testify against him.

SFWired1 >   . . . Ouch.

Anon2993 >   At least I won't be going to jail. Though sometimes I think
              that this might feel worse than that.

SFWired1 >   Right. But—why haven't you gotten in touch with me
              before now? It's been months.

Anon2993 >   I thought you wouldn't want to hear from me.

SFWired1 >   I've been trying to find you. You just . . . disappeared.
              When I got back to Signal your desk was empty and no

	one had a forwarding email address and you'd moved out of your sublet. I even left a message for your lawyer—Rhona something?—when I found her name in the paper, but she didn't return my call.
Anon2993 >	I'm sorry. I figured you hated me. You went to jail because of me. It was my fault.
SFWired1 >	You're missing a critical part of that equation. I was in jail because I *didn't* hate you. I did that to protect you. An impulsive move, and yeah, I didn't really think it through. But it came from a place of genuine concern.
Anon2993 >	So you don't resent me now? For the fact that you have a criminal record?
SFWired1 >	Hardly. They let me go right after you turned yourself in. False confession, not such a big deal in the end. They had bigger fish to fry.
Anon2993 >	I'm glad. And I'm sorry.
SFWired1 >	It's OK.
Anon2993 >	. . .
SFWired1 >	. . . you still there, Esme?
Anon2993 >	Yeah. That's it, I guess. I just wanted to apologize. Take care, Lionel.
SFWired1 >	Wait.
Anon2993 >	. . . what?
SFWired1 >	I want more than that.
Anon2993 >	??? I'm not sure what else I have for you. I wish I could offer you money or something but I'm broke. The last of the cash that I took from my father—it's gone. I gave it all to a victim's fund. It turned out that it was all stolen, and I didn't want anything to do with it once I knew that. I'm working part-time at a coffee shop now. There's not a lot of people who are eager to hire Esme Nowak, unsurprisingly. So I'm just barely scraping by.
SFWired1 >	That's not what I was getting at. What I meant is, I'm still your friend. I still care about you.

Anon2993 >   Seriously? After everything?

SFWired1 >   I mean, you're still yourself, no matter who else you turned out to be. There's always some essential truth to who a person is, I think, despite all the complicating shit that life piles on top. What's important is whether you can dig your way through all that crap and find your way to the best part of yourself. I have faith that you can do that. Seems like maybe you *have* done that, already. So, yeah. I'm not going away.

Anon2993 >   Oh. Wow.

SFWired1 >   . . . That's assuming you don't want *me* to go away?

Anon2993 >   Don't be ridiculous.

SFWired1 >   :)

Anon2993 >   OK, then. If we're friends again, maybe you can help me out with something.

SFWired1 >   What's that?

Anon2993 >   I think that it's time that I find a new name.

54

LIONEL CALLED ME a few days ago.

"Have you been following the news?" he asked. In the background, I could hear dishes clattering in a sink, the whine of a toddler, a whirring blender, the sounds of a household starting its day.

"Not only did I see it, some journalist found me out and showed up on my doorstep looking for an interview about my dad," I said. I was standing at my easel, paint in my hair, squinting at the figure I'd just daubed on my canvas. It was all wrong; I would have to start again.

"Shit, really? Are you doing OK?"

"I'm fine, honestly." I wiped my paintbrush on my smock and tucked the cellphone under my ear. On the other side of my living room window, the squirrels had somehow clambered up to the bird feeder again, and were making quick work of the seeds my daughter had put out. Squirrels, I have learned, are exceptionally clever rodents, adept at the art of misdirection, resourceful survivors; I couldn't begrudge them their treat, even if it meant that the finches would bypass my house this spring.

Lionel set my father's name as a Google Alert years ago, and he still called me whenever something worrisome popped up. For a long time, during the aughts, there hadn't been much for Lionel to call me about. But in recent years, as what was once science fiction has increasingly become reality—AI writing movies, robots delivering groceries, wars conducted primarily by drone, entire career paths wiped out by technological advances—Lionel had been calling me more and more. My father, after living invisibly in his jail cell for decades, just a curious footnote of history, had somehow become part of the zeit-geist. People were once again paying attention to what he'd been warning us about.

I was seeing the same things that Lionel was, the stories that had evidently set Yasmin the journalist on her path to finding me. A news story about how *The Luddite Manifesto* was being taught in college curricula; a Fox News political commentator who'd praised my father on air; an investigative newspaper series about a radical anti-technology movement that called themselves "the Adamites."

This latest story—the one Lionel was calling me about—had made the front page of *The New York Times*. A tech billionaire and self-styled maverick had gone on social media and pronounced my father a "prescient genius" who'd "said what no one else wanted to say." His post had triggered sales of the book version of *The Luddite Manifesto* (published by an unscrupulous press that had snatched up the rights when the government auctioned them off two decades earlier) and launched it to the top of the Amazon bestseller charts. I would have found this laughably ironic—my father embraced by the very people he would have murdered, if given the chance—if it didn't make me ill to think of him sitting in his jail cell, smug in his vindication.

I knew this was coming, of course. I saw it even during the very first days of the trial, with the handful of protestors that sat outside the courtroom every day, cardboard signs hoisted above their baseball caps. *THE BOMBASTER IS A PROPHET. LISTEN TO ADAM. TECHNOLOGY = DOOM.* Rhona said they were loonies, and told me to ignore them; but every time I climbed the stairs to the courthouse, past this phalanx of sour-breathed acolytes screaming their epithets at me—*Jezebel! Traitor! He should have blown you up!*—I felt a chill in my heart. That they were a harbinger of something to come.

"It's just a matter of time now," I said to Lionel gloomily.

"Don't be so pessimistic," he said.

"You know I'm right." And he knew exactly what I meant—we'd talked about this so many times over the years. A conversation we'd had over a bottle of bourbon during the dark days after my father's trial; or during late-night long-distance phone calls when I finally went off to college (art school, not engineering, in the end), or postcoital chats on those occasions when we'd fallen back into bed with each other despite knowing better. Huddled together, whispering about my fears: not that my father's dire predictions would prove correct, but that the wrong people would start to see him as a legitimate theorist rather than a terrorist. That, eventually, some follower would decide to take up his mantle, and start building bombs of their own.

It hasn't happened yet. I'm sure it will.

WHAT DOES MY father think of his renewed infamy? I can guess, but I don't actually know firsthand. I haven't spoken to him directly since that day at Starbucks. The last time we were in the same room together was the long week when I testified at his trial, while he watched me from across the courtroom with his forehead knitted together in disbelief. As if I had inexplicably changed the ending of a story that he was pretty sure he'd written himself.

I decided to stay home on the day the verdict was handed down. I unplugged the phone and turned off the television and cried until I was as empty as a cracked egg. It wasn't until I passed a newsstand the next morning that I learned that my father had been given a life sentence, not a death sentence, but without the option of parole.

After a while, I began receiving letters from the prison where my father was serving his time—letters addressed to *Jane Williams*, always, which caused the mailman no shortage of confusion. I gave these letters to Lionel, unopened, and told him to hang on to them for me in case I ever changed my mind and decided to read them. By the time we got drunk together one evening and threw them in the fireplace, I had at least four dozen.

Eventually the letters stopped coming. I was never sure if that was because my father gave up writing them, or if he could no longer figure out how to get in touch with me.

I've made myself very hard to find.

———

I SUPPOSE YOU'RE wondering why Lionel and I didn't end up together. There are always a thousand reasons why any particular relationship fails—a chain of decisions and miscommunications, impossible to disentangle—but I can probably distill ours down to youth. We were just babies when we loved each other; and each had our own issues to work through before we could find happiness inside a relationship. I hit my twenties and—finally having the freedom to experience life to its fullest—went a little wild; meanwhile, he struggled with finding ways to manage his depression. On top of this, the weight of our complicated history together kept undermining our best intentions. Damage is hard to undo once it's done. And so we broke up, got back together, broke up again. Eventually I went off to art school, was impregnated by a photographer classmate, married him, had our child, became a graphic designer, got divorced.

Along the way, I lost Lionel as a lover. Don't be disappointed by this, though—I'm not. Because I never lost him as a friend, and maybe that was more important, anyway. We still chose each other to be members of the families that we needed, as opposed to the families we were born with.

It is no small thing to have the ability to make that choice; in fact, it's probably the most important decision we get to make in life. Which is why I make it, time and time again. I've carefully built my own community over the years, because if there's one clear lesson that I learned from my hermitic childhood, it's that you need lots of people around you if you're ever going to find your true self. Listening to one voice, and one voice only, doesn't make you a human being. It makes you a parrot.

. . . Or so I remind myself when my own daughter, now a teenager, pretends that she can't hear a word I say.

OTHER THAN MY relationship with Lionel, I lost everything that I had that winter in San Francisco. My name, obviously; and my job; and my father. My mother, too—although maybe you could argue that she decided to lose *me*. Because while she did end up paying Rhona's astronomical legal bills, she never followed up on the other part of her promise that night: *When all this is over, and everything has been sorted out by the legal system, I'm sure we can reconnect and start over.* I spoke to her only once after that abysmal dinner: the following morning, when I called her from a pay phone and asked for her lawyer's contact information. She read me the number, and then hung up before I could even thank her.

Maybe it was hypocritical of me to use my mother's lawyer and take her money. I debated doing neither. But in the end I decided to behave like my namesake, the squirrel, and be pragmatic about my own survival.

Sometimes I wonder if my mother would truly have reached out, after the trial was over and I was vindicated in the eyes of the press. A sympathetic profile of me, written by Janus and published in Signal on the eve of my testimony—the only interview I would ever agree to sit for—had changed the tenor of the coverage. Sentiment tilted in my favor after that; maybe my mother would ultimately have decided that she wanted me as her daughter, after all, and claimed me as her own.

Except that, in the interview, I chose not to keep my mouth shut about her, and so that was the end of that.

. . . Perhaps the strangest part of this saga—in a saga with so many, many bizarre twists—is the role of Tess Trevante. The iconic technologist has refused to speak about her role in these events and has not formally acknowledged her daughter's existence. Her only public comment about the situation came in the form of a statement that she released to the press in the days immediately after Adam Nowak's identity was revealed by CNN. "I was Adam Nowak's first victim, and might have been his last, too, had he not been caught. But beyond this, I have no relationship with these heinous and wrongheaded crimes. Indeed, right up until the perpetrators were finally identified, I believed that my former family was dead. It was quite a shock to discover they were the subject of a nationwide manhunt."

Is this true? Esme Nowak is cagey about what, exactly, happened when she revealed herself to her mother for the first time, reportedly just days before turning her father in to the police. On the subject of Tess Trevante, she will say only this: "I went to my mother and asked for her help. Instead, she chose to help herself. I think that tells you everything that you need to know about her. It certainly told me."

I wonder sometimes what my mother is really like—if there was in fact some more flattering "essential truth" (as Lionel put it) that I would have discovered if I'd actually gotten to know her. Maybe my father's memoirs were an accurate portrait of her—a self-centered woman who'd never wanted a child, until the child became a useful tool; or maybe she was just a human being, flawed in the same ways we all are, who simply wasn't emotionally equipped to handle the stranger who showed up at her door with a backpack stuffed with trouble. Regardless, neither version of her was the mother that I had been searching for. And so, given the unusual ability to choose whether or not I wanted a mother like that, I chose to live without one at all.

I'd be lying if I said that there weren't still moments when I regret this.

CAN YOU EVER escape legacy? Does it define you, whether you like it or not? Even if you consciously flee it, doesn't it still circumscribe the shape of who you are, or are not?

I've spent my life trying to walk the middle ground, to be neither my mother nor my father but someone who is wholly *myself*. But judging by how much I still have to say about the subject—by the fact that, decades on, I'm writing these pages, still seeking some kind of clarity—it's evident that I haven't really escaped either of them. Their shadows loom over my every decision: whether I choose to pick up my smartphone first thing when I wake up, or whether I choose to go for a walk instead. The fact that my daughter and I live on fifteen acres of wooded land in Marin, the fact that I write regular checks to the Audubon Society, the fact that I shun social media entirely—you could draw a line from these decisions straight back to my Luddite father. And yet, the pile of Amazon boxes collecting on my porch are a sign that I am not so very far from my mother, either. She would also surely approve of the electric car my daughter uses to drive herself to school, and the Apple Pencil that I find so critical for my graphic design work, and all the other technology tools that make my life so much easier that I sometimes close my eyes to how they are also making our world harder.

Do I feel guilty about this? Maybe not as much as I should. But if there's one thing I understand at this point, it's that life isn't always a series of binary choices. Sometimes it's not about *either/or* but about learning how to manage the complexities of *both/and*.

I'm sometimes asked, by the handful of people who know who I really am, whether I share my father's pessimistic outlook about what lies in store for us; or whether I agree with my mother that humankind's progress is a one-way trajectory, an arrow going forever up. But I have no answer. I'm not a prophet. I have no crystal ball. But if forced to respond, I think I would say this: that I believe that civilization's path is a pendulum that swings both ways, vacillating between hope and despair, success and failure, and all we can do is hang on for dear life. Because it will never, ever stop.

And so I look toward the future with open eyes, readying myself for whatever comes next. Not Jane, no longer Esme; just me.

Notes and Acknowledgments

ONE OF THE joys of writing novels is that you can liberally mix elements of the truth in with a whole lot of invention. I've done that extensively in this novel, and I hope that those who lived through the nineties dot-com era in San Francisco will forgive me for the many liberties that I've taken.

First off, I should note that while aspects of this novel were inspired by the years that I worked at *Wired* and *Salon,* none of the characters in this book were taken from real life. But I am grateful to all the people that I worked with during those days who shared memories that I mined for details, especially when my own recollections grew hazy.

I was also fortunate to have several books about the early days of the internet that could fill in the holes. Some invaluable resources included *Wired: A Romance* by Gary Wolf, *Burn Rate: How I Survived the Gold Rush Years on the Internet* by Michael Wolff, *The Nudist on the Late Shift: And Other True Tales of Silicon Valley* by Po Bronson, and *Dot.Con: The Greatest Story Ever Sold* by John Cassidy. *Blood in the Machine: The Origins of the Rebellion Against Big Tech* by Brian Merchant is a fascinating history of Ludditism and its echoes in the era of modern technology. I also spent many hours at the Los Angeles Public Library poring through old issues of *Wired* magazine as well as the astute analyses of Professor Dave Karpf of George Washington University in his #WIREDarchive newsletter.

By now you've probably gleaned that Adam Nowak was (very) loosely inspired by Ted Kaczynski, the Unabomber. To fill him out as a character, I found the podcast *Project Unabom* to be tremendously helpful. I also fell back frequently on the thorough reporting by *The New York Times* and the story "Harvard and the Making of the Unabomber" in *The Atlantic* by Alston Chase. *Hunting the Unabomber: The FBI, Ted Kaczynski, and the Capture of America's Most Notorious Domestic Terrorist* by Lis Wiehl was also a helpful resource.

What Kind of Paradise is partly a book about the dangers of living in an isolated bubble with a solitary zealot as your company. In other words, humans need a strong community, and I am eternally grateful for mine, who encouraged me and kept me sane through the writing of this book:

- First and always, Susan Golomb, my agent and my anchor, who has been by my side for nineteen years and six books now. I can't thank you enough for your guidance and wisdom.
- Andrea Walker, my amazing editor, who believed in this idea the minute I pitched it to her, and wisely nudged it into shape along the way. You have been a beacon of calm in a stressful industry, and I'm so happy we were able to finish this book together.
- I constantly marvel at how lucky I am to have so many fantastic people on my Random House team, including Michelle Jasmine, Windy Dorresteyn, Maria Braeckel, Alison Rich, Madison Dettlinger, Andy Ward, Naomi Goodheart, and the indefatigable sales, design, publicity, and marketing departments. Thank you for all your hard work!
- I am also indebted to Brooke Ehrlich, who is no question the most incredible book-to-film agent in the business; Nicole Dewey, my frank and savvy publicist; and Alex Kohner, because the best kind of lawyer is one you can also call a friend.
- The early feedback I got from Angie Kim, James Han Mattson, Tim Weed, Jean Kwok, and Danielle Trussoni was invaluable in shaping the direction of this book. May we all reunite in person again soon.
- I made my first inroads into this book during one writing retreat, and finished it during another, both times with the same group

of incredible novelists who have transformed my writer's life in L.A. Rufi Thorpe, Stephanie Danler, Cynthia D'Aprix Sweeney, Jade Chang, and Edan Lepucki: I raise one of Cynthia's Manhattans in salute to you.

-More thanks: The FlimFlam Hive, Cooler Moms, and Spa Queenz, which despite the inside-joke text-thread names, are very serious friendships that I value tremendously. Everyone at Suite 8, for the popcorn and coffee and pleasant procrastination opportunities during my workday. Bookstagram, for a decade of truly meaningful support and inspiration—I write for you. The Canyon Coyotes, for keeping me on the court and out of my head. And so many others in my Silver Lake (and beyond) community: You know who you are, and I'm lucky to have you in my life.

-Many thanks to Liz Phair for the use of her lyrics.

-To Greg, for keeping the love alive through renovations, fresh starts, and controlled chaos.

-And last but not least, my heart belongs to Auden and Theo. I love watching you both grow and build your own kinds of paradise.

About the Author

Janelle Brown is the *New York Times* bestselling author of *I'll Be You, Pretty Things, Watch Me Disappear, All We Ever Wanted Was Everything,* and *This Is Where We Live*. An essayist and journalist, she has written for *Vogue, The New York Times, Elle, Wired, Self, Los Angeles Times, Salon,* and more. She lives in Los Angeles with her husband and their two children.

janellebrown.com
Instagram: @janellebrownie

About the Type

This book was set in Caslon, a typeface first designed in 1722 by William Caslon (1692–1766). Its widespread use by most English printers in the early eighteenth century soon supplanted the Dutch typefaces that had formerly prevailed. The roman is considered a "workhorse" typeface due to its pleasant, open appearance, while the italic is exceedingly decorative.